Amanda Hickie grew up in Sydney, Australia. She was living in Canada in 2003 when Toronto became an epicenter of the SARS outbreak. That event sowed the seed for *Before This Is Over*. Published in Australia as *An Ordinary Epidemic*, the novel was long-listed for the Dobbie Award for a first published work.

Amanda now lives a brisk walk from Coogee Beach in Sydney with her two computer-oriented sons and husband and two non-computer-oriented cats.

Before *this* is Over

AMANDA HICKIE

REVIEW

Originally published in Australia in 2015 by MidnightSun Publishing Pty. Ltd.
as *An Ordinary Epidemic*

First published in North America in 2017 by Little, Brown and Company

First published in Great Britain in 2017
by HEADLINE REVIEW
An imprint of HEADLINE PUBLISHING GROUP

1

Cataloguing in Publication Data is available from the British Library

ISBN 978 1 4722 4005 7

Typeset in 11.75/15.5 pt Sabon LT Std by Jouve (UK), Milton Keynes

Printed and bound in Great Britain by CPI Group (UK) Ltd, Croydon, CR0 4YY

Headline's policy is to use papers that are natural, renewable and recyclable
products and made from wood grown in well-managed forests and other
controlled sources. The logging and manufacturing processes are expected to
conform to the environmental regulations of the country of origin.

HEADLINE PUBLISHING GROUP
An Hachette UK Company
Carmelite House
50 Victoria Embankment
London EC4Y 0DZ

www.headline.co.uk
www.hachette.co.uk

To K and X, the most interesting people
I will ever meet.

Mon	Tue	Wed	Thu	Fri	Sat	Sun

Hannah drew the sheet around her face and nose so that it caught a pocket of her breath and warmed the air. She sank into the mattress, as if the bed were wrapped around her, around both of them. She felt Sean's bulk beside her, impressing his shape down into the bed and up into the bedclothes. Cocooned together. Her dozy mind moved around the house, expanding the cocoon to encompass the boys as well. She tried to pull herself back into sleep, think herself deeper into the bed – but sleep slid away every time she got close.

She leaned over Sean to look at the clock, making nothing more than a pretense of trying not to wake him.

'It's too late to go back to sleep, hon, too early to wake up.' He whispered but his voice was alert.

'How long have you been awake?'

'Not long. I didn't want to disturb the boys. Don't want them up any earlier than they have to be.'

She felt the hyperawareness and nausea of overtiredness. Every time either of the boys went away, sleeplessness broke out. Ever since they were little. Even for a sleepover. She had woken up last night, she couldn't remember how many times, with some specific dread in mind – a bus crash, a swimming accident, a teacher turning away for a second, Zac following instructions to some terrible conclusion that she just stopped herself from imagining in detail.

Three hours' drive was too far away.

The teachers seemed competent but she didn't know them. If there was a crisis, if hard decisions had to be made, Zac would be just another one of the kids.

She ran through a list of warnings for Zac in her mind. About washing his hands and not kissing anyone (not that he showed any signs of being interested in kissing), not following along if his instinct tingled, the numbers to ring in an emergency. It was important he knew she trusted him, but what if the one thing she didn't tell him was the one thing he needed to know?

And then there were all the things she couldn't influence, the people she couldn't give a stern lecture to. The bus driver falling asleep, the air-conditioning in the hotel spreading germs, something Zac would have no control over, something she couldn't prevent with cautionary words. The luck of where he sat determining how he fared.

'He doesn't have to go.' It slipped out, so softly she wasn't sure Sean had heard.

'He'll be fine,' Sean whispered curtly back. 'He's not a little kid. He went last year, he was fine.'

'The school should have postponed it.'

There was silence for a moment from Sean, an impatient

silence. 'It's not like he's going to Bangkok. There isn't a single case in Canberra. There isn't really even a case here yet. Do you want him to be the only kid who doesn't go?'

'It's not like this is important.'

Sean's whisper became sharp. 'It is to him.'

Why was it so hard to see the times she should have dug in her heels, except in hindsight? It was Pascal's wager, the tiniest chance of danger to her kids weighing heavily against a very large chance of looking a bit foolish.

From deep in the house she heard Zac's bedroom door slam and the sluggish thump of his feet in the hall. Sean dug her in the ribs. 'Time to get up.'

As Hannah came down the hall, Zac was in the doorway of the kitchen, silhouetted by the weak rays of the not-quite-risen sun. His edge was clear and solid. Watching him, her eyes relaxed. Yet again he took her by surprise, his slender height filling the door, his arm up, hand lazily touching the lintel. Her round and squidgy boy had been pulled out to a long strand.

Sean was a few paces into the room, his form dark in the shadows of the kitchen. He seemed solid compared to the slight, bright mirror of his son. They were saying the easy, normal, meaningless, repetitive things that had become habit. Words that started and ended everything. Zac's clear young voice, so light it almost blew away before she could catch it, broke through Sean's soft, low rumble. As she slid past, Zac pulled closer to the door frame to let her by. He loosely held a piece of toast.

'That's not all you're having to eat?'

'It's too early for food.'

The colors in the room shifted blue as she turned on the light. She made herself a cup of coffee to drink while she made Zac's lunch, going back to the cupboard for extras – a muesli bar, some crackers, a bag of chips. Just in case. For whatever situation it was she couldn't foresee. Zac wouldn't eat any of them, and in five days' time the lunch bag would come back with the extra food intact.

She turned the radio down low so as not to wake Oscar. A case in Sydney would have been the lead story, but there wasn't one. All she got was Newcastle and no change, more people sick but no confirmed cases since that lone woman last week. And Thailand and Britain. Actual cases but too far away to be the justification she needed to cancel Zac's trip. Too far away, too hard to grasp, meaningless numbers. There would be nothing official from China, yet again.

When Sean and Zac paused in their conversation, she found herself saying, 'Do you have your phone?'

'Yes, Mum.'

'Is it on and charged?'

'Yes, Mum.' A slightly impatient smile.

'Okay then.' But she couldn't just let him go. 'Be careful.'

'I always am.'

'Do you have some money, just in case?'

Sean, leaning against the wall, swiveled to her. 'I gave him money. He's fine.'

'Don't do anything you don't feel comfortable with.'

Zac turned back to face her, his smile wider now, and good-natured. 'I'm not going to be running around in the middle of the night, Mum. I promise.'

'Of course not. Just stay safe.' She watched him as he rifled through his bag, checking against a list from the school. His face was pinker now, so alive, as the sun took over from the cold fluorescent light. All she had to do to make this feeling disappear was tell him he couldn't go.

Sean watched Zac. 'What's the holdup? I thought I'd be rid of you by now.'

'I haven't got my MP3 player.'

'I thought they said no electronics.'

'Yeah, but they didn't mean it. It's not like it's worth anything.' He rolled his eyes as he closed up the bag, then threw it over one shoulder and loped through the door to the hall.

'Quietly,' Hannah whispered loudly to his back. 'Oscar's still asleep.'

'He's fine, you're fine, we're fine. So relax.' Sean leaned back against the door frame.

'I know, but . . .'

'No but.' He looked her in the eye. 'If you hurry back we might even get in a cup of coffee before Oscar wakes up. A whole cup of coffee with no kids actually in the room.'

She pushed past him and he followed her in silence until she paused at the front door, reluctant to let the day officially begin. 'So, I should drive really fast.'

'That's right, safely and really fast.' He swung open the front door and stepped back to let Zac through.

'And if I had a *real* phone I'd have music because Mum says I have to take my phone. So, you should write me a note, 'cause if I get in trouble it's your fault.'

'Not a hope. Behave yourself and do all the stuff your mum said.'

Hannah gave Sean a quick kiss. As she got in the car, she turned for one more look, but the door was closed.

They drove to the school in comfortable silence. Zac was absorbed in his inner world. Just a couple of years ago it was hard to get a word in edgewise, but now he kept his thoughts to himself until they were well-ordered. He'd done his own packing and she was tempted to check whether he'd had the foresight to take a fleece. It had been on the list and he knew it was a few degrees colder in Canberra. It would be a learning experience – no one ever died of getting a bit chilly, although, at the moment . . . no, they really didn't.

She couldn't help herself. Some things were too important. 'Don't forget the hand goo.'

'I won't.'

'Use it a lot.'

'I will.' He wasn't really paying attention, but she'd said it.

The streets were still empty. It felt odd to pull into a parking space straight in front of the school, as if she were taking something not rightfully hers. Two hours from now the buildings would look the way she was used to, hidden behind double-parked cars as kids jumped out and ran for the gate.

Zac pulled his backpack out of the car as he stood up. He waited for her to come around to the curb, and they walked together into the asphalt yard and stood side by side. A knot of kids congregated in front of the waiting bus, their high, chirrupy teenage voices drowning out the muted murmur coming from the small clusters of parents. She looked around for a friendly face, but if she was being honest with herself, she didn't really know any of Zac's friends' parents.

Zac stood facing no particular direction, as if he didn't know whether to join the clump of kids or be with her. The two of them were matched in their awkwardness. She wanted to push him towards the group, but he had his own pace. His body had started to mature, but every emotion was still expressed, unfiltered, on his face and in the way he stood.

As she stared into the distance, the figure of a woman walking towards her impinged on her thoughts. Someone familiar, someone she had met before, although she couldn't quite place where or who. Possibly Daniel's mother, she thought. She hoped. They had definitely met more times than could justify Hannah's not remembering her name. The woman came to a stop next to her, and side by side, in the moment before either felt compelled to say something, they looked at the kids. Hannah leaned slightly back, trying to retrieve an air gap between them.

'Is Zac as disorganized as Daniel?'

One right at least. 'If there are undies in his bag, it'll be pure chance.'

'This is embarrassing, but I've forgotten your name.'

Thank Christ. 'Hannah.'

'Susan.' Saved.

Hannah stared at the gaggle. Zac had moved to the outskirts, watching. She could see him unconsciously matching his body language to the other kids', laughing at something as the others laughed. The group had widened, fanned out just enough to include him, and while he relaxed a little, he stayed listening, head to one side. Her heart jumped and she realized she was smiling, almost like she was in love.

Susan's hand bumped the back of hers. Cold fingers. The touch was so light that normally it wouldn't register at all. Susan was clearly unaware she'd done it. 'Isn't it terrible, the news from overseas?'

'Oh, yes, horrible.' Hannah tried to think of something more salient to say, but she couldn't get her mind off the spot on her hand, the spot that had been touched. It could be the cold morning, but she felt a lingering sensation of damp. A wet touch would transfer germs better than a dry one. She had to fight the urge to rub the cold away with her other hand. Even if it didn't look strange, it would do nothing but spread the germs.

She edged slightly away. On the Internet it said that she should keep a meter between herself and anyone else. Surely that wasn't enough. Surely a cough or a sneeze could travel farther, but it might at least reduce the accidental bumps and incidental spit.

'What about Thailand? We were there at Christmas. Graeme got sick – Bali belly, and then he was dehydrated – but the hospital was terrific. Last night, there it was on the news. You could barely recognize it, there were people dying in the corridors. And it was so clean and normal when we were there. We were right there.'

Now Hannah's hand was hanging. She fixated on it, couldn't take her thoughts from it long enough for it to move freely. There was a wipe in her bag, but pulling it out to clean her hand now would seem rude.

Zac had broken away from the larger group. He was chatting and laughing easily with two other boys, then stopped to look around. His eyes landed on her, looking for her. He walked over self-consciously and stood slightly too far away.

'Well, bye, Mum.' He generously allowed her to hug him.

'Be good, enjoy yourself, try to learn something.'

''Kay.'

Everyone else was lining up in front of the bus doors. If he didn't hurry, he would be last and end up next to some kid he didn't really know for the next three hours.

His back was pressed against the glass of the bus window. The boy on the other half of his seat was almost touching him. Another two on the seat in front and two behind. At least five kids within a meter of Zac. He leaned closer to the boy in front to say something, breathing the same air. She had forgotten to tell him about the one-meter rule, and even if she had, there wasn't enough room on the bus to keep his distance.

He looked so capable, suddenly so much his own person. She had made him and now there he was – complete, whole, independent.

The bus lurched forward. The kids, some despite themselves, looked out the windows to their parents. Some waved, some just looked. Zac was still talking to his friends and didn't look back, only raising a hand slightly and giving her his confident smile once the bus had almost pulled away. She stood and watched until they were out of sight.

The narrow school gate was clogged with leaving parents who had stopped in groups to talk. She had to weave through, trying not to be touched and not to breathe too hard.

She skirted a toddler hanging on to the tether of his mother with one hand and smearing his snotty nose with the other. Her pulse skipped again. But it was a cold morning – that made noses run. She looked for anything else that might be a symptom, even the memory of a cough or a sneeze. There was no way she would have missed it if someone coughed. The chance that she was looking at the first case in Sydney was minuscule.

Not every sneeze was Manba, that was what she had to keep telling herself. But not everyone who had Manba had symptoms. Any of these healthy-looking people could be in the early stages – or be an asymptomatic carrier – and you wouldn't know.

This was how bad things happened – by ignoring her instincts. If something went wrong, she would always know she'd had a choice to stop him from going. She had to hold herself back from running after the bus.

Every kid did this. All the kids went, the teachers would look after them, Zac was safe. She knew that. She told herself that. But still Hannah felt she had failed him.

It was too late now. It was done.

The cold nip of the car door handle took her by surprise. She glanced at the clock – seven thirty, even though the bus was supposed to leave by seven. Still enough time to get home and get Oscar ready. As much out of habit as anything, she turned on the radio for the news. She felt jumpy, maybe just eager to get home.

There was more traffic on the road now. As she passed Oscar's school, kids were already arriving. A harried-looking father dropped two small girls at the gate of the before-school care center.

The voice from the radio pushed itself to the front of her attention. ' . . . organizers believe they have now identified all attendees. However, a small number have still not been located. The World Health Organization has offered assistance to any government whose citizens attended the conference . . .'

The wind had picked up a little, and the kids looked

like small blue-and-white bundles with their arms wrapped around themselves.

'. . . on farms all over Britain, thousands of animals have already been put down. Protesters gathered in London are claiming that the cull will do nothing to reduce the spread of Manba without a significant drive to identify wild animal vectors. Wide-scale testing of non-domestic animals in the Manchester area has begun . . .'

Gwen had asked her yesterday if their cat caught birds. She'd explained that Mr Moon certainly recognized birds as a source of food, but if it didn't come out of a can, it wasn't worth his effort. Gwen had looked unconvinced. Hannah hadn't bothered to point out that Manba wasn't bird flu and she should worry instead about whether Mr Moon caught bats.

'. . . reports that airport employees are refusing to unload passengers from a plane originating in Bangkok. A short time ago, the minister for immigration said a decision would be made soon on whether the passengers will be allowed to enter the country. In the meantime, the plane is being supplied with food and water . . .'

She thought of all those people returning from holidays. So close to being home after such a long flight, but still stuck in a metal tube. Imagine being sent back to a forced vacation in a disease zone. Well, at least it wasn't summer, so the plane wouldn't heat up too fast as it sat.

'. . . is advising anyone planning overseas travel to postpone their journey. People who must travel are advised to stay away from areas where large groups congregate, including tourist attractions and conferences . . .'

No one she knew would get sick, she had to believe that. The outbreaks overseas would die out. And everyone would complain about panicky scientists, who would insist that we still needed to be prepared for next time. And that would be it.

Or it wouldn't.

And she was prepared. Except that in three hours Zac would be three hours away and she had no control over Newcastle Hospital, airport security, government policy, or viruses.

The news continued – a story about a film star, sports, and weather. She switched it off.

As the car turned onto the driveway, she noticed again the way the facade spanned the property, presenting a united front with Gwen's half of the semidetached house. Its thick front door deadened the sound from the street. Even the side passage between their house and Natalie and Stuart's was barred by a tall wooden gate. An unbroken barrier to keep out noise, dust, draft, people, and germs.

The solidarity was broken only by the paint. Heritage hues of Brunswick green and Indian red on their side abruptly changed to a particularly powdery shade of lavender on Gwen's. Otherwise, they were mirrors.

As she walked through the front door, she could hear the happiness in Oscar's high voice, carried all the way from the back. Sunlight through the kitchen window washed the room in a golden glow. At the stove, Sean leaned over a sandwich toasting in the frying pan.

'You call that breakfast?'

'I see four food groups here, if you count fat.' He lifted the corner of the sandwich with a spatula and a trickle of melted cheese oozed out. 'I'll make you one if you're nice to me.'

She planted a swift kiss on his cheek. 'Will that do?'

'Payment in full.'

The top half of the room was warm and humid, filled with steam from the kettle, but air from outside still crept in under the back door. Oscar sat at the table in his frog-covered flannel pajamas, one size too big. Unlike Zac at the same age, for Oscar five was still young enough not to think they were uncool. He had rosy spots on his cheeks, but his naked feet were pinched with cold.

'Did you see him leave? We wouldn't want him to sneak back.' Sean winked at Oscar, who giggled.

'He was fine. The bus was late but they eventually left.'

'And no one was panicking. They breathed in, they breathed out, the world is the same as it was yesterday, isn't it?' She chose to ignore him. 'Isn't it? Oscar, ask Mummy if the world has changed.'

'Mummy, has the world . . .'

'No, it hasn't, the world hasn't changed.' She begrudged him a smile. 'No disaster struck, the bus left, everything is the same. Today. But tomorrow . . .'

'Tomorrow is tomorrow. Today, nothing has changed.' He slid her toasted sandwich onto a plate and held it out

to her. 'Breathe. You're the only one panicking. He's fine.'
He stopped with the spatula hovering over his sandwich.
'What date is it?'

'The fifth.'

'Are you sure? Crap, I missed my sister's birthday.'

'It's still yesterday there.'

'I'll ring her from work. What's the time difference?'

'I don't know. Day is night, use the Internet.'

She got to the hospital just before her appointment time.
The main building was new – all glass and exposed concrete. Wide public spaces that meant you might be on
time when you arrived on the grounds but were late by
the time you walked through the front door.

Her doctor was housed in a side wing, an old building
that had somehow escaped being knocked down. Its
entrance was homier, less grand than the main entrance,
but today it was covered by a large red X of electrical
tape, holding in place a sign that read CLINIC OPEN. USE
MAIN ENTRANCE.

The main entrance was impersonal and, regardless of
the weather or the signs forbidding smoking within ten
meters of the doors, there was always a knot of gowned
patients, cigarettes in hand, just to one side. As she
reached the edifice, she noticed that the contingent was
larger than usual and all gathered around one door, the
only door that wasn't covered with more red tape. Thicker
smoke to walk through.

The crowd jostled for position in front of a harried

individual wearing a hi-vis yellow vest. A disgruntled woman walking past Hannah said, 'They tell me I can't see my brand-new grandchild. What a lot of nonsense over nothing.'

It became clear as Hannah waded into the crowd that it formed a kind of disordered line. The man in the vest held up his hand to the person in front, who seemed to be berating him, and called out, 'Anyone with an appointment?' Hannah put up her hand tentatively. 'Fill in the form, then go to one of the desks inside.' He went back to his argument.

The form consisted of a plain A4 page printed in black. 'Do you have an appointment today? Have you returned from overseas in the last two months? Have you developed a cough in the last week? Have you had a fever in the last week?' She ticked them off.

Inside, the normally spacious foyer was cut in half by a dotted barrier of white desks. They demarcated the normal soup of life and germs she had left outside from an unaccustomedly empty and sterile world of illness. She handed her filled-in form to the woman at the nearest desk. The woman addressed herself to the form, as if Hannah were a bystander. 'Have you been away in the last few weeks?'

'No.'

'Have you been unwell in any way this week?'

'No.'

'Is this your signature?'

'Yes.'

The woman gestured to a pump bottle of hand

sanitizer on the desk. 'You have to clean your hands before you go through.'

Hannah hesitated. 'Has something happened at the hospital? Is that why all the extra fuss?'

The woman looked up. 'We should be doing this all the time, if you ask me, not just when there's some crisis overseas.'

Past the desks, it was suddenly quiet. In the long corridor through the main building to the clinic wing, she passed only purposeful staff and others like her, late for appointments.

The waiting room was as full as always but eerily silent. Even in normal times, she had noticed, people spoke to each other in whispers. Most came with a companion but they rarely chatted, as if they couldn't find words up to the task of conveying any more than what had to be said. The dominant sounds were usually the crash of trolleys and nurses calling or laughing, but today even those were muted.

The volunteer was missing from the hot drinks trolley. In her place was a piece of printer paper with a handwritten sign reading HELP YOURSELF. Hannah never felt comfortable accepting a drink, especially in recent years. She thought the other patients looked at her, with her head of hair and the spring in her step, questioning whether she qualified for the club. She'd spent so much time waiting in this room that she was no longer a guest – she could make her own coffee. The doctors here gave people great chunks of life that were tithed back in many small appointments.

The woman sitting opposite wore a bright scarf elegantly. Her fingers were thin, the skin dry. The man next to her held her hand gently. He looked worried. She just looked tired. Hannah hoped they got called before she did.

The scarf was vibrant, the way Hannah noticed cancer patients' scarves often were. A small act of defiance, a stoic badge of bravery that said, 'I may look like I'm suffering, but inside I celebrate life.' That was not for her – she hadn't wanted to wear her illness with pride. She had hidden from it instead, trying to pass as one of the ordinary. She hadn't known what to do with strangers' looks of sympathy.

'Hannah?' A mix of question and exclamation. The doctor was looking around myopically, as they often do if they don't know you.

As she stood, he half stuck out his hand. She looked at it for a second, confused, considering the relay of germs, one handshake to another. What about his patients on chemo, did he shake their hands? Did he shake hands with other doctors, and did they shake hands with their patients? He morphed it into a gesture for her to go ahead.

A new doctor always meant having to recount every detail of her diagnosis and treatment, almost justify her presence. The first time, she felt like a friend had stood her up for coffee, that her disease was no longer important. It was at least reassuring that she was routine enough to be handed off to the trainees. She knew nothing good came from that kind of importance.

He browsed her notes while she looked around. The same combination of people – patient and doctor – sat in rooms with exactly the same furniture up and down the corridor, and in other hospitals, and in other countries. Her extraordinary experience was common.

'So, is this a regular checkup, or is there something specific bothering you?'

She pushed aside the mortifying thought that she was almost certainly wasting his time. 'I was supposed to come in a month, but I moved it.'

'I'm surprised you could get in – we've been flat out. Everyone thinks they'll miss their appointment if the hospital closes. At worst you'd be postponed a couple of weeks.' He looked back down at her file. 'How long since your diagnosis?'

'Eight years.' Hadn't he just read the file?

'I wouldn't miss one completely, but you don't have to worry about a bit of slippage.' Reassuring smile.

'I found a lump in my armpit. It's probably nothing, I mean, it was sore one day and then the next it wasn't, so it's probably nothing.'

'When was this?'

'Last Wednesday. I had a bit of a headache last week. I'm sure it's only a raised gland.'

She sat on the long high bed while he prodded gently under her arm with his fingertips.

'I don't feel anything.'

She had to rub around the spot for a few seconds before she located it. 'Here.'

'Has it changed in size at all?'

'No.' Now that she was in front of a doctor, the lump was the same size but felt much smaller.

'Have you had a cough?'

'No.'

'A fever?'

'No.'

'Been in contact with anyone who's had a cough or a fever?'

'They wouldn't have let me in the front door if I had.'

He looked directly and deliberately at her for the first time. 'Well, they would have, but you wouldn't be sitting in front of me.' He pulled off the examination gloves and washed his hands efficiently in the small sink. 'I think we can be fairly confident that you don't have Manba.'

She opened her mouth to object, but he continued along the well-worn groove of his speech. 'There are plenty of minor germs around and they don't take a break because a big one comes along. If it would help you sleep we can do a blood test, but it's extremely unlikely that you have anything. It's quite normal for someone with your history to feel anxious at a time like this, especially given the constant media barrage. The important thing is not to worry too much. It would be a good idea not to listen to the radio or watch too much television news. And don't go home and hit the Internet. I can give you a list of reputable websites for virus information.' He reached the pause for patient reaction.

'I know I don't have Manba. I just want to be sure it's not a return of the cancer.'

He looked surprised. 'Cancer? No, I don't see anything to be concerned about. You're' – he looked down at the sheet – 'eight years and, ah, three months since diagnosis. And while you can never say never, I think you can be very pleased with how well you've done.'

She realized he'd closed her file. There were more important cases, even for him. He had dismissed her.

She threw her keys on the hall table and watched them land on a pile of briefing documents, as if to remind her that they were waiting to be read before she could start on the manual. Soon, if she wanted to be paid for it this month. What the hell, Kate wasn't expecting anything out of her today.

The house could do with a clean and she had to get something for dinner, but right now she needed coffee. She still had an overtired buzz and a slight headache, but she was home.

They should be here. Not only Zac – all of them. The house was empty.

All the years they had saved to renovate. When she got sick, having the money didn't seem so important any-more. And then she realized it couldn't wait. For some people it was a long-deferred overseas adventure, others rang everyone they loved but had never told. For her, it was creating this home that would keep her family if she couldn't.

When she chose the paint color or the size of the pantry, she saw them. The light from the garden fell mottled on the benches and the wall, and the color was happiness. Everything was as it should be. She could hear the echoes of the boys laughing at the table. Here, she saw them making dinners, sitting around for Sunday breakfasts. Sometimes it was the boys and their friends at the kitchen table, sometimes just Sean. She built it for them, and where were they? Not here. No one was here.

With a plunger full of coffee in one hand and a mug in the other, she let herself out the back door and headed to the office in the garage. Like all the houses in this row, theirs backed onto the tiny laneway.

She heard a car pull into the neighbor's garage and, after a pause, the garden-side door open. Hannah considered whether to pretend that the fence provided privacy, but it was Natalie, not Stuart. 'Hi, how's things?' She raised herself on her toes to smile over the fence.

'Oh, extra busy. Everyone thinks they have Manba.'

'Give it time, they probably will.'

'That would be easier, I could send them to hospital. Now all I'm doing is ordering tests and trying to talk them down. Oh, wasn't today the big day? Did Zac get off all right? They didn't cancel it, did they?'

'They got off fine.'

'They are so grown-up at fourteen. I can't imagine I'll ever think Ella is old enough for a school camp. Stuart says he's not letting her out of his sight till she's thirty-five. When he's not saying she has to leave on the day of her eighteenth birthday.' Natalie paused for a moment. 'I guess that's only a few years off for Zac.' She reached her back door but hesitated with her hand on the lever. 'Many of the people overseas, the ones who've died, have had preexisting conditions.'

'I guess that makes sense. It's a relief that we're healthy.'

'So what I'm saying is, you should take care.'

Even though she hadn't achieved anything, by the time Hannah arrived to pick up Oscar, the bell had gone and a fan of kids streamed out the school doors.

Hannah spotted Oscar on the far side of the playground with his friend Dylan, chasing each other like pint-sized satellites around Dylan's mum. She smiled at Hannah as she made her way across the yard. They had almost covered the distance between them before Oscar caught sight of Hannah and broke off his circling to run straight at her, his sprint ending as he slammed into her with a hug that nearly knocked her over. She murmured, 'Careful, Oscar.'

'Sorry, Mum. Can Dylan come over today? His mum says he can, but she says you have to say so.'

Dylan's mum gave Hannah a shrug.

'Please, Mum.'

Oscar had spent the day in a classroom of kids doing she knew not what, but even so, Dylan was a potential reservoir of germs.

'I don't know, Oscar.'

Oscar drew out every word. 'Oh no. You never let me have anyone over.'

'That's not true, Oscar. Dylan came over last week.'

'But that was last week.'

Dylan's mum broke in. 'You know, Oscar, today isn't a good day. Maybe we can do it a different day.'

'But you said—'

'Oscar,' Hannah cut him off, 'a different day.'

By the time they reached the gate, Oscar's dark mood had evaporated. He doubled his journey each time he skipped forward and ran back to her. 'Can I have a chocolate?'

'Sure.'

He ran the length of each block, stopping at the corners for Hannah to catch up. The unalloyed joy he could get from the promise of a chocolate bar made her smile.

The small knot of shops that they passed through on the way home from school would once have been all the necessities – a butcher, a greengrocer, a bank – concentrated around the intersection. Now they were the new necessities – a café, a Thai takeaway, a liquor store. Only the pharmacy and Lily's corner store ignored the changes in fashion.

On the other side of the crossing, a tall, thin woman in a long, straight shift dress meandered in their direction. Hannah frequently saw her around the area, spewing forth obscenities. The woman took an erratic course along the path, peering around as if looking for someone. As they crossed the road, Hannah took Oscar's hand and maneuvered him so as to keep herself between him and the woman. She walked a little faster, tugging gently on Oscar's hand. Her arm jerked back, and she looked to see him picking up something shiny from the ground.

'Come on, Oscar, we don't have time.'

'Why?'

'Don't touch that, it's dirty.'

'It's a bead, it's pretty.'

'Now your hands are dirty.'

Oscar dropped the bead surreptitiously into his pocket and looked at his hands in distress.

'Don't pick things up from the ground. You don't know what's touched them.'

'Can I still eat the chocolate?'

Dirty hands. If she said no, he'd have a meltdown, and the woman was heading straight for them. 'We'll take it home, you can wash your hands before you eat it.' She cursed herself inwardly – this was the kind of situation she should be prepared for.

The woman's hair was cropped so closely that her scalp showed through. Hannah considered covering Oscar's ears, although that would only make it more of an incident for him. If they could get past quickly, if the woman wasn't too loud, he might not even register her. Hannah braced for the tirade.

The woman's voice was high-pitched, piercing, and strangled. 'Are you Jesus today? I am, I'm Jesus today.' She reached a hand out to Oscar, and Hannah realized, with guilty relief, that he wasn't looking. Hannah had never noticed how thin her arms were and wondered if someone looked after her. Her hands were clean enough, but her fingernails were crusted with dirt.

Hannah softly jerked Oscar back out of reach. 'Not today.' She smiled at the woman, trying to divert her attention from Oscar.

'I am. I'm Jesus today.' She seemed satisfied with Hannah's answer. Something on the other side of the road captivated her and she wandered onto the crossing, oblivious of them and the cars. Hannah loosed her grip on Oscar and he shot into the corner store.

By the time she caught up with him, he was picking up and putting down the different bars in turn, slowly reading the words he knew to work out what each was. His hands transferred the germs from the bead onto every wrapper, which in turn would be transferred to the hands of the people who bought them. 'Mouse, look with your eyes and not with your hands.' Since when had she become a compendium of parental platitudes?

Lily leaned over the counter. 'He's fine. It's hard to choose.'

Hannah restrained herself from hurrying his decision-making. That way led only to buyer's regret, tears, and, sometimes, another chocolate bar. Oscar walked all the way along the shelf and back again before he hesitantly stopped in front of a particular box and picked one out. He took it to the counter and put it down in front of Lily.

'He's a good boy,' Lily said to Oscar with a smile.

Normally Hannah would give the money to Oscar to give to Lily, but today she handed Lily the coins herself.

She flinched when Lily picked up the chocolate and pressed it into Oscar's hand, embracing it with her own.

'A good boy.' Lily opened a jar of jelly babies, pulled one out with her fingers, and put it in Oscar's other hand, cupping it with hers. Oscar had popped the jelly baby in his mouth before Hannah got a word out.

Lily's hand had held the coins that Hannah had given her, that Hannah had received from who knows where, that had been held by who knows who, like all the other coins and notes Lily had handled today. And the jelly babies. She didn't want to think how many children's hands had gone into the jelly babies jar even in the last few hours.

Lily watched her looking at Oscar. 'Every day more cases. You make sure you look after this boy.'

Hannah walked the rest of the block and around the corner as if the disease were on her heels. Oscar ran ahead, pulled by the chocolate he couldn't quite have. It was safely unobtainable, in her pocket. He'd never been so eager to wash his hands.

As they came through the front door, Oscar suddenly said, 'Why is she Jesus?'

'I don't know. I guess she thinks she is.' Oscar seemed satisfied and ran to the bathroom, leaving his backpack, his hat, and his fleece dotted down the hall. Hannah let the front door fall back behind her. It closed with a reassuring click.

Oscar came rocketing back up the hall, his hands held out. 'They're clean.'

She looked at the water dripping off them. 'You have

27

to dry them – germs like water. You gave them a big pool to swim in.'

'Okay.' He was already halfway back down the hall.

'And pick up your stuff and put it in your room.' Oscar was gone. 'After you eat the chocolate.'

He was back again, hands wiped but still damp. Holding the bar at the bottom, with the other hand she carefully peeled it like a banana so that the wrapper never touched the chocolate.

Oscar grabbed it and ran off again, 'Thanks, Mum' hanging in the air behind him.

She heard sounds from the living room. The world she had just shut out with the door was leaking in through the airways. 'Television off until you've done your homework.' She picked up the bag, hat, and fleece and tossed them into the bedroom as she passed. When she got to the living room, Oscar was on the floor in front of the blank television, holding the remote.

As a treat, Oscar was allowed to stay up. When Hannah suggested it, Sean raised his eyebrow, said, 'Really?' but didn't take it any further. He was the one who liked to bend the rules. She drew the line closer, so the laxness surprised him more than the bedtime. Calling it a 'treat' allowed her to gloss over the fact that she'd lost track of time on the computer and had completely forgotten to run Oscar's bath.

Oscar came bouncing into the kitchen. 'Can we eat outside, like a picnic?'

Sean frowned. 'It's dark outside, buddy, and your dinner will get cold.'

They ate at the table over Oscar's groans, but he quickly lost himself in retelling his day to Sean. He kept up a stream, Sean only having to throw in 'Oh, really?' and 'What happened then?' occasionally to keep him going. Hannah had already heard these stories this afternoon, which left her mind free to roam. She tripped upon the realization that there hadn't been a single moment in the day when all four of them were together.

The absence of Zac was so strong, it felt like a presence. Watching Oscar now, she found it hard to superimpose Zac's looks and personality on a body that small. But he had been that little once and they had eaten in this kitchen before Oscar was born, three around the table. Two grown-ups and a five-year-old. Then it had just been normal, now it could only be strange. In four years, Zac would be an adult. By the time Oscar was Zac's age, they would be three around the dinner table again.

Before the renovation, where this table stood had been a laundry. Then, the washing machine looked out on the garden. The kitchen had taken up the other half of this room, and its only view was of the side fence. The ghosts of the old Zac, Sean, and Hannah sat at the ghost of the old kitchen table, and the ghosts of the walls she had pulled down cut the room in half.

Sean sat in the dark on the edge of one of the garden beds, backlit by the string of colored fairy lights on the fence.

Next to him were two glasses of wine. He held one out to her. 'Here, I thought you might need this. To recover from your big day.' She sat down on the cold brick and let the tension dissipate as she leaned into him. He was warm, even through their clothes.

Light spilled from Natalie's side of the fence, escaping through the glass doors that spanned the back of her house. Hannah could hear voices – they had friends over, again. The sounds were reassuring, other lives going on, completely independently of her own. She couldn't make out words but the voices rose and fell, sometimes interrupted by an outbreak of laughter, maybe four people in all. From time to time she heard Ella squeal. Hannah was happier to sit in the quiet of her own garden listening to the sounds of Natalie's dinner party than to be at it. It seemed odd that a doctor would have people over now, with the case in Newcastle and everything happening overseas.

A thought drifted across her mind. 'How was your sister?'

'My sister? Oh, I couldn't get on to her.'

Hannah sat up. 'Did you try?'

'It was late there when I got to work, so I missed their day. I tried just now when you were reading, but no answer. I'll try her again before bed.'

'Did you ring work and home? She'll be at work by now.'

Sean shrugged. 'I checked the time. I rang work – she wasn't there so I rang home.'

'Why wouldn't she be there?'

'Because she's on her way to work? Because she didn't go home? Because she drank too much last night and slept through the phone? I don't know.'

'It doesn't bother you?'

'No, it doesn't bother me. She's hundreds of miles from Manchester. Her biggest risk is being scared to death by fear-mongering tabloids. She's in no more danger than us.' He rubbed the back of her hand. 'Which is none, right? Which is as much danger as Zac is in.'

'You and the doctor. You should get together and take turns telling me I'm imagining things.'

'Doctor? Did you have an appointment I forgot? You didn't say anything this morning.'

'You don't need to know about every appointment.'

'Everything all right?'

'Fine. Some young doctor who knows everything. He thinks I'm a hypochondriac.'

'You're paranoid. That's very different from hypo-chondria.'

'You're funny.'

'I know' – he gave her a goofy grin – 'it's my only skill.'

Mon	Tue	Wed	Thu	Fri	Sat	Sun

The noise was muffled, irritating, persistent. She tried not to think about it, tried to go back to sleep.

It was still there. But it wasn't in the room and it wasn't coming from the street. She turned over and hoped it would wake Sean. He could deal with whatever it was.

He didn't.

It invaded her sleep, some kind of an alarm. It wasn't her phone, or a car, or even a burglar alarm. She pulled the pillow around her ears, waiting for it to stop by itself. Hoping. But if anything, it was getting louder. There was no possibility of sleep for her and no chance that Sean would wake. She got out of bed, wrapped her dressing gown tight, and followed the noise.

To Zac's room. And his clock, still set in the absence of its owner.

She whacked it on the top to make it go away. It took a moment for the numbers to make sense. She rubbed her face. Six o'clock. His alarm from yesterday, set early to get to the bus. Why couldn't he have turned it off before he left?

Sean bustled into the kitchen an hour and a half later, well rested. 'Oscar not up yet?'

'You should ring your sister.'

'And good morning to you.'

'Ring her now. It will be getting late there.'

'I have, in fact, already rung her. I'm surprised you didn't hear me. I'm surprised Oscar slept through. We had a terrible line. I had to yell.'

'So why didn't she answer yesterday?'

'She overindulged at her birthday celebrations and turned off the phone. Then forgot she turned it off.'

'And the epidemic?'

'Is literally hundreds of miles from her. Did you make enough coffee for me?'

'I drank it. I've been up for ages.'

'You shouldn't get up so early.'

'Did you tell her to be careful?'

'I told her not to drink so much. London to Manchester's the same distance as Sydney to Canberra. She's fine, she's safe.' Sean contemplated her. 'Zac's safe in Canberra.'

'Says you.'

'My sister and Zac are a long way from anybody who is sick. As are we. Breathe.'

'It will come here. It will get to London, probably before it comes here. In fact, it's almost certainly already in London.'

33

'There'll be warnings, first cases and second cases, and we'll do all the sensible things when the time comes. If you go on like this, you'll be a mess before anything even happens.'

'It will come . . .'

'Yes, it might, and we'll be ready. But that's not yet. I'm not saying ignore it, but you only need to be ready.' He put his arm around her shoulder and rested his head on her hair. 'You taking Oscar to school today or is it my turn?'

'I'll take him. I'm working from home.'

He straightened and threw his hand up in exasperation. 'You didn't go in yesterday. This is what I mean . . .'

'It's Tuesday. I work from home on Tuesdays. I didn't go in yesterday because I had an appointment. It doesn't mean I have to go in today. I'll go in tomorrow.'

'Then I'll do the school run tomorrow.'

They got to Oscar's school seconds before the bell. The footpath was crowded with children in white polo shirts and blue track pants drifting randomly like atoms in a gas. She wove her way between them to the gate, Oscar clutching the tow rope of her sleeve.

The bell rang and the atoms ricocheted around, more vigorous but no more purposeful than before. Oscar hugged her around her middle, and she kissed him on the head.

'Bye, Mum,' and he was off. She watched him run into

the crowd surging towards the school doors until she couldn't tell which blue-and-white back was his.

Hannah turned on the computer with every intention of reading emails, easing herself into work. It wouldn't hurt to have a quick look at the *Herald* and the *Times*, maybe the World Health Organization and Centers for Disease Control websites. And the weather in Canberra. Fifteen degrees Celsius maximum, four degrees minimum. She thought about checking if his fleece was still in his room, but it wasn't as if she could take it to him. She opened her email and looked for something from Zac. Nothing but work.

Mr Moon jumped onto the keyboard and rubbed himself along the monitor. He registered a nonviolent protest by going limp in her hands as she dropped him on the floor, and used the momentum of his fall to spring back up. 'Go and bug someone else.' Half an hour gone and the most riveting information she'd found was that parliament was recalled for an emergency sitting to pass legislation allowing quarantining of individuals. One of the minor parties was calling for a proper debate.

She typed in 'Manba' and scanned down the page of results. The little snippets didn't tell her anything she didn't know.

Manba Respiratory Distress Syndrome – Wiki . . .
www.medical.wiki . . ./Manba
Manba Respiratory Distress Syndrome (also known as MRDS or Manba) is a recently identified disease . . .

Amanda Hickie

Manba Symptoms and Treatment
www.info.medical.manba . . . gov/Symptoms_and_
treatment
The first symptoms of Manba appear within two days
and include coughing, fever, headaches, and diarrhea,
progressing to . . .

Is Manba God's Wrath?
www.trueanswers . . . org/lessons_from_manba
Is Manba a punishment from God? All around us we
see an increase in crime, lawlessness, and immorality
brought about by . . .

Wow! Grandmother discovers this weird cure for . . .
naturalhealth.simple . . ./blog/medicine/manba_cure
Doctors won't tell you this simple cure for Manba. They
make their money from selling you cures invented by
Big Pharma for . . .

She'd read all of these. Somewhere, if she searched
hard enough, there had to be something else, some new
information, something to tell her what was happening
right now.

She clicked on a blog at the end of the first page – *An
Aussie in Paradise*. The last entry was yesterday.

Just back from helping at the hospital. Taking two minutes to let you guys know I am still hanging in there.
Sleep, eat, and back again as soon as I can. Two of my

students are helping out. I told them helping the sick was more important than classes. They told me they could do both. So now they know how to say *I would like a cup of coffee* and *This patient has a purpuric rash and must be isolated*. I'll post again when I can, don't worry about me.

Hannah looked back through the previous entries. One was on the right way to haggle in the local market, another about the students laughing at her attempts to speak Thai, and a lighthearted complaint about the traffic in Bangkok.

She had to stop, clear this from her mind, think about something else. Time to work. As she clicked the little red plus sign on each tab, she tried not to look at the page that appeared below, but as one disappeared, its screaming headline caught her eye. 'First Local Cases – Family Quarantined'. Her fingers fumbled on the keys to reopen it, and there was the headline, stamped across the top of her screen. She skimmed the article for what she really needed to know – where.

The North Shore. So much closer than Newcastle but still with a harbor between them. A harbor and three hundred kilometers between the disease and Zac. And there at the bottom, another reason she should put this out of her mind – they were as yet unconfirmed.

She read the article again, more carefully. Under the headline was a photo of a couple and two boys, a posed family shot in a leafy backyard. Eight and ten, it said. No travel overseas, no contact with any known cases. The parents were sick and the boys had been placed in isolation, just in case.

All those details couldn't calm her. It could be Manba or it could be the flu. It might be a one-off case, but they don't come from nowhere. These people had to have caught it from someone, someone who wasn't currently in hospital, someone who was wandering around coughing, touching door handles and coins and other people's hands. And the people that person had touched in the last few days were touching their children, their children were going to school. Germs have a chain of custody, however invisible it might be. They don't appear spontaneously.

She sat, not reading, not thinking, waiting for something to happen. All she found was a small flame of fear for her family and sadness for the one on the screen. But the first was real, and the second was like the image of sadness. It had the same reality as celebrities on the news. Somehow the screen turned them into fiction. Her legs twitched. She had to stand up, to just move.

She was in front of the pantry, although she didn't remember deciding to walk there. The shelves were loaded with cans and vacuum-sealed bags, but it didn't feel like enough, not enough to keep them safe.

Kate had turned up on her doorstep the day after Hannah told her she had cancer, thrusting a grocery bag at her. 'It's not the most exciting present you're going to get, but it's, you know, to get by. So you don't have to worry about the family not getting dinner or breakfast. I mean, some days you might not even feel like walking around the corner for takeaway. And Sean can't be here all the time. I know it's not gold-standard parenting, but it's just to make it easier sometimes.' Tins of baked beans, a couple of packs of pasta, some jars of pasta sauce. 'I should have brought a scarf.' Hannah had tried inconspicuously to head off the tear by rubbing her eye like it had something in it.

Down at the bottom of the pantry, pushed between some tins of fruit, was a pamphlet she had downloaded from a government website. She hadn't gone out of her way to hide it, but she didn't mind that it wasn't visible. Sean already thought she was obsessed, but it was more like having insurance. The pamphlet said so. The whole back page was a table to calculate how much food, how many toiletries and other groceries they would need for two weeks. Two weeks – a number picked out of the air, good for run-of-the-mill natural disasters like floods or bushfires. A virus didn't simply disappear because some government department had set an arbitrary deadline. When she searched the Internet for 'how long does an epidemic last', it returned the duration of individual plagues in the Middle Ages or the 1918 flu, but Manba was an unknown, and aircraft brought far-flung cities within the radius of local outbreaks. Besides, it never hurt to have an extra tin of tomatoes or packet of rice in the house, although if she looked hard she already had ten tins of tomatoes and five kilos of rice. Just to be safe. Only two weeks' worth would be skimping. Extra food meant extra time.

On the shelves, she saw only what was missing from the nonperishables mandated by the pamphlet. Making the pantry complete might only be a ritual, but it was better than waiting and doing nothing. There had to be food less utilitarian and more fun than tinned tuna and beans. It would be like the big shopping trip before going on holiday, as if whatever small town they were staying in wouldn't have city conveniences like bread.

The pharmacist was losing patience with the woman in front of Hannah. 'If you buy something else to take the total over ten dollars, then you can use your card.'

'But I don't want anything else.'

'Well, do you have exact change?'

'I'm not quite sure, I didn't bring my glasses. Could you add it up for me, dear?' She held out a handful of coins, but the pharmacist kept her hands by her side.

'We're not touching the money, Mrs Mac. You drop it in the disinfectant.' She gestured to a large fishbowl. At the bottom, a layer of assorted coins stood in place of the sand, and halfway up, the notes hung suspended like lazy tropical fish, their colors tinted blue by the antiseptic.

Mrs Mac looked at the collection of coins. 'Well, I'm not sure . . .'

'Hold out your hand.' The pharmacist peered, keeping her distance. 'You've got enough change there. Why don't you drop the coins in one by one, and I'll tell you when to stop. Start with the gold ones.' They counted out six dollars, each one making a small splash and falling surprisingly slowly through the liquid. 'There you go, now you need fifteen cents.'

'I've only got a twenty-cent piece.'

'Well, take the change from the bowl.'

Mrs Mac dropped the coin in and looked doubtfully at the liquid. 'I think I'll leave it. I don't want my hands smelling like that all day.'

'Best thing for them just now, Mrs Mac.'

Hannah hesitated to hand over the prescription she held in her bare fingers. 'I don't know how you're going to disinfect this.' But the pharmacist reached out a gloved hand for it.

'You have no idea how many hands money passes through. I imagine this script has only been touched by two people, at least one of whom should know something about asepsis. They say you can find cocaine on almost every note. Imagine what else gets on them. Not touching the money today.'

The pharmacist came back with Hannah's pills. 'Do you need any hand sanitizer? For regulars I've still got a few bottles. Only two per person though. When they're gone, I'm out and I can't order any more. My supplier says the hospitals are taking everything they can make. So if you want some . . .'

The pharmacist pushed the card machine at her, careful to touch only the back of the machine and with only the back of her gloved hand. Almost every person who'd been in here today must have touched that keypad, and sick people went to pharmacies. Hannah knew she looked ridiculous, but the pharmacist was wearing gloves and there was no one else in the store to see her. She pulled a wipe out from her bag and cleaned the machine.

The pharmacist rang up the script on the cash register. 'Do you want cash out? I'm only giving what's in the jar.'

'I'm fine.' As Hannah picked up the plastic bag with the pill bottle inside, she couldn't help but feel a vague contamination. 'I need to fill another script in a couple of weeks. Will you still be getting things in?'

'So long as it's not antivirals or vitamin C, you should be fine. Oh, and the hand wash is only for regulars. Don't tell people.'

As she left the pharmacy, she briefly considered going back for the hand wash. There was some in the pantry, as specified by the list, but she had no idea how much they might use. Either it would sit there taking up space or they wouldn't have enough.

A car honked its horn and she looked up. It swerved around two people walking down the middle of the road. A man and a woman, maybe late fifties. They were involved in their conversation, just as if they were walking on the footpath. When they came to the intersection, a mother and her two small children were on the pedestrian crossing. The couple waited a few meters back until the family was on the other side. They carefully looked both ways before crossing directly through the middle of the roundabout.

She picked up Oscar from school, rushing him into the car. Her instinct was to get back online and check what had changed in the last couple of hours, but she had to resist that ever-present obsession. She ferried her bags of groceries from the car to the kitchen.

As she unpacked them, she made two piles, one for the kitchen cupboards and one to go back up the hall to the pantry. A cornucopia. Eggs, dried chorizos, some salami-like things that had been hanging at the deli and looked like they would keep well. Fresh meat, fresh fruit, fresh vegetables. She could throw into a shopping trolley a better life than almost anybody who had ever lived. Even a king might well have ruled all he saw, but without greenhouses or airfreight it wouldn't have done any good to demand out-of-season fruit.

The big block of cheddar would make sandwiches, but she'd also bought fancy cheese, something they would relish. She imagined sitting around the kitchen table with Sean, Zac, Oscar, a glass of wine, and some Brie and crackers. That's what she wanted, for her kids to say to her years later, 'Remember that time we shut the front door, and didn't go out for weeks, and we had cheese and crackers and played cards all day.'

With all this food, the only thing she hadn't thought about was tonight's dinner. It hurt to think of using any of the bounty in front of her. All this was for storing, not eating. She would rather make a meal of leftovers than start depleting their stock. In the freezer, she found a plastic bag of excess mince. A tin of tomatoes would make a Bolognese sauce, but that meant using a tin. Only one tin, but the pasta as well.

Oscar was watching her from the doorway where Zac had been standing yesterday. He took up so much less space. Where Zac's body stretched tall, Oscar still had a solidness and stood firmly in contact with the ground. Zac's movements were awkward but leisurely. When Oscar ran, each foot hit the floor with a thud that reverberated along the floorboards throughout the house and under the party wall to Gwen's. Just as well she was a bit deaf.

'Can we play a game? Can we play cheat?'

'You can see I'm putting away the shopping. Maybe we could do something when I'm done.'

'I don't have anything to do.'

'You've got a roomful of stuff. Look on your shelves, there must be something there.' Oscar stomped away, joists shaking. 'Try not to disturb Gwen.'

She put all the packets and tins back in the green shopping bag and carried it to her pantry. It took up one side of the small vestibule in front of the bathroom, presumably intended as a linen closet before she co-opted it. The rows were soothingly neat. She took her time lining up the new tins, making sure the flour and sugar and oats were in one area, the different kinds of tinned vegetables in another. On a whim, she moved the packets of lentils and kidney beans from next to the dried fruit and put them next to the tinned beans. Satisfying, as if each tin were another brick in their defenses.

There was an unusual lack of noise from Oscar while she finished. That often meant trouble, but if she checked up on him, he'd instantly lose interest in whatever he was doing. Better to trust he was occupying himself well.

When she looked at the pantry, she saw meals. Large bags of rice and pasta, calculated out to be so many dinner, lunch, and breakfast servings. She had allowed extra flour for making treats like biscuits or scones, to go with the jars of jam stashed away. She had jars of anchovies, olives, little things that could be added to the basics. Cubes of vacuum-packed coffee and long-life milk calculated out at so many cups a day. With all these she had made her preparations, but she couldn't be sure that they were enough. There had to be flaws in her plans, if only she knew what they were. She needed confirmation, more information, another checklist. She needed to look online for new websites on emergency pantries, to find the thing she had missed.

But not yet.

On the way up the hall, she could hear Oscar talking to himself in two voices. She paused just outside his open door. In the middle of his floor was a big pile of playing cards. On one side, a neat hand of cards lay facedown, on the other sat Oscar, holding his. He announced to the room in a high voice, 'Two kings,' and placed two cards on top of the discard pile. He lay his hand facedown and moved around to pick up the other hand. In a deep voice he said, 'Three aces,' and put three cards on the pile.

'What are you playing, Mouse?'

'I'm playing cheat.'

'How can you play cheat by yourself?'

'I play both sides.'

'But you know if you put down kings or not.'

Oscar looked outraged. 'But I can't say "cheat" just 'cause I know. That would be cheating.'

'Maybe I could play?'

'Okay.'

She allowed herself to become engrossed in trying to cheat obviously enough to get caught but not obviously enough that he knew she wanted to be caught. It was harder still to pretend not to notice the grin on Oscar's face every time he sneaked six cards onto the pile saying it was three. Or when he put down his eighth queen. He didn't cheat by halves.

Oscar threw his last cards triumphantly on the pile. 'Two sixes!' A third card peeked cheekily from the two he had fanned out. She was holding three sixes in her hand. He'd thrown them into the discard pile just before she picked up, saying they were tens.

'You win.'

'Can I watch TV?'

'Sure.'

The instant he was out of the room she knew she needed something to distract her from the subliminal craving to get back to the computer. Too early to start dinner, too late for another coffee. All the shopping packed away. She stared out the kitchen window at the office, and found herself walking across the yard.

The home page of the newspaper had changed again, two new Manba stories. Several schools shut awaiting test results, and the government asking promoters of concerts and sporting events to consider postponing 'until the situation was clearer'.

She searched for Manba again. The same list of results, even down to the *Aussie in Paradise* blog. She made it through to the third page before she found something new – the website of a math student who had created a program to trawl Facebook, Twitter, and blogs for instances of Manba-related words.

Two months ago, cough and fever were all a flat line. Then seven weeks ago, 'cough' and 'fever' rose, slowly at first and, close on their heels, 'diarrhea'. Around three weeks ago, the curve rose sharply. The word 'rash' followed the same curve, but smaller and lagging by about four days. 'Manba' came from nothing two weeks ago, but quickly caught up. The student noted that the uptick in blogged symptoms predated the first medical report by about a month. Hannah clicked on the 'separate by country' button. China was responsible for most of the early curve, but the word 'Manba' itself barely registered.

She checked the weather in Canberra. Fourteen and overcast.

There was only one new email. The same form letter the school had sent every day this week giving hygiene advice and its exclusion policy for kids who had traveled recently. She wondered if the school was excluding kids who had traveled across the bridge. If Zac were here, she'd close the door behind him. She'd keep them home from school, and work from home. If only Zac were here.

Hannah was partway through reading Oscar his bedtime story when the phone rang. She listened out for Sean to answer it.

'You missed a bit.' Oscar looked at her darkly.

'Oh, did I? What did I miss?'

'You missed that bit there.' He pointed to a paragraph she had indeed missed.

'I think you can read. If you can read, why am I reading this to you?' She was trying to catch the tone of Sean's voice even though she couldn't make out words, to get a sense of who was on the other end.

'No, I can't.' Oscar smiled mischievously. 'I can't read.'

'Except when you see ice cream. I think you can read the words "ice cream".'

Oscar pushed his hands over his mouth, trying to hide his smirk. She could hear Sean's steps in the hall. And Gwen probably could too, the way he was thumping.

Sean's head appeared around the door. 'It's for you.'

'Is it . . .' Hannah made a little Zorro 'z' in the air with her finger.

'It's Kate. I'll finish the book.'

It was never going to be Zac. He'd been gone less than

two days. It wouldn't occur to him to ring, and neither should it.

'Hi, Kate.'

'Hi, stranger – we missed you at work on Monday.'

'I had some errands and Zac had a thing.'

'And I had to have lunch by myself. So you can make it up to me tomorrow and take me out. We'll call it a business meeting and you can charge it to the company.'

'Tempting as that is, I was planning to work from home tomorrow.'

'Seriously?' Kate sounded a little annoyed. 'We've got stuff we have to go over. I've got a technical document covered in notes to give you.' Her voice changed again. 'You had an appointment, didn't you? I forgot, a doctor's appointment. Is anything wrong?'

'Fine, no problems, I'm fine. I'm just keeping Oscar home from school.' Better get it out of the way now. 'Probably for a few days. Maybe you could post it. No, don't post it' – fingers on paper, someone licking the envelope – 'scan it. When you've got time, there's no hurry. I've got plenty to be getting on with.'

'Have you taken him to the doctor?'

'No, he's fine. Just, you know, a kid thing.'

'You have to take him to the doctor. If he's sick, you absolutely have to take him to the doctor.'

'He's not sick.'

'Then why would you keep him home? Hell on wheels. Send him to school, come in to work tomorrow. Whatever it is, he can tough it out.' Not even Kate got it.

'Hannah, we've got work to do, we've got deadlines. If he's sick take him to a doctor, if he's not send him to school. Or bring him in if you must.'

'Don't give me a hard time. It's what I have to do. There's nothing wrong with him, I just have to keep him home. The work will get done.'

'You're insane.'

'I'll meet the deadline, which is an age off, and I'll be in in a few days.' *Liar, liar, pants on fire.* 'I get more done from here anyway. I'm not distracted by long lunches.' As she hung up the phone, Hannah felt like the naughty girl caught skipping school.

The living room was dark but for the light from the television flitting across Sean's face. He had the sound turned down so as not to disrupt the delicate ritual of Oscar falling asleep. The silence made the images seem abstract, a random collection of pixels. Two boys, one bigger than the other, sitting on a hospital bed behind a set of glass doors. A nurse swathed in disposable paper clothing carrying a tray with sandwiches, sealed pots of juice. The boys from a different angle, sprawled out on the floor, surrounded by Lego pieces, for all the world like a pair of brothers playing. Quarantined from the fuss they were creating.

Hannah watched from the door frame, still holding the phone handset. 'Can you stay home?'

'Tomorrow?'

'For a while, a few days.'

'Is there a reason?'

'It's just time. Two cases in Sydney. Four, really.'

Sean didn't take his eyes from the screen for a second. 'Literally less than one in a million. Suspected cases. Who are in hospital.'

'And four million, nine hundred thousand, nine hundred and ninety-six people who haven't been tested. The North Shore is only a bridge away. The teacher of those two kids might shop at our supermarket. The children of their doctors or nurses could go to Oscar's school.'

'Two suspected cases that might turn out to be nothing.'

'It's here. Manchester was out of control in less than a week.'

'We're a much bigger city. Your chance of crossing paths with even one person who met somebody who met them is tiny.'

'Someone has to be unlucky. I'm keeping Oscar home until this is over.'

'Fine.' He pulled his eyes away from the television. 'He can watch TV and kick a ball around the park, if that's what makes you happy.'

'He's not going to the park. He's not leaving the house. They're shutting up kids in hospital.'

'To stop it spreading, and it worked, it hasn't spread.'

'That we know of.' She put the phone back on the cradle. 'At least there haven't been any cases in Canberra.'

'Well, why would your foreigners want to bring their smelly germs to Canberra when they can see the glorious sights of Sydney Harbor. Very discerning, your foreign

51

germs.' Sean waited for a laugh or at least a smile, but Hannah was distracted by the TV and a photograph of a confident middle-aged man with a reassuring face, a neatly trimmed beard, and glasses, posed as if for a pass card or an annual report.

'Turn up the sound. Turn it up.'

He fumbled with the remote.

'. . . was one of the team who treated the initial patient and was the first to recognize her symptoms. Until becoming ill, Dr Gilchrist was closely involved in her treatment and that of several patients at Newcastle Hospital suspected of having Manba. Hopes were high last night that he had turned the corner, but his condition deteriorated suddenly this afternoon . . .'

Sean turned the sound down.

'Hey, why? Turn it back up.'

'He's one guy in one hospital that's two hours away.' The images changed again. Grainy cell phone footage. The backs of people running, somewhere in Asia, a knot of police in riot gear taken from a low angle, one of the police lifting his visor, a paper mask underneath. 'I don't think it helps to watch this.'

Hannah shook her head. 'You think pretending it's not happening gives you some sort of magical protection?'

'I think it's happening whether I know about it or not. It's just not happening right here.' He looked at her with gentle puzzlement, as if he was unsure how to explain. 'You have to live the bit that's right in front of you. When it's time for this' – he gestured at the TV screen, and the image of soldiers patrolling a suburban street, maybe Manchester – 'we will do what we have to.' She crossed her arms, didn't say anything. 'They think they might have isolated the virus. That was on before. Someone in Melbourne.'

'So they can look at the little bugger under an electron microscope.'

'And work out ways to treat it. You said we have to hang on for a vaccine. So they make a vaccine and we'll be fine.'

'What about the people in Thailand, England, Newcastle? Those people on the North Shore? A vaccine won't help them.'

'They're not us. You can't save everyone.'

She stared past him, at nothing. 'Is Zac safe?'

'He's safe.'

'He should be here.'

'And he will be, Friday. Come on, let's leave this, do something else.' He tried to pull out her crossed arms.

'I'll' – she pulled away from him – 'I'll check on Oscar.'

'He's fine. He's sleeping in his own bed and he's fine.'

Mon	Tue	Wed	Thu	Fri	Sat	Sun

The early-morning quiet of the sleeping house was broken only by the slowly building hiss of white noise from the kettle and the intermittent hum of the fridge. There was nothing Hannah had to do today, at least nothing with an appointed time. The day was hers to spend.

She pulled a loaf of bread out of the fridge and with the tips of her fingers folded the bag on itself two, three times to make a barrier between the slices and the outside of the plastic. She washed her hands before taking two slices and dropping them in the toaster, wondering if toasting would sterilize them, then decanted the rest into a Ziploc bag.

Sean wandered in, looking bleary. 'The alarm didn't go off.'

'I didn't set one.'

'Oscar will be late.'

'He's not going, remember?'

'Oh.' Sean got a mug from the cupboard and poured

some coffee from the fresh pot. He stared at it. 'Are you sure?'

'Yes, I'm sure.' She took her coffee and toast and sat at the kitchen table looking into the temptingly clear, bright garden. One of those autumn days with no clouds to keep the warmth in. 'I read that they're not letting any planes come from Thailand or the UK. One of the airlines made all their London passengers change planes at the stopover to make it look like that's where they came from. It got turned around in the air.'

'See, they are doing something.'

'A bit late. We're brewing our own batch of bug here – we don't need to import an epidemic.'

He shuffled over in his socks and sat down. 'A couple of days off school won't hurt Oscar. It will fizzle out, or it'll turn out that one guy had something else and the rest ate a bad prawn, like last week. But whenever someone sneezes, people will jump. Are you going to keep him out of school every time?'

'He's staying home until the disease is gone.'

Sean put his mug on the table and started turning it in circles. 'It can't be gone if it hasn't got here yet.'

'I mean *gone* gone. Gone from everywhere.'

Sean looked back down at his mug, seemingly fascinated by the irregular coffee ring it had created. His forehead was furrowed and his eyebrows pulled together as if he had a headache. Hannah waited for him to say something, willed him to say something. His heavy silence gathered weight. She wanted him to be the one to break it, to give her something she could argue with. But she couldn't leave the obvious unsaid, when he was so clearly ignoring it. 'We should all stay home.'

'What if there is never again a time when there are no cases? People get all sorts of things . . . Toddlers get meningococcal disease, but we didn't keep him away from daycare.'

'I want you to stay home.'

Sean banged his coffee mug, sloshing the contents onto the table, drowning the coffee ring. 'I will not stay home today. That's mad. Just because people I have never met might have some disease.' He stood abruptly and walked to the door, as if the movement could express the words trying to pour out. He paced back towards her. 'It's not bloody voodoo. You don't get sick by bad vibrations through the air.'

'Gwen will hear you.'

'Gwen is a deaf old lady who wouldn't hear us shouting "fire".'

'I didn't make this situation. Don't get angry at me.'

Sean rubbed his forehead with his fingers. 'The only situation is the one you're imagining.'

'It wouldn't matter what I say. You've decided nothing is wrong.'

'Nothing *is* wrong. Here. You think it's wrong because you can see it going wrong somewhere else. I get that you don't want to take risks, but I can't live by your paranoia.'

Her instincts were pushing her to walk away, but she

needed something, at least a small something, from him. She slowed her breathing and lowered her voice. 'Could you at least stay home for long enough for me to go to school and get Oscar's books?'

'I have a meeting at eleven.'

She was very calm. 'Then I'll be back by ten thirty.'

'Hon . . .'

'Don't wake Oscar, he can sleep as long as he likes.' She walked awkwardly across the room, marshaling her eyes to keep them from drifting in his direction – straight into the protection of the bathroom and the privacy of the shower.

In the deep distance, a tinny piano started the national anthem. The light, raw voices of the kids dragged behind. A loud and warbling woman's soprano led the piano by half a beat, trying to push them forward without success.

Here Hannah was, standing in the school office, facing a woman who asked questions that she hadn't thought of answers for, when all she wanted to do was sign in and get Oscar's books. She was trying to construct a coherent sentence about the disease and shutting the door, but when she ran it through her mind, it came across as a little bit nutty.

'Oh no, he's not sick.' The truth sounded unconvincing, even to herself.

'You'll need a doctor's certificate if he's away for more than three days. If you've seen any symptoms at all, you should be taking him to the doctor.'

Just stick to what you came for. 'I only want to get his books.'

The woman looked at her with determination, an implacable obstacle. Hannah returned the look. *Say as little as possible, press on through.* She could feel her cheeks redden.

'You're not doing him or the school any favors if he's sick.'

'He's not sick. I'm just keeping him at home.'

'If he's not sick he has to be at school.'

'He's taking a break for a few days from school for' – *be nonspecific* – 'personal reasons, and I want to keep him up to date with his schoolwork.'

'Any non-urgent absences from school need to be pre-approved by the principal.'

Acknowledge what she said, don't argue or justify. 'I'll remember that for next time.'

The woman dismissed her with a gesture to the sign-in book. As Hannah left the office, she tried to walk softly, to avoid drawing attention to her victory won through obstinacy.

Oscar's classroom was on the first floor, in a functional fifties-era wing that had been grafted on to the original Victorian building. As she started up the tight, airless concrete staircase that had been wedged in between, she heard a clatter of small feet on the hard treads above.

Around the bend of the stairs, a stream of tiny children jostled each other, descending towards her. She took the last few steps to the landing and tried to press herself into a corner, in the hope that their turbulence would flow by. Their teacher followed at the rear, issuing random instructions in a booming voice. 'Jason, don't run ahead. Two lines now. Clementine, turn around and keep walking.' She gave Hannah an apologetic smile. The buzz and chatter of high voices reverberated on the hard walls, leaving Hannah to smile back mutely while a procession of black-smudged hands, grimy from schoolwork or the playground, Hannah couldn't tell, brushed against her.

In the corridor on the first floor, stripped of the camouflaging cacophony, her heels clacked on the wooden boards, certain to draw the attention of the whole school. A pair of little kids hurried by, one jiggling with the involuntary twitch of an urgent toilet need, and stared at her in curiosity. She hadn't planned to crash into Oscar's classroom like this – she'd assumed that the woman at the desk would send up for his books and they would appear.

She stopped at the door of Oscar's room. The children were working, books open. Some stared off into space, some purposefully filled an answer into each box on the page. One girl diligently colored all the capital letters, chewing on the end of each pencil as she thought, then returning it to the communal tub before exchanging it for another. At the front, Mrs Gleeson bent down to help one of the children with his work. As Hannah wasn't in a hurry, it seemed polite to wait for her to look up. She scanned the room. One of these chairs must be Oscar's, one of the three or four that were empty.

Already several kids were staring at her. From close by,

she heard a very audible whisper, 'Oscar's mum's here.' A couple of the kids tittered. One of the boys at the back turned around to look at her. 'Is Oscar coming to school today?'

'Not today.'

'Is he sick?' Now the whole row was looking at her.

'No, he's not.'

'So why isn't he at school?'

'He's just not.'

She made her way towards the teacher, along the narrow gap between the children's chairs and the wall. Occasionally she had to shift one and its unexpectedly heavy occupant to get through. She tried to make sure she touched the chairs and children with only the cloth of her sleeve. Her nose started to itch.

The disruption of the chairs made Mrs Gleeson at last glance up. 'Can I help you?' she said sharply.

'I'm Oscar's mum.'

'Oscar's not sick,' came a voice from the back of the room.

'Thank you, Mitchell.' She said the name with two distinct syllables. 'Get on with your work now.'

'I'm sorry to interrupt, but Oscar's going to be away for a few days and I want to pick up his books so he can keep up with his work.'

'Has Oscar got the flu, Mrs Gleeson?' came another voice.

'It's not flu, it's called Manba,' a small girl near her said with great gravity.

'Oscar hasn't got the flu. He's just having a few days at home.' She smiled at Mrs Gleeson in the hope it would smooth the way.

'You'll need to inform the front office.' Mrs Gleeson looked slightly more annoyed and less distracted. 'And we'll need a note.'

'Oh, I talked to the woman in the front office.' Her cheeks were hot again.

'Melanie, could you help Oscar's mum find his workbooks?' The grave girl got up from her desk.

Hannah leaned down to the girl without getting too close, and spoke softly. 'Which desk is Oscar's?'

As Hannah pulled the top book from the shelf under his desk, a mass of books and papers tumbled out, landing on the floor with a thud. All the kids looked. She got down on her knees and sorted through the pile, pulling out anything that looked like a textbook. The rest she pushed haphazardly back, an approximation of how Oscar had left them.

'Is there anything else?' she whispered to Melanie. The girl nodded solemnly and led her to a row of boxes at the far side of the room. Behind her, Hannah heard one of the children sneeze.

Melanie flicked through the books in one of the boxes. Her hands touched every one before Oscar's. Hannah was grateful for plasticized covers and the disinfectant wipes she'd brought with her. She quietly thanked the girl and shuffled sideways out of the room, trying to catch Mrs Gleeson's eye, but the teacher didn't look her way.

As she walked briskly away along the echoing hall, she felt each step shaking off dust, contamination, the press of human contact. Making her lighter. She was not beholden to teachers, friends, organizations. Not constrained by any outside requirements. She didn't care if the school wanted written notice in advance, she didn't care if Mrs Gleeson disapproved, she didn't care if she'd been economical with the truth, or if anyone thought she was ridiculous. Her boys – that was all she needed to consider.

The front door was closed again. For now, at least. She would have to work on keeping it closed. The burble of the TV leaked from the living room, where Oscar lay, zoned out, watching a primary-colored and overtly educational cartoon.

She found Sean in the kitchen, seated at the table, absorbed in a magazine. Without waiting for him to look up or finish what he was reading, she said, 'So, how long has he been watching TV?'

'Not long.'

'Really?'

Sean looked up, his face set. 'Yes. Really.'

'What's he been doing?'

He stared at her impassively. She expected him to say, with Zac's defiant intonation, *Stuff.* 'He played. In his room.'

'With you?'

'He didn't need me, he was fine by himself.' Sean stood, stretching as he got up. 'I'll be off.' He stalked stiffly past her. 'I've already spent half the day here.'

She caught up with him just as he stepped into the living room. 'I'd rather you didn't go.'

He stopped, turned, and with a deliberately everyday tone said, 'I don't get to choose. Turning up is not optional. I have a contract. If I don't show up they don't pay me.' An edge was starting to creep into his voice.

Hannah glanced over at Oscar, who was still engrossed in the cartoon. She took in the unveiled annoyance on Sean's face and decided to ignore it. 'I can't keep him safe if there's a chance you're bringing home the very thing I'm trying to shut out.'

'And I can't drop everything because you're a bit freaked. It's not a school full of kids, it's an office. We don't swap spit.'

Oscar shifted his legs and scratched the side of his face, and they both froze. Hannah pulled Sean through to the hall and shut the door behind them.

Concern couldn't completely drive away Sean's look of impatience. 'I think you like the idea of us all staying home. And if we have to, we will, but until then I go to work and I get paid.'

'We don't need the money.'

'We don't? I'm glad you think so. I'm not so sure. What happens when they decide not to renew me because I didn't show? What happens if one of us gets sick? We don't have anything in reserve. We've still got debts, we've got bills. I'm going in today.'

'Money is not as important as being alive.'

'Let's save that thought until we need it, because the

bank thinks differently.' He rubbed his fingers gently along her cheek. 'When the time comes, I'll stay home. But we're not there yet.'

He kissed her lightly, and she pulled him into a close hug. 'The school looked so normal . . . I don't know what to think.'

He squeezed her tightly. 'Have fun with him today. Try not to worry.' She let him go and he unlocked his arms from around her. 'I'll see you tonight. I promise not to kiss anyone.'

She had a plan, for everyone to be under the one roof. For the door to be closed, with all the problems outside. But Sean was at work, Zac in another city, and the front door was flapping open and closed, wafting in the outside world.

Oscar still lay on his back, stretched out across the floor. His head was near the television with his neck extended to see the upside-down image. He appeared to be in the same zombie-like trance, although the program had changed.

'Hey, I picked up your schoolbooks.'

'Okay.'

'Tell you what, why don't we do some painting?'

'Okay.'

Out on the patio she set up the paints and brushes and tacked up some sheets of used printer paper on the glass door in lieu of an easel, just like last year, before he started school. She even dug out his painting smock, an old shirt of Sean's that on Oscar nearly reached the floor.

The third time she called him, he came from the TV, sluggishly, but refused her help getting into the smock – a self-sufficiency clearly learned at school. Even rolled up as far as they could go, the sleeves were too long and he flapped his hands around in the wide openings, engulfed in billows of fabric.

'What should I paint?'

'I don't know. What craft were you doing at school?'

'People we know. We made a chart of all the people we know, and how they go with us. You know, lines that say who they are.'

'Well, why don't you paint someone you know who isn't here. Maybe you could paint where they are as well.'

Oscar gave intense concentration to the featureless stick figure he was creating. She guessed it was a boy only because it wasn't wearing a dress. He made two brown dots for the eyes and, with the brush, he scribbled the same brown all around the top of the head. Brown eyes and brown hair could be Sean or Zac, or lots of people.

After a burst of effort, Oscar stopped, as if turned off by a switch.

'What is it, sweetie?'

'I don't know how to paint a Canberra.'

'It's a city, it's got buildings and trees. You can imagine it.' Oscar looked dubious about the propriety of 'making up' Canberra. He painted a tree without much enthusiasm, then moved to the next sheet.

In the top left corner, he constructed a stick figure. Around it he painted a wonky black box and another much narrower box next to the first. 'That's Mr Turner's class. Dylan's in that class.'

'You could paint you and Dylan playing.'

'But I'm here.'

'You could pretend you were there.'

Oscar gave her a scornful look and went back to his work. This was like a gift of a few more moments of toddlerhood. Just him and her, and nothing that had to be done. When she thought back to last year, already she couldn't remember how they had filled the time. Naps helped, but she was certain he wouldn't be going back to naps. All those hours in a day. She started making a mental list of things they could do together and, more important, things he could do by himself. At least at the end of the week, Zac would be home. If she could prevail on him to do stuff with Oscar, they could be company for each other.

She was deep in her thoughts and didn't quite hear when Oscar said, 'Am I going to die?'

'Hmm, what's that, Mouse?' She replayed the sentence. 'No. Why would you die?'

'That's what happens. You have to stay home if you get sick. And then you die.'

'Who said that? You're not sick.' He stopped painting to listen. 'You're staying home so you don't get sick.'

'So will the people at school die?'

'Has someone been scaring you about getting sick?'

'At assembly they told us to wash our hands and not to eat anybody's lunch 'cause you'll get sick. Jack said Rose ate Anna's apple at lunch and she was going to die, but she didn't.'

Hannah pulled Oscar and his paint-splotched smock into her arms. 'I hope no one we know is going to die. The government is going to do everything they can to keep us safe.'

'Will the government come to our house? You and Daddy can keep me safe. Then the government doesn't have to do it.'

'When we have to, we'll all stay at home, just Zac and you and me and Dad, and we'll be fine, okay? You don't have to worry. But for now, we're going to have a holiday, just you and me.'

'Okay.' And suddenly the need to finish his painting completely replaced any thoughts of death.

He abandoned the painting as enthusiastically as he had undertaken it. It was only just twelve, but she figured they could stretch out lunch for at least half an hour. And then he could start on his schoolwork. That would give her a chance to make progress on the manual. Enough, hopefully, to appease Kate.

She rummaged around in the fridge for food she could use up. Half a cucumber, some cabanossi sausage. When she added the crackers to the slices on the plate, she noticed that everything was round, so she searched out foods that would continue the theme and added some dried apples and a cheese stick cut into tiny wheels. The apples were particularly pleasing – their circles within circles would tickle Oscar's fancy.

'Time for lunch.'

He appeared in the door as soon as she called. 'Can we have a picnic?'

'Sure, why not?'

Oscar lay on the blanket in the sun, nibbling at a dried apple ring he'd pushed on his finger. His eyes closed for a moment – she could hope that nap times were back – but they popped open again. How easy it would be to curl up in the sun as well, but she had promised Kate a first pass by the end of the week, a draft she hadn't done any work on yet.

Hannah set up his schoolbooks and a couple of puzzle books on his little table and chair behind the door in the office. He stirred from the blanket, followed her in, and sank his head onto his table, undisturbed by the clack of her keyboard. After a few minutes, he raised his head and started looking through the activity books.

'Hey, let's do the schoolwork first and then you can have some fun.'

'I like doing this one.' He pulled out a math book. For five minutes she read in silence, until the sound of a page turning broke her concentration.

'Finish the first page, Mouse, before you start the next one.'

'I have.'

'Already?' *What did they do at school all day?* 'Save the rest for later. What about doing some mazes? You like those.'

That kept him quiet for just enough time for her to reread the last sentence before he popped out of his chair.

'Look at this.' A thick scribbled line, crossing and crossing back through the boundaries of the maze.

'Great, good job.'

He kept up an almost constant chatter, narrating his every action, but if she dropped in a 'Hmm' or 'Is that so?' sporadically, she could read and keep him happy at the same time. Until she realized that he'd just said the same thing twice. 'What, sweetie?'

'Well, can I?'

'Can you what?'

'Play outside now?'

'Sure you can.'

The plastic clamshell filled with sand sat in one corner of the grass, pushed against the garden bed. She gladly took a break from working to open it for him and then left him, reluctantly. If she could only get another hour of work done, she'd take a break.

But first she rang Sean and was sent to voicemail. 'Hi, it's me. If you have time, could you stop at a bookstore or a newsagent and get as many activity books as you can find? I'm going to need them.'

Only half past one and already she was fighting the urge to crawl under her desk and sneak a nap, what with the trip to the school, the argument with Sean, and keeping Oscar occupied. But her exhaustion was overlaid with the nagging feeling that maybe somewhere something was wrong.

She needed new words to make her calm, to know that right now everything was okay. But right now didn't last long. Minutes, nanoseconds. In fact, maybe right now someone was typing terrible news, just about to click the 'post' button. It was an unsatisfiable addiction.

First Canberra's weather. Fine and sunny. Minimum of three, maximum of sixteen. A nice day, but a bit chilly tonight. Zac would be at Parliament House now. Maybe walking around the grassy hill.

The front page of the *Herald* snapped in place. 'Eleven More Suspected Cases'. She scanned the article. More than what? More than last night? If she'd checked this morning, she would know.

The story was full of vague assertions and paragraphs lifted from previous articles. The only real detail was at the bottom of the page, a table of hospitals and cases. Newcastle still only had two deaths – the doctor and the very first woman who'd been at that conference – but they now had nine confirmed cases. On the North Shore, all seven cases were unconfirmed. And at the hospital just down the road, the hospital she had been at on Monday – her hospital – four unconfirmed cases.

She looked around for Oscar. As if she would see a haze of contagion drifting towards him.

He was standing with his toes on the middle rail of the fence, his chin not quite reaching the top. His head was tilted back so he could see over. Blanched tips and red knuckles betrayed the strain in his fingers as he held up his weight. On the other side, Gwen was patiently listening to what appeared to be a long and convoluted story. Through the glass, Hannah could barely hear the sound of their voices. Gwen smiled at Oscar, gently patted his small hand, then picked it off the fence and held it in hers.

The very old and the very young, that was who the Internet said were most at risk. Oscar climbed down from the fence and ran back to her in the office.

'Gwen asked why I wasn't at school. She said I don't look sick.'

'What did you tell her?'

'I said I'm not sick. I said I'm home so I don't get sick.'

'Sweetie, it's probably best if you don't touch anyone over the fence.' She guided him back to the house, the bathroom, and soap. 'Not Gwen or Ella or Natalie, not until you go back to school. You can talk to them, that's fine, we don't want to be rude. Just don't go near the fence.'

Wedged between Hannah and the sink, Oscar stood on a low stool, washing the carrots while she reached her arms around him to scrub the potatoes. It kept him occupied and he liked to feel useful, grown-up. The carrots came out clean, if dripping wet, and most of the water ended up on the counter or down the front of his T-shirt.

'Mouse.' She tried to sound stern, at least stern enough to impress Oscar. 'Be a little careful. Try to keep the water in the sink, okay?'

'I can see Natalie. Is she making Ella's dinner too?'

Through the window and over the top of the side fence, Natalie's head silently bobbed around in her kitchen. Here they both were, doing the same things at the same time, no more than a couple of meters apart. A mirror life, in spitting distance and yet totally isolated from hers, intersecting only to pass conversation on the front step or in the back lane.

'Don't stare at her, Mouse, it's rude.'

'But that's where the window is, and I'm standing here. I can't not look there.' Fair point, neither could she. He twisted himself so his hands were in the sink and his head pointed at the ceiling.

Hannah glanced across to see Natalie laugh as she floated across the room and out of sight in the direction of the garden. Through her own back door, Hannah heard Natalie's back door open. She heard her call Ella for dinner and Ella call back.

They could have moved this window when they were renovating to give a view of the garden, but she'd had other distractions that year. The time she had now with Sean and Zac and Oscar had been paid for by putting one foot in front of the other when her feet were as far as she could see. She had done what was required of her, been through all the hard stuff. She should get to sit this one out, right here, with her family. Other people could deal with this virus, other people could get sick – she had paid already.

Sean offered to do bedtime, but that meant giving up the last moments with Oscar before sleep claimed him. Still, the day had worn Hannah out, so she chose a short book, and by the time she kissed him good night, his eyes were nearly closed.

She sneaked into their bedroom. Sean had already told her once tonight not to bother, but it was Wednesday and Zac hadn't rung. Independence was important, but all she had to do was press the dial button.

'Hi.' He sounded bright and alert.

'Hi, Zac, it's me.' She spoke softly, so as not to wake Oscar in the next room. 'How's Canberra?'

'Mum.'

'Were you expecting someone else?' She was mortified to hear herself sound so much like a mother.

'Well, we had to go into a room for four, so Daniel and Ben ended up in a room with two other kids, and we're not allowed to walk around the corridors unless we're going to the activity room, and their room's the other way, so we can't go there and they can't come here, so they keep ringing us. They rang everybody else's phone.'

'So are you having fun?'

'Sure.'

'Is Canberra interesting?'

'I guess.'

'Is everybody well?'

'Mum' – she could hear the sigh – 'no one is sick here. What do you think?'

She waited for him to say something more. 'Well, stay safe. Have a good time.'

''Kay. Bye.' And he was gone to more immediate things.

She opened the living room door quietly. Sean was half-way between standing and sitting on the edge of the sofa, his face screwed up and flushed behind the blue reflected light of the television. He took a step towards the images and turned a face to her as if about to pour out what he had just seen, but she put her finger to her lips. She softly closed the door behind her, but he had already slipped out the other way. She followed his shadow through the unlit kitchen and found him silhouetted by the moon and the fairy lights from the garden.

Hannah tried to read his face in the gloom. 'Are you okay?'

'It's an island. It's an island. How hard can it be to keep something off an island? Germs can't swim. Sick people can't swim. You shut the fucking airport and we're all okay.'

'So we shut *our* door, and *we're* okay.'

'Someone died today. There are people dead. That's not okay. One or two dead people' – his figure shrugged with contempt – 'well, that just happens sometimes. Nothing anyone can do about that. If it was ten people all at once, that would be a disaster. Enact a law, rebuild a highway.' Sean punctuated his anger by pummeling the darkness in front of him. 'But if you space them out, ten dead people just not all at once, that doesn't require any action.'

'Ten. I didn't know it was ten.'

'Not yet, but this is how it started in Manchester. Just an isolated infection yesterday, an unfortunate death today. Neatly spaced out, but each one sooner than the last until it explodes.'

'It's not like this wasn't coming. I said this was coming.'

'So are you happy about this? Are you happy that you're right?' His raised arms shook slightly.

'Why would I be happy?' Hannah took a deep breath to try to slow herself down. 'I don't want there to be an epidemic, but since there will be, maybe you could listen to what I've been saying. And stay home.'

'It didn't have to come here. The government could have cut it off before it started, but they missed a chance. They should have shut the airports. Someone has died. It's already too late.'

Hannah soothed his arm down and held his hand, as if she could anchor him. 'And in this reality, they didn't, so there's no use wishing for a different one. We work with what is, we have to if we want to get through. Please. Stay home.'

'That doesn't solve it.'

'It does for us, which is all I can care about now.'

'What about everybody else? It doesn't have to be a crisis. They could slow it down, they could buy time, they could shut the damned airport.' He walked off into the dark of the garden, and she let him go. She didn't have anything to say except *yes*.

Mon	Tue	Wed	Thu	Fri	Sat	Sun

Ten thirty. Two and a half hours of doing something that looked approximately like work to anyone looking into the office from the outside, and still no nearer to completing the reading she'd planned for herself this morning. But the only people looking in from the outside were Oscar and Sean, roughhousing on the small patch of grass that passed for a backyard. She was enthralled by their physicality, something she noticed between Sean and both the boys that she could only imitate. It seemed to come naturally to the three of them.

In two hours' time, by agreement, she would break for lunch and Sean would get the uninterrupted office time for the afternoon. Sean's heartbeat was in the house now, and she could feel it. There was a rightness in the three of them being within the same walls. And in six hours' time, she would have Zac too.

Canberra, windy, clouds clearing in the afternoon, fourteen. She tried to think herself six degrees colder, to feel what he was feeling. Tried to imagine the walls of the

National Gallery, the paintings he would be looking at. She tried to think herself into his thoughts – coming home, the art in front of him, or some computer game. Even when he was right in front of her, she had no access.

Twenty past eleven. She watched Oscar carry a can of cat food out to the patio. Mr Moon followed, weaving in between his legs, fawningly rubbing against him, as if Oscar were not already feeding him. Oscar squatted on his heels and put down the can, engulfing Mr Moon in a hug, and the cat took the opportunity to stretch out his neck and lick the top layer from the tin. He had become Oscar's in the last few days, to be found demanding pats while Oscar watched TV on the sofa, or hidden at the bottom of his bed before lights-out. A furry substitute for friends or a brother.

Twelve fifteen. She reached the end of a paragraph and forced herself to start the next section. Twelve twenty-seven. Close enough.

The kitchen was oddly quiet. No Sean or Oscar in the living room, but through the closed door to the front of the house she could hear puffing and panting, giggling and little feet thudding. She opened the door to the sight of Oscar sprinting up the hall and back down again. He slammed into Sean, who was watching the stopwatch on his phone and barely swayed back.

'Whoa, six point three. What's five minus three?'

'Two!'

'Point two of a second faster. That's the fastest yet. Good job.'

Hannah made a face at Sean. 'Fitness and sums – what are you, Superdad?'

'I'm doing it for you.' He gave her a kiss. 'I've drained all the energy out of him. He should be an angel this afternoon.'

'What about poor old Gwen? The noise is probably driving her nuts.'

'I haven't heard her. Maybe she's not home.'

'Maybe *she* doesn't go running up and down the hall.'

'She adores Oscar – she wouldn't begrudge him a bit of exercise. Anyway, she's a bit deaf.'

'Do you think she's' – Hannah lowered her voice although Oscar was right there – 'all right?'

'I haven't heard any coughing.'

'I mean coping, by herself.'

Sean shrugged. Oscar was splayed out on the floor at her feet, his still slightly chubby arms and legs flung out. 'I'm' – *pant* – 'so' – *pant* – 'hungry.'

She reached down and tickled his exposed strip of belly. He contracted into a convulsing, laughing ball. 'Well, lucky for you it's lunchtime.'

Oscar stretched himself out. 'What's for lunch?'

Sean picked him up and hoisted the wriggling boy over his shoulder. 'I don't know. Let's see what we've got.'

'Toasties.' Oscar wiggled his legs in the air.

'Let's go look.'

Oscar got toasties. When Hannah looked in the fridge, it was full to bursting, but all she saw was the food they didn't have, so she cut the ham and cheese in paper-thin slices.

Sean asked as she handed his plate to him, 'Did you put mustard on that?'

Oscar paused from eating his way frontward into his sandwich and looked at it with horror. The food dropped out of his mouth. 'I don't like mustard.'

'Don't be disgusting, Mouse – it won't kill you. Anyway, there's no mustard on yours. Did you taste mustard?'

'I need some milk.'

'There's no mustard.'

'Some milk!'

'Just one cup, or a glass of water instead.'

Sean came back with the tumbler of milk. 'Your mum's right – water after this. The carton's empty.' Sean looked over at Hannah. 'I'll get some more after lunch.'

'Where from?'

'Around the corner.'

'Through the front door, around the corner?'

'That's where the corner store is.'

She gave him a look.

'I need a cup of coffee. I mean *need* a cup of coffee after wrangling Superboy this morning. I can live without it being a cappuccino, just, but I can't live without the milk. I'm all for not dying, as long as I don't have to do it without coffee.'

'It's not a joke.'

'Come on, five minutes. I spent the whole day at work yesterday. Five minutes outside today won't kill me.'

'You can't be half in quarantine. It's all or nothing.' The way he looked at her, he knew she was right, but she thought the coffee might still win. 'I'm serious. It's *all*, including the corner store.' She turned her back on Sean, focusing all her attention on Oscar. 'Eat the rest of the sandwich. The crusts aren't poison.'

Oscar threw his head back in his best theatrical display of despair. 'But I hate them. They're revolting.'

'They taste exactly the same as the rest of the bread.'

Oscar pushed the thin right angles of crust across his plate and stuck out his bottom lip.

'I mean it, that's lunch. You're not getting anything else.'

'I'm not hungry.'

Sean butted in. 'A couple of crusts don't matter. We're not going to starve for a couple of crusts.'

'We'll regret those crusts before this is over.' She waggled a finger at him, only partly in jest. 'Who knows how long this is going to go on for. Eat your crusts, Oscar.' Hannah gave her best mother face and Oscar jammed them into his mouth with a look of distaste.

'You said you planned, but you didn't think about coffee?'

'There's plenty of coffee, but milk doesn't last. Things we need fresh we can get delivered from an online supermarket.'

'I know I'm arguing against my own interests here, 'cause if I have to go without coffee there'll be trouble, but they have germs online too. They'll be packed by people who will touch them. And you'll have to answer the door to some delivery guy with germy hands. How's that different from picking up a carton of milk from Lily's?'

'You can pay online, they drop them on the porch. We leave them as long as necessary before we bring them in. I'll ring Natalie – she can tell us how long.'

'Fine, you do that, but right now I need milk for coffee.'

'Because I planned, there's long-life in the pantry. Make sure you write it on the list so I can order some more.'

Oscar begged to be allowed to watch TV. It was early afternoon, he'd already done his schoolwork with Sean, and the only thing on was programs for toddlers. She told him he could have one hour and if he used it up on little kids' shows now, he couldn't watch something else later. He spent several minutes with the schedule, hand on chin with a furrow of concentration on his brow before firmly announcing that he wanted to watch now. All the big-boy trappings were falling off, and for a few days, in the privacy of his own home, he didn't have to live up to anything. He didn't even have a big brother to want to be like.

She watched a few minutes of the brightly bobbing puppets. It wouldn't be the worst thing in the world if she checked the news, quickly. Sean wouldn't come in, Oscar didn't need her. He didn't even notice as she got off the sofa.

As she snuck back through the living room door with her laptop under one arm, the TV didn't sound right.

The reflected light on Oscar's face didn't look right. She turned to the screen. The image wasn't right. Instead of primary colors, it was filled with a photograph. The two boys she had seen in the newspaper on Tuesday, with the word ORPHANS blazed across the top and underneath, BREAKING NEWS.

'. . . parents died this morning within hours of each other . . .'

Hannah couldn't stop staring at the picture. Two boys.

A feeling welled inside her, old and familiar. When her doctor had sat her down and clearly, patiently said the unambiguous words that had been implied by mammograms and biopsies, she waited to cry. That was the expected response. What had blindsided her instead was overwhelming anger, a convulsion of rage. She had looked for her fear of dying but found in its place anger on Zac's behalf. That a stupid, random mutation might stop her from finishing what she had started when he was born. That she might be forced to let Zac down.

On the screen, an older woman looked pale and lost. 'I just want to take them home. I promised my daughter, but they won't let me take them home.'

Hannah rubbed away a tear. These two boys had lost the people who were supposed to be there for them. She blamed the universe for doing stuff like this. She blamed the television for bringing it to her. She pressed the off button to shut it out.

Oscar looked up at her, grave, the TV spell broken. 'That's not good.'

'No, it isn't.'

'That's sad for those boys.'

She tried to look behind the serious face, to gauge if turmoil lay underneath, whether he saw himself and Zac in these brothers. 'I think they're very sad now. But their grandma will look after them.'

He was too young to know so much about death. And whether he knew or not, events would continue in the outside world. The best thing she could do for him was to keep it from invading their space.

'Oscar?'

'Yeah, Mum.'

'I think I'd like you only to watch the kids' channels from now on. Okay?' She turned the TV back on and changed the channel. Thank goodness for cable.

She was saved from any need to explain by the phone ringing. 'I'll only be a minute.' He went back to watching cartoons, savoring what was left of his hour. He seemed no different.

She scrabbled around the kitchen, looking for the handset. 'Hello?' She sounded more flustered than she would like.

'Hi, is that Hannah? It's Allison. I'm Mitchell's mum? Mitchell is in the same class as Oscar? They play together a lot.'

Hannah couldn't bring to mind Mitchell and only had a vague idea who Allison was. 'Oh, hi.'

'Mitchell tells me that Oscar's been away from school. I hope everything is all right.'

'Yes, fine. He's fine. I just decided to take him out for a few days, that's all. You know' – she really needed to work out her story – 'a few days to recharge his batteries.'

'Aren't you a good mother.'

Hannah said nothing, waiting to see what Allison was leading to.

'So, I was thinking, you know, how smart you were to see what was coming, and since you're already at home, I thought Mitchell could come over to play.'

'We're very busy this weekend.'

'But you're home Monday.'

'Monday?'

'You must have heard – they're closing the school today. And I have to go to work, but two are easier than one anyway. I'm sure Mitchell would keep Oscar out of your hair.'

'So you could go to work?'

'Exactly. I mean, I don't know what the government is thinking. Who's going to watch the kids? What do they think, we're all going to stay home?'

'Oscar's not seeing anyone at the moment. That's why he's at home.'

'Right, that's the point. But he still needs to play, doesn't he? Mitchell would be no trouble.'

'No, the point is, we're not having contact with anyone.'

'Mitchell's healthy.'

'I'm sure he is, but you're still going to work.'

'If I wasn't, I'd look after him myself. I'm very careful. I use a tissue when I open the bathroom door.'

'No, I'm sorry. We're not having any visitors at all. I'm sorry I can't help.'

'I can't just take time off – I have a job to go to. And you're already at home, so he's not going to put you out. I think we all need to help each other at a time like this.'

'I have a job to do too. Why don't you take holidays or work from home? That's what I'm doing.'

'Well it's nice for you that you have the option of not turning up to work if you want . . .' Hannah hung up. Her hand was shaking.

The living room was empty, the TV off. Oscar wasn't in his bedroom. She found him in the small square of garden, standing expectantly, one foot on his soccer ball. 'Can we play now?'

'Sure, but you're going to win.'

The sun and the running quickly heated her up and she was puffing within minutes – she wasn't used to running around, and it was hard to catch her breath when she was laughing at the same time. Oscar's moves tickled her. He had learned to use his small size and greater maneuverability against Zac, who far outclassed him in strength and speed, and he ran under her legs, doubling back around her full tilt. Zac would be back tonight, a much better soccer partner.

Angry school parents, work deadlines, pantry lists. That was the outside world. This was real life – chasing a ball according to some random rules Oscar made up as he went along. Lying on the grass trying to catch her breath. As she lay, she heard the familiar sounds of Stuart's car arriving home. She sat up to see Ella, seemingly floating in midair, emerge from the garage. Underneath her, Stuart's head and shoulders rose as he straightened on the way out.

'Hi, Stuart, you're home early.'

Stuart had a thin, angular face that looked a little like something unpleasant had just happened but he was too polite to mention it. He was a hard man to get to know, especially as Hannah couldn't shake the feeling he found her in some way disappointing. Today he looked particularly put out. 'Nat can't get away. Too many patients to see and no one else to do it, and I couldn't get the sitter to come – she says she's busy, has to pick up her own kids. And apparently, they're closing the daycare, so they wouldn't even keep Ella an extra hour. You'd think they'd only just heard of Manba the way they're going on. If it was safe enough to be there this morning, I can't see why it's not safe now.'

'The daycare too?'

'They could have kept her until five. Now I'm going to have to go back to work when Nat finally comes in. This whole thing is a complete screwup.'

'It must be a worry, Natalie seeing so many sick people.'

'They're doing house calls, for God's sake. You're not allowed into the clinic with a cough because you might be infectious. Or you might only have a cold, in autumn. So she's driving from house to house and has to suit up for each consultation. It takes her an extra half an hour, a ridiculous waste of time. I told her to send one of the junior doctors, but she says they're her patients.'

'If she's got a moment tonight I wanted to ask her a question about how long the virus would last on, you know, plastic. Like a shopping bag or something.'

'There'll be a website. The government is very good at websites and public awareness campaigns.'

'It's very vague.'

'That would be because they don't want to look like they've got nothing to say. The only thing they're good at is platitudes and press releases. Nat says assume nothing is safe.'

'Daaad.' Ella pulled at Stuart's hair.

'I'm told it's snack time. Usually she has it at daycare but they were worried about contamination. They could have at least thrown a biscuit at her. Okay, Pumpkin, snack time.'

Hannah watched them disappear into the house.

'Mummy.' Oscar tugged at her jeans. 'Can Natalie be my mum when you die?'

'I'm not going to die anytime soon, Mouse.'

'I like Natalie. I like going to Ella's house. They have ice cream after dinner. When you and Daddy die, I want to live with them. When Zac comes home he can live with them too.'

'We're not going to die. Of course we're not going to die.' She was making promises she couldn't necessarily keep. 'We'll be careful. And you could live with Aunty

Cindy.' It wasn't the first time she'd had to consider the ramifications of having no family left beyond one sister-in-law on the other side of the world. 'It's very, very unlikely.'

Before she finished talking, Oscar was back kicking the ball around the grass. He was a difficult kid to read sometimes. He would kick the ball across the grass, then turn suddenly and steer it in the direction of the garage, all while keeping up a commentary to himself, just under his breath. Without breaking step, he punctuated his run with 'I done it!' – although she couldn't tell what the 'it' was that he'd done – followed quickly, and just as unaccountably, by 'Ohhh nooo.'

He came running over to her. 'Did you see that? Did you see that?'

She wasn't sure what 'that' was, but he looked so pleased with himself. 'That's great.'

The phone, the home phone that no one called, started to ring for the second time today. She pelted back to the kitchen.

The machine clicked on, and she listened to her own voice give the message as she fumbled for the handset. For an instant she thought they'd hung up, then a distorted voice came from the answering machine. 'Oh, hello, Mr and Mrs Halloran. It's Paul Abrahamson, Zac's teacher. There's nothing wrong, Zac's fine. I just rang to let you know . . .'

Hannah got the phone to her ear. 'Hello, hi, yes. I'm here.'

'This is Zac's teacher, he's fine. I'm ringing around all the parents to let you know that we won't be back at five.'

Her heart was thumping from running, but to her body it felt like panic. 'What's happened?'

'Nothing, all the kids are fine. There's a bit of trouble with the bus. We're trying to organize to get home tonight, but at this stage we couldn't be back until at least eight. We may have to stay the night.'

'But surely the bus company has a responsibility to get you back?'

'As soon as I know something more definite, I'll email everyone with the details.' And with that, he hung up.

She stared at the handset. No. That was not how things went. Zac was coming back tonight, and everything would be under control. She had let him go reluctantly and she'd lasted five days – five days – with the dread of having done the wrong thing because tonight it was supposed to be all right. There was a plan, a timetable to be adhered to. This was how things go wrong, one small setback at a time. One quizzical look from a doctor who says, 'It's probably nothing, but let's check it out.' One slightly flustered X-ray technician who says, 'I didn't get a good image, we'll take a couple more.' She didn't want to be on this train.

She scanned through her mobile for Zac's number. He answered right away.

'Hi.'

'Zac, are you all right?'

'Hi, Mum, I'm good.'

89

'What's happening? Is everyone okay?'

'The bus driver won't take us. He says he won't go back to Sydney, he's safer here.'

'What?'

'It was so cool, 'cause we were all on the bus and everything, and the bus driver made us take all our stuff off. And then Mr Abrahamson came, 'cause he was looking for Simon, and he told us to put our stuff back on. And Brandy was crying. I guess she's really homesick. But Mr Abrahamson swore at the driver. You should have heard him. And the driver said he wasn't risking his life for someone else's kids.'

'So what's happening now?'

'Mr Abrahamson says we need to find another bus company, but Ms Eisler says that we won't find anyone on a Friday afternoon.'

'Where are you?'

'We're in the park across from the hotel. They said we can't come back in, but they're trying to find somewhere that can take us. They're really nice. They had some conference that was canceled, and they brought us all the cakes and sandwiches and stuff, and some juice.'

She gulped a breath. There would be a time to give in to how she felt, but not on the phone, not to Zac.

'Hey, Mum, I have to go, okay? I'm holding up the soccer game.'

'Ring me as soon as you know anything. Ring me.'

'Course.'

'Bye, Zac. I love you.'

'Yeah.' And he was gone again.

She took a few rapid steps towards the garden, the office, and Sean, then stopped. The school would look after it. She'd met Mr Abrahamson. He was a sensible man. But if they got in the car now they could be there and back before midnight.

Mr Abrahamson was looking after it.

She picked up the notepad lying on the counter. The top sheet had the beginnings of a shopping list from this morning. It needed to be finished. She stared at it blankly. Nothing came to her beyond that she needed to make a list and Zac was stuck in Canberra.

She strode across the lawn, past Oscar still playing solo soccer, and into the office. Sean looked up. 'Hiya.'

'We're going to Canberra.'

Sean looked nonplussed but not surprised. 'You planning on waving to Zac when we pass him at Campbelltown?'

'There's a problem with the bus and they're looking for another and somewhere to stay.'

'So, they might come back tonight?'

'It didn't sound promising. If we set off now—'

'Nothing has changed since Monday. There are still no cases in Canberra. He's still having fun with his mates. So he spends an extra night. It'll be good for him. It'll teach him to cope with adversity, give him a bit of resilience.'

'Because nothing has ever gone wrong in Zac's life.'

'This is not the same.'

Only one thing had changed – the time she had to wait.

Zac didn't need his mother turning up like a crazy woman. For now he was safe, away from the cases. He would be back tonight and if he wasn't back tonight, then he would be back tomorrow.

Notepad in hand, she stood in front of the pantry. Oscar, like a small shadow, was standing just behind her. He stared seriously at the shelves. She knew what was there – after all, she'd only topped it up on Tuesday. She ran her hands along a row of cans. Meals. Meals that allowed them not to go out. She straightened a can of tomatoes that was sitting halfway between its row and the tinned beans. She pushed each row so the last can hit the back of the cupboard.

'Now they're all squiggly at the front. You should put them back.'

'This way I can see the holes I need to fill up.'

'Well, you should count them and then put them back. They don't look neat.'

'What do you want for snacks?'

'Muesli bars, chocolate biscuits, ummm, chocolate.'

'We can get those.'

She shooed him into his room and sat down to order from the online supermarket. The process was pleasingly simple, a series of questions and all she had to do was answer. Suburb? She filled it in. Delivery time? She didn't care since they weren't going anywhere. But the weekend was already booked out, and there were only two times free on Monday. One first thing in the morning and one later with a slightly cheaper delivery fee. It made sense to get the cheaper one, since they were home all day. Her finger hesitated over the mouse button. But what if they canceled deliveries between the morning and the afternoon? What if she saved two dollars but lost the groceries? She clicked on the morning slot.

The website opened up in front of her. Choice, possibilities. She worked methodically through her list, pulling down each menu and burrowing through, getting a little shiver of satisfaction as each item on her notepad transferred to her online cart. Now that she'd collected the things she had to have – rice, muesli, oats – she relaxed a little. Some things could be controlled. Now for things they didn't need – microwave popcorn, chocolate, sugary breakfast cereal.

She clicked through to the checkout. A pop-up blocked the page, with important letters blazed in red.

The World Health Organization advises that the Manba virus lasts less than two hours outside the human body. We have taken every precaution to reduce potential exposure of our products. All our service personnel wear gloves while handling your order. Please continue to store cold items in the fridge immediately, as delay risks spoilage.

Words on a screen were no guarantee of protection. She'd go to the WHO website and check for herself. And if it was true, the delivery time slot was before the day warmed up, so the milk should survive. But if she had to, she could use gloves to bring it in and forbid anyone to touch the carton. The rest could sit on the porch until it was safe.

She typed in her credit card number, clicked submit, and leaned back on her chair to enjoy the warm satisfaction of having kept them safe for a few more days.

Pans everywhere. Every bowl cluttering the countertop. When Sean made dinner, she stayed out of the kitchen, driven in only to suggest that Oscar could do with some food soon. An open packet of almonds sat squashed between the onion skins and the plastic supermarket tray the chicken came in. 'You're putting almonds in that?'

'I was peckish.'

'Then finish making dinner. And don't graze on the contents of the pantry while the rest of us go hungry.'

'It's only a handful of almonds.'

She tried to suppress a sigh of exasperation. 'You eat it and it's gone.'

'Dinner's ready now. You could go and grab Oscar.'

While they ate, Oscar analyzed in great detail the television programs he'd watched. Hannah listened closely, hoping the newsbreak wouldn't come up. Maybe he'd forgotten it.

Sean cooked a good meal, but when she looked at her plate, she saw food taken out of the pantry. The chicken and the cream would go off if they weren't eaten, so they had to be used. Begrudgingly she admitted that the noodles had to be there to bulk it out, and the couple of mushrooms left in a basket were not enough to make anything on their own. Herbs from the garden pots. That was fine, herbs grew. She picked through the food on her plate, sorting the ingredients. He'd added a tin of tomatoes, a small handful of capers, and some leftover olives. With every olive she tasted, she couldn't stop herself from thinking of pasta puttanesca. Tomatoes, capers, and olives, a meal all by itself, a meal of things that could be kept in the pantry and didn't spoil.

Oscar went for his shower, Sean put the meal that would have been Zac's into a plastic tub, and Hannah scraped the waste into the bin. All of Oscar's olives and capers. Sean finished stacking the dishwasher and she ran a sink to wash up the things that hadn't fit. Still thinking about olives, tomatoes, and capers.

Sean picked up the tea towel and started to dry. 'You seem a bit quiet.' She went on with washing up. He studied a glass carefully before placing it on the counter. 'Is there something?'

She said nothing.

'Is it Zac?'

'You really don't get it.'

Sean threw the tea towel over his shoulder and leaned back. 'This is because I wouldn't go to Canberra.'

Hannah dropped the saucepan back into the sink, splashing the dry glass. 'You didn't listen to what I said, so I must be angry?'

'About the almonds? You're pissed off at me because I ate a handful of almonds? That's what I heard you say. I don't know what that means.'

'It means what I said. You wasted food.'

'I know it's been a long day. Oscar can be draining and you wanted Zac home. The week didn't work out exactly the way you planned it, and I think you're taking it out on me because I ate a handful of almonds. A handful, enough to keep a mouse going for half a day.'

'You didn't have to use the olives and the capers.'

'I thought it tasted all right. I liked the capers. I thought you liked capers.'

'It's not about like – it's that they're gone, like the almonds. Once they're eaten, you can't get them back.'

'There's still half a packet. We'll buy some more. We're not buying takeaway, we can afford to have a spare packet of almonds. Just add some to the delivery.'

'The order is done and they weren't on my list.'

'So, next order. It's not a big deal.'

'Zac's bus driver won't come back to Sydney. How long do you think before it's the truck drivers?'

'At which point the government will be forced to do something. They're not going to let the food supply fail.'

'You have an awful lot of faith. But I'd rather be in a position to look after ourselves.' She shook her wet hands into the sink, more vigorously than necessary. 'I didn't buy a load of random stuff. I worked it out. You use a tin of tomatoes and we don't have it for dinner another day. We didn't need tomatoes and capers and olives as well as the chicken. Next time don't put in anything you don't need.'

Sean looked at her, the tea towel suspended in midair

above the saucepan. 'I'll ask permission before using seasoning.'

'We have to plan. I mean, we *have* to plan. The pantry is there to keep us safe. But that counts for nothing if you don't think.'

'How was I supposed to know? You didn't say.'

'Before this week it was just a pantry. I shouldn't have to tell you our situation. Can't you see for yourself what's happening?'

'What I can see is a lot of things that might happen but haven't yet. We can't plan for everything that might happen.'

'I do.'

'And then you never get to live. Then you're always planning for disaster, planning for the next lump. Can we at least move past the last one?'

She pulled the plug out of the sink with force, splashing water on herself and onto the floor. It could stay there for all she cared, a puddle of water to stand in for the words she couldn't find. Let him clean it up.

Her anger carried her loudly out of the room, but with the slam of the door behind her, it vanished. All she was left with was the sound of the shower running and Oscar's light tuneless voice singing to himself through the bathroom door. She breathed out the tension as she leaned back against the wall. The pantry door was ajar, and through the crack she could see the incomplete wall of supplies. Those gaps should be filled right now. So many things could go wrong between now and Monday.

Amanda Hickie

And where was Zac? He was supposed to be here. The front door couldn't be shut for good until she had Zac and a full pantry. She would happily fast-forward through this part of her life. Couldn't it just be agreed that she had done everything right and they could skip the next bit?

Oscar poked his head around the bathroom door. He was shiny and his hair dripped.

'You're making the floor all wet – what are you doing?'

'I want you to dry me.'

'You're a big boy. Big boys are perfectly capable of drying themselves.'

He closed the door behind himself and through it she could hear a cheerful monologue that drew her in. When she opened the bathroom door, the towel was loosely wrapped around him but the water had dripped into a puddle just off the bath mat.

'Here you go.' She gave him a good rub. He wriggled as if she were tickling him.

It wasn't her turn for a story, but right now the thing she wanted most was not to go back to Sean. Surprisingly, Oscar didn't notice, or at least didn't object, to the change in routine. The act of reading the story, a Dr Seuss she almost knew by heart, was meditative. Each nonsense word relieved her of some of her adulthood.

The light was off, Oscar was quiet. Stranded here in the hallway, still she craved a few more moments before confronting Sean and her own bad behavior. She rested her head against the front door, feeling the cool of the evening conducted through the wood. No sound found its way in. She felt a pressing need to see what was on the other side. With the door open, the breeze blew through the security grille and onto her face. The street was quiet and empty, the only movement a man walking his dog down the dotted lines in the middle of the road, mask over his face. Her eyes followed him to the corner, tracing his invisible path when he disappeared.

She missed the daytime, the beautiful crush of humanity, the human contact by osmosis. The passing schoolgirls, ringing mobile phones, the leaked music from iPod headphones, and the steady stream of people, now absent, who walked down her street on an ordinary day.

The quiet was gradually replaced by a rumble. In the gloom, she could just make out a street sweeper at the far end of the road. It passed her door, spraying the gutter, and she smelled hospital.

As she followed the sound of the television back into the house, all she wanted was to delete this bad mood between them. But when Sean looked away from the screen, his forehead was lined. In his eyes she saw a disturbed sadness, and it was her fault. She had infected him with this.

The image of a reporter on the scene was superseded by a beaten and bloodied face.

'What happened?'

'He coughed. He didn't cover his mouth and he coughed in front of some guy's girlfriend and they beat him.' Two men in handcuffs, glowering at the camera.

99

She sat down close to Sean. 'Where?'

'In town, some shop in town.'

She was crying, but not for the beaten face on the TV, or for the two boys whose parents had died. She was crying for things that might never take place. She was crying because every day, everywhere, small tragedies happened and she didn't know how to care about every single one, and so they aggregated and magnified and became incomprehensible.

Sean put his arm around her and pulled her in, swathing her in his shirt. She felt heady, gasping and rebreathing the warm recycled air caught in the folds. She could do nothing but hold on until the sobs subsided. Her head ached and she wiped her face with her sleeve.

The phone was lying on the sofa beside him, and he turned it over and over slowly, as if looking for some answer hidden on it. 'The teacher rang. They're staying the night. They opened one of the local schools and the kids are camping in the hall. Apparently a pizza place around the corner donated dinner for them.' He sounded unsure of the truth of it. 'They sound like they're having fun.' He looked at her, debating whether to go on. 'The Department of Education has told them to stay put until the situation here is clearer. Mr Whatever thinks they're going to be there all weekend. I talked to Zac, he's fine with it.' He pressed ahead a little more firmly. 'I think it's the right decision. I think it's good for him. I don't think we should go and get him.' He looked set, like he was ready to dig in.

The choice had been made and she couldn't find the energy to do anything but go along with it. There was a comfort in being handed a decision she didn't like instead of fighting against events she couldn't affect.

'Hey, I know this sucks.' Sean pulled a strand of damp hair from her face and smoothed it back. 'But maybe it's the best thing. If it will help, you can yell at me or break some plates. I think there are some old ones in a box in the garage.'

She buried her face in his neck, warm and familiar. 'It's okay. I'll be fine.' She breathed in his smell. 'Where are they?'

'In a school.'

'Which school?'

There was a moment's pause as if Sean were trying to assess the significance of his answer, but he had only one to give. 'I don't know.'

The phone rang. He answered, then handed it to her.

'Hi. It's Susan, Daniel's mum. Has Zac called you?'

'Sean talked to him, but I think the teacher called.'

'I don't know what to do.'

'I don't think there is anything we can do tonight.'

'We should be doing something.'

How wrong and weird it was to be the one urging caution now, so opposite to her real feelings. 'There's nothing to do. We have to wait.'

Mon	Tue	Wed	Thu	Fri	Sat	Sun

Sean's voice woke her. She stared stupidly up at him with no idea what he'd just said. 'Huh?'

'We're going.'

'Are we?'

'Get up.'

'Where?'

'Canberra. Now. Get up.'

She stumbled into the kitchen. Sean looked at her sharply. 'You're not dressed.'

'Where are we going?'

'Canberra. I told you. To get Zac.'

'Did he ring?'

There was a pile of random food on the counter. Water bottles, apples, some bread. Sean was throwing it all into a backpack.

'Why are we going to Canberra?'

'They're going to close the roads.'

'I thought you said he was safer there.'

'They will close the roads. And when the disease gets to Canberra he will be alone.'

'They told everyone they were going to close the roads before they did it? That doesn't make sense.'

'It will happen. Today. If we don't get going, he'll be stuck there.'

Hannah knocked on Gwen's door. First she rang the bell, but when she couldn't hear the chime from inside, she knocked, not too loudly, on the door. She didn't want to be knocking on Gwen's door. She thought they should all go. Sean had seriously suggested leaving Oscar in front of the TV with a bag of chips and a bottle of soft drink. 'And what happens when we get killed on the highway because you're in a panic to get there?' Sean's answer was: 'Then he won't be dead.'

They should have gone on Friday. Hannah knocked on the door harder, but willed Gwen not to answer. Gwen's deafness worked in Hannah's favor, that and she was probably still asleep.

She walked back to the kitchen. 'We're taking Oscar with us.'

'For fuck's sake, leave him with Gwen. Or the two of you stay, that works. That makes sense.' He was throwing his hands around.

'She's not answering and he's not staying here by himself. And you going alone is not an option.' She had plans to get them through, and every one required that Sean still be around.

Hannah swilled the remains of Sean's coffee. It was bitter and sweet but better than a headache. She took a piece of bread from the bag on the counter, smeared it with peanut butter, and bit into it. Chewing, she pulled out another one.

'What are you doing?'

'Eating breakfast. Oscar needs something too.'

'He's eaten. We're going now. Bring breakfast with you.' He grabbed the backpack and called Oscar in from the garden. 'Go to the toilet. We're going now.' She was already in the car when she remembered the shopping.

Sean called after her as she ran back to the house. 'What now?'

'A moment, that's all,' she yelled back. She fumbled with the key in the lock, pounded down the hall, the joists bouncing underneath her. Gwen was surely awake now, but there was no way she was leaving Oscar. She flung open the kitchen cupboard and grabbed a cooler bag, threw some ice bricks from the freezer into it. Running past Oscar's room, a crayon on the floor caught her eye. She grabbed it and a piece of paper he had drawn on. At the front door, she leaned the paper against the wall of the porch and wrote in crayon over the top of the printing on the back, 'PLEASE LEAVE SHOPPING BEHIND PORCH WALL BEHIND YOU, COLD BAG FOR MILK. THANKS,' and wove the paper in between the bars of the screen door.

She doubled back, grabbed masks, gloves, and hand sanitizer from the hall table, and sprinted to the car.

'Burglars can read.'

'They have eyes to see a pile of shopping on the door-step too.'

As Sean backed out into the road, Hannah faced the front door and her note. It seemed easy for someone to pick up flagrantly unattended groceries and a lot more effort to break into the house. Right now, she cared more about the groceries. The engine idled as Sean checked up and down the road, then pulled out in an arc. On the corner, Mr Henderson was weeding the patch of lawn that made up his front garden. He was a soft-spoken, diffident little man, who seemed to live in that yard. As they drove past, he straightened himself up and gave a wave salute. She waved back. The only noise was the short synthetic chirps from Oscar's game. Hannah leaned back against the headrest.

'Are you okay there?'

She rubbed her face with her balled hand. 'Still asleep.'

As they approached the tunnel under the airport, Sean called out to Oscar to look up and watch for planes landing above them, but it was unsettlingly peaceful – the last moment of interest before the long featureless road. Concrete sound barriers embossed with waratahs and abstract sea patterns were interspersed with warehouses, clusters of shops, and endless rows of open, identical backyards. After an indeterminate time of letting her eyes roam, Hannah broke the silence. 'Where do you want to change drivers?'

'What about Goulburn? That's about halfway.'

'Not in the town.'

'Obviously – round there, outside the town somewhere.' Hannah turned her back to the window, watching Sean's rhythms as he drove. His eyes flicked from windscreen to dashboard to mirrors and then started around again. At the end of one cycle, he glanced over at Hannah. She gave him a small smile before he turned his gaze back to the road. Sean's eyes took another circuit, seemingly hypnotized.

Hannah looked out the windscreen. The asphalt was as dark gray as always, the concrete of the sound barriers as white. They could be on any stretch of highway – she had no sense of how far they had to go. She glanced at the clock. For eight on a Monday, it didn't look like peak hour. 'What makes you think they're closing the roads?'

Sean broke the pattern to look over at her again. 'I woke up early and couldn't get back to sleep. People were tweeting about trucks moving those plastic barriers. It seems a bit pointless now. Three people died yesterday in Sydney alone. That's as many as we've had so far. Talk about shutting the stable door after the horse has bolted.'

'So why will they let us through?'

'I'm hoping it takes a while to set up a roadblock.'

'You woke me up on a hunch that the government is incompetent?'

'There's a chance.'

Oscar's voice broke in from the back. 'When will we get there?'

Hannah twisted herself around to look at him. 'It's going to be a while.'

'Oh.' Muted electronic sounds came repetitively from the backseat. 'When will we have lunch?'

Sean answered impatiently. 'I don't know – there's food in the backpack if you're hungry.'

'I'm not hungry.' The sound from the game stopped. 'I need to do a wee.'

'Didn't you go before we left?'

'I need to go again.'

Sean was scowling. 'Can you hang on?'

'No.'

'Damn.' He stared at his mirror, as if it were the fault of the car behind. 'I'll pull off at the next exit, we can find a petrol station. I could do with a coffee and we can get petrol.'

Hannah couldn't believe Sean would even consider it. 'He can't go into a petrol station toilet.' She turned back to Oscar. 'You'll have to go by the side of the road.'

Oscar's face clouded over. 'People will see me.'

'No one will look.'

'People will see me.'

'If you need to go, that's what you have to do.'

Hannah scanned the side of the road for a suitable spot while Sean kept driving. Oscar wailed from the back, 'I need to go now.'

'Hang on, hang on.' Sean pulled over near a clump of slightly thicker roadside planting. 'Out you get.'

'You'd better go with him.'

Sean held the car door open. 'Come on Oscar, no one will see you. You can go behind one of the bushes and the car's in the way.' Oscar stayed in his seat, looking defiant and crestfallen. 'I'll stand between you and the traffic, with my back to you. And the cars are going so fast anyway, they won't see you.' Oscar forced himself deeper into the seat, and looked at Hannah with a silent appeal on his face. She restrained herself. Sean was dealing with this.

Sean started to close Oscar's door. 'Fine. You can hang on until you burst.' Oscar unclicked his belt, pouting.

They were parked at the apex of a long curve with a wide tree-filled divider hiding the other half of the road, cutting Hannah's view to a few hundred empty meters forward and back. A car passed them at highway speed. Nothing remarkable, although she couldn't see into the back window over a stack of belongings. An old red sedan drove by, slightly slower, and she found this time she could examine the occupants. They were all so young. The driver couldn't have been more than seventeen or eighteen. The windows were rolled down, releasing the bass beat of music, but there was something about the way they looked, a stillness, a realization. The red car was eclipsed by a rental truck. She thought she saw a man and woman in the front, possibly the top of a child's head and expressions of grim resolve.

Time was escaping. Everyone was moving except them. She could just make out Oscar's bared bottom and strad-dled legs behind Sean, who was standing, feet apart, arms crossed, like a bouncer at a nightclub and just as formidable. He pulled a face at her and she pulled one back. She saw his shoulders shake as he tried not to laugh. Oscar walked back to him, hands held out from his body. She saw Sean bend down to his level, listening attentively. They both turned to the car and came to her window.

'Oscar and I have discussed the hand-washing situation and we may have a problem. I don't recall packing any wipes.'

'Didn't you just. As it happens, I picked up the hand wash.' She passed it out the window.

'Hand wash it is, then. That will do, won't it, Oscar?' Oscar nodded seriously as Sean squeezed the pump pack for him. 'And we've decided that he'd better not need to do doo-doo – otherwise we're in deep doo-doo.' Oscar snickered.

Sean indicated and pulled out into the sweeping curve. Around the bend, the road became a long straight stretch. In the distance, orange traffic cones dotted across the fast lane, choking the road, and behind those, an electronic sign flashed alternately SLOW DOWN and PREPARE TO STOP. As they drove closer, they saw that the rental truck was pulled up at the narrowest point of the shoulder and behind it sat the red car. A policeman with a lighted baton waved them into the single lane. A few car lengths on, the traffic cones dotted back the other way, opening up the road again until it was cut by two police cars parked across the traffic flow.

In front of the truck, a man stood and gesticulated angrily at a policewoman. In the front seat, a woman looked out rigidly over the top of the scene, as if she saw Canberra in the distance. Her daughter was a ball of clothing with two pigtails sticking out, huddled into her side.

Four of the five teenagers were standing around the back of their red car, looking lost. One of the girls was wiping at her eyes. The boy next to her was standing close, slightly turned away, as if unsure of how he could give comfort. The young driver was standing near the open door of the car looking serious and attentive while a policeman not much older than him gave instructions.

A third policeman sauntered around the car to Sean's window. Sean leaned out and spoke a little too genially. 'So, what's happening?'

'The road's closed. Where are you from today?'

'We came from the city. We're only picking up our son – he's on a school camp in Canberra.'

'You're not going through now. The road's closed.'

'For how long?'

'It won't be open today. There's no point waiting – you should go home.'

The officer raised his voice over the escalating anger of the man from the truck but continued without otherwise acknowledging the commotion. Hannah kept her eyes on their policeman, although it made her uncomfortable to have her back to the ruckus.

'If you drive on, sir, there's an emergency vehicle

turning bay before you get to the patrol cars. You can make a U-turn there and you'll be back on the other side of the freeway. Have a safe trip home.' He nodded to Hannah and Oscar.

Sean rolled up the window and put the car into gear.

'Is that it?' Hannah shook his arm.

'What do you want me to do?'

'We came all this way and that's it? We leave Zac by himself in Canberra?'

'What do you want me to do? Ram the police cars? I don't think that will work.'

'I want you to fix this. I want you to get Zac.'

Sean's face was closed, as if he was watching the road but not seeing it. As they pulled around the teenagers, the one angry voice was suddenly joined by three or four others. Hannah looked to the noise and caught the gesticulating man's fist meeting the policewoman's face. The other two police had their guns drawn, pointed at the man. The younger one looked to his older partner and back to the angry man. He held his gun as if this was not the day that he had prepared for this morning. Hannah's eyes were drawn to the guns and she was surprised by how calm she felt and how much like toys they looked.

Sean turned his head to follow her gaze and braked hard. She said quietly, 'Sean, I don't think it's a good idea to stop.'

He dragged his eyes back to the road.

'Sorry.' He broke his gaze and looked at her. 'I've never seen a gun except on television.'

She gestured towards the backseat with her head. 'And Oscar doesn't need to.' Oscar was hunched over his game.

As the car eased forward, she willed him to bring the clutch up slowly, not to jump the car. Twenty, thirty more meters to the EMERGENCY VEHICLES ONLY sign. He took the rough gravel track between the two sides of the freeway more smoothly than she imagined possible – only a few hundred meters to retrace until they reached the bend and the trees again. The guns, the police, the truck, the red car, and whatever was about to happen would be out of sight.

She saw the teenage driver walk slowly towards the circle of police, his hands up in front of him, a barrier and a plea for peace. In his elongated, languorous movements, he reminded her of Zac.

'I beat the boss.' Oscar's voice made Hannah jump.

'What's that, Mouse?'

'I beat the boss. He's really hard.'

'Good for you.' They had reached the bend. This boy in the backseat was hers, and that's all that mattered. Whatever happened at the roadblock wasn't her concern.

Oscar's face glowed back at her. 'I'm going to show Zac when we get there.'

'Was he tough?'

'You have to shoot all the spikes off his side, and he kept whacking me with his tail, but I got him.'

'Well done.' She smiled at him. Marbled with a bubbly feeling of happiness was the sobering knowledge that Zac was stranded and they had failed him.

Sean turned the car sharply into a side road so small that Hannah hadn't seen it. The asphalt gave way to corrugated dirt and Oscar let out a long vocal breath, which vibrated with the bumps.

'Do you know where this goes?'

'Not a clue. But it's the only option I can give you that doesn't involve a confrontation with the law.'

Hannah pulled out her phone. No signal. For five or ten minutes they passed nothing but fences and dirt access roads blocked by gates. The only break from the monotony was provided by a tractor stopped in a field. As they pulled in front of a rough track into the property, they could make out two figures standing next to it.

Sean rolled down his window. 'Hey!'

The figures didn't move.

He leaned out and yelled. 'Excuse me!'

One of the figures turned around and ambled towards them, head down. He rubbed his nose, examining the powdered dust on his boots as he reached Sean's open window.

Sean leaned out. 'Is there another way through to Canberra?'

'Not on this road.' The man was paying more attention to the fencing running into the distance than to them. 'The road to Canberra's back that way.' He thumbed in the direction of the highway.

'If we didn't want to take the main road, is there another way?'

'You could go through town, but it'll only take you

back to the highway thirty clicks on. And I can't see why the fuck you'd want to. Turn your head around and you can see the road to Canberra. The town's not much and the back road's nothing at all.'

'What about a way that isn't on the maps?'

'You're not something to do with drugs, are ya? 'Cause that's not right, with the young fella in there.'

'We need to get to Canberra, to our other boy. The highway's closed. They'll have closed the road through town too, by now.'

'You could cut through Davo's property. I'm done here, I could do with a ride.' He lifted his hand without turning around, and the man in the distance echoed the gesture before turning back to the tractor.

Hannah was about to object, tell him that he was putting himself at risk, for all he knew they were infected. Or he was infected. Every first case comes from somewhere. But he'd already opened the back door and settled himself in. 'How are ya?' He nodded to Oscar as if they were two blokes at a pub.

'Fine,' Oscar said, without commitment. Hannah kept her eyes on him in the mirror.

They drove the narrow dirt roads. No one spoke except their guide, and then only to give terse directions. 'Left in twenty.' 'Watch the ditch.' He wound the window down and rested his arm on the sill. The track was not more than a car and a half wide, and Sean tried to hug the side, jockeying the wheels along the seam of compacted earth and weeds. A beat-up station wagon covered in dust approached from ahead at speed. It sat solidly in the middle of the road and swerved only as it reached them. Their passenger raised the fingers of his hand a millimeter and the hand in the station wagon did the same.

After half an hour or so, the man leaned forward almost congenially. 'Just pull over at the next gate, that's me.' He jumped out of the car. 'Go straight for a click, turn left at the T, and that takes you back to the main road. You can't miss it.'

'Thanks,' Sean called to his back, and the man gave the same curt wave.

Hannah watched as he became nothing more than a detail in the pastoral scene reflected in her side mirror. They weren't sick, she knew that. He wasn't walking off to wipe out a whole country town. And he hadn't coughed or sneezed. He looked healthy. That was all the reassurance she had available.

As they approached the promised T intersection, Sean slowed to a crawl and scanned the road in both directions.

'What are you looking for?' She tried to follow his eye line.

'Even if we meet one now, we must be beyond the barrier. Who's to say we weren't always here?' He looked at her as if she knew what he meant. 'We should get petrol.'

Hannah gave a resigned shrug. She wasn't going to carry the load of this decision.

'Come on, you were happy enough to have the guy in the back. We need petrol.'

'Not happy.'

'Well, he was in the back, and there'll be a station on the outskirts of town.' No answer. 'We can't make it to Canberra and back on what's in the tank. That's not me being difficult, it's reality. This is probably the safest place to get it. So which way am I going? Town or freeway?'

She glanced at the petrol gauge. Not enough to get home from here, certainly not enough to get to Canberra and back. It was a long way from anywhere, off the trucking route, and there were no reported cases this far out. They were probably the only non-locals to pass through in weeks. If they had to . . . and they had to. 'Use gloves on the pump and hand wash when you're done. Pay with cash, and don't take any change.'

'If I use gloves, why do I need hand wash?'

'That's the deal.'

Sean took the turn back towards the town, and half a kilometer on, they found it. It had been built for the main road this had once been and in its new circumstances was oversized and sun-faded. Part of the hardstand had been reused for a 'fresh produce' stand so long ago that it was empty and broken. They pulled into the wide, potholed drive, built for the trucks and buses that now took the freeway. They were the only car. Hannah looked through her wallet while Sean worked the pump. 'You can put in fifty dollars' worth. After that we'd have to go up by twenty.' Hannah watched the counter turning over by cents as Sean squeezed and released to get to exactly fifty.

A paper towel dispenser hung by the pump. Soaked in

hand sanitizer, paper towel was at least something she could use to wipe down the seat and seat belt where their guest had been sitting. Oscar looked on as if his mum disinfected their car whenever they filled up.

The rest of the trip was easy, fast, uncongested. On this side of the roadblock, their yellow license plates stood out like flashing signs of guilt among all the local blue-and-white plates. Hannah was afraid they would be stopped for that alone.

Oscar grizzled from the back. 'My legs hurt.'

'We're nearly there.' And it was enough truth to postpone the grumbling. There was no need to tell him that when they got there they'd be turning around and doing it all again.

As they drove past the WELCOME TO THE ACT sign, she felt like they had made it. Each remaining step seemed trivial, a process that had to be gone through. There was nothing standing in the way but the doing of it. She ratted through her bag for her phone, the next step. It rang out to voicemail. Damn it.

'Zac, we're nearly there. Get your things and come out the front. Ring me back to let me know you got this message.'

Hannah watched the phone for subtle signs of Zac that it couldn't possibly convey. She held it until they pulled up across the road from the school gym. It looked just like any school day – behind the gym, the schoolyard was filled with kids, some of them playing soccer, some standing around in groups. Along the footpath in front, people walked, like they would on any day, so close she could touch them if she wound down the window. So strangely normal that it felt wrong. She pressed redial. 'Zac, why do you have a phone if you don't answer it? Get out here, we're waiting outside.' She hung up and stared at the phone again.

Sean started to open the door. 'I guess I'll have to go over. Why don't you take Superboy for a run up and down the footpath while I'm gone.'

'What, with all these people around? He can run all he wants when we stop for lunch, somewhere isolated. Give Zac another minute.'

'A minute won't make any difference.' Sean shook the wheel with exasperation. 'He can't hear his phone.'

'Thanks to your detour, for which I am grateful, it took us more than four hours to get here. Five more minutes won't hurt.'

'Five minutes won't make any difference either.' He pushed the car door all the way, and she put her hand on his arm, a gentle restraint.

'You're not going like that.' She held a pair of gloves out to him.

'Look at all these people.' He pointed to the pedestrians, the soccer players. 'Not a glove, not a mask between them. That's how normal people behave.'

'Not a chance. If they want to take a risk . . .'

'They're not taking a risk – there is no risk. There's no panic because there is nothing to panic about. No disease here.'

'Gloves and mask. Please.'

'This is absurd.'

'Humor me.'

'When there is a reason, I accept it. But I refuse to give in to irrationality.' He got one leg out of the car but she gripped his arm tighter.

'Let me try one more time.' She let it ring until it went to voicemail. And again. And again.

'If he was going to answer, he would have.' Sean pushed the door open again. 'Give me the damned gloves.' Hannah's phone rang.

'Yes. Zac.'

'Hi, Mum. There are a bunch of missed calls on my phone.'

'I've been ringing and ringing.'

'It was still under my pillow and we were playing this board game.'

'We're here, out the front. Get your things together and meet us out here. You can tell me the rest then.'

She watched the digits change on the dashboard clock. Ten minutes at most and then she would . . . and then she would . . . *not* get out of the car and get him.

The double front doors of the gym bulged out. The left fell back, the right swung open, and for a moment they saw Zac's outline in the doorway, before the door swung closed.

'Where's Zac?' Oscar's light voice spoke for all of them.

Sean pushed his door open and swung his leg onto the

asphalt. Hannah squeezed his arm but he pulled away. 'I'm only going to put his stuff in the boot.' He took the gloves, slipped them over his hands, but tossed the mask back to her.

Both doors opened together this time. Zac came out of the right and another boy from the left. Behind them, slightly taller, was their teacher, Mr Abrahamson. He had always looked young to Hannah, but today his face was overwritten with tiredness and a certain air of responsibility. Mr Abrahamson stopped on the far side of the road, his arm out in front of the two boys, keeping them in place. A couple walking down the street hesitated, looked to Sean and back to the boys, then chose to make a wide arc around the group.

'Mr Halloran, Zac's got all his things and he's ready to go.' Mr Abrahamson looked at Zac with genuine affection. 'He's been great. A real help with some of the other kids. I've told him how impressed I've been with his behavior.'

'That's good to hear.' The two men perched, leaning forward on opposite curbs. They looked courtly and ludicrous, as if observing some arcane etiquette.

'If you want to leave him, the school here has offered to look after us. They're going to try to find billets for the kids today.'

'We're here – we'll take him back.'

'Mr Halloran, I'm thinking about the kids. It's very safe here. I think maybe you should consider your options before Zac comes across the road. Do you have someone you can stay with in Canberra? I've made arrangements for the children that I think are in their best interest, and we don't know what's going to happen back in Sydney. You could try to get into a hotel if you don't know anyone, but you'd better not say you came from Sydney.'

Hannah put her head out the window. 'We're taking Zac home.'

She could see how earnestly he believed what he was saying. He seemed to give her statement more consideration than it deserved. 'Even if you can't stay here, you should still consider leaving Zac. Sydney isn't the best option for him now. And you might not have a choice. The story is they're closing the highway. But once he's crossed the road, the school is no longer responsible for him. If you can't find anywhere to stay, I can't ask any of the families here to take him in.'

'*From* Sydney,' Sean said firmly. 'It's closed *from* Sydney. Unless you've heard of someone being turned back.'

Mr Abrahamson shifted on his feet. 'One of the kids left here with their parents a couple of hours ago. They haven't come back.'

'So we're going home and we're taking him.' Sean spoke with firmness.

'Dad, can we take Daniel? His folks aren't coming.'

'How do you know they're not?'

'He rang them this morning – he wants to go home but they said they couldn't get here. He thinks his mum is sick and they don't want him to be in the house. We have to take Daniel.'

'I guess . . .'

Hannah cut Sean off. 'We'll talk about it, Zac.'

'When, Mum? If you leave him here, he's stuck. You came all this way for me – how do you think his folks feel? We're going now, so you have to tell me now.'

Daniel's mum had been so eager to come on Friday and had sounded fine. Hannah tried to read the boy's face. He was staring at the ground, his eyes turned away from them, although there was nothing unusual about the patch of concrete he was studying. His hair flopped forward, hiding any expression that might give her a clue to his feelings.

'Zac, we can't just kidnap someone else's child. It sounds like they want him to stay here.'

'And I can't let him go without his parents' permission,' Mr Abrahamson said to Zac. 'You understand.'

Sean cut in. 'Daniel, what's your parents' number?'

Hannah pulled Sean down so he could hear her whispers. 'I think we should talk about this before we ring them.'

'If they are happy for us to bring him back, why wouldn't we? He'll be better off with us than with strangers.' Sean stepped onto the road and held the phone out to Daniel.

'Just hang on, no closer.' Hannah would have been out the door if she hadn't been on the wrong side of the car. As it was, she was stretched across the seat. 'He can ring them on his phone.'

Daniel dialed, spoke a few words, then passed the

phone to Mr Abrahamson and stood with his arms crossed, quarter turned away from everyone. Zac, next to him, still faced forward, shuffling foot to foot. Mr Abrahamson hung up the phone and nodded to Sean.

'That's settled. You're coming with us, Daniel. Sling your bags in the boot. In you hop.' Sean hesitated a beat. 'Your mum'll be all right. I'm sure she's only got a cold.'

'Wait, wait, wait.' Hannah was almost falling out of the car with urgency. 'There are masks and gloves for you both.'

'Mum!' Zac rolled his eyes at her. 'We're not sick, no one's sick here. We've been here all the time.'

'Meanwhile we've been breathing all over the car. So, better to isolate you.'

She put on her own gloves before getting two pairs out of the packaging, at arm's length. Zac put them on self-consciously, looking to Daniel from time to time to see if he thought it was stupid too. 'If it's so dangerous, why did you even come?'

As Zac slid into the backseat, Oscar tried to leap at him but was jerked back by the seat belt he forgot he was wearing.

'Don't touch him!'

Oscar jumped, startled by the seat belt and Hannah's screech. He looked to her with tear-filled eyes, not sure what he'd done wrong. She tried to calm her voice. 'It's okay. You just can't touch him.' Oscar's face was a mix of guilt, fear, and embarrassment.

'Hey, Mouse.' Sean leaned into him. 'Zac's been away

for a few days, so he's got different germs from us. His germs are probably fine, and ours are too, but for a few days we have to keep our germs to ourselves.' Oscar unclenched a little.

'I want to hug Zac.'

'Not today, Mouse. Save your hugs for a few days.' Oscar drew himself in, trying to put space between himself and Zac.

Half of Canberra seemed to consist of dusty tracts of land beside the road, dotted with gum trees. The best Hannah could find was a triangle between nowhere and nowhere else, with no houses or office buildings nearby. It wasn't pretty but it was isolated.

On a parched island of grass, Oscar waited for what would happen next on this strange day, cross-legged, a big smile on his face. As Hannah unpacked the eclectic assortment of food from the backpack, Zac stood looking down at it.

'You can't expect us to eat with masks on. So what are we supposed to do?'

'Take your sandwiches over to the next tree. You can take off the mask and gloves there.'

'I bet you made the sandwiches, didn't you? So they have your germs, so that would be really dumb.' Zac rolled his eyes at her. 'What's the point of the stupid masks if we're going to eat the germs anyway?'

The sandwiches should be safe. She'd made them more than two hours ago. And eating germs was not the same as breathing them or rubbing them in your eyes. Her imperfect understanding was based only on snippets of information. She rummaged through the bag for anything in packets, in case she was wrong. 'Here you go. Hygienically sealed in a factory.'

'Muesli bars? Muesli bars aren't lunch. And the masks are still stupid.'

'There are cheese snacks in here too. Don't take the gloves off and don't touch the food before it goes in your mouth, hold it with the wrapper.'

'Dad, she's mad.'

'Yes, she is. Do as she says.'

Food eaten, detritus gathered, and back on their way, Zac and Daniel kept up a joint monologue, reliving the school trip in shared cryptic three-quarter sentences. 'And then he,' 'but Simon wanted to,' laughter. Oscar tried to join in by retelling the bits of stories that he thought he understood, but Zac would cut in halfway through. 'You weren't there, Oscar, you don't know what happened.' And each time, Oscar would hug his wounded silence to himself for five or ten minutes until his infatuation for the older boys overcame him.

Hannah let it all wash around her, concentrated on the driving and the mostly empty road in front of her. Even Zac's snarkiness made her happy to have him back. Their only stop was for a toilet break at Zac's request. Oscar took to the trees with enthusiasm, proud to show his brother that he was an expert at peeing by the side of the road. Zac wrinkled his nose and declared he'd hold on, but Daniel sheepishly admitted that he needed to go. Hannah took the break to stretch her legs behind the car. She listened in to the exchange between Sean and Zac in the al fresco men's room.

'We're not going to stop again, so if you hold on, you're holding on for two hours.'

'I don't need to go.'

'You asked to stop. I mean it – we're not stopping again, and if you think we'll give in and stop at a proper toilet, you're wrong.'

When Daniel came back, Zac stomped up to the trees, engulfed in a cloud of resentment. Hannah accidentally glanced over and whipped her eyes away again, but all she'd seen was Zac struggling to work out how to juggle the gloves and the hand wash.

The open road – they had made it, they'd escaped. Hannah relaxed her grip on the wheel, turned on the radio, and twiddled the dial until she found a classic hits station. The sounds of the seventies, the seventies, and the seventies from what she could hear. She stared straight ahead but out of the corner of her eye she could see Sean doing disco moves to stadium rock. He took a bow to the backseat. As the next song started, they made sideways eye contact – it was a gift – and in unison broke into 'We Are the Champions'.

Daniel's face mask looked blankly at Hannah in the rearview mirror, but Zac had thrown himself back in his seat. 'Stop the car, I want to kill myself.' Sean and Hannah launched into the second chorus with gusto.

The spot where they had been turned around that morning came slowly into view, visible each time the hills rose and fell. It seemed different now, more organized, more structured, blocking a stream of cars stretching towards Sydney. It was surprising how solid a temporary barrier could look. Sean flicked off the music. 'Not champions yet.' He put his hand over hers on the gear stick. 'We were fine this morning, we'll be fine now. At least we're all together.'

The important thing was to behave normally, which shouldn't be hard. After all, they hadn't really done anything wrong. But even the act of thinking about looking innocent made her feel guilty. They hadn't put anyone in danger – except the farmer, and he knew they'd come from Sydney and still got in the car of his own accord. And it's not as if they had broken through the barrier. They had just taken another route. But still, she felt her cheeks burn.

The roadblock on this side of the highway, new since this morning, looked more ad hoc. A man with a light baton waved them over to the shoulder. She slowed into the line of cars waiting to be processed. A handful of police walked from car to car, poking their heads into the drivers' windows. After a brief conversation, the car would peel off from the line to either wait for the emergency U-turn bay back to Canberra or, occasionally, continue straight on. As the police moved between cars, they called out to each other, 'You taking a break now?' or 'Save some coffee for me.' They didn't look back to see where the drivers they had spoken to went.

While Hannah waited to move forward, she watched the road ahead. On both sides, police cars obstructed the road before the U-turn bay. When a small line of cars had gathered, the two nearer police vehicles would move, leaving a clear path to the other half of the divided freeway, back to Canberra. Once they were through, the police moved back into place and the first few in the long line of Sydney-bound cars took their turn. She wondered if anyone else had found their cross-country route and whether it had been barricaded off.

The far roadblock looked very different from the makeshift checkpoint of this morning. Traffic cones had been replaced with an unbroken line of large orange-and-white plastic barriers. The four casual police from this morning were now a patrol, efficient and coordinated. And although the police officers lounging against the vehicles blocking the road looked bored, there was also a watchfulness under their feigned indifference as the Sydney traffic took the turn. As the last car reached the bay, a small white hatchback swerved out of the line waiting to be processed and roared towards the policemen. One touched his gun, the other waved his arms and yelled, a third pulled out a walkie-talkie as the car spun around them and on towards Canberra, disappearing in a cloud of dust. Hannah heard the detuned rev of its engine as it passed, followed by a squeal of tires and a siren. Through the clearing dust, blue and red lights flashed and she could just make out the back of the renegade and its pursuer.

Sean gave her an impish look. 'Maybe I should have tried that this morning.' He bumped her on the elbow and nodded forward. She hadn't noticed that the line in front of her had cleared. In her haste to bring no attention to herself she clashed the gears and lurched forward.

She turned to Sean. 'Am I flushed?'

'No.'

'I don't look red?'

'Stop talking, here he comes.'

She rolled down her window a little too eagerly, while the policeman was still several meters off. But not rolling it down might look aggressive. It was down now, she couldn't change that. And they wouldn't care, would they? Best to just say nothing and speak when spoken to. If she took the lead, she was afraid she'd blurt out something incriminating.

'How's it going?' He was young and walked awkwardly, as if the weight on his belt threw him off-balance.

'Fine. It's fine.'

'Where are you coming from today?'

'We've come from Canberra.'

He nodded at her.

'We're heading home. We met my son and his friend there – they had a school camp.' *Shut up, shut up, before he asks you when.*

He looked them over with less interest than she expected. 'Are your boys sick?' He motioned to the masks.

'No. No, not at all. No one's sick. It's just a precaution in the car. We've been trying to keep the kids apart because, you know, little kids are germ factories. But he's fine too. It's just . . .' She trailed off. 'You know kids.' But at his age, he probably didn't.

He leaned his head in a bit more and talked to Zac. 'Hey, mate, say something to me.'

'Like what?' Zac was muffled by the mask.

The cop seemed satisfied and turned back to her. 'So are you from Sydney?'

Don't volunteer anything. 'Yes.' She willed him not to ask when they left. Her brain went blank. Just when she needed a believable lie, nothing came.

'We're advising people to stay out of the whole Greater Sydney area. Were you staying with friends?'

'No.'

'You might get back into your hotel. We can give you something to say you never left the zone.'

'Our home's in Sydney. If there's any way, we'd like to go back home.'

'Your funeral.' The policeman looked sobered by the inappropriateness of his comment. 'Once you go in, you won't be coming back out until it's all over.' He looked at Sean, shrugged, and handed him a sheaf of Health Department pamphlets. 'Keep your little ones safe.'

'We will.' Hannah gave a genuine smile, the first emotion she'd allowed onto her face since they'd reached the roadblock.

The boys in the back were quieter now, even Oscar was staring out the window. A wave of tiredness crashed over her as the adrenaline drained away. They had the boys, they'd made it through the roadblock. Everything was done. Getting home was a formality.

'Hey.'

Hannah jumped. 'What did I do?'

Sean smiled at her. 'Maybe I should drive the rest of the way.'

'It's not far.'

'We did it.' He gestured his head to the backseat. 'We've got a full house.'

They were ten minutes from home.

'You'd better pull in so we can fill up again.' Sean waved his hand in the general direction of the petrol station.

'We're not stopping again.'

'Be serious – we've got less than a quarter of a tank.'

'We'll make it home. Too many risks today, no more.'

'And next time we need to take the car out? When it's worse?'

'I'm not going to change my mind.'

Sean looked thunderous but said nothing.

As soon as they pulled into the driveway, the boys bundled out of the car and bounced around the small paved front yard.

'Zac, Daniel.' Hannah was still summoning the energy to haul herself out of her seat. 'You're going to have to stay in your room for the next two days.'

Zac's eyes were a mixture of outrage and dismay. 'What if we need to go to the toilet?'

She sighed. 'Then you can go to the bathroom, of course. But that's all, and definitely no playing with Oscar.'

Zac pulled a face at Daniel, although the effect was hidden by his mask. 'As if.'

Sean held the door as the two boys ran through, Oscar chasing them. He bent behind the low wall of the veranda. 'Home delivery.'

She hadn't noticed that the note was gone. He took two bags, and she took the last one and the cold pack. 'I need a coffee. And you can have real milk.' She smiled at him.

'I bet you wish you'd agreed to buy the espresso machine. Fully automatic, beans in the top, touch one button, a perfect café cappuccino out the bottom.'

She lingered on the step. The last light of the day was golden on the rooftops. In his front yard, Mr Henderson rested against his fence, chatting to Gwen. He lazily raised a hand to her without breaking his conversation, and Gwen looked around and gave her a smile and a wave. Gwen should know better. She should know to stay indoors. And Hannah could only imagine where else Gwen went. Just as well they hadn't left Oscar with her – she'd have had him gallivanting all over the suburb. Hannah ducked inside before Gwen could come over and talk to her.

She found Oscar lying outside Zac's room, his ear

pressed to the crack at the bottom of the door. More than an espresso machine, Hannah wished she could know for certain that she was disease-free. She wanted more than anything to open Zac's door and give him a hug. It was such a small risk, such an infinitesimal possibility. But if she and Sean were sick, she needed Zac safe. An image flared into her mind, one she hadn't had for a while. But instead of Sean's shoulders supporting her family, now it was Zac's slender frame.

Mon	Tue	Wed	Thu	Fri	Sat	Sun

Her back ached. She turned carefully onto her other side and it eased slightly. She stretched her left leg over her right, trying to push her toe forward as far as she could without hitting Sean's back. The pain disappeared and she let herself sink slowly back to sleep. But as she sank, the pain reasserted itself. She rolled on her back and stretched out her hips. Again the pain receded. Not really pain, more insistent discomfort.

She listened to Sean's rhythmic breathing, trying to distract herself. But after a minute or so, she found she was actively listening to him. She couldn't stop herself from listening. It was as annoying as snoring. How was it possible that she ever slept next to the endless purring of his breath? There it was again, a dull ache in the small of her back. A need to move a muscle, which she couldn't satisfy. Tonight, last night. She couldn't remember if she'd had it the night before.

It was Monday's long drive. More than eight hours sitting cramped in the car. And the anxiety. That would cause this kind of pain. Surely Monday must have been the first night.

Symptoms had to start somewhere. The cancer that kills you begins as one wayward cell. As far as she knew, there was no way to tell the normal grind of life from warning signs. She could ignore it and regret it, or she could lie here obsessing about a backache.

After all, she hadn't had a clue when she first saw her mammogram, a night photograph of the earth, bright white patches connected by well-illuminated corridors. The doctor worked his way around the image on the light box, until he got to one densely lit area. 'That's the one. We're going to have to take that out.' But the other clusters looked exactly the same to her, cities, more or less populous, but with no way to tell which were the nice neighborhoods. Unless they were all bad and he was just pointing to the worst of them. Her eye caught on another patch that was, as far as she could see, the twin to the problem. 'And all the others? Will we have to deal with them later?' He looked quizzically at her. 'Like this one?' She pointed to the twin. He shook his head kindly. 'No, no, no. That's normal tissue.'

She turned again, twisting herself into a yoga pose, the only position in which nothing hurt. There it was, the sleep, if she could only grab hold. Something jolted her. *Concentrate on the sleep.* And again. Something out of place, a noise. She let go of the sleep. She opened her eyes to listen better. It came again, a car door opening. Someone coming in late or going out very early. On a weeknight. In the middle of the night. She heard voices.

It was someone else's problem, out in the street, nothing to do with her. Sleep was more important, if only she could get her mind away from the car. They would close the car door and drive away and that would be it.

The sound of the car door didn't come, her mind sharpened, trying to make out the smallest changes. She slid gently out of bed, tripped over her shoes lying on the floor, and banged into the wardrobe door. Sean snuffled, rolled over, and went back to breathing loudly.

She put her hand between the curtains and made a gap to look out. Four doors up on the other side, she could see a silver sedan with its doors and boot open. The porch light of the house was on, and the front door ajar.

She recognized the man who lived there, a nodding acquaintance, leaning into the car. When he stood up, the weak light spilling from the house fell on his daughter in the backseat. From the boot he pulled out what appeared to be a blanket and tucked it around her. The girl's mother was coming down the stairs with a large cardboard box, heavy by the pull of her arms. As the woman reached the open boot, the nearest streetlight caught its contents, and Hannah saw a carton of cereal sticking out the top. The woman put the box in and tried to close the lid. She pushed down on the box and tried again. She shoved on the boot lid as it sprang back, then started unpacking. Out came a suitcase, a small kettle barbecue, and another couple of boxes.

There was a sharp noise from the house, like the door closing. Hannah saw the man push his shoulder against the front door and, satisfied, make his way down the stairs. He pulled the driver's-side door closed as he slid behind the wheel, and as they drove off, the woman's face was lit in profile by the streetlamp.

Hannah wondered where they were going. Anywhere, she supposed, if they had a tent. Sean had found a website the day after their trip to Canberra, of people sharing circuitous routes out of the city that hadn't yet been closed, but it seemed likely from the follow-up tales of failure that the police had found the site too. Maybe the family was just going to another suburb, farther south, farther away from the hot spots.

Her back ached. There was no point going back to bed.

Light fell dimly through the panes in the front door, giving her a sketchy outline in gray to navigate by. She guided herself past Oscar's room and into the living room by the tips of her fingers on the hallway wall. The curtains let through a small glimmer, but outside Zac's room, the hallway was windowless and engulfed in inky darkness. She paused to listen for noise. Her stern voice through the door had had little effect on Zac and Daniel, since they knew she wouldn't come in to follow through on her threats. Now they were quiet, finally asleep. She tripped and jumped as her foot hit something just outside Zac's door.

The bundle on the floor made little murmuring sounds. She felt her way to the light switch outside the bathroom, shuffling her feet against further surprises. Oscar lay across Zac's doorway, in a nest constructed from his duvet and pillow. His face was pale and empty and left her feeling disquieted and sad. He snuggled further down into his makeshift bed and looked so comfortable, she decided to leave him be.

In the kitchen, her laptop was where she had left it that afternoon. It had been nine hours since she checked the Internet. Seven of those before she went to bed. And it had been hard, steeling herself not to look. Nine hours of news that she didn't know. There might be an explanation of why her neighbors were doing a flit in the night. Or some of it might even be good – there had to be progress sometime.

The blue light of the screen barely lit the walls. She scanned down the newspaper's website, and registered that it was after midnight. Today was now yesterday. She found the number. Eighty-one. That had to be a typo – they meant eighteen. There were only thirteen dead on Monday. Only. Thirteen people dead in one day. But eighty-one. It had to be wrong. She snapped the laptop shut. Until the morning. The paper would notice their mistake and fix it by morning.

In the bathroom, she looked at her wan and fearful face. Through all the years of worrying and scanning her body, of being on high alert, this much she knew about cancer pain – you couldn't make it go away by bending or stretching. She told the panic merchant in the mirror firmly, 'This isn't what cancer feels like.'

In her experience, cancer didn't feel like anything at all. It was a blob on a mammogram, a wrinkle in the skin, but she still didn't know the difference between hysteria and prudence.

She took two painkillers and made her way back to bed, stepping over Oscar. She gently swiveled him so that he lay along the hall, not across it.

Oscar was stretched out on the sofa, in thrall to cartoons, when she got up. His duvet and pillow were still in a pile outside Zac's door. As Hannah passed, Zac called out, 'Can we get some breakfast in here?'

'In a minute.'

'Mum, Oscar's been up for hours and he won't get us anything. We're starving.' His voice was muted by the door.

Her head was muzzy from lack of sleep, but at least the pain was gone. 'In a minute.'

'Can we at least come out?'

'This afternoon. Two days is this afternoon.' Zac said something that she couldn't hear and wasn't supposed to.

Of the bag of bread, only enough full slices remained for the boys' breakfast, leaving her the crusts. In place of gloves, she used the bag to hold the bread as she dropped it in the toaster, a fork to lift the slices out and hold it in place as she smeared a trace of jam across each piece. A teaspoon of chocolate powder floated in a glass of long-life milk for each of the boys, the powder encapsulated in bubbles of air that divided as she stirred harder, remaining bone-dry inside the translucent skins.

The tin of coffee felt light. She shook it, as if somehow that would make it heavier. Her calculations were off.

Unlike the bread, she couldn't blame it on Daniel. That had better be added to the next order. She filled the base of the ancient stovetop espresso maker with water, screwed the two halves together. The hiss and spit of an explosion of steam and shrapnel waiting to happen was exactly why she had retired it to the back of the cupboard years ago. Now that there wasn't a barista around the corner, they both craved a proper cappuccino, and since they had time available for coffee-making, it had been recalled from exile.

She knocked softly on Zac's door and, without waiting for a reply, opened it and slid the tray in. As she closed the door, she heard Zac's whine. 'Mum, toast? I hate toast – it's like cardboard.'

Daniel's voice was softer, not designed for her to hear. 'More for me.'

'Yeah, right.'

The painful brightness of the yard darkened the unlit office more, so that she could barely make out Sean hunched over the keyboard. 'Knock, knock.' He looked up at her, but his mind remained in the virtual world. 'Coffee.'

He put a hand out for the mug and took a sip. 'Improving.'

'How's work?'

He snapped into focus. 'Do you know there's not a single case in Melbourne? The whole office down there is working normally. They're going out to lunch today.'

'Are many people still going in to the Sydney office?'

'It's been closed.' He looked away and shrugged, as if it was unimportant. 'One of the guys from another department lives in that block of flats. So they closed the office, as a precaution. After he was quarantined, like that's going to help.' He rubbed a spot of dirt from his screen.

'What flats?'

'You haven't looked at the paper yet? Ten people dead yesterday all in one block of flats. He was in yesterday. I was supposed to be in a meeting with him.'

'Is he all right? Is he sick?'

'I don't know. I don't really know him. An email went around earlier saying he was doing okay but . . . the whole block's quarantined. There are soldiers standing outside the building. It's all over the news. And it's not like the ten knew each other – they just live in the same block. They say it could be getting through the sewerage system. Aerosolized when you turn on the tap too hard or flush the toilet.'

'How the hell could that even be possible? It spread through the toilet?'

'Who knows? Maybe it's an old building with dodgy plumbing. Maybe they're secretly partying together. No one knows.' He ran his hand through his hair. 'But I'm safe and everyone who went in yesterday is going to spend today and tomorrow waiting for symptoms.' He looked around the room, as if for a solution. 'Eighty-one dead yesterday and someone I work with lives in the same block as ten of them. The guys in Melbourne keep telling us to forget about work. But what am I going to do?' He put his arm around her waist and gave her a squeeze. 'I'm okay and you're okay and Zac and Oscar and Daniel are all okay. But I have to keep doing something, pretending that it matters, otherwise it's not okay anymore.' He looked into his mug. 'Is there more? You'll be rivaling the café in a few days. It's good.'

It was good because they had the old espresso pot. Because the air was fresh and voices of people were in the distance. Because Zac was in his bedroom and Oscar was watching cartoons. So the coffee tasted good.

Hannah sat on the arm of the sofa, watching Oscar watch TV. Waiting for him to change position was almost a meditation. Just about the only way he didn't sit was flat on the seat. Now he was lying with his legs draped up over the back, feet flat on the wall behind, his head hanging backwards over the front of the sofa. Two minutes earlier, he had been on his front, crouched like a mouse with his knees pulled up to his chin underneath him.

An ad came on for a 'special' meal with a movie tie-in toy. 'Hey, Mum. I really want that. I really like that movie.'

'Sorry, Oscar, can't go out the front door today.' The perfect answer.

Now on the screen, a woman poured laundry powder into a washing machine. From the machine, a bubble squeezed, enveloping the woman and floating her into the air. Below her, a sea of animated germs, black and scowling, threatened to reach the bubble. One by one, the

bubble enfolded the members of the ⸻
them from their own home. It was a s̶⸻
so appealing. To be in that bubble, with C⸻
and Sean.

She was jolted from the daydream by the sou⸻ ⸻he
doorbell. As she walked down the hall she realized no
one had come to their door for a week, no one unexpected. She took a step back as she opened it, to keep a
meter between her and whoever was outside. It took an
instant to recognize Gwen, backlit by the sunlight from
the street, peering in.

'Oh, Hannah. I'm so sorry to interrupt you.' Hannah
was still wearing her pajamas. It was not as if she was
going anywhere today.

'Not a problem, Gwen.'

Gwen stood as if waiting for something, her eyes
focused on the grille.

'I'm not opening the grille, Gwen. Sorry, we're not
letting anyone in or out.'

Gwen looked surprised. 'What a lot of fuss over nothing.' She talked fast, as if continuing a conversation
already started. 'No one's come. Meals on Wheels didn't
turn up this week and I can't get on to my daughter. She's
probably gone away.' That would be thoughtless, to leave
town without telling your elderly mother. But thoughtless
was better than the other possibilities. 'I can't get to the
shopping center, and Lily's is only a corner store – you
wouldn't expect her to have everything. So when you go
to the shops I've got a list of things for you to pick up.'

. m not going to the shops, but I'm getting some things delivered. If you give me the list, I'll get them to put your things in too.'

Gwen had her purse in her hand. 'I don't want much, a few tins. I'll give you some money.' Money that had probably been through Lily's till and the hands of Lily's customers.

'Later. We don't know how much it will be.'

'Fifty dollars should more than cover it.' She had the note out, one hand on the grille.

'I'll get it from you later. I'm not opening the door right now. Not until the epidemic's over. It can wait until then.' Gwen looked affronted. 'Gwen, do you cook for yourself?'

'I manage. The Meals on Wheels man comes and my daughter brings me a casserole on the weekend. Or a salad.'

'When did the Meals on Wheels man come last?'

'I think it was Thursday. Maybe Friday.'

'And your daughter?'

'Oh, she's always busy.' Gwen dismissed the thought with a wave of her hand. 'She has a family of her own and everyone is making such a fuss about this illness.'

'What have you eaten since Friday?'

'I'm not incapable of looking after myself. I've been doing it for a long time and I haven't starved.'

Gwen moved closer to the grille as she became engrossed in the conversation. And each increment sent Hannah farther into the shadow of the hallway, until Gwen was an outline haloed by the light.

'I can't let you in, Gwen. People are dying.'

'I hope you don't think I'm one of them. Except from hunger if the Meals on Wheels man doesn't come back.'

In Hannah's mind, the shelves of food in the pantry rearranged themselves, smaller somehow, clustered for six now when they had been designed for four. 'I'll make sure you have food.' She looked beyond Gwen to the street outside, willing the Meals on Wheels car or Gwen's daughter to appear and make this not her problem. 'Gwen, you can't go out, especially not to Lily's. It's dangerous.'

'Oh, I don't go far and I'm right as rain.'

'I'm serious. It takes two days to see symptoms. You could be sick, or Mr Henderson could be, and not even know it. That's why you have to stay home and not have contact with anyone.' Gwen looked unimpressed. Hannah continued, a little weakly, 'Will you be all right at home, on your own?' All she was prepared to offer was food, nothing more. And yet even that made her anxious. Each meal she gave Gwen, gave Daniel, was a meal's less protection for her boys. Offering too much and not enough.

'Of course I will. I've been on my own for fifteen years now – I think I know how to stay put.' She fumbled around in her pocket and pulled out a torn envelope with florid handwriting. 'Just a few things.' She gave the grille an offended look that traveled down to the gap at the bottom. 'My knees aren't what they were.'

'Why don't you leave it in the letterbox and I'll get it out later.' It could stay there for a few hours.

When Zac was little and she'd listened to just about as much Wiggles as she could stand, she made him a CD for the car. She'd spent a night going through their music collection, finding all the silliest songs that were still acceptable to her. He had loved that CD and only grown out of it when he realized that Oscar in his turn had come to love it. And now she needed something to cheer herself up, make her feel as if there was still fun in the world. As if she was five again and didn't have to worry.

Oscar only knew one dance, the Macarena – the Hokey Pokey of his generation, taught to him by the teachers at school who were just old enough to have learned it when it first came out. Whatever song she put on, he insisted they dance it, and she followed his lead. In unison, they swirled hips, clapped hands, flicked thumbs, and stamped feet. Ending with a quarter-turn jump in whichever direction Oscar chose.

Oscar kept up a monologue the whole time, punctuated by giggles. 'And Mrs Gleeson stood on Mr Turner's foot when she jumped and Mr Turner yelled but no one heard him 'cause the music was so loud and . . .' She could barely hear him over the stamping.

A thumping came from somewhere other than their feet and Hannah paused the music to hear teenage fists pounding on Zac's bedroom wall. 'TURN THE MUSIC DOWN.'

Oscar and Hannah looked at each other and laughed. 'Stop being such killjoys,' she yelled back.

'We're trying to play a game here and every time you elephants jump on the floor everything goes everywhere. We have to yell at each other.'

Hannah winked at Oscar. 'We won't jump so much.'

'It's two days! With no one sick.'

'Two more hours.'

Even without being able to see him, Hannah knew Zac's eyes were rolling. 'Two hours, I'll be dead. From boredom, not from a cough.'

'At least you'll stop griping at me when you're dead.' Too well brought up to bust out, she guessed. A tick in her column. 'Hey, Oz, let's do a dance that doesn't use our feet so much.' She taught him to twist, lifting one heel and holding his weight on the other. She flapped her arms, like the Eagle Rock, waved them around above her head, any silly pose to get him to laugh.

They were caught midtwist when Sean walked in, coffee cup dangling from one hand. 'Can you turn the music down? It's too loud.'

Hannah smiled at him. 'Across the yard in the office? No way.'

Sean continued to frown. 'I came in for a coffee. And you're loud.'

'You and Zac. The two of you can move into the garage when we let him out and never make a sound.'

'You're the one who's always going on about not disturbing Gwen.' Sean waved at the party wall. Oscar had already engrossed himself in the pile of Lego bricks in the corner, shutting out the adult noises. 'Serious things are happening. You might be having a good time, but out there' – he shook his hand in the direction of the street – 'out there people are in trouble. Real people.'

'Me being miserable won't change that.' She had her hands on her hips, ready to defend herself. Oscar took apart and put back together the same set of bricks, but she knew he was listening, trying to pretend that somehow he wasn't part of this. It wasn't fair on Oscar, scaring him like this. 'Why don't you finish early today?'

'I finish early every day now. I've still got stuff to do.' Sean turned to Oscar and said with all the force of his bad temper, 'This place is a mess. Is that any way to treat your toys? Look at them, all piled up. They'll get broken.' Oscar's eyes started to well.

'We'll tidy it when we're done, won't we?' She tried to jolly Oscar.

'The mess was here yesterday. It was here the day before. You shouldn't be picking up after him, Oscar should be doing it.'

'He did. Yesterday was a different mess. Every day we pick up the mess, then we make a new one.'

Cancer makes you a better person. It must be true – people said it to her all the time. But Hannah couldn't take in the whole neighborhood, she couldn't feed everyone, and yet there would always be someone in need and more that she could have done. Wherever she drew the line, she would fail someone. If she was a better person now, she must have been a truly inadequate one before.

She'd lain in bed exhausted from throwing up, her whole body alien, fighting her. Modesty, privacy, were jettisoned. Any sense that her body was her own was abandoned, its sovereignty ceded to doctors and technicians.

The sharp certainty that she was going to die still sometimes ambushed her, but it didn't make life sweeter. It was a mosquito buzzing in her ear at night, no more creating happiness than a mosquito creates sleep. She'd suffered and not suffered and knew for certain that she preferred the not suffering. All that cancer had left her with was a fading anger that she'd wasted a year of her life on a posse of renegade cells.

Her only task had been to make it to the other side, back to the life she already had, the person she had chosen to be. And here she was, eight years on, the same person, wishing that she didn't feel responsible for Gwen.

A little before dinner, just shy of two days since they'd arrived home, she changed out of her pajamas so as not to embarrass Zac in front of Daniel. With her finger to her lips, she got Oscar and Sean to follow her to Zac's door and knocked quietly.

'What? Go away.'

She turned the knob and opened the door. 'You think I'm not going to come in there and make you regret that?' She smiled at him and he looked back, bewildered.

'It's not time.'

'It's past time if you count from Canberra.'

She had expected a champagne cork pop, but the two boys picked themselves up from where they were lying and sauntered out. Oscar bounded around them like a puppy. 'Do you want to play outside? We could play soccer. I could be on Daniel's team. I'm good at goalie.'

'Tell you what, Oscar and me against you two.' Sean looked down at Oscar. 'We'll slaughter them. Your mum could play for our team too.'

Zac snorted. 'If you want to make it harder for yourselves.' Hannah gave him a look. 'I'm joking. It's a joke.' But he muttered to Daniel, 'We're set.'

Zac and Daniel played to win. Sean played to let Oscar have fun. Hannah played to avoid looking like a wet blanket. Oscar just played. The older boys knew that five people on a couple of square meters of grass had to wing it, but Oscar stopped play for every infringement.

'Hey, Oscar.' Sean bent down to Oscar's height, to camouflage his puffing, Hannah suspected. 'Let's imagine that this isn't soccer.' Oscar gave him a questioning smile. 'Maybe this is a different game, one called lawn ball. It's very simple. You kick the ball, you don't touch the other people, and you don't go off the grass.'

'Who throws in when it goes off?'

'You do.'

'What about when we go off?'

'The youngest player always throws in.'

'What about when—'

'Anything' – Sean took them all by surprise by belting the ball in front of him with his foot – 'goes.' The ball slammed into the fence. 'Goal. One, nil.'

'Hey!' Zac turned from amusement to outrage in a second.

'My rules.'

'Hey, new rule – you don't have to be nice to your dad.' Zac and Daniel pushed across the lawn, dancing around Sean.

Oscar neatly stepped out to the ball and punted it to Sean, who kicked it across the grass and onto the fence. 'Two, nil.'

At first, Daniel steered away from her, too polite to crash into someone else's mum, but after a few minutes the need to not be beaten by Zac's little brother and mum took precedence. In between dodging the boys, Hannah noticed Ella's head poking over the top of the opposite fence, big toddler eyes silently watching the game. She wondered if Natalie or Stuart knew where she was.

As Daniel's foot connected with the ball, aimed square on for a slam goal against Gwen's fence, he jumped in triumph. His joy morphed, in seconds, to embarrassed shame as the ball curved too high, missed its mark, and sailed clear over to Gwen's backyard.

'I'm sorry, I didn't mean to.'

Four sets of eyes scanned Gwen's garden. Oscar tried to scramble up the crossbeams of the fence to join in. Sean contemplated the mission. 'The coast is clear. The rule is, if you sent it, you get it.' Sean locked his hands together to make a step and boosted Daniel to the other side.

Hannah stood near Ella's still-mute bobblehead. Caught in the passage between their houses, she could see a slice of sunset. Orange clouds with a purple underbelly.

'Hey guys, look at this.'

They gathered to watch the display in silence and she discreetly held Oscar away from the fence and Ella. The colors changed, now red, now purple – spectacular, gaudy, and baroque. The color drained, leaving the overly ornate clouds a steely lavender.

Oscar said, 'The clouds didn't look like that yesterday. Yesterday they were pink and yellow. They're different every day.'

In their little cube of space, nothing big happened, only small changes, variations on a theme. These ephemeral moments gave her an awe of existence – the rightness and gratitude she felt with these people who were her world.

Now gloom hid the ball, leaving only its glowing white patches for them to track. Oscar ducked and weaved, an invisible motion in the failing light. Sean kicked at the ball, missed, and just pulled himself up as he was about to connect with Oscar. He twisted, tried to recover, and, with something approaching grace, landed square on his back. Oscar was in awe. 'Cool, Dad. Do it again.'

'Hey, we could turn on the lights.' Zac moved towards the house.

'Ow.' Sean laughed and gasped from the grass. 'I think it's dinnertime.'

'Yep.' Hannah picked up the ball. 'Past dinnertime.' She looked at the fence. Ella had gone without her noticing.

'Hey,' Zac called from the patio door, 'the light's broken.'

'Here.' Sean flicked the switch a couple of times. He tried the switch just inside the kitchen, up and down. Nothing.

'The fridge's not working.' Zac leaned on the white door and stared into its dark void.

Hannah lurched forward. 'Then keep the door closed, you'll let out the cold.'

'You can't let out cold. It's not a thing. You can let out cold air, but you're not letting out cold,' Zac said with all the force of two years of high school science.

'Shut the door!'

Oscar came running back from the hallway. 'And the TV's not working.'

'Never mind,' she said with forced gusto, 'it's an adventure. We don't need electricity.'

She rummaged on the bottom shelf of the pantry, looking for her emergency candles, with Oscar hovering behind her like a foreshortened ghost. 'Here you go, you can take those to Daddy.'

Zac stood in the passage from the kitchen, arms crossed cockily, Daniel slightly behind. 'How are we going to cook dinner, on candles?'

'We can use the barbecue. It'll be like camping.' Zac gave her the world-weary teenage look of someone burdened with lame parents. 'Or we could break up the furniture and burn it in the backyard. I'm starting with your bed.' In response, she got a bit of a smirk.

The door opening from the hallway took her by surprise, unaccompanied by the usual light that announced Sean's entrance. 'They're playing cards by torch light in the living room. Oscar begged for candles but I can see that ending in disaster.' Sean leaned back against the kitchen counter. 'Did you know children can function without electricity? I don't think they knew. At least without the TV we can be sure they won't see the news. We can hope we've seen the worst, that tomorrow the numbers will go down.'

'Do you think so?'

'No.' He fished a wine bottle out of the recycling, jammed a candle in the neck, and handed it to her. 'I think for you something more romantic than a torch.'

They split the task of dinner. He took a candle out to the gas barbecue to cook some rice, she had the job of working out what to add to it. It was a toss-up whether to eat everything out of the fridge first or the freezer, but it was late and anything in the freezer was going to take too much time to defrost without the microwave. The trick was to picture the contents of the fridge like a memory puzzle, open the door, and pull out everything she needed in one fluid move. It took her a few seconds to orient herself, but the cold creeping along her hand forced her to take what was in easy reach as quickly as possible.

A carrot, a couple of sticks of celery, th... bage, some spring onions, the tail of an ... ham. She slammed the door and looked at the ... her mind she tried to reconstruct where she h... the things she needed, then opened the door again to scoop up leftover roast chicken and a couple of eggs to fill it out.

The candle cast a warm light around her hands and the chopping board as she diced the vegetables. When she looked out the back window, she could see Sean standing over the barbecue. His face glowed orange, the rest of him invisible in the darkness. Their warm pools of light connected, working together but separated.

He came back once he had the rice started. 'So what are we cooking?'

'Impromptu Fried Rice Leftovers.'

'Yum.' He nuzzled up to her neck, she leaned into him. She mixed soy sauce and fish sauce into the beaten eggs, put each of the ingredients in a bowl, and all the bowls on a tray, a patchwork of food, to take them out to the patio table. Sean carried the candle for her like a butler. Its small light disappeared into the voluminous darkness. Each bowl looked meager, but fried up together they made a huge mound. The leftovers would in turn be more leftovers, someone's breakfast.

Hannah portioned out the fried rice onto six plates, putting aside one for Gwen, and scraped the rest into a bowl. She called the boys. Oscar skipped into the room, Zac pushed in after him, but Daniel followed sedately and seated himself at the far end of the table. He picked up his knife and fork, then awkwardly put them down when he noticed no one else was yet ready.

'Can I help?' His hands were clenched in his lap.

There had to be something she could give him to do, to make him feel less like a guest. 'You could carry some things over for me. What about the salad?' The salad was leftovers as well, the last of the fresh, leafy greens. If the power came back, she should look on the Internet to see if you could eat any of the weeds in the garden. Anything to be able to stay out of the world a bit longer. Not that two square meters of weedy lawn would keep even a caterpillar going for more than a day or two.

Daniel watched his hands while he ate, as if keeping himself in check. She wished he wasn't quite so well behaved. But this was his first meal out of his room. Candles on the table. For all he knew, they always ate this way. 'There's salad too, Daniel. Dig in.'

'Thanks.' He handled the salad servers awkwardly, scooping a mound of lettuce between the two spoons. She could see a look of anxiety on his face as he held it suspended over his plate. He tried to put it back into the bowl, but a few leaves fell on the table. His hands held the servers so tightly, he had trouble releasing them. 'I think I took more than my share,' he mumbled.

'Never mind. Dig in,' she said. Daniel inhaled his food – she had only looked away for a moment and it was gone. 'Help yourself to some more.' This time she didn't need to urge him.

'Thanks, Hannah, it's really good.' The second plate vanished nearly as fast.

Zac scraped everything remaining in the bowl onto his plate then stopped to watch Oscar pushing his food around, eating it half a spoonful at a time. 'Are you going to finish that?'

'Mum, Zac's telling me what to do.'

'I asked you a question, I didn't tell you anything. If you're not going to eat it, I might as well have it.' Not that long ago, Zac would have died rather than eat someone else's food.

'Oscar's food is Oscar's and he's going to eat it. You had two helpings – you can't still be hungry.'

'Well, not hungry . . .'

'Zac, you've had your fair share.' Hannah injected a warning tone into her voice.

'Dad! He's going to waste it. What good will that do?'

'What about Daniel – have you considered if he wants more?' Sean was uncommonly stern.

'He had seconds. And he doesn't want Oscar's leftovers. That's gross.'

'Well, your mum hasn't had seconds – what about her? I'm surprised at you, Zac. You're usually more considerate than this.'

'I'm fine,' Hannah jumped in. If it came to feeding herself or Zac and Oscar, she'd go without. And Daniel, of course – she should be ready to give up her food for Daniel too.

So much for the leftovers. Her recalculations had

assumed six people ate one and a half times as much as four. But she'd never realized how much of their food was consumed by Zac. Gwen subtracted very little, but another teenage boy . . . All her plans for making biscuits and cakes to keep their spirits up were naive if she couldn't keep enough bread and meat on the table.

Daniel had reverted to sitting up straight with his hands neatly folded. When it became clear there would be nothing left on Oscar's plate, Zac slouched back. Daniel shifted a little. 'Could I be excused from the table?'

Sean looked at him with surprise and awe. 'Did you hear that, Zac? Daniel has manners. He asks if he can leave the table.'

'That's only because he's a guest. He doesn't do it at his place.'

'Is that true, Daniel? Because if it is, you shouldn't be a guest. Behave as badly as you would at home. But if you're just well-mannered, try to influence my son.'

'I wonder whose job it was to teach me?' Zac grinned.

Daniel was still looking politely at Sean.

'Of course you can go.'

Hannah cut in. 'Stack your dishes in the dishwasher. We can live in hope that the power comes back on.'

'But if it doesn't, you'll have to take them out again and we wasted our time.' Zac looked smug.

'If it doesn't, you boys will get to do the washing up, so why don't we assume it will?'

Despite the grumbles, the boys threw themselves into the stacking with vigor, and Hannah bit her tongue. They were doing what she asked, so if plates got broken, it was no one's fault but her own.

'Great job.' Sean stood sentry as they finished up. 'Go run around for a bit, burn off some energy. You could play Murder in the Dark or something.'

Oscar and Zac were gone, but Daniel held back at the door. 'I'd like to ring my mum, if that's okay.' Sean, behind him, shook his head at Hannah slightly.

'Sorry, Daniel, I don't think any of the phones work without power. Because they're all cordless, you know.' An excuse with so many holes in it, she could only imagine that Daniel was too polite to point out all the mobile phones they had.

'And, you know, mate, it's getting late,' Sean jumped in. 'We don't want to wake your mum up. She needs all the rest she can get just now. We'll ring tomorrow. That'll be better.'

Hannah held the words in until Daniel had followed the other boys out. 'And we're not ringing why?'

'She's pretty sick. I got an email from his dad today. Maybe tomorrow she'll be on the mend. There's no need for him to worry until he has to.'

They watched the boys from the kitchen door. Oscar had endless energy, pent up from so many days with only his feeble parents for company, and Daniel was a new playmate. An unknown quantity to be tested to destruction. As Daniel sat in the middle of the lawn, pulling strands out of the grass, Oscar threw himself at Daniel's back, as if to climb it. Daniel gently rolled himself sideways, depositing Oscar on the grass. Oscar took another leap and held on tight. Daniel patiently peeled Oscar's hands from his shoulders, and once he had himself free, moved to the wall of the garden bed, out of the field of play. Hannah wished for something that could distract him from whatever inner conversation he was engaged in.

In one of the kitchen drawers, she unearthed a scrunched box of bent sparklers, left over from Oscar's last birthday. 'Hey, guys,' Hannah called from the doorway, 'look what I've got.'

Sean helped Oscar hold his steady in the flickering flame of the candle. Zac and Oscar leaped and whooped, made afterimage circles and wrote their names with light. Zac challenged Daniel to a sparkler duel and the two boys danced around each other, thrusting and parrying, Daniel without much enthusiasm, for the few seconds the sparklers spat.

The transitory joy was broken by a wail from Oscar. 'I stubbed my toe.' Punctuated with sobs. 'I stubbed my toe!'

'Hey, mate, I think you've had too much fun. You haven't cried like this since you started school with the big kids. It's nothing.' Sean held out his hand to stop Hannah from rushing to comfort Oscar. 'It's nothing. He'll be fine.'

But as his sobs subsided, Oscar crept into Hannah's arms. She didn't think his tears were only for his sore toe.

'Right, time for bed.'

'Oh, what? It's too early. Come on, Dad.' Zac was filled with moral outrage at having his new freedom arbitrarily removed when it was barely dark.

'Okay then, not you two, but definitely you.' Sean picked up Oscar from Hannah's lap and tossed him over his shoulder. 'Time to wash this sack of potatoes. You can't eat dirty potatoes.' Oscar was grinning again.

Zac and Daniel were company for each other and she could use the moment of freedom to find out what was happening about the electricity. At least the battery in her laptop had power. She set herself up at the kitchen table by the light of a candle. The hum was reassuring as she turned on the laptop, but she couldn't get any further than opening a browser. The phone line, and hence the Internet, was still connected, but the router needed power. The bits and bytes she needed were right there, in the wires behind the wall – she just couldn't tap into them.

People got information before there was an Internet. There must have been – must still be – information lines. Except that she no longer had a phone book because any number she needed was on the Internet and she wasn't prepared to use her mobile if there was a chance she couldn't charge it.

She stood outside Oscar's door, listening to the end of his bedtime story. The lights came back on as dramatically as they'd gone off. She pushed open the door to let in the hallway light and flicked on the light switch in Oscar's room. Sean blew out the candle, and Oscar burst into tears again.

'What's wrong now?'

'I liked it dark. It was so much fun.'

'The lights will go off again – I can just about guarantee that.' Sean tucked the sheets tight around Oscar and slipped Teddy into the bed, even though Oscar had left him on the floor for months. 'We don't need to wait for fun – we can make it ourselves.' Oscar suspended his tears as he gave this proposition careful consideration.

Sean's arm lay along the back of the sofa, his hand resting on Hannah's shoulder, a small patch of body warmth. He held her tighter, pulling her in. The two of them looked out of the cave of their house through the small portal of the TV screen at the strange world they had left.

The minister for energy made a statement trying to paint the outage as just one of those things that happens, even at the best of times. An unfortunate coincidence. His image gave way to the opposition spokesman, wearing an equally audience-tested costume of sober suit and dependable tie, declaiming that the day's events only served to demonstrate how woefully underprepared this government really was.

Images of large machinery, tired men and women hunched over panels in some sort of control room, the bulbous cooling towers of a coal power plant. The face of a woman – the grainy picture froze and jumped, presumably an interview by webcam.

'Do you resent your colleagues who didn't volunteer?'

The dark shadows under her eyes gave her a look of

exhausted desperation. 'The people here, we're mostly the ones who don't have family depending on us. We all agreed to be locked in. I don't resent the others. I know them, I've been to their houses, I know their kids. We get food brought to us, we're being looked after. In some ways it's easier. Everyone has to make hard decisions now, do what's important to them. Here, we're working hard, but we can catch up on sleep when this is over. My friends out there are on their own. I only hope they're all right.'

Sean had the remote in his hand, finger resting on the channel button. 'She should go home.'

'The power plant's probably safer than her home.'

'The newsreader. Look at her eyes. She's been on every news report this week. She needs to sleep.'

The mayor stood on the empty steps of Sydney Town Hall and cheerfully declared, 'I can tell you that today the council has unanimously voted to remain here, in the city, until this crisis is over. This city, our city, has the best hospitals, the best infrastructure in the world.' Footage of the mayor glad-handing smiling patients in hospital beds. No footage of her being doused in antiseptic the second the cameras were turned off. 'And I challenge the prime minister to join us here to show her support for the citizens of this, the most vibrant city in the world.'

'I've had enough.' Sean kissed Hannah's hair and smoothed it down with his hand. 'You look done.'

'I miss going to work. No, I miss having downtime when the kids are at school, even if it's at work.'

'I know. They're so . . . there. All the time. I ended up

bribing Oscar to stay quiet this morning. A biscuit for every five minutes he didn't talk to me.'

'You are the worst parent.'

His eyes softened as he smiled at her. 'I am.'

'How many biscuits did he get?' *From my pantry.*

'One. And that was an incentive – he didn't last two minutes.' Sean stretched as he stood. 'Come on. Bed.' He pulled her up from the sofa, snaked his arm around her hip, and rubbed his face into her neck. It sent a shiver down her side and made her laugh.

She tilted her head in the direction of Zac's room. 'We'll disturb them.'

'God forbid his mother should laugh.' He was still smiling. 'Come on.' With his arm still wrapped around her, he guided her to the hallway.

She liked being so close to him, feeling him through her clothing, smelling him. The time they spent the last few days wasn't together, it was side by side. It was Mum and Dad, always monitoring what they said in case small ears were overhearing.

She looked closely at him, wondering if some remnant of this morning's bad mood still hid in his face. 'Is everything okay?'

'In the whole wide world?'

'In your world.'

He didn't answer right away, but opened his mouth to speak, stopped, then gave a mirthless 'ha' and shook his head.

'What?'

'You're going to tell me you told me so.'

'Told you what?'

'A bunch of people from the office are sick.'

He watched her face for her reaction. She felt an icy anticipation. 'How sick?'

'Two in hospital. Three more got turned away.' She could see him struggle to dam the words in his mouth, hold them back. 'Apparently being turned away is good – it means you're not going to die yet. There's no room in the hospitals for anyone who isn't dying.'

She didn't have any more emotion to call on. The cold dread that sat between them was not part of her and she had no words to dispel it.

'I didn't know whether to tell you about them. It's been on my mind, but there's nothing I can do.'

Voices in the street. Natalie under the streetlight, facing her house. Stuart holding Ella, perched on the wall of the veranda. Ella leaning forward with her hand out, squirming in Stuart's arms.

Hannah moved sideways, shifting the narrow view presented by the curtains from the street to the veranda and back.

Ella twisted around and said something to Stuart as he leaned into her. Natalie blew a kiss to Ella, who caught it and kissed her hand where it landed. Ella wriggled down from the wall and away from Stuart's grasp. Natalie took a step towards her and then one back with her hands up. Ella was halfway down the steps before Stuart caught her.

Natalie wiped tears off her face. She took a chocolate bar out of her bag, gave it a kiss, then put it in the mailbox. She gave a wave and got back into her car. Through the window, Hannah could just hear Ella, struggling to get out of Stuart's arms. 'Mummy, Mummy.'

Mon	Tue	Wed	Thu	Fri	Sat	Sun

Daniel hovered in the kitchen, stiffly moving from one spot in Hannah's way to another. He silently observed her getting breakfast ready, not quite comfortable enough to offer to help, not quite relaxed enough to leave her to the preparations.

'Have a seat, Daniel. Breakfast will be out soon.'

'Would I be able to ring my mum?'

Sean answered from the kitchen table. 'Why don't you wait until after breakfast, mate.'

Daniel glanced at Zac for support. 'My mobile's out of charge and I want to ring my mum.'

Sean picked up the phone, shifted it from one hand to the other. 'I think I should . . . I'm going to talk to your dad first and see if she's well enough to talk.'

'I can talk to my dad.'

'Just let me speak to him first. After breakfast.'

Daniel had an expression on his face that almost approached resolve.

'Why don't I ring him now.' Sean took the phone into

167

the garden and Hannah followed him out. He held the phone sideways to let the sound escape. It rang and a voice answered. 'Hi, is that . . .' Sean stamped his foot to get her attention and raised his shoulders in a question. She shrugged – she'd never actually met him. ' . . . Daniel's dad?' An inaudible reply. 'It's Zac's dad. Daniel wants to talk to his mum. I don't know what to tell him. Is she, is she all right?'

Hannah heard the sobs on the other end of the phone and the tinny, strangled voice. 'Susan's alive. Oh God, she's still alive. Last night, I didn't think . . . She was so bad, I couldn't see how she could last the night. But she's still here.'

The kids were lined up behind the glass of the back door, watching. Sean turned his back, a shred of extra privacy. 'What do you want me to do? I can tell him she's okay but she can't talk if you want.'

'No, she can, she can, she wants to. Put him on, I'll tell him.'

'Do you want a moment to get yourself together?'

'We're so . . . we're so grateful you've got him. That's what Susan said last night. He's safe with you – she couldn't have borne it if she'd put him at risk.' The thin voice was crying again.

'Maybe you should put her on first, give yourself a moment. You know.'

Sean forced a smile before he turned back and beckoned to Daniel. Hannah turned to see Daniel's reaction as he took the phone. She saw the hope become confusion and concern.

Oscar came running across the yard. 'Mum, Mum. Someone's at the front door and Zac says we can't open it. Zac told him to go away, but he said he wants to talk to you.'

'I'll go.' Sean took Oscar's hand.

'No! He says he wants Mum, he has to talk to Mum.'

Hannah sighed. 'Maybe it's Mr Henderson. Maybe he needs groceries too. We can start a co-op.'

Oscar ran in circles around her, getting under her feet as she tried to walk. 'I was scared he might try to break the door, but Zac said the grille was made of metal and he couldn't break that.'

Zac and Daniel formed a concerned huddle halfway down the hall. Zac pulled himself a bit taller as she pushed past. She could hear someone moving on the other side of the door. 'Who is it?'

'Groceries.'

Her forehead creased and her lips pursed even though he couldn't see her. 'Just leave them on the porch like it says on the instructions.'

'It's not that.' He sounded hesitant, not dangerous. She tried to imagine what dangerous sounded like – probably nothing like her imaginings. 'I'm trying to tell my regulars and you've ordered from us a few times now.' Don't let him be one of the end-timers that she'd been reading about on the net, ranting about Manba being a punishment for, well, pretty much anything.

'What about?' He said something that she couldn't make out. 'I can't hear you.' She turned to the boys, just in case. 'Why don't you go bug Daddy in the office.'

She swung the door open, stepping well back. The grille was locked and she held the keys in her hand. Its mesh was the only barrier between her and this man and his germs.

'I'm trying to talk to all my regulars.'

She'd only ordered once and that had been delivered when they were out. He could be anyone under the paper face mask and gloves, the paper hospital gown.

'This is my last run and I don't think they'll find a replacement.'

'I guess it's not safe. Well, thanks for all you've done.' *Now go away from my front door.*

'I'm going to be driving trucks for the government. Delivering food and coal to the power stations. I don't have to get out of the cab, so it's safer, you know.'

'Uh-huh.' She could see someone looking out from behind a curtain across the road. Drawn by the sound of a car engine.

'Anyway, I can't get petrol for my van. The petrol stations are all shut. Reserved for emergency services. I had to drive halfway across Sydney to fill up this morning, from a mate who still had a bit in his tanks, and once that's gone, I'm done. I'm no use for deliveries without a truck.'

And just like that, Hannah felt the Internet calling her to see if other supermarkets were still delivering.

His paper mask hid his mouth, but his gray eyes looked older than his jet-black hair would suggest. There was a sad acceptance in them. 'I haven't been home this week – I wouldn't do it, wouldn't put them at risk. Not with all the houses I go to. My wife puts the little ones on the phone every night. It breaks my heart. But if I'm working for the government, they'll do the right thing by my family. I can look after them this way.'

'That's good.' She wondered what his kids looked like, what his wife was doing right now. She hoped he didn't pull out photos.

'It's not going to get better anytime soon.' He talked like they were old friends. 'Have you noticed? The number of dead is going up every day. Not so much around here yet. I wouldn't be going door-to-door if they were. More in the north, but it's moving. And it'll break two hundred by the end of the week, for sure. Nice kids, your kids. Course I knew you had kids from your order.'

He had been through their groceries. It gave her a shiver, to think how much this stranger might know about them. Where they lived, her name and phone number. She felt a strong need to slam the door.

'Your kids were very polite. I've had lots that aren't, people screaming at me, and I'm bringing them their food. You'd think I was robbing them.' Hannah smiled. A small, unhappy, go-away smile. 'You're doing the right thing by them, staying inside. But I wanted to warn my regulars. If things start getting tight, you might find someone to deliver, but don't have a grocery van pull up in front of your house. It won't be too safe. We've already stopped delivering to a few areas. Some of our drivers have been mugged for the food in their vans. Police can't do anything. There's not enough of them, even for the bad areas.'

'Sure. I'll do that.'

'Oh, and there's a few things missing – they'll credit your card. No deliveries coming from interstate.'

Her stomach lurched. 'What's missing?'

'They give me a list of what's in the delivery. You're supposed to check it off and sign to say it's all there.'

'Can you leave it with the groceries? I'm not signing.' Her hand trembled on the grille handle. Two hours out there – she wasn't going to get it for two hours. She tried to pull herself together. The same things would be missing in two hours. 'Is it the rice? Did you see if there was any rice? Turn the plastic bags around – I might be able to see.'

He shrugged and spun each bag around. 'If it's not here, there's nothing you can do.'

'Ha! Rice, there, I can see it. What about the cold things? The milk and the fresh meat. That bag needs to be out of the sun.'

He looked at his clipboard. 'No refrigerated delivery noted.'

The milk. The meat. 'Are you sure? Could you check in your van? Maybe you left something in the van.'

'It's on the form. You have to sign it.'

'I'm sorry, but I'm not opening the door.'

'Look.' He pressed the sheet against the grille. 'Down at the bottom – no refrigerated delivery.' He slipped it into one of the bags.

'Wait, wait. I didn't read it all, bring it back.'

'I have a full van to deliver. The form will be there when you're ready to come out.'

She tried to see into the bags. If she could work out what was missing, she could plan. Curse Gwen and curse Daniel and curse the people who had ordered before her. Curse the two hours when she wouldn't know for sure.

Back in his van, checking his clipboard, he was just a stranger who cared about people he knew only through their groceries.

No meat, no milk. All she had was one face of the bags, frosted images of the groceries through the plastic. She could only see one cube of coffee grounds and no chocolate. As if staring hard enough could give her X-ray vision, she pressed her face against the grille and willed herself to make sense of the diffuse shapes and colors.

The sound of the delivery van disappearing in the distance was overtaken by another car turning into the street. She hauled herself up from the cold wood floor to get a better view. The silver sedan pulled back into the spot it had left less than two days ago, in the middle of the night before last. The doors opened lethargically. The little girl trudged to the front step and sank down onto it. She watched her parents without interest as her father opened the boot, unpacking the boxes onto the curb. The suitcase, the barbecue, only one cardboard box, nothing sticking out the top. The mother, passing the girl, took her hand and languidly led her to the front door.

From the kitchen, Hannah could see the boys in the office. Both doors were open and across the small lawn she could hear them serenading Sean. He had his hands over his ears, trying his best to look angry, failing to cover his laughter. Their untuned voices jumbled over each other. Daniel was trying to follow Zac's lead, with half an eye nervously on Sean, afraid to be left out, afraid to get in trouble, a little at sea. The singing faded in and out, depending on which way they faced. For a few seconds they clicked into staccato unison and she caught '. . . just like cherry cola'. The inappropriate things she let them learn when it didn't matter, when they were too young to understand, and how well they remembered. If she was lucky, those were pretty much all the words they knew.

As the breeze blew the sound away, she heard a rustling from the direction of Natalie and Stuart's garden. Through the gaps in the paling, she could just make out Stuart in a garden chair. If he wanted to talk he would have said something, but not to acknowledge his presence bordered on rude.

He moved again.

'Hi, Stuart, how's it going?'

He stood slowly and stiffly. 'You know, it's going. Ella

just went down for a nap.' From his face, drained of color, he could do with one himself.

'Has Natalie come home yet?'

'She won't be back till this is over. It spreads like wildfire. You know most of the people who have died so far have been medical staff.'

'I'm sure she's careful.'

He stared into a distance that went all the way to his garage. She knew she was intruding on the only break he got from Ella all day, but she thought it would seem brusque if she walked away. He was nice enough, but if Natalie hadn't been so personable, if there hadn't been Ella, if they weren't neighbors, she wouldn't have tried.

Just as she was ready to make her excuses, he broke his silence. 'You should get rid of that cat.'

She looked around for Mr Moon, but he was off somewhere. 'I'll try to keep him inside if he's bothering you. But he's not sneezing, he's not off his food.'

'He doesn't need to seem sick. Shut him in or shut him out. I'd be happier if he wasn't hanging around.'

She couldn't keep the cat in – it was like storing mercury in a sieve. 'The boys love him. I don't think they'd understand.'

'Tell them he ran away.'

'Oscar's not that easy to fool anymore, and Zac, well, you know, teenagers.' Zac had that peculiar teenage sensibility to loss, the awful new awareness of permanence.

'You can't seriously think a cat is worth the risk.'

'What makes you think that cats spread it? Did Natalie say so? It's bats, that's what I read. They think it's bats.'

He gave a condescending laugh. 'Maybe they're wrong about how long it lasts outside the body or how it's transmitted, because somehow it's spreading. You can pin your hopes on it being bats, but are you sure your cat doesn't catch them? When this is over there's a PhD in there for someone.'

There were so many rumors on the Internet, more or less outrageous or ignorant. Just contemplating all the possibilities was enough to drive her back to the computer.

Stuart spoke again. 'Not everything you read online is the truth.'

'Well, that's no surprise.'

'I mean the official stuff. There's no point getting people into a panic about things they can't change. I don't think Natalie tells me the truth, either. I know she doesn't. What could "being careful" possibly mean when you're standing at the epicenter of the end of the world?' Stuart leaned down and picked up a coffee cup from beside his chair. 'Back to it.'

Mon	Tue	Wed	Thu	Fri	Sat	Sun

The street was too big, the distance from the door to the car much greater than it used to be. Walking across her own front yard was the strangest thing she'd done in days. The pools of light under the telegraph poles were large and sinister, and their presence made the shadows and crevices more likely to harbor harm. She should have filled the script when she had the chance last week. Sean thought she should leave it. Today's news didn't help – a doctor on a house call, beaten in the street for the medicine samples in her bag. Sean said cancer didn't come back because you missed a few pills, whereas desperate people hung around isolated pharmacies. But who knows what triggers one little bastard cell to start dividing. Who knows how you tell. Of the two, at least you could see the strangers coming.

She pushed the petrol cap back into place as she passed. Had they left it open last time they filled?

The sound of the car door reverberated indiscreetly, the sound of the engine filled the street. She looked around for the twitch of curtains, or shadows at the front doors of her neighbors' houses. The needle on the petrol gauge still hovered around a quarter of a tank. That didn't tell her much. It had never been very reliable and she could drive for several days without its moving before it precipitously dropped to empty. She should have listened to Sean and filled up on the way back from Canberra. But even in the unlikely event she saw a petrol station that still had petrol, she'd promised Sean not to stop. If she hadn't shut the door on him, they'd still be arguing about whether it was safe to go. She winced at the thought of how she'd flounced out, punishing him for disagreeing by refusing to let him shoulder the risk.

On the main road, she was surprised by how many people were about. The pedestrians were sparser than usual but she didn't think it was right that anyone at all was out. Riders spilled off a bus that had stopped in front of her, heads down, masks over faces, repelling each other like magnetic poles. Each one stepped sharply to one side to avoid a knot of four men leaning against a storefront. Their lack of masks shocked her, and they were passing cans of beer, pulled from the carton that lay between them, from hand to gloveless hand. The pedestrians kept their eyes to the ground, but from the safety of her car she stared and pushed down the door lock button. One looked straight at her and laughed. She looked around for any police presence, but knew they were already spread too thin.

For long stretches, the only signs of habitation were lights in the houses, punctuated by thin clusters of people near the shops. Those scenes could pass for a quiet but normal evening if the shops and cafés weren't almost all shut. The farther she got from home, the more, irrationally, she felt threatened by these islands of activity. Too late to admit Sean was right. She ran the orange at a couple of intersections rather than stop. Or at least she told herself it was orange and not red as she put her foot down, stomping on her well-bred instinct to obey the rules.

She had no trouble finding the street she was looking for – it was the biggest road, with streetlights and a row of shops running in both directions, empty of people. The storefronts were lit, but dimly, as if the shopkeepers had left one light on only. Up on the left she could see a store that glowed more brightly. She drove along the empty curb and pulled up in front of it.

Although the pharmacy had all its fluorescent lights blazing, there was no sign of anyone inside. She put on disposable gloves, one pink, one yellow, fished her wallet out from under the passenger seat, took out thirty-five dollars in notes as she'd been instructed, and hid her wallet again. The script lay on the passenger seat.

She rapped on the shop window and pressed the script against the glass. Inside, a door along the back wall opened a crack. Through it, she could see a young man talking to someone behind him. He came to the window to read the script. After he had examined it, he yelled through the glass, 'Push it under the door, with the money.'

She folded the money and put it inside the script,

scrunching it as she shoved it through the narrow gap. The young man unfolded it with the toe of his shoe and squinted. 'One minute.'

She was exposed, lit by the store like the leading lady of the footpath. She should have parked facing the wrong way. As it was, she was going to have to walk all the way around the car to get to the driver's side. Farther than she would like in an emergency.

One of the hospital pharmacies might have been a better idea, less isolated. But they would have been crowded by all the people who needed heart medicine, antibiotics, antidepressants, insulin. The very reason they were kept open was for sick people. Here, alone, the dangers were more obvious but less likely.

She must have rung half the pharmacies in Sydney. Less than one in ten answered, and only after she'd let the phone ring and ring.

When one of the calls was finally answered, the man on the other end was tired and suspicious and asked for her name. He was only open for regular customers, but Hannah had talked fast and eventually, reluctantly, the man had admitted he could fill the script.

And here he was, the voice on the phone, coming back out to the glass front, much younger than she'd expected. He came right up to the window to yell again and she instinctively moved back, even though the glass between them blocked everything but the sound. 'There's a planter around the corner, it's in that.' He scurried to the anonymous safety of the back room.

No matter how profligate it was to drive ten meters, she couldn't muster the courage to walk around the corner alone. She did a U-turn, took the corner, and pulled up next to the planter. One hand on the car door, she felt under the plants for the package, threw it on the passenger seat, and took off, her heart pounding.

She was suddenly a very long way from Sean. Ahead, all she could see was the dark street. She fumbled to plug her phone into the hands-free kit. The ringing of the phone on the other end sounded thin in the metal box of the car.

'Hello?' He sounded like himself. Warmly, comfortingly like him. She should record him saying just that word, 'hello', and carry it around with her.

'It all went fine. I'm on my way back.'

'Oscar's asleep. Zac and Daniel are in Zac's room. They're ready for bed.' Everything he said, the way he said it, was strangely, inexplicably normal.

'I won't be long.'

'I'll be here.' She could picture him in the light of their living room, watching TV. The whole house would be lit up. She saw it before her, an island of light in the vast threatening dark, and she set her course towards it. She imagined this was how firefighters felt. Lots of nothing happening, waiting for something unlikely but catastrophic. She was twitchy and bored at the same time.

When she'd been diagnosed with cancer she'd sat in the specialist's consultation room nodding. *Yes, yes, I understand.* Her doctor had explained what would happen next, who she would see, what the procedures and outcomes were, and Hannah had listened carefully, academically. The doctor had watched her, Hannah assumed looking for a reaction, but his words had no more weight than air.

On the way home from the doctor's it struck her. So this is what I get – it's not what I was expecting. How had she not noticed that all her life she'd been waiting for the one thing to happen, the one thing that you can't recover from?

She was still expecting something. She always expected something. This virus wasn't it either. Whatever it was wouldn't be long and drawn out – it would be a sharp axe. A call from school telling her to go to the hospital. A work colleague of Sean's on the phone with a catch in his voice. She'd spent all her time mentally preparing for things she couldn't bring herself to think about. If one of the boys died, if Sean died … She couldn't think beyond that point. This wasn't it yet, and whatever it was, it was still out there waiting.

The bright bubble of cleansing light kept them safe for the time being. She couldn't control school, she couldn't control Sean's work, she couldn't control other drivers on the road, she couldn't be there when Zac was out with his friends. She could only hope to be in their heads, telling them to take care, not to take risks, that the most important thing was coming home at night – nothing else came close. As she turned on to their street, she could almost see a radiance around the house.

She took the steps in one jump, afraid of the darkness

nipping at her heels. Nothing behind her but the oppressively silent shadows of her neighbors' houses as she put the key in the lock.

The gloves from her hands fell to the mat, joining the growing pile of discarded contamination from the outside world. She shut the door on it all.

There he was, lit by the TV just as she pictured. He shifted over to give her room on the sofa. She didn't say anything. He didn't look up from the news. The images were sickeningly familiar. People with face masks walking past bodies in the street.

'Manchester?'

'Somewhere in America.'

'I didn't realize it had got that bad there.'

'It took hold quicker, I guess. They don't get to cut themselves off from the rest of the world.'

Piles of corpses being burned by figures in hazmat suits. One of the spacemen tossing a body on the pyre. The discarded shell of a life. That 'infection risk' had been going about her business only days before, having breakfast, worrying about paying the rent, complaining it was too hot to sleep. The effort we expend on the minutiae of life when we don't know it's too late to matter.

The scale precluded comprehension. One person had a story. Gather them in hundreds, thousands, and they became a bonfire to prevent contamination.

Another city, another pile of bodies. Children, old people, driven into the streets by necessity. The well carrying the sick, looking for medical help that in some countries wasn't there even under normal circumstances. But she had to witness this. It was the penance she did for being safe, for now, with Sean and her children. It was the payment for still being alive.

The same newsreader. The dark circles under her eyes, grown too deep to be hidden by her makeup, were highlighted by the mask she hadn't been wearing a moment ago. On the other side of the desk sat a similarly masked man.

'. . . while it appears that the cumulative fatalities this weekend may approach a thousand, I think that needs to be taken in a context where . . .'

'Aaaaaagggh.' Sean was on his feet. The remote made a pinging noise as it hit the screen. 'Tell the dead about context, you fucking liar. Tell them how to put a thousand in two days into perspective.' He grabbed a handful of Lego bricks and hurled each one, machine-gun rapid, at the man on the screen.

'Sean.' She tried to pull him down to the couch.

'Tell my sister that. Tell her to take a historical view. Half the people she works with are dead. But put it in perspective and it's not as bad as the Black Plague or the Second World War.'

'Is she all right?'

Sean collapsed back onto the couch. 'She emailed today. She's all right, she's surviving.' Hannah curled into him, wanting to make it better.

Now the television framed a photo of the two boys who were in isolation. ORPHANS DIE. She waited for the emotion to hit her, the grief, the fear. Nothing came. She didn't know these boys any more than she knew the remains being thrown on the fire. They lived in the same town, spoke the same language, wore the same kinds of clothes, played the same computer games as her kids. That didn't make them any more real than the thousands. The thousands were not less loved by their families, the friends of each of the thousands felt their grief just as deeply. She couldn't stay on the couch, not without seeing for herself that her boys were safe.

Mon	Tue	Wed	Thu	Fri	Sat	Sun
▓	▓	▓		▓		
▓		▓	▓		▓	
▓						

'There's a poo.'

No, no, it was too early. If she didn't move, she wasn't awake.

'It's floating.'

All she had to do was out-sleep Sean.

'It's really big.'

Not my turn, not my turn.

'In the toilet.'

'Flush it, Mouse, just flush.' She lost – she'd given herself away.

'It won't work.'

'Jiggle the button.' Sean still hadn't moved.

'I did. I jiggled. It won't flush.'

She fell out of bed and followed Oscar to the bathroom. There it was, floating. She pumped the handle a few times and listened for the cistern to kick in. Nothing. The sink tap spluttered and spewed a teaspoon of rusty water, no help there. Sooner or later the sensitive eyes of teenagers would be up, so, to protect them, she respectfully concealed the offending sight with a few squares of toilet paper.

Sean peered around the door as she was contemplating her handiwork. 'This could be a problem. No water in the kitchen.'

The Internet was full of people tweeting about lack of water – it looked like the whole city. The water website had no specific information, only an emergency number, and Sean waited on the line for half an hour before he reluctantly hung up. 'The water will come back or it won't. Knowing when won't change anything.'

'I haven't run the laundry tap, but at most there'll be a cup of rusty water in the pipes. Even if you boiled it, I wouldn't drink it. There's bottled water in the pantry – that should get us through a couple of days, but not if we flush the toilet with it.' The downloaded list had mentioned water, although not for flushing, but that was surely for cyclones and earthquakes, not anything that happened here. It was no excuse. She should have followed the list.

'If the water doesn't come back by tomorrow, we might have to drink our own urine.'

'That won't be popular.'

'It would solve the flushing problem.' Sean smiled like an idea had gone off in his head. 'What about the rainwater tank?' He looked pleased with himself. 'You haven't been using it to water the garden or anything useful, have you?'

Sean filled the kettle from the tank, to prove he could, scooped out the coffee grounds carefully, leveling off the top with a knife. He sniffed at the dregs in the milk carton. There was just enough that they could pretend they were drinking macchiatos.

Sean made a salad for lunch. The last few cherry tomatoes, a couple of papery spring onions, a handful of olives, half a small tin of salmon, and some leftover pasta. He stared at the tomatoes.

'Do they need to be washed? Is it worth the water or does wiping them with a damp cloth get them clean?'

He served out onto six plates, five for them and a paper one for Gwen. For six days they had taken her lunch and dinner, knocking on her door and leaving the cling-wrapped meal on the step. What a bad neighbor Hannah was, a bad human being, making Gwen live all alone. But she was alone before the lock-in too, so if Hannah was failing her, she'd been doing it for a long time.

In the living room, Zac, Daniel, and Oscar were playing cards. They sprawled out on the floor, Zac leaning against the sofa leg. Oscar sat upright, cross-legged, examining each card in his hand. The pack was sitting in the middle, the top card faceup. Each boy had a messy pile next to him, the won tricks, Hannah guessed.

'Come on, Oscar, put something down.' Daniel's legs splayed out in front of him, his cards in a fan by his side. Oscar screwed up his face, his hand hovered over one card, then another.

'Give him a chance,' said Zac. 'He's littler than us. Hey, Oz, take your time.' That was her Zac, the one who didn't admit to enjoying his brother but at least tolerated and looked out for him.

'Zac, I've got lunch for Gwen. Do you want to take it round?'

Oscar played a card triumphantly. From the surprise on Daniel's face, it was a good move.

'It's my turn and this is the last hand.'

She was already holding the plate and the boys had been so well behaved, it wouldn't hurt to take it herself.

As she walked up the hallway, the diffuse sunlight through the security grille hit the glass in their front door, forming a golden geometric glow. She balanced the lunch in her left hand to grab the doorknob with her right, her eyes on the plate, trying not to let it tip. The light unfolding around the edges as it opened dazzled her for a moment, and she smiled, thinking how nice it was to really pay attention to the small things. She unlocked the grille. No pockets, nowhere to hold the keys but on the tip of her pinkie under the plate. The grille handle jerked away, pulling her with it. Her hand pivoted to keep the plate flat, and she landed heavily on her right foot, just on the edge of the step.

By instinct, she grasped the handle harder as it juddered. A high-pitched voice, chattering in distress or anger, issued from the silhouette of a person. Hannah couldn't integrate the unformed sensations. They moved around then snapped, without changing, into Gwen. On their doorstep. Tugging at the grille. Screaming at her.

Hannah grabbed the handle tighter and tried to wrestle the grille back to the frame. Gwen's practical clothes were clean and well presented. Her hair was in its usual gray bob. Hannah couldn't reconcile the navy canvas lace-up shoes, their white rubber soles pristine as always, with the inexplicable rage in Gwen's face.

Gwen tugged hard at the grille. At the end of each tug, the steady pressure of Hannah's weight brought the grille nearer to being closed. Hannah tried not to hear the stream of abuse and accusations, tried not to think that this was Gwen, her pleasant neighbor, Gwen, whose garbage bin she'd always put away as a neighborly gesture.

Gwen yanked, the grille banged, hitting the frame and jumping away again. Hannah considered shouting, but Sean was out the back and she didn't want the kids to come running. She didn't want them to see this, to be part of this.

She couldn't let go of the grille until it was locked, and the paper plate was beginning to sag. There was no way to get the keys into the lock without letting go of the handle. If she dropped the plate, the cling wrap wouldn't hold. One whole meal gone. How dare Gwen, after all they had done for her?

She gave the handle an almighty shake and sent Gwen flying back. Hannah was shocked that someone could treat an old woman like that. She had an impulse to look around for the culprit. Surely it couldn't be her.

Gwen spun around and grabbed at the veranda wall to stop herself from falling. She was on one knee.

Hannah considered only for a split second letting go of the handle. She swung her body around in hope of finding help in the seconds before Gwen stood up, a solution, some form of twister that would let her hold the handle and the plate, and move the keys. But the only thing she saw was Zac, halfway down the hall, quiet and still.

'Take the plate!' she screamed at him. He darted forward, eyes down, and took it with both hands. She twisted back, still holding the handle fast. The key turned with a metallic snap just as Gwen got to her feet.

Hannah pushed down on the lever, hard, and when the lock held, she forced herself to let go. She took a step back, a meter's distance between her and the grille. Her hand was cramped, her knees were weak. She put her hand to her face to stop it from shaking. Her face was cold and clammy. She turned her back on Gwen and there was Zac, still standing there, still quiet, still looking down, still holding the bowed plate. 'Take it to the kitchen.' He took a step backwards. 'Everything's fine.' She forced herself to speak slowly and calmly. 'Thanks, you were a great help. Everything's fine now.' Zac took off.

Gwen pressed against the grille. Her palms had bloody grazes from the fall. 'I know what's happening. I know.'

Hannah took a breath before speaking, and struggled to keep her voice down. 'Do you? I have no idea.'

'They've turned off my water. They've turned off my water and you're happy to let them.'

'Everybody's water's off. It'll be on again by dinner, like the power.'

'I went over and talked to Roger Henderson. His water is off too. It's not an accident. They'll help people like you. But you won't help me or Roger Henderson because it doesn't suit you. Easier to shut yourself in with your water and food and shut us out.'

'You have to go two days, two days, without seeing anyone. How hard is that? How can you not do that? Who else have you talked to? And who else has Mr Henderson talked to? And who have those people talked to? My kids' lives are more important than a chat with Mr Henderson.' She couldn't stop. 'And what difference does it make which side of the wall you're on? We're full up – we're not a bloody hotel. We've given you food, we'll give you water. Stay inside your bloody house if you want to live.'

Gwen shook a finger at her. 'And who'll look after Roger Henderson? There won't be enough to go around, not enough medicine, not enough food, so let's get rid of the old people, let's turn off their water. You know and you don't care what the government's doing. More for you.'

Hannah gently closed the door on Gwen so she didn't have to see the hatred directed at her. It shut with a soft click. She felt herself being submerged by exhaustion. Her legs and arms felt heavy and spent. Gwen's shape was still behind the glass, still yelling at the door.

The extra meal sat on the counter, covered with a tea towel, accusing Hannah of heartlessness.

'I'll take it around later. I can jump the fence and put it at her back door.' Sean kept his voice low even though the boys were sitting at the table with them.

Daniel whispered to Zac, who batted him away with a black look and snarled. 'Nothing, just nothing, okay?'

Oscar looked up from his fork. 'Everyone is grumpy today. Zac's grumpy and Gwen was really grumpy. I heard her yelling.'

'Gwen's a bit scared and sometimes scared people get angry.' Sean spoke soothingly and Oscar seemed satisfied.

She had tried to do everything right, to do right by everyone. She'd relaid her plans when Daniel joined them and again when Gwen needed help. Bloody Gwen. Without Hannah, she wouldn't have food at all.

Gwen was an adult. Even her children were adults. Zac and Oscar, not to mention Daniel, relied on Hannah, and she owed it to them not to risk their lives for someone who wouldn't help herself by keeping indoors.

They should have stayed out of it. There must be some government service to look after people like Gwen. Or Gwen's kids, but apparently they cared less than a neighbor did.

From time to time, Oscar raised his eyes to give her a sideways look before flicking a cherry tomato at Daniel, two fingers propped on the table like a mini soccer player. Daniel kicked it back at him and Oscar blocked it from rolling off the edge, dribbling it between his fingers.

'Oscar, eat the tomato. It's not a toy.'

'I can't, it's slimy.'

Sean jumped in. 'It's not slimy, those are fresh vegetables. Old fresh vegetables, but they're perfectly good, see?' He put a forkful in his mouth.

Oscar pushed the salad around his plate. 'I'm not hungry.'

'You have to eat, Mouse. You don't want to waste away, do you?'

'I want something else.'

Daniel picked up the tomato and pushed it into his mouth. 'See, I ate my salad, it's good.' He looked to Hannah for approval. 'We're lucky – your mum and dad are really looking after us. Not every kid has someone to look after them.'

She imagined Gwen cleaning up the blood on her palms. Washing them with Dettol and water, the blood still oozing from the skin, fumbling with a Band-Aid. And then, with dried blood on her hands, with gravel rash on her knees, sitting down to drink her solitary cup of tea. If she had any water. Gwen was by herself and no one was coming for her. Hannah, her last hope, had shut her out.

Hannah rubbed her face, trying to pretend she wasn't wiping away a tear of self-pity. Zac scowled at his empty plate. Oscar and Daniel were saving a new cherry tomato from leaving the playing field. Only Sean looked at her.

As the boys left the table, Hannah mumbled quickly to Zac, 'I'm sorry you saw that – it wasn't appropriate.'

Oscar looked over with round eyes. 'What's not appropriate? Did Zac do something wrong?'

Sean put his arm around Zac's shoulders. Hannah noticed they were nearly the same height. 'Zac didn't do anything wrong. Why don't you guys go and watch TV? I want to talk to Zac for a minute.'

'He did do something wrong.'

Hannah had to push the words out of her throat. 'Zac didn't do anything wrong. I did. Zac helped me, but he's not the one who did the wrong thing.'

She called Daniel back just as he was leaving the room with Oscar. 'Daniel, your mum's going to be fine, you know that? You're here to be safe, but she's getting better.'

'I know.' He held himself stiffly and his reply was unconvincing. She thought how much it sucked to have to be grateful to the people who were keeping you away from your mother when you thought you would never see her again.

She stood as close to the back door as she could, to put distance between herself and this conversation that had to be had, that she wanted to be no part of. Zac mirrored her by the hallway door, slightly stooped, like a sprinter ready to make his escape. Only Sean held his ground in the middle of the kitchen.

'You're pretty pissed off at Mum.'

'No.'

'Yes, you are. And that's okay.'

Zac shrugged, avoiding eye contact.

'What would you have done?' Sean glanced at Hannah as he asked the question. 'Would you have let Gwen in?'

Zac opened his mouth but said nothing. His eyes were shiny with incipient tears.

'Would you?'

'I don't know. No.' Zac almost looked at her but stopped himself and looked squarely, defiantly, at Sean.

'But she could have done it differently. She didn't have to yell at her. Gwen fell over – she's an old lady.'

'I know. I'm sorry.' Hannah felt a deep mortification, deeper for Zac's witnessing.

Zac spoke to Sean as if she weren't in the room. 'You wouldn't have done that. It's not right.'

'I don't know what I would have done. I wasn't the one at the door.'

There was a tightness about Zac's face. His cheeks were hollowing out as his child chubbiness was being reordered into lean young manhood. His lips were pressed firmly together, to stop him from betraying himself, but that only made the slight quiver of his chin more pronounced.

Hannah took a step closer to him, but he still didn't look at her. 'That's not all that's bothering you. Do you think you should have done something?'

'Zac, it's not up to you to deal with this stuff.' Sean spoke man-to-man. 'Try to understand – it's hard for us too. Don't stay mad with your mum too long. She did her best.' He gave her a glance again, as if looking for confirmation.

Zac kept his eyes on his feet but his reply hid teenage contempt. ''Kay.'

Hannah spoke hesitantly. 'This is bad stuff. It's all right for all of us not to know what to do.'

''Kay.'

'Now we have to work out some way of getting food and water to Gwen.' Hannah sighed.

'We can put it in a takeaway container and leave it for her. Take it around sometime this afternoon. She can't lie in wait for us all the time.'

Hannah dug in the cupboard for a container and decanted the salad into it. From the pantry, she got a small plastic water bottle.

'So, how do we deliver this?' Hannah stared out at the fence again. 'To her back door I guess.'

Sean walked out to the backyard and stepped on the horizontals of the fence, craning around to get a good look through Gwen's small back window. An old lean-to laundry blocked most of the view. 'I can't see any movement. I can't see anything. Maybe I should take it to the front door.'

'I don't think that's safe. She'll expect it. We always take the food to the front door. And the blinds are drawn all day. You can't see in.' She stared at the blank back of the house. 'Maybe we should try to talk to her when she's calmed down, take it around then.'

'You're not going to her place. That really defeats the lock-in.' Sean contemplated the yard, the fence, and the door.

Zac looked from one to the other. 'We can't let her go hungry.'

Sean put one hand on the fence. 'Well, here I go.' He pushed up with his arms and tried to swing his legs over. The fence wobbled back and forth. Once he got one leg up on top, the fence settled into a more graceful sway. Hannah could see the palings digging into his gut as he shifted his weight. He gave a large heave and slid both his legs and most of his heft to the other side. The fence gave a lurch. He dropped over, leaping up just a little too enthusiastically, then stumbled again.

'Are you all right?'

'My knees are fine. They are absolutely fine because I'm not old.'

'Quick.' Hannah held out the salad and water to him.

He hobbled at a jog, his frame lumbering from side to side. At the back door, he bent to put the food down, creaked back up, and knocked. Back to the fence was a sprint and a scrabble up the smooth side. Hannah pulled at his torso but only managed to grab his shirt, half pulling it over his head. She laced her arms under his armpits and gave a tug. It got him to the top of the fence and he half tumbled down the other side.

Gwen's back door opened. Zac ran one way to the house, Hannah and Sean the other to the office. They slammed the door, huddling in its shadow. Hannah was shaking silently, tears running down her face.

Sean put his arm around her, drew her in to his shoulder. 'It's okay. It's okay.'

Her breathing came in deep gasps, not quite like sobs. She was having trouble drawing air, she was laughing so hard. 'You' – she gasped again – 'are so' – another almost sob – 'uncoordinated.'

They stayed behind the door, arms wrapped around each other until they were quite sure Gwen had gone inside. Hannah could feel the vibration of her voice against his chest. 'I screwed that up. And I don't know how to fix it.' Her face became somber.

He kissed her damp cheek. 'What could you have done?'

'Something different.'

'What something?'

'Not push an old lady over. I screwed up.' She rubbed her wet face on his shirt.

The moonlight turned the lemon tree and the garage into ghosts. The boys were in bed. There was no sound from the TV in the living room. No car noises from the street. No banging of pots or voices from the neighboring houses. The intermittent improvisation of a wind chime and tin roofs creaking in the breeze stood in for the silent occupants of the neighboring houses.

She pulled the heater closer to the table. The kitchen lights were off. Only the bars of the radiator glowed against her legs and warmed the room with a faint orange light. In the strange quiet of the night, Hannah could hear every soft footfall on grass as Sean emerged from the dark of the office, across the garden, and into the gloom holding a bottle of wine in one hand and a piece of paper in the other.

He held up the bottle as if it were a hard-won trophy. 'We might as well drink the least valuable liquid we have and save the water.'

They drank slowly in comfortable silence, savoring the astringent, full flavor. Hannah lost herself in the deep red of the wine in the low light.

'I could do this every night.'

'You could do this ten more nights. Or, given we have nothing to do tomorrow and no one to answer to, five more nights.'

Hannah rested her feet on his knees. 'Just as well we can't wash the kids in wine. What a beautifully useless drink this is.'

'Speaking of which.' Sean smoothed out the sheet of paper on the table. 'Somewhere on here it says how much water we use.' He held it sideways to the radiator and squinted.

All Hannah could see by the glow was that it was one of their bills. 'You could turn the light on.'

'And ruin the ambience? Not a chance.' He ran his finger over the columns. 'I think it says a hundred and sixty-three, or sixty-eight, I can't tell. Does that seem right for a day?'

'I have no idea.'

'Let me see, average daily usage. That's the one. So that's how much we use in a day.'

'For four of us, but there are five of us. Or six.'

'Right, so, that's about . . . I don't know.' Sean looked befuddled.

'You've only had a glass.'

'Ah, my love – the wine, the moonlight, and you are all intoxicating.'

She pushed his leg with her foot. 'You think that will get you somewhere.'

'I think I will impress you with my towering intellect.

I believe, if my calculations are correct, that means we use about forty liters of water per person per day. But we just won't wash the kids. Or their clothes. If we all stay dirty we'll all stink the same.'

'We still need water to cook. So, thirty liters each?'

'No, much less. No water for the garden or the dish-washer. We can reuse cooking water.' Sean looked over the bill again. 'But we have to factor in the toilet.'

'Any idea how many liters the bucket holds? I used the whole thing but maybe we can get away with less.'

'We'd be screwed if we still had the old toilet. I think the new one is supposed to use six liters at a time and the bucket holds around ten. I told Zac just to use a half – it worked for me.'

'He must have loved that.' Hannah considered how lucky she'd been to get out of that particular parenting moment.

'He loved it even more when Oscar danced around him chanting "If it's yellow, let it mellow, if it's brown, flush it down." ' He grinned at her. 'So, I think if you look sideways and squint, we could get away with fifteen per person.'

'More like twenty-five.'

'Twenty, and that's my final offer.' Sean raised a bidding finger.

'We plan for twenty-five and work our hardest to make it twenty.'

'Sold, to the tipsy lady in the woolly socks.' Sean stared, defocused, into the garden with a contented smile. 'I feel peckish. What do we have in the way of goodies?'

'I will allow you to get a tin of smoked oysters from the pantry. The kids don't like them anyway.' Hannah lifted her feet to let him get out and held them suspended until he came back with a plate loaded with crackers and the oysters.

She slipped a cracker into her mouth and licked the oil off her fingers. 'I never thought a natural disaster would be like this. I didn't think there would be parts I'd want to remember.'

Sean refilled their glasses and considered the contents with a subdued and bitter smile that they didn't seem to warrant. 'That assumes we make it to a time when we can look back and remember.'

'Right.' The path that idea led down was unnerving. She diverted her thoughts to the things she could control. 'Which depends, in part, on the water. How much do we have in the tank?'

'More than if we'd bought the tank you wanted.'

'It's three-quarters full.'

'So it would have been three-quarters of a thousand liters. Now it's three-quarters of two thousand.'

'You were right, I was wrong.' She smiled. 'Which makes how much?'

'A week and a half, if it doesn't rain, but it's going to rain.' He considered the glass, twirling it by the stem. 'The water wouldn't do us any good without the pantry. That's all you.'

'Ah, but I didn't think to buy a case of wine.'

'One of us has to be about the fun.'

'Do you think Zac's ever going to forgive me for this afternoon?'

Sean frowned.

'I'm not even sure he should.' It was a confession, and she hoped for absolution.

'We'll survive this because of you.' Sean squeezed her hand. 'After all that we've been through, together, we're practically indestructible. Zac will just have to learn that you can't solve the unsolvable, but you can endure it. He'll forgive his mother for not being superhuman.'

'I'd die for Oscar or Zac, if I had to, but I wouldn't die for Gwen. I hope I would for Daniel, but I don't know. Does that make me a bad person?'

Sean shrugged. 'What about me?' He flashed her a smile. 'Would you die for me?'

'I assumed you'd die for me, boyo. That's the way I saw this relationship.' She slipped her feet back onto his lap.

He smiled. She sipped her wine. They listened to the silence.

Sean shifted in his chair. 'There's a funeral tomorrow for one of the guys from work.'

'How well did you know him?'

'Not well. I know what he looked like.'

'You can't go.'

'Is that how we measure our compassion, by how well we know someone?'

Hannah considered the moonlight. 'What if some of us have smaller souls? What if I was just born with less?'

'I imagine your soul is full-figured.'

'Maybe no matter how hard I try, even if I expend all my energy, the most I'll ever be is a not completely crappy human being.'

'Or maybe we never had to make decisions like this before. Maybe all over the city these kind of decisions are being made.'

'By people who are better, more compassionate.'

Sean rested his hand on the foot that lay in his lap, staring at it as if it held an answer. 'How do you measure compassion? Is it an unthinking reflex, even if that achieves nothing? Or is it careful and considered and planned? You can only do what you can do.'

'What happens when we run low on water? How do we decide who gets what?'

Her leg was warm where Sean's hand rested on it. The branches of the lemon tree swayed, dappling the light falling on the kitchen table. She stretched out her toes and he pushed back against them.

He looked at her with gentle concern. 'The water will go back on. It's a city – you need water. Lots of people don't have a tank – they'll have to bring the water back. Or we could leave the water to the kids and drink wine. But we do it together.'

Mon	Tue	Wed	Thu	Fri	Sat	Sun
▓	▓	▓		▓		
▓		▓	▓		▓	
▓		▓				

She looked at the clock on the car dash. It was ten past twelve, later than she thought. She could see Sean drumming on the shelf of the ATM, waiting for it to spit out the cash. He had been calm as long as he was doing something, but now he couldn't speed up the money counting, and his head darted left and right.

She looked at her phone. Still ten past twelve. The boys were home alone. Every second spent here was another second they were not protected.

This was the second machine they'd hit tonight. They had waited until they were sure the kids were asleep, like Christmas Eve, then had driven up to the local shops and done a circuit around the block to make sure no one was there. The shops had looked strange, but only in the way they would on any Tuesday night around midnight. Vacant, shut up, waiting for people. Bright shores on a dark street.

Sean had taken out the daily limit. And how pleased he had been with himself as he had pointed out it was a *daily* limit, that midnight was the end of one day and the start of the next. Which is why they had sat in the car for another half hour, waiting for the day to end.

'Are you sure this will work?'

'No, but we're here now. Where else do you have to be?'

'Home.'

'At home, we'd be asleep. How much protection would you be providing then?'

'We were only going to be ten minutes. They're alone, and we got what we came for.'

'If the banking system goes down, we'll need cash for food, petrol . . .'

'Fine, five minutes more.'

That afternoon they had spooked themselves with the thought that they had almost no cash in their wallets and that the ATMs might not always be refilled. And then they spooked themselves with the thought of carrying large amounts of money through almost empty streets. Sean had spent half an hour going through the boys' things looking for a baseball bat.

'Why would they have a baseball bat? They've never played baseball.'

'It doesn't have to be baseball. Anything threatening and hard that you can wield like a bat.'

'They play soccer. The soccer ball is in the garden.'

'Someone gave one of them a cricket set, didn't they? I remember plastic stumps in the garden. Zac made me play with him. I'm sure.'

Zac and Daniel had watched, still and silent, as Sean

had pulled everything out of Zac's cupboards. They had followed him to the garage as he emptied every box. They had looked on, Zac embarrassed and Daniel bewildered, as Sean had arisen triumphantly with the tiny plastic bat.

Now that they were actually here, she worked hard to reassure herself that these were her local shops the same as always, but the dark midnight shadows in empty shop windows made it hard. She was parked diagonally, to see down both roads, watching all directions, jumpy, ready to yell. The idling engine was a magnet for anyone looking for trouble, but if she turned it off, she would lose seconds starting it. They weren't teenagers – they were parents of a teenager. If they met trouble, a quick getaway was their best bet.

Sean stood at the ATM, in a well-lit recess in the glass front wall of the bank, hand out, looking down to the money dispenser. She watched the shadows, hoping that any danger was here and not at home. He was clear as day to anyone in the street. The bat was in his left hand, dangling at his side. It barely made it to his knees. She wanted him to hurry up. Leaving the boys alone was a mistake.

As they drew up, the house gave nothing away, dark and silent in solidarity with every other house in the street. A light drizzle shimmered in the cones of the streetlamps.

'Hey.' Sean rubbed her knee. 'We're safe. Even thieves stay home when it's wet.'

'Your run-of-the-mill career thief, maybe, but desperate people don't care about a few drops of rain.'

'What are the chances that someone would pick our house, in the one hour in the middle of the one night we're not there?'

Worry was a talisman – it kept the evil at bay, but it didn't make leaving the boys behind anything but a bad decision. As she put the key in the front door, she thought about how pointless the lock was, how flimsy the house's defenses were. They were defenses of convention, politeness. A general agreement to go in through the front door, not smash the window next to it.

Her first impulse was to place a hand on Oscar. By the light that seeped around his curtains, she could see his forehead forced into a little pucker that seemed out of place. Concern, Hannah thought, for a future he wasn't aware of yet. But he had thrown his arms wide, as if they lay where they fell, and his body oriented itself without heeding the direction of the bed. He breathed heavily, a child's version of a snore, like a baby clone of Sean. She let herself watch him.

She couldn't do more than take a step into Zac's room. The door opened only a fraction, wedged hard against Daniel's mattress, which took up most of the floor. Even in sleep they defended their right to privacy. Two lumps in two beds, two sets of breathing sounds, and two mops poking out from the sheets. They were safe.

Her nerves jangled but she ached with tiredness. As Sean stuffed the wad of fifties into one of his weekend work boots, it bothered her that it looked like nothing more than a roll of paper. Hannah wrinkled her nose at him. 'Couldn't you pick a nicer shoe?' As if that would make a difference. Any thief worth his salt already knew all the places amateurs like them hid their money. They were trying to second-guess themselves.

'We can go again tomorrow night.'

'Getting home and finding the kids still safe is a reprieve, not license to keep doing it.'

'I'll go by myself.'

'The petrol gauge dropped below empty. You'd have to walk.' She could picture the long walk, him standing alone at the ATM, everything that didn't happen tonight happening. She turned away from the thought, like a sharp wound.

'Let's see how things are tomorrow.'

She slid into bed, hunkered down under the duvet, and turned towards the luminous numbers of the clock. Half past one, much chillier now than it had been when the kids went to bed.

Oscar would be up in five hours. Five possible hours of sleep. But her muscles were full of stored energy. She had an itch to get up, expend the tension, but she was pinned in place by her need not to wake everyone. Tomorrow she should run up and down the hall like Oscar did.

A quarter past two. Four hours until Oscar woke. The streetlight through the curtains made patches on the ceiling, like a map. She traced paths between the islands of light.

The clock said five to three. Her mind presented her with all the hiding places in all the heist movies she'd ever seen. In the freezer, inside a fish fingers box. The cistern. Images, connections over which she had no control, came to her. The toilet flushing, all the money squeezing through the pipes, floating out to sea. Her mind grasped in passing at the idea that there was no water but was distracted by the thought of the sea only just down the hill. She tried to relax her body, let it sink into the bed.

She thought it was nearly four.

Hannah woke up to a gloom that felt like seven, but the clock told her it was ten. A thin, steady hiss of rain fell, its low gray clouds scattering and attenuating the sunlight.

In the living room, the boys were in their pajamas, surrounded by Oscar's toys, books, playing cards, interspersed with plates and bowls. The remains of breakfast.

All the glass in the kitchen windows and door let in the chill in place of morning light. She brought a cup of tea and some toast into the living room. With both hallway doors closed and the little fan heater going, the living room was pleasantly toasty.

Yesterday, Zac had announced his intention of reading ahead in case classes were going on in Canberra without him. Judging by his place in his textbook, he was making progress.

Daniel had clearly shanghaied Oscar's coloring pencils and a sketchbook. The fat triangular pencils and cheap pulp paper were no match for his artistic abilities. He was sprawled out on the floor, lying on his stomach. The pages were divided into irregular panels like a comic, the contents roughly sketched in lead. He methodically worked his way across and down the page, bringing each frame to colorful life. From time to time he stopped to look over what he'd done with a critical eye, sometimes going back and adding to a previous frame.

All the schoolwork they had brought home for Oscar had been finished days ago. He lay on the sofa with Zac, curled up in a ball around his video game. His only movement was the rapid tapping of his thumbs and the occasional jerk of his whole body as he moved with the screen. Zac said, without looking up, 'Turn the sound off, Oz. I can't concentrate.'

She picked up the book she was halfway through. There was never going to be a better opportunity to work her way through all the books she'd bought and never finished. Although she yearned to be like Oscar and cast off the *shoulds*, for the time being she persevered. If she couldn't concentrate, the flaw was in herself. She was going to get right to the end.

Oscar fidgeted and she lost her place. He hadn't done anything she could legitimately tell him off for. She tossed the book on the lounge. Her brain was fogged with tiredness. This morning all she could handle was a simple plot that went from beginning to end and characters she didn't have to think about. The room was too small, the house was too small.

She leaned forward, trying not to be obvious, in an attempt to make out more detail in Daniel's drawings, but his arm was crooked around the top as if shielding it. Zac looked over at her a couple of times, disapprovingly.

'What are you drawing, Daniel?'

'Just, you know.'

It could be a window into how he felt. She should try to show an interest. 'Can I have a look?'

Daniel looked pained. 'It's not really ready.' He colored self-consciously. His art was the only space that was his in the whole house.

She picked up her book again. If she made it all the way through to the end, she'd reward herself with a kids' novel. Zac had a shelf full, starting with everything she'd ever read him, moving on to the ones she didn't know, the ones he'd read himself. Those would be the books she'd read next. Oscar fidgeted again – she lost her spot again and shot him a cross look. He didn't notice.

Zac said, 'When's lunch?'

'I don't know, are you planning on making it?'

'I made my own breakfast, didn't I?'

'Well, you get a gold star then.' For that, she received a sour look. 'We're all home all the time. You can take some responsibility and pull some weight. I don't need to do everything for you.'

'Yeah, like that happens.'

Pencils scratched, buttons clicked, pages turned. The quiet was irritating, distracting her with the absence of noise. She got to the end of a paragraph and realized she had no idea what it said. The words slid across her eyes. She yawned.

Sean swept into the room, laptop in hand, all noise and bustle. 'It's freezing in the office. I can't feel the ends of my fingers.' He looked around the room, satisfied with the independent industriousness of the boys. 'Shove over, I need to finish this thing. I can't even think, my brain is so cold.'

Sean's cheerfulness grated on her nerves. 'I don't know why you bother. What difference does it make if you don't get it done?'

'The guys in Melbourne are waiting for it.' Sean barely looked up from his screen.

'The guys in Melbourne are safe and get to go to the office. The guys in Melbourne can do it themselves.'

Sean stopped typing and considered the idea. 'While I can still do something useful, that's what I'm going to do. I can't see why I wouldn't.'

'As if moving electrons around makes any real difference at all.'

'I'm not sure this is the time or place for that conversation.' Sean nodded his head in the direction of Zac and Daniel. 'Anyway, I'll just say the words "mortgage" and "bills".'

Zac's head twitched, almost as if he was trying not to look at them. Daniel studiously continued his art, with a kind of alert obliviousness.

'It's not even that cold.'

'And yet you have the heater on. It was okay when I

started, but I think I sat still so long the blood stopped pumping to my extremities. The way the damp gets into that room . . . Still, rain means more water in the tank.' Sean rubbed his hands together in an exaggerated motion. 'So much better.' His cheerfulness was noisy. 'You look wrecked. Maybe you should go back to bed.'

'I don't feel like it.' She wasn't going to give in to her body's needs. Instead she forced herself to reread the last paragraph. Each word made sense but she couldn't join them to make anything meaningful. She closed her eyes and rested her head back on the couch.

'Sean, could I ring my mum sometime this morning?'

'I'd like to talk to your dad first, so wait until I'm finished. Then, for sure.' Daniel looked at him quietly, waiting for more. 'She's getting better. Your dad said yesterday, remember?'

'Yeah, whatever.'

Sean ran his hand over Hannah's hair. 'Why don't you lie down?'

'I don't want to lie down.' But she did. She wanted to sleep, but in here. Here in this safe, warm, quiet room, with her boys around her.

She curled up in the corner of the sofa with her head on the armrest looking for the sweet spot, the exact place that would let her drift off. She fidgeted and turned, the noisiest person in the room. The syncopated clacking of Sean's keyboard added to the rhythmic quiet. She stretched herself out, nudging Sean's laptop out of the way with her head to rest on the edge of his leg. He perched the laptop sideways on his knees, arching his arms over her to reach to it. She drifted off.

She woke on the sofa. A crust of drool had dried in the corner of her mouth. Her neck complained as she tried to return it to a normal angle. The room was lit up, with the kind of vibrancy no electric light could produce. The sun streamed in the window through the pulled-back curtains. A warmer, clear noon sun.

She eased her head onto the armrest and poked around in her mind for the bad mood of the morning. It had gone, leaving nothing in its place.

She felt vacant as she followed the sounds to the kitchen, thinking about last night. They shouldn't risk that again. The cash they had was enough for emergencies, and she had to believe that the banks would keep going.

'It moves!' Sean laughed at her as she came through the kitchen door. 'Just in time for a pikelet.' He clumsily turned the golden pancakes, smearing uncooked batter across the frying pan.

'Is this lunch?'

'Lunch? I'm sure it's not lunch. This would be a terrible lunch.' The boys giggled, even Zac. Sean gave her a smile that melded with a supplicating light in his eyes. 'We'll get to lunch eventually. Lunch is only a time of day. We are not slaves to the clock.'

Oscar was heaping jam on his pikelet with a spoon. The jar was half empty. Drips meandered down the side and pooled on the table. It had been nearly full yesterday.

The blob of jam glided across the pikelet as Oscar stuffed it in his mouth. Before she could get a protest out, he had wiped his jammy fingers on his pajama pants.

'Eww, gross.' Zac rolled his eyes.

'What?' Oscar's mouth hung open, still stuffed with red-streaked pikelet.

'Double gross. I can see the food in your mouth.'

'Next batch.' The boys rushed for the plate. 'Ah-ah-ah. Your mum hasn't had any yet.' They held respectfully back while Sean took one and put it on a small plate. As soon as he was done they descended on the remaining two pikelets to argue about who had had how many. In the happy noise, her apprehension leaked away.

'Hey, Mum.' Zac didn't have a pikelet in his hand – he must have deferred to the guest and his younger brother. 'Dad thinks you can whip condensed milk like cream but he wouldn't do it without asking you first.'

Oscar paused, a jam-laden pikelet halfway to his mouth, not wanting to waste another bite if there was going to be cream.

Sean looked around at the eager eyes, slightly guilty. 'Well, I think my grandmother might have done it once, but I don't know how. Sorry.'

'We could try.' Hannah mentally tallied the cans in the pantry, weighed the happiness apportioned against the worry of running out, all while Oscar's pikelet hovered. 'Next time.'

'Aaw.' The pikelet disappeared into his mouth.

Sean dropped another set on the plate and poured more batter into the pan. She took his hand and gave it a squeeze. 'Thanks.'

'S'okay.' He looked at the small bubbles forming on the top. 'It's a terrible lunch. Lucky no one can see. I'd have my parenting license revoked.'

'We can have lunch later.'

'Hey' – Sean raised his eyebrows theatrically – 'Daniel's mum rang us. Isn't that great?'

'That's great. How is she?'

They all looked at Daniel, who chewed uncomfortably, trying to finish the pikelet in his mouth so he could speak. 'Good.' He swallowed. 'She's out of bed. It's good. Dad says I can come home soon.'

'Well, that's great. I think that's great.' Hannah smiled at Daniel and snuck a glance at Sean for confirmation.

Sean pushed the pikelet around the pan, scraping with the metal spatula. 'Yeah, well. You know, of course. As soon as it's safe. But you're fine here. We should ring your dad and tell him you're fine here.'

'Did your mum see a doctor today, Daniel?'

'Dunno.'

If she hadn't seen a doctor, Hannah couldn't convince herself Susan wasn't infectious. But a doctor visited other patients, brought new germs along. So, knowing about the doctor couldn't tell her how safe it was, but the information would be comforting if useless.

Oscar absentmindedly munched his food, staring out

the window. Something about his look, a suppressed, distressed comprehension, made Hannah follow his gaze to the lawn. There, with one paw up on the patio, was Mr Moon. Oscar twitched slightly. The small pucker between his eyebrows that he had when he slept dented his forehead as he looked down at his plate with great concentration. He got up from the table and put one hand up on the windowsill. On the other side of the glass, the cat silently meowed. Mr Moon looked less kempt than he'd been a week ago, but not particularly thinner. She felt bad for the cat. She felt bad for the birds and mice he'd probably eaten.

Sean moved swiftly but calmly to grab the water blaster that sat next to the back door. Oscar's head turned at the click of the key in the lock. Sean took aim and let fly a long stream of water that caught the cat side-on. It jumped at the first drop, but Sean kept the stream going, following it along the fence and over to Gwen's yard. A full cup of water at least.

Zac and Daniel observed silently. Oscar looked at Sean with thunder in his face.

'I have to, mate. He has to find somewhere else to live.'

'I know.' Oscar stared at the blaster. It was his. His blaster had driven away Mr Moon and he had done nothing to stop his dad. He looked from Sean to her. They were his parents, and she could see he wanted to believe them when they said it was the right thing to do, but he was struggling. She grieved for the lesson he had just learned – how to be hard-hearted.

Zac put his arm around Oscar and looked at Sean with distaste. 'Mr Moon will come back when this is over. He came to show us he's all right, didn't he?'

'I guess so.'

Sean was back at his post, over the pikelet pan, as if nothing had happened. Hannah took it as his attempt to stay out of the boys' way for a few moments at least. She felt guilty that he'd had to do it, that he was the object of their disapproval. The two of them had made the decision together.

She rested her hand on his shoulder, both their backs to the boys, and whispered, 'They understand. They know it has to be done. You won't be the bad guy for long.'

He lifted the frying pan to the sink and wiped it quickly with a damp cloth. 'I should get some work done.' He went through the door without looking back.

Daniel grabbed the blaster. 'Hey, Oscar, let's get Zac.' They backed him into the corner near the door. Zac cowered with his hands over his face, a wide smile behind. He could grab the blaster from Oscar if he wanted.

'Get him, Oz, get him.'

'Hey, hey, what on earth do you think you're doing, wasting water, and in the house?' Hannah confiscated the water blaster. 'Don't you have any sense? What are we going to drink if you squirt each other?'

Zac stood his ground directly in front of her. 'Dad did.'

'That's different, you know that. We're not talking about that now.' Squirting a cat was straightforward. It was something that needed to be done and so you did it. This was the hard bit, the explanations, the accepting responsibility for it, and Sean had bailed on doing that.

'Outside.' Hannah unlocked the door again. It had been kept locked since they shut Mr Moon out to save Oscar from the impulse to let him in. Hannah looked around the yard to make sure Mr Moon was gone, and murmured to Zac as he passed her, 'Come straight in if you see Mr Moon. Don't let Oscar touch him.' The boys ran into the empty space where the cat had been.

One pane of glass, two layers of fabric, that's what separated her from the miasma of the street, the fresh, free air swarming with germs.

'I thought you were working.'

Sean stood in the bedroom doorway. 'I'm taking a breath.'

He pushed back the curtain – a pane of glass and now only one thin layer of fabric. The scrim gave a misty sheen to the view despite the full daylight. Something down the street caught his attention. Hannah strained to listen and thought she heard the sound of a distant diesel engine. Whether it had been there for a while, she couldn't be sure.

'Can you see anything?'

Sean lifted the scrim. Nothing but the brittle pane of glass between them and the world. The sound of the engine stopped. Light from the street bounced off the bonnet of their car, the asphalt. To the right, the view was blocked by the wall to Gwen's. Diagonally up the road she could only just see the corner of the house where the family with the silver sedan lived. To the left, nothing. She strained to make out anything in the cross street by Mr Henderson's house.

Sean's arm dropped. Hannah swiveled around to follow his look. Climbing their stairs was a balloon figure in gloves, mask, hazmat suit, and paper booties. The figure clutched a clipboard to its chest and waved some sort of ID in the other hand. From the way the figure walked, Hannah guessed it was a woman. She came close up to the window and pressed the ID against it. Her gloves left trails in the dust on the glass.

'From Sydney Water. Could you come to the door so we can talk?' She spoke loudly and distinctly, as if to an old person, the sound fighting to penetrate the mask and the window.

'We can talk here,' Sean shouted, his hands cupped to the glass.

'It would be easier on my voice at the door, sir. I'm no danger to you. We've all been screened.'

'Here is fine.' There was a stiffness about Sean, an anticipation.

The woman's shoulders sagged. She took a deep breath and leaned right into the window. 'I am going door-to-door to let people know their options. We are aware that the water has been off in this area for more than a day now.'

'Three days. And just us, then, is it?'

'Sorry, sir?'

'Everybody in Sydney has water, just not our neighborhood.'

'Viral contamination was detected in routine testing of client supply. The supply was shut down as a precaution until the situation could be assessed. In the meantime . . .'

'What does that mean?'

The woman looked at her clipboard to gather her thoughts or her strength, or just more information.

Sean pushed on. 'So all the water in the rest of the city is safe, except ours. Why is that? How long's it going to take?'

'Well, sir' – the woman's eyes drifted to the empty road – 'we are still testing in a number of areas and everything that can be done is being done.'

'But it's not coming back on for us, is it? Or you wouldn't be here. What's so special about us?'

'I just know what they told me, and they didn't tell me that.' Even in her balloon outfit, the woman looked out of scale. Either she was tiny or the outside world was too large. 'There has been some contamination. Most areas have been cleared.' She fiddled with her clipboard, as if uncertain whether to continue. 'It's just what I heard people say, but they think maybe bats got into the local system somehow and contaminated the supply, but they're not sure where.'

'So what do they need to do to fix it? When will that happen? And why can't we just boil it?'

'No one wants to take a risk with people's lives, sir. They would have to be sure they've located the source.'

'Why aren't they filtering it or something?'

The woman looked past them into the room, avoiding their eyes. 'I think – I'm not an expert, they just gave me a sheet of paper to read – but I heard someone say – I'm not sure I'm right about this – that there was some equipment they could get from overseas and – you understand, no planes are flying here, although the air force, I mean, of course, since it's an emergency and you know – but the places that they have to get them from, they're having their own problems, with the' – her paper mask inflated and deflated as she spoke – 'outbreak.'

'When?' Sean bellowed so hard, it hurt Hannah's ear. 'Just tell me when.'

'We're doing everything we can. They've turned the school into a shelter.' She'd found a way back to her script and slipped into a well-worn groove. 'And we will be providing water, food, everything necessary. So we're urging you, if you have any doubts about your ability to stay in your home, to come to the shelter. We ask that you don't bring any belongings other than clothes and sleeping bags or blankets. New arrivals should expect to be quarantined for two days.'

'Why aren't you bringing water round?'

'There's water at the shelter, sir.'

'If you brought water round, people wouldn't have to leave their houses.'

'We're doing what we can, sir. It's not easy. If you decide to stay, we are organizing water trucks, but I have no information on how long that will be. You are strongly urged to make your way to the shelter. Can everyone here walk that far?'

'We're staying.' Hannah didn't give Sean a chance to answer.

'I've got some information.' She pulled some sheets off her clipboard.

'Leave it near the door.'

The woman pinned the paper down with the doormat but hesitated. She trudged back to the window.

'There's someone next door, an old lady or something. She wouldn't answer at all. You try to help, because that's the right thing. I'm knocking on people's doors to help and she screamed without even opening the door. Someone like that, someone who can't look after herself, needs to be in the shelter. I left some info, but if you talk to her, try to make her see she'd be better off there.'

'She's got us,' Sean said firmly.

The woman made her cumbersome way down the steps, along the footpath, and then up to Natalie and Stuart's door. They watched her knock. She waited, knocked again. Sean let the scrim fall, frosting the view. He walked towards the front door.

'You don't know who she's touched. Leave the pamphlet there. We can read it tomorrow.'

He stared at Hannah with a strange look of sadness. 'The cat can't understand.' She tried to make sense of the words coming out of his mouth. 'Things just happen in a cat's life. Someone gives you food, they don't give you food. They rub your tummy or they kick you. A cat can't have a concept of compassion or betrayal. It has habits. Someone gives it food, it keeps coming back. When the food stops, it's not emotional for the cat, it's about finding another source of food. Do you think he's getting food?'

'Yes.'

'Then cats are not very bright, because they don't understand betrayal or loyalty. It's about having to do the least worst thing, even when that thing sucks. Do you think it's worse to do a bad thing, or to do nothing and risk a terrible thing?'

'We did the best thing.'

'I did it. The least worst. And now the boys know their dad doesn't care if Mr Moon dies. They don't know that I only care that they live.'

'I think they understand.'

'I don't want them to. This shouldn't be part of their lives. I know worse things happen every day, but not to my kids, the ones I'm supposed to look after.' He wiped his face with the back of his hand. 'I hope Daniel doesn't understand. Because his mum is like the cat. If they'd rung and said she was dying, we wouldn't have let him go to see her and he would have hated us. And I don't know what's in his head. He's just here, being polite and well behaved . . .' Sean fell silent before the words burst out again. 'If I thought I was dying, if I thought I wouldn't see Zac and Oscar again . . .' He couldn't follow the idea through. 'We've been acting like it's a long sleepover. He's a smart kid – he knows what's going on.'

'Maybe he talks to Zac.'

'Every decision I've made so far, I've messed it up. I don't seem to be able to grasp the real stuff. What's wrong with me that it takes this long to work out what that kid's going through?'

She took his hand and stroked the back. It was still damp from wiping his face.

Mon	Tue	Wed	Thu	Fri	Sat	Sun

Pulling the tins to the front didn't hide that the shelves were half empty. Two tins of tomato soup for lunch now left only two more. One more lunch, one more reasonably unsatisfying lunch. Every meal eaten now was one that wasn't there later. Every meal she managed to conjure out of leftovers was another half a day they could stay inside. She forced herself not to count how many tins, how many packets of pasta, just closed the pantry doors.

Despite what it felt like, not every meal was leftovers. Odds and sods from the fridge and the cupboard – a couple of flabby carrots, a stick of wobbly celery, some dried beans she used for holding down baking paper, half an onion – lay on the counter. Together they looked like soup. Some barley, which she had no recollection of buying, would do instead of bread.

This was what her grandmother used to talk about, saving jars and making soup. If only she had a chicken carcass or a ham bone. Hidden at the back of the fridge she discovered a couple of dried sausages that Sean had brought back from a farmers' market. For six months they had been waiting to be made into something sophisticated. Now they completed a farmers' market Depression soup. The sausages probably cost more than her grandmother spent on a whole meal. She smiled.

At the kitchen table, Oscar colored-in. Lots of the coloring, not so much of the in. This was the last of the activity books Sean had bought on the first day. Left for last because it was the most uninteresting, rote, uncreative. He did it only as an excuse to sit near her, and to watch for Mr Moon. The instant she laid out the ingredients, he hopped down. Something, anything else, was more interesting than the book. 'Can I help?'

'Sure.' She looked out at the deserted garden. 'You could pick me some herbs. Anything you like the look of in the herb pots. Remember to break the leaves off, not pull them up.' She handed him a bowl and moved the chopping board to the kitchen table so she could keep an eye on him.

He came back with the bowl full, mostly of parsley. 'What do we do now?'

'Um . . .' If she let him chop veggies they would be eating lunch at dinnertime. 'You could get some water for the soup from the rainwater tank.' She searched out a clean soft drink bottle. 'Fill it up, and remember to put the lid on.'

'Okay.'

He walked across the garden, swinging his head from side to side, scanning for feline danger. It reassured her that he jumped when a bird lighted on the fence. She could trust him to be cautious. It was safe to look down for a few moments at the sausage she was cutting up.

She heard what could have been a wail of surprise from Oscar and on its heels the slam of the office door. She dropped the knife and bolted to the back door. Oscar lay splayed face-forward on the grass, his T-shirt soaked with water, the bottle flattened underneath him. Sean spoke in a harsh tone.

'You weren't looking where you were going, were you?'

'Yes, I was.'

'I was watching you. And why wasn't the lid on tight?' Sean stood over Oscar.

'It was.'

'What were you even doing? That's a day's water for someone and it's gone.'

'It wasn't my fault.' His face streaked red with tears.

'This isn't a game, we can't get more at the store. You want chocolate, you want another drink? There isn't any more when it's gone. Do you understand?'

'I didn't mean to, it wasn't my fault.' Oscar's voice rose higher in proportion to the injustice of the situation.

Hannah ran to put herself between Oscar and Sean. 'What do you think? He'll learn by being yelled at? I told him to do it. Yell at me.'

Sean turned away and trudged back to the office. She helped Oscar up from the grass.

'My' – *sob* – 'pajamas' – *sob* – 'are wet.' He choked on his indignation.

She knelt down to pull him to her, but he held himself stiff.

'I'm wet.'

Sean's voice took her by surprise. Crouched next to them, he took Oscar's hand and looked him in the eye, modulated his voice to make it soft and calm. 'I'm sorry, Oz. That was unfair of me. I didn't know Mum told you to get the water.' Sean didn't make eye contact with her. 'It wasn't fair of me to get mad at you.'

'Okay.' Oscar's sobs abated and his body softened.

Hannah shepherded Oscar inside and hung his wet pajamas over the back of the kitchen chairs to dry. They weren't really dirty. Not bits-of-mud-on-them dirty. Not worth-wasting-more-water-on dirty.

Once the soup was finished, she would have to ladle out a container for Gwen. Daniel and Zac were taking turns to bring her food. They changed which door they left it beside each time, knocking and running away like pranksters. Oscar wanted to take his turn as well, but not after yesterday's incident. Against Hannah's better judgment, they had let him take it to the front, but he thought he saw the door opening and dropped the meal. When Sean dashed around, there was no sign of the dropped container. She spent the afternoon listening for noises from Gwen's side of the hallway wall without hearing her. But then they never did.

There were only a couple of takeaway containers left. She wrote a quick note. *Gwen, could you please leave the water bottles and food tubs outside so we can reuse them?* She couldn't bring herself to put *love*, and *cheers* was too jaunty under the circumstances. So she didn't put anything. It was obvious who it came from.

When Oscar came running into the living room, she jumped, barely catching her laptop as it slid off her knee. He was gone again before she registered what he said. She entered the kitchen prepared for bad news, but all she saw was Zac and Daniel standing by the back door, ominously silent. Whatever the problem was, it was in the garden. Please, she thought, don't let it be Mr Moon dead or, worse, injured or sick.

But in the middle of the yard stood Ella, like a statue busker at the Quay, in pink from head to toe. Riotous, discordant shades of pink. One chubby foot was shod in a strappy, sparkly sandal, the other in a pale pink runner. Her legs were firmly planted on the ground, covered in long stripy fuchsia-and-mauve socks that nearly met her hot-pink shorts. Over the shorts, a net fairy skirt stuck out like a shelf, covered in more sparkles. Her purple T-shirt sported a mass of flowers in pastel shades on the front, and Hannah could just make out, peeking over her shoulders, fairy wings to match the skirt. A plastic tiara was pushed in among her tangled curls, set at a rakish angle. And around her face, elastic knotted through her hair, a white surgical mask covered her mouth, nose, and chin. In the absence of the rest of her features, her eyes peeping out over the top appeared impassive.

Sean broke the trance by calling through the window.

'Ella, sweetie, what are you doing here?' Hannah hadn't even heard him come into the room.

Ella shook her head.

'Are you cold? Where's your dad?'

She shook her head again.

Sean looked to Hannah and shrugged. Hannah murmured so the boys wouldn't hear, 'Is she crying?'

Sean called out to her again. 'You have to go home, Ella. Your dad will be worried.'

Next door might be farther afield than she was prepared for any of them to venture, but it was only at the other end of a copper wire. Hannah dialed.

'We finished our game and she was there. I'm sorry, I'm sorry. We weren't watching the garden. She might have been there for ages. I'm sorry. We didn't see.' Zac tripped over his words trying to explain.

The line connected and Hannah willed Stuart to pick up. Simultaneously, she could hear a faint ringing from next door. 'Ella, did you leave the back door open?'

'Yes.' At least she had said something.

'Does Daddy know where you are? You should go home.'

Sean touched her on the elbow and said softly, 'She can't climb the fence. There are no footholds on our side.'

'You're not going out there to give her a boost.' She looked at Sean, at a loss as to how a grown-up would act in these circumstances.

Sean called out in a reassuring tone, 'Honey, I'm going to open the side gate and you can run round to your front door. Your dad will let you in.'

'Daddy's not home.'

Hannah tried again. 'Where's Daddy gone?'

'He went to Mummy.'

Hannah hoped that meant to the hospital.

'Stay there, honey, just for a tick.' Sean sprinted, as much as his father-of-a-teenager's frame would allow him, down the hall. Hannah tried to gain some insight into the boys' thoughts through their faces. Faces that reminded her of the two boys who had died, who had known, before they died, that sometimes parents leave, sometimes you can't rely on them when you need them. But her boys already knew that – they'd known for years, no matter how much she explained in a neutral tone what cancer was, no matter how much she told herself that Oscar was too young to understand, really understand the implications of what she told him, no matter how much she hoped that Zac was so used to the words that they were meaningless to him. They knew what Daniel had learned in the last two weeks – that sometimes parents fail in the worst possible way.

Sean jogged back in, puffing. 'I think I can see their car in their garage.'

'He could have walked.'

'Maybe someone came for him, like an ambulance, or Natalie,' Zac piped up.

'Yeah, maybe.' Sean didn't sound convinced. 'What do we do?'

Hannah took the phone into the living room for privacy. She dialed the hospital.

'Hi, yes, I'm trying to find Dr Cope, Dr Natalie Cope. No, I don't know the extension. She doesn't normally work there but I know she's volunteering.' The receptionist transferred her to emergency, who transferred her to a ward and then another ward. Each of them was helpful but some things were clearly important – the status of the patients, how many beds were available, how much antibiotic they had on hand, the number of doctors they needed to staff the wards. Keeping track of the names of the doctors who had turned up to help was not. Eventually, one woman transferred her to human resources. She hung on until it rang out.

Back in the kitchen, everyone was still in the same place although now wet patches on Ella's mask traced her tears sinking in.

'Her mobile rings out, his rings out. The home phone rings out too. But we know that, we can hear that.'

'Ella, do you know your grandma's phone number?' A tiny shake of the head. 'What's her name, sweetie?'

'Nana?'

'Does she have another name?' Head shake. 'What about Mummy and Daddy's friends, what are they called?'

'Sue?'

'Sue who?' The head shake again.

There was no way out, there was no one to hand her to. If there was some way to make the little girl standing on their back lawn not their problem, they couldn't find it.

Oscar pushed at the back door, but Zac took firm hold of his hand and called through the open crack. 'Hey, Ella, can you spell?'

'She's not even in school, Zac.'

'Ella, do you know how to play I Spy?' Ella nodded. Oscar tucked himself into Zac's side, watching. 'Well, I spy with my little eye something beginning with, I mean, something that's red.'

Ella looked around the garden with big eyes. It was clear to Hannah that Zac was thinking of the bright red wind vane on the garage. Ella, her feet rooted to the spot, was never going to turn around to see it.

'I know, I know what it is.'

'Give her a minute, Oz.'

'Umm.' Ella looked around more frantically. 'Ummm.' She looked harder at Zac. 'Umm, your shirt?'

'Cool, you got it.' Hannah had to smile – Zac had learned how to cheat like an adult. 'Your turn.'

Sean leaned into Hannah and murmured, 'We need to talk where they can't hear us.'

She whispered back, 'I'm not leaving them unsupervised.'

'Zac's got it under control.'

They tiptoed to the other end of the kitchen, Hannah keeping her eyes on the boys, ready to jump if Oscar made a move.

'So what do we do?' Although Sean whispered, from his stillness she thought it likely that Daniel was eavesdropping.

'She can't come in. She's probably seen Natalie and who knows what's happened to Stuart. For all we know, she's infectious. She'll have to stay outside till we find someone to take her.'

'There is no one.' Sean was firm.

'She can go to a shelter.'

'Are you kidding me? You won't let us walk around the block, but a three-year-old can go to a shelter?'

'You can't have forgotten. One and a half thousand' – she noticed Daniel twitch and dropped her voice – 'dead, yesterday. Nearly three times Monday.'

'Out of five million. Less than a tenth of a percent. She's one little girl out of five million, and you want to send her into that.'

'Her mum's working at germ central and her dad ditched her. I guess Gwen could take her.'

'Gwen's a crazy lady. I'm not knocking on her door and I wouldn't give Ella to her.'

'So . . . what?'

Hannah waited for Sean to say something. And waited. And then she cracked. 'So, she has to stay here.' Sean seemed relieved that she had said it. 'She can sleep in the office for a couple of days. We'll have to work out some way of keeping her in there when we're delivering.' Sean looked at her with horror and she felt she had to explain. 'Like Gwen. We'll have to take meals to her like Gwen.'

Sean was clearly struggling, trying to find the right words. 'She's three. She's' – his eyes slid away as he shook his head in disbelief – 'three. You can't seriously expect a three-year-old, a three-year-old, Ella for Christ's sake, Ella, not some stranger, to sleep all alone, to be all alone for the next two days out in the office. Can you imagine how terrifying, how mind-fuckingly' – Hannah glanced at the boys – 'terrifying that would be? You can't treat her like the cat. Even if she wasn't someone we know, even then, she's a human being, a little girl whose parents have disappeared and *you* think it would be appropriate to incarcerate her in the garage?'

'Why do you think Stuart dumped her here? He's not my favorite person, but he wouldn't ditch his own kid without a good reason. And why do you think he put a surgical mask on her? Because he was sick and she's probably got it too. He's gone off to hospital and he hasn't taken her. Why would he? If there's any chance she's not sick, the hospital is more likely to kill her than save her. But we have three kids here, one of them not even ours, and we have a responsibility to them. To keep them safe. We *know* she's been exposed.' Sean looked at her coldly. 'I'm not going to apologize for putting my kids first. I can't be responsible for everyone.'

'Not even for the one toddler in your backyard.'

'I'm not throwing her out in the street. I'm not going to starve her. She just has to sleep in the office for two days.'

'And if she gets sick?'

'Then I was fucking right, wasn't I?'

'And you'd leave her to die out there.'

'No. I don't know. But how does it help her if Oscar and Zac and Daniel get it too?' The boys had stopped playing their game and were watching them in solemn silence.

'So you won't let her in?'

'No.'

'She has to sleep out there alone.'

'For two days.'

'Fine.' He strode out the door, shoving Zac and Oscar out of his way. Hannah saw Oscar on his toes, ready to follow. She sprinted over and slammed the door. The four of them huddled together at the glass, watching.

Sean put his arm around Ella's shoulders, talking to her quietly, gently, but they couldn't make out what he was saying. Hannah felt an ache, a physical pain as he moved away. She was angry at him, angry for making her feel her actions were wrong, for making a decision that she wouldn't have. For putting Ella ahead of his own family. He was right there, but gone. Just to the end of the garden, but maybe never to come back.

'Right,' she said loudly to a spot over the boys' heads. 'Well, this is an adventure. Just us for two days.'

'Yeah, some adventure.' Zac turned his back and led the walk away from her.

The TV went on in the living room, too loud. She didn't care. She could go in and rouse on them, but it would achieve nothing. Her aspirations had changed. She didn't have to worry about whether they ate right or did their homework or played violent video games at their friend's house. There was only one thing she had to achieve – to get the boys through this.

By now it was done, even though she could see Sean, just across the lawn, even though he looked the same. By now he had the virus or he didn't. And she had to decide, at this instant, that if he came back in two days she would celebrate, and if he didn't, then he was gone from this very moment.

She was startled from her thought by a fist banging on the glass of the door. Sean, belligerent but slumped. 'I need gloves. I need disinfectant. I need a face mask.' He colored slightly. They both knew he should have thought of these things before he gambled his life on his principles. 'And something to put water in, a bottle or a jug.'

'You can't come into the house, not even to use the toilet.'

'I know.' He looked worn. 'We'll improvise. There's the back lane.'

'How does she seem?'

'Scared, sad.'

He was going to make her ask. 'Is she sick?'

'She doesn't look sick.'

Sean had spent time in the office before, and even though she couldn't see him, she had still been aware of his presence. Now she was only aware of his absence. The kitchen drove her out – it was filled with her angry yearning for the other end of the garden, so she exiled herself to the isolated safety of their bedroom, curled up in the duvet that smelled of them. The cold of the room crept in under its edges.

The street was quiet, the room was quiet, there was no way to escape herself. The noise of the television lured her back to the living room.

She caught Zac's face contorting into a scowl as she walked in. Oscar had a contented, almost Mona Lisa smile as he cuddled into Zac. And Daniel, Daniel looked blank. Attentive, polite, amenable, but blank.

'Hey, Daniel' – she winced at her own lameness – 'how are things going?'

'Fine, Hannah. It's good.'

'Watching something on TV?'

Zac looked thunder at her.

'Yeah, you know.' Daniel gave her a polite smile and a half nod. 'We've seen it before but there's nothing new on. They keep looping the same couple of days' programs.'

She worried that he recognized her attitude towards him in the way she had reacted to Ella.

'You know, Daniel, I'm glad you're here. I'm sorry about your mum, but you're always welcome here. Like one of the family.'

'We're watching TV, Mum. Can't you see?' Zac snarled. 'Like he doesn't know. He knows, so if you don't have anything important, can we get back to watching?'

But what Daniel knew, and she knew, was that she wasn't telling the truth. She would do everything humanly reasonable for Ella and Daniel. For Zac or Oscar she'd do the unreasonable. She would risk her life for them. Daniel and Ella weren't her family.

She made dinner by herself, cleaned up by herself. From

now on, she was going to have to do everything by herself. At the end of the garden she could see the two plates she had left outside the office door, empty and abandoned. Ella was perched on the office chair. Sean must have adjusted it to its highest to let her reach the computer.

Sean came out of the garage – not once looking towards the house – with two sleeping bags, an old bar radiator, and an almost new plush purple teddy bear that Oscar had never taken to. They each stood in their own pool of light at the ends of the dark garden, but he didn't look towards hers.

Zac was standing next to her, smacking two empty hot chocolate mugs on the counter.

'You finished them quickly.' She plunged them into the opaque washing-up water. It was tepid now but it would be a waste to boil more just to heat it up. 'I need you to do something for me. Fill up some bottles from the water tank so we don't have to keep going out.'

'Dad might die.'

'We don't know that Ella is sick.'

'Why didn't you stop him? You order us around enough.'

'He's a grown-up. I can't make his decisions for him.'

'Yes, you can.' Zac's chin wobbled. What was endearing on Oscar was distressing on Zac. The possibility that he might lose control, her self-contained, independent boy, unnerved her. She put her arm around him and he didn't pull away. He opened his mouth twice, and though she thought he was going to say something, she knew he wouldn't let himself talk until he was sure he could do it with no signs of childishness. 'He might die. He's my dad and he might die. Don't I count for anything? You keep saying you're protecting us, but he's my dad and I want my dad to live.'

She pulled the plug out of the sink. The rest could wait for tomorrow. She wiped her hands on a tea towel. 'I don't think he thought it through. You wanted us to take Daniel and I don't regret that. It's kind of the same.'

'Daniel wasn't going to kill anyone. Doesn't Dad care enough about us not to die?'

She ran her hand through his hair, and he only turned his head away slightly. 'Some decisions are more complicated than that.'

'Whatever.' He twisted out of her arm. 'It's his life, right?'

But it wasn't just his life. She knew it and Zac knew it and one day Oscar would know it. He owed them something, he had a duty to them, a terrible duty to stay alive. She'd been doing it for eight years. Blood tests and mammograms and drugs that made her tired, made her sweat, made her feel sick, even now. She did anything the doctors told her, because it was her duty to Zac and Oscar. Sometimes it exhausted her, the process of living. How could Sean not realize, even now, the commitment he made when he took part in creating them, to do everything he could to stay alive?

Keeping a happy face was wearing, and the kids didn't buy it. She was drained. She needed peace, needed this to be over. Her mood sent a subliminal ripple of anxiety through the house. What she wanted was to send them all to bed so she didn't have to present any kind of face to anyone. She hated that she was deceiving them with her fake enthusiasm and plastered-on smile, but she comforted herself that whatever she did with her face, it wasn't really a lie. She needed them to believe that things were what you made them. This time could be miserable or it could be bearable, depending how they saw it. Right now, all she wanted was to fast-forward through this. Tomorrow she would look at it all in the new light of the morning. She would do her damnedest to be a good person tomorrow.

The boys were draped over the sofas, interlocking like a barrel of monkeys, watching TV.

'Okay, that's it. Bedtime.'

'Oh, what? It's not even Oscar's bedtime.'

'Well, get ready for bed. I think everyone needs some quiet time.' The resentful teenage eyes looked back at her again. 'All right, you don't have to sleep. You can stay up so long as you don't bother me.'

'Yay!' Oscar was wide-eyed and too loud. 'I don't have to sleep.'

'*You* have to sleep.'

'Aaaawh.' His protest ascended a scale.

'Wash. Pajamas. No arguments.'

She boiled a jug and carried it, steaming, into the bathroom. Oscar jogged in front of her, forcing her to swerve to avoid tripping and spilling the water. She poured it into the sink and added some cold from the bucket on the floor, swishing it gingerly with her fingers.

'That should be cool enough.' She left him stripping off.

In her corner of the sofa, in the hostile silence of teenage contempt, she hid behind her laptop, pretending she was working. She only opened emails with businesslike subjects. They allowed her to escape, for a short time, from this small box. Somehow it made it better that out there other people were living their lives. She let her eyes slide over the other messages. She didn't want to know the bad stuff. She didn't have anything that would help them.

A chat window opened in front of everything else.

Hey babe.

Kate. She'd left herself logged in. If she ignored it, Kate might go away.

You there? I haven't heard from you in a while.

Hi Kate.

Are you hanging in?

We're surviving.

You got enough water and food?

She couldn't share any more. She couldn't take anyone else in. Her fingers hung above the keys. Kate's words formed on the screen with a rush.

The water's back on here, but word is the east is still out. How are you making do?

We have rainwater.

Tasty.

She typed, *How is everyone?* then backspaced over it. Typed, *I can't cope,* then deleted it. *We'll manage.*

Hey I could get my cheese and crackers and you could get your cheese and crackers and we could pretend we're out to lunch.

You have cheese and crackers?

I stocked up on junk. When we get back to work you'll recognize me – I'll be the one with hardened arteries.

Oscar jogged into the room.

Have to go. Wet boy to tend to.

Hug them all for me.

'Oscar, you're naked, that's gross. Put some clothes on.' Zac's voice was full of older brother outrage.

Hannah barely looked up. 'He's not technically naked, he's got a towel on.' The bath sheet went around his small waist several times. He clutched tightly to a handful of the folds in front of him and the towel sagged loosely around his back, making him mostly naked from behind. 'Go get your pajamas on.' He meandered in the direction of his bedroom. 'Go on. Bedtime.' She hadn't told Kate about Sean, but she needed to hear that she was right and he was wrong. If only she could be sure Kate would think so.

Oscar came back damp and pajamaed. Zac submitted to a good night hug from him, but played no part. Hannah put her laptop on the sofa to let him give her a kiss and a cuddle. 'Do you want me to read you a story?'

Oscar silently stood his ground.

'You don't want a story?'

'It's Daddy's turn.'

'You know he can't read to you tonight. He'll read twice when he comes back.' She got up and expected him to follow her to his room, but he didn't budge. 'Come on. Bedtime.'

'I haven't said good night.'

'You just did.'

'I haven't said good night to Daddy.' His small, smooth face was set with determination.

'Sure, of course. You have to say good night to Daddy. He'd be upset if I'd sent you to bed and he missed getting a good night.' She called over to Zac. 'Hey, you want to come say good night to Dad?'

Zac's lips curled dismissively. 'I'm fine.'

She stood with Oscar at the back door. The glass was cold. They could see Sean clearly at his desk. Oscar jumped up and down waving his arms, yelling 'Dad, Dad!' so loud it hurt her ears.

'Wait here. I'll ring him.'

Oscar reached up to the kitchen light switch and flicked it on and off rapidly. 'Look. You don't have to ring.' Looking at him stretched out on his tippy-toes, she could see how he could grow into Zac.

Sean looked up at the pulsating of the lights.

'Oscar, he's seen us.' Oscar went back to pogo-ing wildly with his arms waving. He was so revved up, she thought he might never get to sleep.

Sean leaned over to the sofa and said something. He slowly crossed the small patch of grass, watching where his feet fell. Fatigue draped over his shoulders and pulled like gravity. He stopped about a meter from the door and only then raised his eyes to them.

His mouth moved, but she couldn't hear him through the glass.

'What?' She cracked the door open a little, making sure she held it firmly and that Oscar was behind her arm. 'Oscar wants to say good night.' For a shocking second she thought Sean was going to cry.

She leaned on the back door, watching the ghost of Sean's face lit by his computer screen. She could stand here in the dark all night, her face getting colder against the glass, but she would still be here and he would still be there. What she needed was sleep.

Outside the bathroom, the floorboards were wet where Oscar's undried body had dripped. She threw a towel down to soak it up.

The dry toothpaste was rough in her mouth. She poured a centimeter of boiled water into the tumbler and swirled it around, then spat. She could still feel the grit in her teeth.

The hallway was dark and silent, but Zac and Daniel were, surprisingly, already asleep, and she wasn't going to risk reanimating the house by turning on a light. Something snagged at her foot. She tripped forward, flailing her arms to keep herself upright. The towel wrapped itself around her leg and she stepped heavily sideways, slamming into the door of the pantry. The handle thrust itself into her ribs. She gasped, the air knocked out of her. She held in the pain that she wanted to howl out, waiting for a sound from Zac's room. She hugged the bruise on her side, pulled the towel from around her feet. The pain stabbed as she stumbled down the hall and fell into bed.

The cold of the sheets clung to her. She curled, trying to minimize contact with them. The thin layer of air around her slowly warmed, but the bottom of the bed stayed icy, her feet numb. If Sean were here . . . If Sean were here . . . to hold her for warmth, to take the ache away. But his side of the bed was cold. She tried to lift herself out of the pain in her side, inhabit a spot just above her body. Her mind drifted, moving around the house, the books strewn on the living room floor, the clean plates in the drying rack. Her thoughts snagged on the back door. She couldn't conjure the memory of locking it, and if she hadn't, no one had.

Surely she had. The door was locked.

Unless it wasn't.

Someone in the backyard only had to turn the handle to let themselves in. She could almost picture them, an indeterminate shadow, all threat. And here she was, at the far end of the house, a useless first and last defense. The room contracted, but the house echoed its vast emptiness.

This is what Sean had done – left her with the hard, ordinary job of carrying on while he, dramatically, took the easier route of acting on principle. Heroic gestures didn't ensure the back door was locked, that there was enough food and water.

She felt her way by proprioception and memory through the darkness, jumped at the figure of a person sitting on the sofa – a cushion and its shadow.

The handle of the back door channeled the cold of the night from outside. A slight pressure told her it was locked. On the far side of the short garden, deep shadows engulfed the dark office. No sign of life but the slow movement of the wind in the lemon tree.

She turned back to the kitchen, looking for something to anchor herself, armor herself with. Her eye lighted on the knife block, the large wooden-handled chef's knife. Its heft was familiar in her hand.

She needed to calm herself, to convince herself everything and everyone was secure, that it would be safe to sleep. Through the door, Zac's room was still. She put her head far enough into Oscar's to hear his slow breathing. Although she remembered locking the front door, she couldn't let go of the thought that the grille could be unlocked, even though she knew it wasn't. The cold air from the street flooded in the moment she opened the front door. A movement caught her eye. A few doors up on the other side, someone was coming out of a house, leaving the door ajar. He stepped off the porch and into the moonlight, the man with the silver sedan and the daughter, coming out of the wrong house, carrying something – a white plastic shopping bag overfull with what looked like groceries. His hand splayed, trying to hold both handles over the boxes that stuck out the top. Except that the plastic was ripped down one side, he could have been stepping out of a supermarket.

She slipped the knife under her pillow as she slid back into bed. Her head lay gingerly on top and her hand rested against the handle. As her muscles relaxed and sleep overcame her, an alarm sounded deep in her brain, fear of rolling onto the knife. She moved it under a book on the bedside table and touched the handle for comfort.

Small noises came from Oscar through the wall – his bed creaking as he rolled over. She thought about the cold, she thought about the empty space beside her. She listened to the restless boy, she touched the knife handle. She didn't remember falling asleep.

Mon	Tue	Wed	Thu	Fri	Sat	Sun

She woke to the gentle white noise of rain on the roof. Cold seeped into the house, the air, and her bones, the kind of cold that her body mistook for damp. The light that oozed through the curtain was gray, no sun to burn off the chill. The bottom of the bed had been sucking the heat out of her feet all night, and as they hit the icy wood of the floor, she felt the chill shiver up through her.

She dragged her body down the hall, as if piloting an automaton, a broken-down, clapped-out automaton. Here at the controls, she was disconnected from the machinery. This body had no sentimental value. She hadn't forgotten that it had tried to kill her.

Oscar leaped at her as she came through the living room. 'Can we have breakfast now?'

'Give me a chance. You can see I just got up.' In the kitchen, the dishes from yesterday were still in the sink, and there were more than there had been last night. Could it be possible that Zac had tidied his room and added to the heap? The stack overflowed the sink and spread onto the kitchen counter. She pushed aside one of the plates and only just caught the glass that, Rube Goldberg-like, teetered over the edge. It was a mess. A big horrible pile.

She banged on Zac's door.

'What?'

'Are you guys up?'

Zac opened the door a crack. 'Yeah, we're up.'

'Wash the dishes.' She put in the polite word to make up for the tone of demand in her voice. 'Please.'

'What, now?'

'I'm not making breakfast till it's done.'

Zac muttered to Daniel as she walked away but, nevertheless, the door opened and she heard them stomp to the kitchen. She threw herself on the sofa next to Oscar, watching television again.

'Haven't you seen this one already?'

'Yes.'

'Do something else then.'

'What?'

'Something else.' He kept watching. She picked up the novel she was reading and tried to concentrate. 'Turn the volume down. It's too loud.'

Oscar turned it down a little. She nestled in the corner of the sofa, trying to pretend that reading was like sleeping.

Oscar crawled across from the other end. 'Can we have breakfast?'

'You already asked me that.'

'Can I have toast?'

'We don't have any bread. We still don't have any bread. So we can't make toast. We had this conversation yesterday.'

'We could make bread, like last week, that's fun.'

'We don't have any bread flour.'

'What are we going to have?'

'I don't know, Oscar. I don't know what's for breakfast. When the boys have finished the washing up, I'll go make it. Then I'll know what we're having and you won't miss out. But right now I want to read, okay? I just want a little bit of quiet.'

Zac slouched into the room. 'Yeah, done.' He slouched away again.

The healthy packets of cereal were long gone. As were the unhealthy ones. Most of what they had left was grains. By trial and error, she had discovered that powdered milk tasted better if it was cooked into some sort of porridge, but they'd used up the oats as a makeshift muesli while they still had tinned fruit and long-life milk.

Rice would do, or couscous. With spices – she still had plenty of spices – all boiled up with some water and the powdered milk. A little bit of dried fruit, rationed out.

Breakfast couscous, it sounded like something from a café. With fresh milk and toasted slivered almonds. Fresh berries on top. Sitting in a café in the morning sun, someone else doing the cooking. That would be good. Sean would take the boys for a walk and she would linger over a second coffee, reading the paper. And at the end, she could get up and walk away, no washing up.

As she spooned the coffee grounds into the pot, she could see the bottom of the tin. One more really good pot or three very weak ones. She'd based her plans on feeding four, not six. Seven now. As she drank, she watched the saucepan bubble like hot mud.

Oscar was at her elbow again. 'I don't like that.'

'You don't know if you like it – you haven't tried it.'

'I'm not going to eat that.'

She put out one takeaway container and a couple of plastic bowls, searched out a thermal cup hiding in the back of the cupboard, and put a spoon of powdered milk in the bottom of the cup, dissolving it with the coffee. It looked gray and unappealing, only half full. If he wanted a whole cup, he could have stayed here. She didn't pour one for Gwen, there wasn't enough. And Gwen got a big bag of tea and a few liters of long-life milk in the last load of shopping, all to herself. Gwen didn't have to share with anyone. Hannah spooned the mush into the container and the bowls. No berries, no slivered almonds, no sun.

'Hey, Zac.' She yelled out. 'Zac.' She yelled louder.

He appeared at the kitchen door, Daniel, his shadow, behind him. She held out a tray with the mug and bowls. 'Take this to the office for Dad and Ella.'

Zac looked her square on. He didn't hide his disdain. 'You take it.'

For an instant, anger overtook her. Not at Zac, at Sean. If she took the food to him, she could give him not just the tray but all the words she was trying so hard not to say, that she was trying not to unleash on an undeserving Zac.

'I will, I can.' Oscar bounced. 'I'll take it.'

She looked at his enthusiastic face and knew he wouldn't be able to resist stealing a hug. 'Daniel will have to take it.'

'Why?' His face changed from puppy eagerness to crushed disappointment in a blink. 'Why can't I?'

'It's too hard for you to balance the tray.'

'But I . . .'

'I said no. Zac, you can take Gwen's.' She handed the container to Zac.

'Yeah, whatever.'

'Pick a different door.'

Zac flicked his eyes and stomped away.

'Wait.'

Zac turned stiffly back to her. 'Yes?' He spoke the word cleanly and crisply.

'If there are containers there, don't touch them, okay? Leave them there.'

'Why did you ask her for them if you're not going to use them?' He had a snarky smile, pleased he'd caught her in an error.

'Two hours, genius. They need to have been out at least two hours.'

'But he gets two computers. He gets the one in the office and his laptop, that's not fair.' Zac was well under way.

'What's he going to do with two? It's not fair, we don't have one and he has two.'

'I don't think he's using them both.' If she didn't look up from her work, Zac would stop. The laptop was a shield.

'So why did he take them? He could have given us one.' Daniel stood, as always, just behind him.

'I don't think the computers were uppermost in his mind. He had other things to think about.'

'But,' Oscar cut in, a self-satisfied smile on his face, 'you have a computer, Mum. We could use your computer.'

'Or I could use my computer. Because it's my computer.' Zac slumped his shoulders in exaggerated despair. Daniel looked intently sideways to avoid making eye contact. 'Why?' Zac took a belligerent pose and she could see Daniel shrinking, as if he thought Zac had gone too far.

'Because I said so, Zac. Give me a break. You're supposed to be big enough to look after yourself, so act like it. You can't possibly be so devoid of imagination that you can't find something to do without the computer for two days. Just don't bother me.'

Oscar nestled into her side, creeping his arms around her waist. He pushed himself under the edge of her laptop, trying to get closer to her, tipping it.

'I don't want to find something to do. I want to be with you,' he whined.

'I didn't mean to yell.'

He burrowed into her and she felt a sharp pain as he

dug into the spreading bruise on her ribs. She twisted herself away from it but the ache had reawakened.

'Will you play something with me?'

'It might seem to you like I have endless time, Oscar, but there are still occasionally more important things for me to do than play.' She needed time, privacy, peace. 'Don't look like that – you've got Zac and Daniel. You've got a roomful of games.'

'Don't expect us to babysit him.'

'Come on Zac, half a day. How hard is it to be nice to each other for half a day? I'm doing it all here, with no help.' She shook her finger at him to drive it home. 'When I'm done with what I have to do, I'll spend time with you. But not now. Try to show a little maturity.' Oscar sulked, Zac gave her a defiant stare, Daniel looked like he hadn't noticed there was a conversation going on. 'I'm going to my bedroom. Don't disturb me.'

She stood sharply and marched away, depriving Zac of any chance to retort. At the door to her room, the thought ambushed her that Oscar might take the opportunity to visit Sean. She marched back through the living room to the kitchen, locked the back door, and returned with the key in her dressing gown pocket.

The laptop teetered on her knees as she tried to perch on the edge of the bed. The springs wobbled underneath her, and typing was a random hunt for the keys. The only stable solution was to lie, teenager-like, on her stomach with the computer in front of her. The stretch down her front made the bruise ache. She pulled up her pajama top to inspect it, a large burgundy stain spreading away from the blanched impact spot.

She occupied herself with the things that had to be done, like paying bills. There was no excuse, even at the end of the world. The electricity. No matter how dodgy the supply was, she was grateful for the intermittent trickle of electrons. The water. Maybe she shouldn't pay that. What were they going to do, cut the nonexistent water off, stop them from not flushing the toilet? Thank God for a bucket and the water tank. The phones, the Internet, the council rates. She paid them all, pulling down the boxes on the bank page, filling in the amounts, verifying and submitting. Writing all the details on the printed bill. Boring, stupid grown-up stuff that never went away.

She rewarded herself with a bit of net surfing. Or punished herself with exactly what she wanted. She found a website called *Abandoned Down Under*. The front page was a mosaic of stories, and she clicked on one at random.

We had our last delivery of pine boxes a week ago, now it's all cardboard and we're having trouble getting even them. I rang the factory three times yesterday because my boss won't bury without a box. He says you can't ask a family to just put their loved one in the earth. So we stopped answering the phone in the afternoon because we've no more space until we bury some of them. I can't face telling one more person to take them into the street and call the hotline. Just now a woman knocked on the door, crying because her father was laid out in her living room. I told her she can't keep him there, it's not safe. She thinks the government will bury him in a pit with a bulldozer. I don't know if she's right.

If it were Sean or Zac or Oscar . . . She pushed out of her mind the thought of sitting in the living room with their shells. Clinging to their empty wrappers, having nothing else left.

Click.

It's all very well for the government to say work from home but who can do that? We're builders. You can't do that from home. The tradies, the factory workers, all of us that actually do something, that make all the stuff for everyone else, we're stuck at home. How am I supposed to pay my subbies? And who's still getting paid? The people who are pushing paper, staring at their computer screens in their own homes, typing something now and then. It's not like that's real work. Meanwhile the rest of us are going out in it, risking our lives, for what? To keep things going for the nerds. They could all die tomorrow and who would know the difference?

Click again.

We only got here to the shelter yesterday, but they stopped taking new arrivals this morning. Halfway through the night, one of the staff told me to move my kids to the other side of the gym and not let them near anyone. In the morning, they tried to keep it quiet, but I saw some bodies lined up on the floor in the hall next door. An ambulance pulled up and I saw a woman begging to be taken to hospital. They said if she could walk, she wasn't sick enough. There's only one other school in walking distance inside the quarantine zone. We didn't go there yesterday because someone said it was already full. Even if it wasn't, now they won't let us leave for two days.

One clearly wasn't a local.

Yeah, I'd like to be able to complain about having to work from home. It must be nice for all you Aussies on your nice little island. You don't know the first thing about compassion. I'm disgusted that you can whine about a bit of inconvenience when there are people in the rest of the world trapped in their houses because their government declared martial law. Looking after their dead and dying families. So why don't you just go for a walk on your perfect beaches in your Aussie sunshine and whine a bit more . . .

She forced herself to read the whole post – gruesome details of the worst that people had to endure – and felt duly shamed. At the bottom of the page was a breakout box. 'From the Health Department website.' A column of dates and beside each a number. The last entry was yesterday – 2,826 dead, all in Sydney, all in one day. She tried to think about just one person, the one that made six, and wondered how they could be sure there wasn't another one, uncounted, that made seven. If Ella had carried it into the house, if they all died here, who would know? She looked out the window at the row of houses opposite. Were any inhabited by the dead? She felt their threatening presence pushing against the front door.

She shivered. The room was cold but the world outside was colder. She should have been crying but all she felt was a chill.

A window appeared on her screen.

I hoped you might bring breakfast.

And after a brief pause.

It would have been nice to see you.

I'm not the one who walked away.

How normal it felt, to be chatting on the computer.

How did you sleep? How's Ella looking?

No temperature, no cough. Slept fine. A bit upset.

Then she forgets. Then she remembers. She's three.

She wanted him to keep typing. It was like getting a note passed in class from a secret crush. Even with the heater, it must have been freezing in the office, but he knew better than to expect sympathy. She started to type *I want us to be together* but another line from Sean scrolled up.

Stuart told her to keep her mask on. She had a tantrum when I tried to take it off so she could eat dinner. In the end she wore it around her neck. She may never take it off ag

The cursor sat blinking after the 'g', waiting for the computer to catch up with the rest of Sean's sentence.

That's fine by me.

Sean's sentence still wasn't complete. She went back to browsing while she waited for him to think. 'Page not found.' She clicked another tab – 'Page not found'. She clicked, fast, through all the tabs, opened a new page – 'Page not found'. The network icon had a red line through it. She rebooted the machine. Still no network.

She walked back to the living room where the boys had arranged themselves in parallel lines on the floor in front of the TV. Oscar jumped up.

'Mum, can we—'

'Just a minute, Oscar, I have to check something.' The phone was dead. She unplugged it from the wall, plugged it back in, and rang the home number from her mobile. In her ear, the line rang, but the home phone didn't. She tried Sean's mobile.

He started speaking before she'd even heard a ring. 'Something happened to my computer. I'm not seeing the network.'

'The phone line's not working either.'

'It might be us. Try ringing Gwen.'

'I don't want to talk to Gwen.'

'Just ring it – you'll be able to hear her phone through the wall. You can hang up.'

'I don't know her phone number.'

'Look it up in the book.'

'We don't have a book anymore.'

'Look her up on the net, then.'

She waited a moment to let that sink in.

'I'll try Stuart. You ring anyone, they're all stuck at home.'

She rang Kate, counted twenty rings, another twenty, and another. Then Daniel's home number. Again it rang out.

Her mobile rang. Sean. 'I can't hear Stuart's phone, but if the door's blown shut . . .'

'What if the phones are working but there's no one to answer?'

'Take a breath,' he said. 'More likely it's the phone network.'

'If it's the whole city, people will be blogging about it. See what you can find on the net.' Her turn to forget. 'The TV's still working.' She looked at the clock. 'The news will be on in half an hour.' There was an uneasy silence from the other end. 'We're safe inside for now. There's nothing we can do and no hurry to do it.'

'Text if you need me for anything.'

'I miss you.'

'I haven't gone anywhere.'

'I know.'

Zac was standing in front of her, speaking before she'd even hung up. 'So, Mum, if you're not using your computer, can Daniel and I have a go?'

'All the games are in the office and you're not going out to get them.'

Amanda Hickie

'We'll surf the net. Come on, there's nothing else to do.'

'The net's out.'

'Aw, what?' He was indignant. 'You can't be serious.'

'It's not a punishment. It's just life.'

'And Dad gets the computer and all the software,' Zac muttered loudly as he moved off.

'Live with it, Zac. He didn't cut you off from the computer on purpose. We didn't disconnect the Internet to spoil your day. You know what's going on out there, don't you? You've noticed what's happening outside our front door? People are dying, Zac.' She tried to stop herself, but her voice kept saying the things that were crowding her head. 'People are dying. There are people starving to death in the same house as their family because the people who love them are too scared to bring them food. You know what's crappy about losing the Internet, Zac?' He looked defiantly at her, raising his eyes, though his face was turned down. *Stop*, she told herself. 'It's not that you can't flush away the next two hours of your life playing a game. That's not what's crappy. What's really crappy, what's terrifyingly crappy, if you stopped to think about it, is that now we have no way of knowing what's going on out there. And when we run out of food, we'll have no way of knowing what's waiting outside.'

He raised his head and looked her full in the face. 'Gwen and Dad and Ella are out there. You're scared of them.' He sneered the word 'scared' but his tone became offhand, as if he didn't care what she thought anymore. 'You could ring someone on your mobile.'

'No one is answering.'

'You were talking to Dad. Dad answered. On *his* mobile. I bet you didn't ring another mobile. You can't get to the Internet because your computer uses the phone lines to get to it. You want to check the Internet? It's on your mobile.' As he stalked away, she noticed how his feet fell more firmly.

She could ring someone – there just wasn't anyone she wanted to ring. She stared at the contact list on her mobile. Each of them was someone she knew, someone she was connected to. Sophie, who she went to school with. They still grabbed a coffee when their paths crossed and they had time. Damien and Yvonne, friends she could rely on, but since they lived on the other side of the harbor, their problems were just as big as hers and too far away. She hadn't spoken to Deb, just around the corner, since this had all started. Too busy, she told herself. The list scrolled on. Kate would talk, if that's all she wanted. But no conversation could change what was happening in her house right now. There were no words that someone could speak down the phone that would make Sean safe.

Her head ached – from the tension, from the pain of the bruise, from clenching her muscles to stay warm. Even if she sat with them almost on the heater, her feet were still cold. Every part of her was still cold. And when she wrapped one hand around the other and blew into them, the warmth stopped the minute she did.

The only thing she needed to say was *I feel alone*, but if she rang someone to tell them her problems, she owed them, she had to listen to theirs. And if they didn't have food or masks or water, what would she say then? 'Come over, we've got plenty'? Everything she needed to survive was in the house, and her plans depended on all of it. She felt the urge to throw the mobile to the ground and stomp on it. Better to be unable to ring anyone than to have to admit she didn't want to ring anyone.

Her mobile rang and she snatched it up. Sean would tell her she wasn't such a bad person, that it was okay to have such a strong desire not to share. 'Sean.'

'Oh, hi.' The voice on the other end sounded disconcerted, and she was taken by surprise, as if strangers no longer existed. In the moment of silence, she could hear the speaker's doubt. 'Um, is this Hannah?'

'Oh,' she tried to sound businesslike. 'Yes.'

'It's Danny's dad.'

Beep. The line died. She looked at her phone, a blank screen. She couldn't remember when she had last charged it. Through the house, through the living room, startling the boys, to the kitchen, to the charger next to the kitchen window. She was leashed to an area three paces along the counter, a tether to the outside world. Hannah fumbled the phone, trying to find Daniel's dad's number. The phone rang again.

'Hi, yes, sorry. My phone ran out of charge.'

'We're nearly there. Could you ask Danny to get his stuff together?'

'You're taking him home?'

'The doctor's just left. She says it's safe. I'll be there in five minutes.'

'But isn't that a risk? If you've just had a doctor in the house?' He'd hung up.

She was standing in the living room, saying the words, 'Daniel, your dad is coming to get you.'

Daniel said nothing. He stood, as if empty of intent, in the center of the room.

Zac gave him a subdued dig in the side. 'Hey, that's great.'

Daniel blinked.

'You need to pack your stuff.' Daniel still didn't move. 'Zac, can you give him a hand?' Was she doing this because it was the right thing to do, to let him go? 'He'll be here any minute.' And who was it right for?

Daniel followed Zac passively, Oscar buzzing around them. She could hear Zac in the bedroom, bossing Daniel into organization.

The doorbell rang and Daniel was past her like a streak. It rang again. 'Don't open the door!' She yelled after him. His mother, the doctor . . . she had a responsibility to keep him safe. Although with one less mouth to feed . . . She was appalled that the thought was hers. 'Don't. Don't open it!' She ran, her muscles cold and stiff and refusing to recognize the urgency. Daniel was on the balls of his feet, a few steps back from the door, looking to her for permission. Someone was knocking. She jogged up behind Daniel.

The door had to be opened, Daniel had to go. This was his dad's decision. She wasn't his parent. 'Don't open the door, I'll do it.'

Daniel stood like a taut spring, still not quite sure this was happening. She wasn't prepared.

'Hi, who is it?'

'Danny, are you there?' At the sound of his dad's voice, Daniel's eyes lit up.

Zac came trotting up the hall with Daniel's bag. He looked sheepish, shy, as he held it out. 'I might have missed some things.'

Daniel took it from him firmly. 'It doesn't matter.' He looked down at the bag in his hand and then back at Zac. 'Thanks.' The word fell between them, inadequate. 'Thanks, man.'

She grabbed the handle firmly and opened the door. A sharp, damp breeze blew through the grate and down the hall. 'Hi.' She sized up the stranger on the other side of the grille, unsure if he was responsible enough to be handed the care of Daniel.

'Come on, Danny, we've got to get you back to your mum. Quick as you can.'

He wasn't even talking to her. She had a responsibility to, to, to . . . Daniel's parents, to the man on the other side of the grate, to keep Daniel safe. 'Are you sure that it's a good idea?'

Daniel's dad was shaking his head as if he hadn't allowed himself to believe what he was saying. 'Susan's desperate to see him. When she woke up this morning, she couldn't think of anything else. She's been count-ing down the days.' He looked back to his son. 'The sight of you is going to do your mum a world of good.'

Daniel already had the grille unlocked. Zac took a step towards him. 'Hey, bye.' Hannah pulled Zac back, a meter back.

'Yeah, bye. Thanks for having me, Hannah.' Daniel was already on the other side of the screen door, his dad's arm around him.

'Thanks, we owe you. I don't know what we would have done without you looking after him.' Daniel's dad looked at his son, almost the same height as him, and Hannah could see the sheen of tears in his eyes. 'I don't know what we would have done.'

They walked to their car, got in, and drove away. Just like that. While Hannah and Zac watched. Oscar trotted up the hall full of naive curiosity. 'Where's Daniel gone?'

'Home, sweetie.'

'Is he coming back?'

'No, he's gone back to his mum and dad.' She was relieved and ashamed.

'I bet they were sad without him.'

'I bet they were.'

Zac was still standing, staring at the empty place on the concrete in front of the house where Daniel's car had been. His arms wrapped tight around himself.

'Are you okay?'

His body turned to her, but his eyes stayed glued. 'It's a bit cold.'

As they walked down the hall, she was shivering.

She asked Zac to keep Oscar in the front of the house. He flicked his eyes in contempt, but they were deep in a board game when she let herself into the kitchen. She pulled a chair up to the counter next to the window that was her portal to Sean, next to the charger that kept her phone going. She texted, *I need to see you.* Her phone trilled at her instantly. **Coming out for playtime.**

Ella kicked the ball around the yard. When it came too close to the house, Sean kicked it back. He leaned against the outer wall of the kitchen, two layers of brick separating them. Through the window, open a crack, Hannah told Sean calmly, matter-of-factly, about Daniel leaving. She promised herself she wasn't going to wallow in how badly she'd behaved to Zac about the phone, but her head hurt and air blew through the open window, encasing her in a blanket of cold. As much as she tried to hold them back, the words fell out. And the tears. She couldn't stop the tears although there was nothing to cry about. She cried for everything, the whole horrible mess. The fight, letting Daniel leave, her cold feet and hands, Ella playing alone in the yard, the window between her and Sean. She shifted in her seat, bumping her bruise against the edge of the kitchen counter. She cried for the pain.

The ball strayed off the grass and Hannah was bereft for the seconds it took Sean to retrieve it. Her nose was streaming, mixing with her tears. Her face was flushed, her eyes were swollen, hot, red. She swallowed down phlegm, snorted as she tried to breathe. The hotter her face got, the colder her body became. She gulped, tried to stop crying, but choked as another sob came. She was gross and pathetic.

On the other side of the glass, Sean watched her as he listened, shifting from foot to foot, and when he couldn't look at her anymore, they both watched Ella.

Hannah calmed her breathing long enough to say, 'She looks healthy.'

'Better safe than sorry.'

Hannah wiped her face with her hands and her sticky hands on her jeans.

'Now you have one less to look after. That has to be good.'

'Daniel and Zac looked after each other. Zac will miss him.'

'Yes.' They fell into silence again. Sean sighed heavily. 'At least the rain filled the tank.'

'Yes.'

Hannah splashed a little of the water from the bucket in the kitchen on her face to try to make herself look normal. It sent a shaft of cold through her. Her reflection in the window was still red and swollen, but she couldn't waste any more water.

She would stay in the kitchen forever if it weren't for Ella's stripy socks and pink shorts, soaked through from the damp grass. The fairy skirt did nothing to keep her warm. Hannah rifled through Oscar's wardrobe, hoping to find some old clothes small enough not to fall off Ella. He had socks, at least, and one pair of his pants with a belt could be cinched tight. Oscar watched from the doorway. Her face still felt hot but she hoped it didn't show.

'What are you doing?'

'Getting some clothes for Ella.'

'I don't have girls' clothes.'

'She can wear boys' clothes. She won't mind.' He eyed her disapprovingly. 'Why don't you play with Zac?'

'He's in his room. He told me to go away.' Oscar wandered over to his bookshelf and started pulling things off. 'Does Ella like coloring?'

'I think so.'

'I don't think she would like this book – it has trucks. Girls don't like trucks, they like fairies. The other book has fairies but that's my favorite.'

'Girls like all different things. If you want to give her the one with trucks, give her that one.'

'It's a really good one. I'll give her that.' He looked at Hannah seriously for a few seconds. 'Does she have her teddy? She might not be able to sleep if she doesn't have a teddy, but I don't need mine to sleep.'

'I'm pretty sure Daddy found her a teddy.'

'You could get her teddy from next door. And some clothes.'

'I bet Stuart locked the house when he went out.' She

hoped. Oscar was making a small pile of toys in the middle of the floor. 'That's plenty, Mouse. She's got the computer and I think Daddy got some toys from the garage.'

Oscar unstacked and restacked the pile, turning the toys over and examining them. 'Can I take these things out to Ella?'

'I think it's best not to. You can play with her tomorrow.' Oscar shrugged and wandered off.

The house was so much quieter with one less, or two if she counted Sean. Daniel had barely said a word, but now Zac had no one to talk to. Except Oscar and Hannah. And today talking was only a snarl. When he eventually came out of his room, he lay on the sofa, his eyes sad and vacant.

'Justin says the phones are out all over.'

'Who's Justin?'

'A kid from school.'

'You've never mentioned him before.'

Zac looked blank. 'There are a lot of kids at school.'

'How did you talk to Justin?'

'He texted me.' Zac was being patient with his slow mother. 'Everybody else has a smartphone and I don't even have Internet.' The whole thing was clearly her fault.

'Zac, do me a favor – make sure you keep your phone charged.'

'Sure.' She could see the cogs turning over as he tried to process something. He stared at the turned-off television and, as she was about to get up, he blurted out,

'Daniel must be really happy to be home. It must be really great to be with his mum and dad.'

She waited but he said nothing. 'Yes.' It was the most she could bring herself to say.

Hannah opened her bedroom curtains to give herself a view of the street and a little weak sunlight, too insignificant to add more than psychological warmth to the room. Clouds built high into the sky above the houses on the other side of the road. Everything felt damp, everything felt cold – it had worked its way into the whole house. Down the intersection next to Mr Henderson's, she could see blue sky breaking through. The clouds were struck by the last of the day's light. She crawled into bed. In the peace of her bedroom, enveloped tightly in the bedclothes, she watched the clouds turn from orange to pink to deep purple to steel blue. Gaudy, artificial colors. Nature had no restraint.

The street might be full of people silently watching the sunset, or it might be unobserved except by her. There was no way to know how many silent inhabitants filled the houses in the street, how many Gwens. Not everyone could be lucky, but she had done everything she could to make sure they made it through. She had to have blind faith that doing everything was enough, had to believe it was just endurance now. Eventually she would reach something that could not be endured, but she told herself not this time, not for them. The moment was ephemeral – she couldn't even lock it in her memory. At best she could hope Sean was watching too.

Her feet were cold, her face hot. She shucked off the duvet and the icy air hit the light sweat on her skin, sending a chill through her.

Dinnertime soon. Lentils and rice. She used to enjoy food, the cooking and the eating, before it became an endless drudge of meal making. Dried beans were almost all that was left. And rice. A couple more cups of lentils and then they were down to the black beans and kidney beans that needed to be soaked but hadn't been. She tried to remember how much rice, exactly, they still had to bulk out the beans.

The sky had faded to shades of purple-gray. The light was almost gone. From florid to sepia had taken no more than twenty minutes. Out of the wardrobe, she pulled big thick mountain socks and a fleece jacket to put over the jumper she was already wearing.

She dragged herself to Zac's door. He was swathed in his headphones.

'Could you give me a hand with dinner?'

He looked around, surprised. 'Sure.'

Oscar was right behind her. 'I can help too.'

'You can't help, Mouse.' Zac used his older-brother tone. 'Cooking is too dangerous for a little kid.'

Oscar's shoulders slumped and he dragged his feet away.

'Zac, I know you can find something for Oscar to do.'

She sat at the table and watched as Zac followed her instructions. Oscar snuggled up to her, leaning his head on her shoulder. He wriggled, his arms bumping and digging into her. Her stomach started to cramp, her mouth filled with saliva. The act of trying to swallow made her gag. She tried to stand but Oscar put his arms around her. She shoved him away.

The spasm in her stomach urged her to get to the sink, the bath, the toilet, anywhere. Now. Oscar made another attempt to hug her and she pushed him aside as she stumbled through the doorway. Oscar tugged at her fleece – nothing registered but the taste in her mouth and the knot in her gut. She was nearly there, she was at the bathroom doorway.

'But, Mum.'

Turning to look at Oscar was enough. She was on her knees, retching. The remains of lunch spread across the timber floor in front of the pantry, a fishiness behind the acid.

'Oz!' Oscar fell back like he was on an elastic, pulled roughly by a horrified Zac. 'Get away, Oz, don't touch her.'

Oscar looked at her with wide, confused eyes. 'I'll get Dad.'

'No.' It took everything she had to talk. 'You can't get Sean.' She coughed and spat. Zac wrapped his arms around Oscar's shoulders, holding him away from her. Her two boys looked down on her, like a formal portrait, as she knelt on the floor. Zac's hug was comfort and restraint. Oscar couldn't see the panic on Zac's face, but she could – the way he was afraid of his own mother and afraid for her.

'I'm feeling a bit better.' Her head was clearing, her

stomach settling, but trying to stand made the world start to turn. She collapsed back to the floor and rolled away from the mess she'd made, until her back rested against the cool pantry door.

Zac stepped farther away, pulling Oscar with him. 'Oscar, go to the living room, stay there until I tell you.' He guided Oscar around her legs, around the edge of the pool of vomit, making sure not to touch anything. He was too young, only fourteen. He had always been too young. Too young at six to understand what cancer meant. Too young now to have to protect his little brother from her, from Sean. He skirted around her with a businesslike manner that brought her failure home to her. 'I'll get you a towel.'

'Can I come in yet?' Oscar's light voice carried from the living room.

'Stay where you are, Oz.'

'I want to help.' His voice was high and uncertain.

'I'll look after Mum. You stay there.'

She wanted to pull him into a hug, like he had hugged Oscar, but even the thought of sitting up was a challenge, and she was the danger.

'I'm all right.' She tried to look reassuring from her position on the floor. 'Really, I'm fine. It's something dodgy I ate.'

Her stomach spasmed again. She stumbled at last into the bathroom and threw up into the toilet. The tile floor was cold, cleansing, and smoothed away her nausea. She shivered. Zac gingerly stepped over her and put a towel on the side of the bath. She closed her eyes but she could hear him sloshing water from the bucket into the toilet.

'Could you get me a glass of water?' She could lie here forever. Until the epidemic was over, until Sean came back. Zac put a plastic cup next to her head. 'Thanks.' She tried to smile.

She felt better again, a trick her stomach played on her, lulling her into believing she could sit up. Safer on the floor. Zac looked down at her, considering. He went away and returned with an old grubby blanket that lived in the car. The woman lying on a bathroom floor that hadn't been cleaned in weeks couldn't afford to be picky. Gently, he laid it over her, careful not to touch her.

'I don't need it, I'm too hot.'

'You'll get cold, Mum.'

She tried to push it off and he jumped two feet back.

'You have to stay warm.' He leaned over her to straighten the blanket. The distress on his face was visceral. He was afraid and determined, and if she struggled, she risked touching him, so she let him finish covering her.

She closed her eyes and tried to let the nausea happen to the woman on the floor. It was a trick she learned during treatment, a way of enduring time without experiencing it. She concentrated on the senses that weren't ambushing her, that she could dissociate from the suffering body. The random play of light on the inside of her eyelids, the banging of pots and utensils in the kitchen.

After a stretch of time, short or long, she couldn't

measure, she heard a quiet voice at the door. 'Mum, where's the recipe?'

Zac didn't know that there are no recipe books for whatever's in the pantry when the world stops making sense.

'Fry up the onion. Put in a cup of lentils.' Saying it made her gag. 'Some spices . . .'

'What spices?'

'Smell them, whatever smells good. Two cups of rice.' She stopped to breathe and regain control. 'Twice as much water. Boil twenty minutes.' She spat the words out so she could go back to trying not to exist.

More banging. Even muffled by the walls, it went through her. The soft voice at the door again. 'Twice as much water as the rice or the rice and lentils?' She couldn't think, she didn't want to think. 'Mum?'

'Both, twice as much as both.'

She could hear them talking to each other and could tell by Zac's tone that he was bossing Oscar around. His voice was deeper and stronger than it had been a few weeks ago. He was becoming the thing he pretended to be for Oscar's sake. Oscar's childlike voice answered back, happier the more Zac bossed him.

There was a change in Zac's tone. A hidden concern, more dictatorial. She pulled herself along the floor, closer to the door to catch the words.

'You can't go to the bathroom.'

'But I have to pee.'

'Well, you can't do it in the bathroom.'

Oscar sounded desperate. 'I need to pee. Where am I going to pee?'

'Just hold on.'

Oscar's voice rose to a wail. 'I can't hold on.'

The back door opened and sent a shock through her. What would Zac do now – where would he go if he didn't know what to do? Sean? She tried to get to her feet, but her stomach rebelled. She could hear the emptiness of the house. It was beyond her control.

The sound of the door again, followed by Zac's voice. 'That's gross. You can't do that.'

'You said to water the plants.'

'Not the pots. We eat the herbs, Oz. If you pee on them, we'd be eating your pee.'

'Oh.' The word carried all the disappointment of a little boy who had let down his big brother.

'It's okay, I stopped you, but you have to think.'

'Okay.' The disappointment was gone.

She fell asleep and woke up cold. Not feverish cold, just cold. The blanket lay to the side, thrown off while she slept. Her stomach felt like she'd been punched, but it wasn't mutinous. The clatter from the kitchen had been replaced by the white noise of the television. She took a swig from the tumbler of water to wash the bitter taste from her mouth and crouched to spit in the toilet. Her head hurt, her bones felt like they were made of lead, and her muscles barely worked, but she wasn't going to throw up.

More than anything, she wanted a shower to wash

away the rancid sweat, the smell of sick. She pulled herself up to sit on the side of the bath and turned the tap on. It sputtered. She'd forgotten about the water.

She wiped up the floor outside the bathroom with the towel Zac had left. The smell made her dry retch. She splashed the floor with disinfectant and pulled Daniel's towel off the rail to spread it around. The towels were two heaps of potential infection she couldn't leave in the bathroom for Zac and Oscar. She opened the window and heaved them into the side passage. The effort made her sweat. With toilet paper dipped in the little water that was left in the tumbler, she wiped her face.

She ached all over.

She dragged herself down the hall and through the living room. Zac and Oscar were side by side on the sofa, watching some cartoon only Oscar would be interested in. Zac sat closer to the hallway, his arm around Oscar, a barrier between his brother and the door. The way he braked Oscar's attempt to get up as she came through . . . it wasn't by accident.

One foot in front of the other, she kept walking. Halfway up the hall, thinking of nothing but the need to get to bed, she heard Zac's voice behind her. 'Mum.' She turned around – he was deliberately closing the door to the living room.

'I need to lie down, Zac. Talk to me later.'

'You have to stay in your room. You can't come out.' He was grave and strange. 'I can't keep my eyes on Oz all the time. You have to put something behind your door so he can't come in.' He must have been working this out, thinking of all the possibilities while the bright colors of the cartoon passed over his eyes.

She nodded. 'Did you have dinner?'

'I had to take Oz with me to Gwen's. I didn't tell Dad.' She nodded again. All she had to do was follow instructions. 'There's some food left if you want it.'

'Maybe tomorrow.'

She was nearly at the bedroom door when Zac's voice came again, this time with a note of desperation and doubt. 'I'm going to make him sleep in my room tonight.'

'Good idea.'

'He's good. We're both good.'

'I know you are. You're doing a good job. You're a good boy.' She meant it, but she would have said anything to get to bed.

She closed her eyes and tried not to feel the pounding in her head, the furriness in her mouth. She slept and woke and slept. In her dreams, she was awake, hearing Oscar's and Zac's voices. And when she woke, she heard them still. They should be in bed – she was the one who should tell them, but she remembered what Zac said, to stay away. He was right and her muscles ached and just turning in bed made her head throb.

It wasn't fair, it wasn't right. She had done everything, everything asked of her, everything she had asked of herself. Taken every precaution. It should count, that she had already done the looking death in the face. All the chemo, all the radiation, the shots and the pills and the side effects. All done. The people with cheery faces telling her that cancer was an opportunity. Not one of them had she smacked. So why had she bothered to survive only to die now, from a bug she should have been able to avoid?

She went through all that for Zac – made a bargain with the empty air around her that she would do what was asked in return for enough life to see him through to adulthood. That was the very least she was owed. Staying alive long enough to infect her boys wasn't the deal. All those times, she had told herself that anything could be endured, that she just had to get through it. But this was too much. Her anger and despair could muster nothing more than tears. If this bug was going to kill her, she didn't have the energy left to go through the actual dying. All she wanted to do was sleep until it was over.

And yet she woke, eyes gummed, salty crust around her nose and mouth. It was dark and quiet, sometime in the early morning, she guessed. The room was cold from the night, but the bone-chilling shivers had gone. The thought still hung in her head that she didn't have the energy to die. And it struck her – she wasn't going to die. She was going to puke and feel like the insides of a drain, but she hadn't coughed or sneezed, she had no diarrhea. Her nose had only been running because she'd been crying and throwing up. Her temperature was normal.

The stomach cramps and vomiting were hours ago now. That wasn't Manba. Ella hadn't turned up until yesterday, and Daniel's father this morning, so it was too soon to show symptoms if it came from them. And the taste of fish. Because there hadn't been quite enough to go around for yesterday's lunch, she had given the boys more and taken for herself the last two unappealing sardines from a tin she found at the back of the fridge. The sardines were now in a towel in the side passage. She felt weak and alive and very tired.

Mon	Tue	Wed	Thu	Fri	Sat	Sun

The morning was jarringly ordinary. She followed Sean through the front door, right on his heels. It was open and airy outside, bright after being in the house so long. Her eyes took a couple of seconds to adjust. Sean had disappeared from sight. Where he should be, a man stood on the porch. He said, 'Sean's dead.'

She could see he was telling the truth. 'When?'

'Just as he came through the door.'

'Then we go back.' She felt a rising wave of desperation. 'We go back, back before we came out, and we stay inside.'

The man shook his head.

A storm of panic and grief broke out in her chest. Her head could only look on, fight to keep herself from drowning in it. She looked at the street, empty of Sean like every other part of the world now. She knew the man was right. Sean was dead and there was no undoing it.

There was shouting but no one in sight. An angry, frightening screech. She woke with a start. The room was barely lit and the dread from the dream still lay heavy on her. It felt more real than the voices coming from the street. Her legs held steady, if weak, as she tentatively tried her weight on them. She lifted the corner of the curtain slowly, inconspicuously.

Three burly men, maskless and gloveless, stood around Mr Henderson's front door. The shrill, chattering sound came from Mr Henderson, throwing himself at the back of one of the men like a demented lapdog. The front man delicately picked his way down the steps. He was older than the other two, midfifties, casually dressed in a baggy cream jacket that looked like it was meant to be worn crumpled, and dark gray slacks. His silver hair was casually long, not unkempt. The middle man carried a bedsheet tied like a large sack. He heaved it onto a pile in the back of a worse-for-wear white tradesman's van. The last man tired of Mr Henderson's noise and pushed him backwards, like he was flicking off a fly. Mr Henderson scurried up his stairs and slammed the front door behind him.

From beside the van, the older man pointed to the house next to Mr Henderson's. The front door was off its hinges, swinging open. One of the younger men disappeared inside. The older man's gaze roamed the row of houses on Hannah's side, passed the front of hers, then doubled back.

She jumped away from the window. The knife was on the bedside table – she grabbed the handle tight. A dumpy middle-aged woman in her pajamas waving a knife in their faces was no real threat. She ran down the hall to the living room and screamed at the empty space. 'Get to the backyard.'

Zac appeared on the other side of the room, Oscar's head poking out from behind him.

'Go to the backyard. If I scream, run.'

Oscar was startled by her wild appearance and shrill panic. 'But Daddy's in the backyard.'

Zac froze. He could only protect Oscar from their mother or from their father.

'Get Daddy. Get Daddy now.'

'But it's not two o'clock.'

'I don't care.' She tried to fill her voice with command, as she had when they were little and naughty. 'Now.' She bolted back up the hall. All she wanted was to shepherd them to safety, but danger was at the front door and she was their only defense.

She moved her head back and forth across the gap between the curtains, trying to see as much of the street as she could. The younger man emerged from the house, hands empty, shrugged at the older man, and sauntered over to the third man, the one who had pushed Mr Henderson. They stood next to the van, talking. Relaxed, prepared, in work clothes and sturdy boots. The older man ambled diagonally across the road. She willed him to choose Stuart's house. Stuart was fastidious in his tastes and never parsimonious in satisfying them. His house had better pickings and no one was home to resist.

Gwen. She was a bit deaf, probably heard none of the

ruckus from the street. She would be even more of a push-over than Mr Henderson. The only thing standing, obliquely, between Gwen and these men was Hannah and her chef's knife. For a stomach-lurching second, Hannah feared that yesterday's lunch was going to bring her down again, but this was adrenaline, not food poisoning.

There could be no doubt, the man's path ended at their front door. He was followed, a step behind, by the man who had carried the swag, a sheet billowing loose in his hand. From nowhere, Sean was next to her, puffing, child-sized cricket bat in hand. 'What is it? What happened?' Hannah stood back to let him see through the curtains. 'Is the security grille locked?' She nodded. 'Then they can't get in.'

'They could smash the window, they could come down the side passage.' Her stomach dropped. 'I sent the kids to the backyard.'

The rattling metallic sound of the grille was followed by a man's voice, 'Hey. Open up.'

Hannah and Sean waited. Now there was banging. Hannah stole a sideways peek down the porch.

The younger man was kicking the grille. The older one supervised him with indifference. 'There's no one home. I'll take out a window. Let me get the hammer.'

She whispered. 'We have to answer.' Sean nodded.

The bedsheet man lost interest in the grille and backed down the stairs to survey the whole house. 'Boss, there's a side gate.' The one across the road looked on with amused boredom.

The side gate was only bolted, with a cutout to let it be opened from the street side. 'We have to do it now,' Hannah whispered.

Sean flung the front door open and they were face-to-face with the older man, separated only by the mesh of the metal grille. Up close, his jacket was more than fashionably wrinkled, and his face had a puffy wash-and-wear look. Under the jacket was a crumpled open-necked business shirt palely checked in blue. His expression snapped into exaggerated conviviality. 'Hi. Sorry my colleague made so much noise. We weren't sure if anyone was in. We don't mean to bother you, but our van broke down and we need to ring a friend to pick us up. Wouldn't you know it, the mobile's battery is flat.' He smiled, which would have been convincing if she hadn't witnessed him robbing Mr Henderson's. 'Could I come in and use your phone?' He was leaning into the grille companionably. Both Hannah and Sean pulled back.

'All the phones are out around here.' She answered a little too quickly and spoke too fast. She could feel the muscles around her mouth pulling down and trembling, giving her away.

'Oh, yes. You don't have a mobile?'

Sean broke in. 'Tell us your friend's number, we'll ring him for you. Quarantine, you understand.'

'He's a cautious man, like your good selves. I'll need to talk to him. Just open the screen door and pass the phone out. You can see I'm not sick.'

Hannah turned very deliberately to Sean. 'Darling, I

told you last night, the phone's dead. The battery won't charge.' She turned back to the man and forced a smile.

'So we have a long walk in front of us.' He gave a weary shrug. 'At least you could spare us a cup or two of water.' She could see he was running through his lines.

Sean brought the cricket bat up sharply and banged it hard on the grille. 'Bugger off and don't come back.' The young man pricked up his ears at the action. 'We've called the police.' The thug snorted with contempt – none of them believed this any more than they had the lie about the mobile.

She raised her knife firmly and held it in front of her. Her voice wavered. 'You can bully an old man, can't you? That's all you're good for.'

The young man threw himself bodily at the grille. Hannah and Sean jumped back. He threw his heft at it again but it didn't move.

She froze, terrified that she would involuntarily glance at the bedroom window. All the men had to do was turn their heads to see it had no bars. If she and Sean fled, abandoned the house to these men, they protected the kids but lost the last of the food. All the time shut in would have been for nothing. That made her angry, angrier than she was about Mr Henderson, angrier than she had been last night at the thought of dying. These people were beneath contempt, added nothing to the human race, yet threatened her family, threatened her preparations.

But they were bigger than her, and ruthless. When it

came to the crunch, she didn't think Sean could whack someone hard enough with that bat to do damage, and she wasn't sure she could sink a knife into human flesh, not even if it belonged to these thugs.

She held the knife more firmly, hoping she was doing a better job convincing them than herself. The younger man broke off his attack on the grille to stare. The older one watched, as if curious to find out what would happen next. Sean shifted his hold on the diminutive bat.

The man across the road called out, 'What's taking so long?'

The older man considered them, sizing up whether they were worth the bother. 'We're just chatting to the householders.'

'Don't waste your time, we're full anyway.'

The young man on their doorstep smiled, a leer that made Hannah shiver, then turned and lumbered back to the van. The older man gave a slight nod of the head and said, 'Catch you next time.' They watched him saunter across the road. As the van took off, Hannah and Sean scrambled to the bedroom window to watch. Once it was out of sight, they spilled onto the veranda and leaned over the brick wall to check that it hadn't stopped farther up the road. It was gone.

They watched and waited, Sean checking both ways in case the van had circled the block. Across the road, Mr Henderson's front yard was deserted, his door closed. If they had taken his valuables, that was heartbreaking. If they had taken his food . . . there must be someone else, surely, who was capable of helping him. She pushed away the bad feeling. Zac and Oscar came first.

She looked at Sean and saw a ghost. She put her hand on his arm to make sure he was real. He smiled at her and slipped his arm around her shoulder.

'You're here.'

'I wasn't far away.'

It felt only like a reprieve. The men at the door, she surely must have dreamt them. They strained belief. But Sean dying? People died every day – that was easy to believe, that was real.

He kissed her head. She felt his touch indirectly through her hair, his hand was on the fabric of her pajamas. She put her hand to his face, to feel the warmth and solidity.

'It's okay, they're gone.'

'You're here.' She kissed him on the cheek. 'You're here.'

'That's a problem, isn't it? I can go back to the office. I haven't touched the kids.' He looked down the hall. 'We'd better let them know it's safe.'

She held on to him as they crossed the threshold, just to be sure, and only let go to lay the knife gingerly on the hallway table. He continued down the hallway and she scurried after him. When she caught up in the backyard, his face was clouded by a grim determination. 'I can't see them. They're not out here.'

They moved through the house methodically, punctuated by calling out Zac's and Oscar's names. She looked

292

in Oscar's toy box, in his wardrobe, under his bed. Despite the camouflaging piles of clothes, books, and games on the floor, they weren't there.

She met up with Sean as he was coming out of Zac's room. On their way to the kitchen, she opened the pantry and pulled back the shower curtain in the bathroom, just in case. Zac wouldn't take such a little kid's hiding place unless he was desperate, but there weren't many places big enough to hide three.

She hesitated at the back door.

'What's the problem?'

'They'll unload the truck and come back.'

'How many houses do you think they did? Somebody might have rung the police. That's a risk they won't want to take. They'll move on. I would, if I were the kind to turn over other people's houses.'

'Or they've gone to get something to break down the door with. How can you possibly know what they have planned?'

'As if they needed something to break down the door with. If they wanted to take us, they would have. You can obsess about this, but in the end it doesn't matter. What matters is finding the kids.'

'I had to stay at the front, you understand that. I couldn't be with them.'

'I'm sure you made the best choice and I'm sure they did whatever it was you told them to.'

'I told Zac to run if I screamed. And it's possible I screamed.' They both stared at the empty garden.

Sean pulled her into a hug and spoke into her hair. 'I wouldn't have done different. Now let's find them.'

Sean held her hand as they walked through the backyard. He stood on his toes to look over the fence to Ella's house. 'The door to Stuart's is still shut. They could have gone anywhere.'

They wouldn't go to Gwen. They wouldn't go *to* anyone. She'd made them afraid of people. Danger at the front door, danger from their parents.

Sean got down on the office floor and pivoted on his stomach, looking under the desk and the secondhand sofa, even though the spaces were too small for three. Hannah's eye caught on every possibility, however impossible. The filing cabinet drawers, the gap next to the bookshelf. Sean pushed himself slowly up and she could see a smeared circle of dirt on his T-shirt and a look of defeat in his eyes.

They had to be in the garage. She held her breath and instructed the universe – *They will be in the garage.* The roof made soft metallic clicks as the sun heated it. Behind the clicks, she heard a deeper silence than they had found anywhere in the house, as if the walls were holding their breath. She looked past the car to the roller door. If they had let themselves into the back lane, there was no knowing where they could be.

'Zac? Zac? They're gone.' No sound, no movement.

The garage was filled with old furniture and boxes. Things they had no use for but she couldn't bear to throw out. Old toys, the kids' old clothes, a shelf filled with tools and pieces of wood, ready for some DIY emergency. One wall was covered with a ziggurat of storage boxes, a neat aggregation of paperwork and castoffs, all labeled.

Sean grabbed the box at the nearest end and wrenched it forward, then the next and the next. The fourth box sat slightly out of line, and as Sean pulled, Hannah could see a dark gap, and Zac looking back, his body making a shield between the two little ones and the outside world.

In front of him, Zac grasped a hammer with both hands. He crouched, primed like a cat ready to pounce.

Ella burst into tears. 'I breathed, I couldn't help it.' Even her sobs were muted. 'I'm sorry, Zac.'

'You can come out, it's safe.'

Zac looked warily at Sean. 'What happened?'

'Some . . .' Sean was struggling to find words that would convince Zac without scaring the little ones. 'Some people came to the front door. They're gone now.'

'What people?' He held the hammer like a light saber.

'No one. No one we know.'

'Mum chucked.' Zac threw it out like a challenge. Sean didn't look surprised, just spent. He looked to her for an answer.

'I wouldn't be better this morning if it was Manba. And I don't have a cough.' But what she was thinking was *Too late now anyway.*

Zac shook his hammer at Sean with less resolve. 'You might be sick. It's not two days.'

All three children were watching Sean. 'It's possible, but I don't think so.' The hammer wobbled in Zac's hand as his grip loosened. 'You're standing next to Ella, you're breathing her air, so there's no point worrying about me.' Zac twitched and his eyes were forced wide. He opened his mouth to speak, but nothing came out. Sean put his hand on Zac's shoulder. 'You did a good job. You found a safe place for Oscar and Ella.' The hammer fell to the ground. Zac wrapped his arms around Sean's middle and buried his face in his clothes. 'How did you keep them so quiet?'

'We're good at hiding. Zac said so.' Ella's voice was soft and solemn.

'Is it two o'clock yet?' Oscar looked for permission from Hannah. 'Do Daddy and Ella have to go back in the office?'

'No. It's fine.' She enfolded Oscar and Ella in a tight hug.

'Mum, you're squashing me.' She let them go, reluctantly.

Zac, with relish, rigged up a trip wire along the front path, complete with a booby trap of empty cans salvaged from the recycling bin. When he had no choice but to move from the shadow of the house, he darted out and ran back. Only once the front was booby-trapped could Hannah feel safe out of earshot of the front door.

They laid a blanket out in the backyard. The sun infused into her cold bones. It felt like days since any warmth had reached them. Ella and Oscar lay on either side of her. They spread their arms and legs, turned their tummies up to collect the sun's rays.

Sean mixed some peanut butter and soy sauce with water, poured it over a mess of rice and leftovers, and called it satay. Even when it was placed on the blanket in front of her and a fork was in her hand, Hannah didn't feel like food. All she felt was exhausted and shaky. It was an unappetizing mess, but the need not to waste food overrode her instincts.

Ella prodded the mashed-up pile on her plate. She swirled it around with her fork, and when she lost interest, she wandered over to the lemon tree and started pulling off the lower leaves, scrunching each of them and putting them to her nose.

'Ella,' Sean called over to her, 'come back and eat lunch.'

'I don't like it.'

'That's fine, honey. I'll make you something else.'

'Hang on.' Hannah made annoyed eyes at him. 'She has to eat what everyone else eats.'

'I can't blame her.' He pushed his own food around. 'It's slop.'

Zac stiffened slightly, listening more closely, and Oscar leaned in, not bothering to disguise his interest.

'She has to eat what everyone else eats. It's only fair.'

'She's barely eaten anything in two days.' Sean's face was stony. 'She didn't like anything.'

'None of us like it, but it's what we've got. She won't starve.'

'You think.'

'She'll eat when she's hungry. For God's sake, we don't have anything else.'

Zac and Oscar both eyed Ella's plate while they wolfed down their food. The instant the last forkful went in his mouth, Zac leaned over and scooped up some of Ella's.

'Hey.' Sean pulled the plate away from him.

'You're making her something else. I'm hungry.'

Hannah put the plate back at Ella's spot and called out. 'Ella, come sit down now. Leave the tree alone.' Hannah dropped her voice and turned to Sean. 'Give her more time to eat. She has to eat what we eat.'

Zac and Oscar watched Ella lift every slow forkful from the plate to her mouth.

'Righto, kids. You're going to help me tidy up while your mum gets to enjoy the sun.'

As Sean shooed them into the house, Oscar was explaining the intricacies of his room to Ella like a good five-year-old host, but Ella was unmoved by the enticing description of Oscar's toys.

Hannah closed her eyes and indulged herself in the sensations of the garden. The irregularity of the grass beneath the blanket, the rustle of the lemon tree's branches in the breeze, the back door slam. She opened them again to the sight of Sean bearing two mugs. As he put one on the blanket, the smell reached her, warm and bitter.

'I don't know that I want any.' She picked up the mug in her hands just to steal the warmth. 'I don't want to test my stomach too much after yesterday.'

'Ah, but I couldn't be so mean as to not share it. It's the last pot. Unless you're hiding a packet somewhere.' He looked hopeful.

'How will you cope?'

'I've convinced myself that this is the best coffee ever, even though I am completely aware of the process of its creation.' He took a sip. 'It's not bad. It comes close, even with powdered milk and not enough grounds.'

'You could put mine in the fridge and microwave it tonight.'

'Then this cup wouldn't be special. And there's only so much the magic of the moment can overcome. I think being three hours old and reheated as well would be a stretch too far.'

Zac wandered through the open door, ambled across, and dropped down on the grass beside Hannah. 'That smells good.'

'Do you want it?'

'No, but it smells like breakfast on Saturdays.' He pulled out a blade of grass. 'You know, real breakfast. Bacon and eggs and toast. And some mushrooms.'

'If we had a mushroom farm, we'd have fresh mushrooms,' Hannah said. 'A fresh vegetable. Do you think mushrooms stop you getting scurvy?'

'A big bottle of vitamin C will stop you getting scurvy.'

'Daddy's so romantic.'

'What about eggs, Mum? If you'd bought some chickens and a mushroom farm, we could have a cooked breakfast.'

'I think even factory chickens get more space than this.' Sean considered the yard. 'There's a tiny green lemon on the tree. We could all suck on a slice.' He gave Zac a big grin.

Zac looked mildly concerned. 'Are we really going to get scurvy?'

'We're not going to get scurvy. This will be over soon.' Sean didn't sound completely convinced.

Oscar appeared at the back door, his trousers held loosely around his waist. His face was a mixture of outrage and despair. 'Didn't you hear me calling? I've been calling and calling and no one came.' He threw his hands up in a theatrical gesture, quickly grabbing his trousers again as they started to fall.

'What's up, Mouse?' Sean sounded offhand. If he hadn't had a restraining hand on her arm, she would have been up, trying to comfort Oscar. She couldn't be responsible for everything and she didn't have the energy to argue.

'There's no toilet paper.'

'Well, get some from the cupboard outside the bathroom.'

Oscar looked affronted. 'I looked – there isn't any.'

Sean looked to Hannah for the next move. She creaked up from the ground with effort. 'Let's look again, Mouse.'

'I looked.'

And he had. Another set of eyes couldn't conjure any hiding among the sparse, well-organized tins. All she could find was the last tissues, a small pocket-sized pack.

She stared at the remaining tins and packets. So much

for carefully calculated rations, so much for average consumption multiplied by four. Her self-reproach was interrupted by Sean, peering over her shoulder. It still didn't make any more toilet paper appear. His voice mirrored her own recriminations. 'We have weeks' worth of hand wash but no toilet paper? I thought you planned this out.'

'It turns out kids use more toilet paper but wash their hands less. That shouldn't have been a surprise.'

Zac followed them down the side passage. The concrete was dark, slimy and green from all the rain. Sean stepped over the squelchy towels outside the bathroom window. Before this started, they produced enough waste for a whole bin every week. But now almost all they added was an empty bag and a couple of tins once a day. Sean dived into the recycling bin, digging through the tins to retrieve the last copy of the local paper that, up until a few weeks ago, was left on their doorstep every week. It was still in its plastic sleeve, protected from moisture.

Zac followed them back to the patio table and watched their every move as they tore the newspaper into squares. 'What are you doing?'

'Making toilet paper.'

'I'm not using that to wipe. Gross.'

'It's this or nothing.'

'The bits with photos are shiny. That's not going to work.'

'Then don't use the shiny bits.'

Zac stared at Sean as if he had gone mad.

'Don't waste it' – Sean waggled his finger at Zac – 'or you'll have to use the shiny stuff.'

The chime of a text message came from Zac's pocket. He pulled out his phone, gave the message his serious consideration, and then turned to Hannah gravely. 'You don't have Manba.'

'Your phone told you that?'

'Sophie's dad.' He spoke matter-of-factly, as if Sophie's dad was the usual source of such knowledge.

'Who's Sophie?'

'A kid in my year.'

'And you rang her dad?'

'No.' She sensed that he felt his mother was clearly an idiot, even if she wasn't infectious. 'I texted Simon, but his parents didn't know, so he emailed Lachlan because his mum works at the university, but she didn't know. But Lachlan used to go out with Sophie, and her dad's a doctor at the hospital, so he emailed her. And she texted me. Her dad says it gets worse for the first three days, at least if you don't treat it. You don't get better overnight and you don't throw up. You have, you know, kind of the opposite.' The phone went off again. 'He says you ate something bad.'

'Food poisoning. All that technology and your mother could have told you that.'

'And you could have searched the Internet. You're the one with the smartphone.' He muttered under his breath, 'They all have smartphones.'

'How often do you text people?'

'I don't know. Whenever.'

'I guess it's not much fun for you now Daniel's gone. Do you text him much?'

Zac shrugged.

As the fog and lethargy of illness left Hannah, it was replaced by a gnawing fear – that their food wasn't safe. She was supposed to be resting on the sofa. Her feet lay, comfortingly, in Sean's lap as he read, and her eyes were closed but her mind revolved through possibilities. Although it seemed, in cool reflection, that the men from this morning were more interested in conning their way in than breaking their way in, she kept coming back to the thought that if they abandoned the house, the food was lost. She opened her eyes. Sean was watching her instead of reading.

'You should be sleeping.'

'I was.'

He gave her a skeptical look.

'We have to do something. Maybe a more secure house . . .'

'You want to break into someone's house and squat? Seriously?'

She got up and walked to the pantry, as if staring at it could somehow solve the problem. As she stood there, hugging herself tight, Zac passed on his way from the kitchen. He faltered in his path when he saw his silent sentinel mother, then kept going. Hannah felt as if she couldn't leave, as if the very act of not staring at the pantry would put them in danger. Her trance was broken only when Zac dropped a motley heap of wooden planks at her feet.

Sean and Zac's quiet industriousness was amplified by the din of the cordless drill and the clatter of the hammer. She wouldn't let herself question whether their fortifications would be of any use. It was all they had. And when they were finished, the edges of the pantry doors were haphazardly reinforced with an assortment of planks. At the middle edges, Sean had drilled large holes through both the reinforcing and the doors underneath, threaded through the D-lock from Zac's bike, and locked it with a click.

'You are the official keeper of the key. Keys. I also put a padlock on the side gate. And we are officially out of locks.' Sean handed them to her. 'No one's getting to our food without smashing the doors.'

She wanted to say, *And what if they smash the doors?*

'I know, I know, the front window is a problem, but I can't magic up longer planks without dismantling the fence.' He put his arm around her and gave her a squeeze. 'I will, if you want me to.' She shook her head. 'Next time we can upend the bed.' He looked her in the eyes. 'Not worth a smile?'

'Go on, Mum, try it.' Zac gestured at the pantry, not looking as happy as he should.

She tried to slide the key in, but the angle was awkward. 'I can't see the slot. Could you turn the light on for me?'

Sean flicked the switch. Nothing happened. 'Damn. Do we have a spare bulb?'

'Inside the locked pantry.' Hannah tried to tilt her head upside down and sideways to get a better look, but was hit by a tired dizziness.

'I'll get you the torch.'

She heard him click the living room switch on his way through, but no light came on. As she stepped into the kitchen, the fridge was forebodingly silent. Ella and Oscar looked up from the jigsaw on the kitchen table. The pieces were too small for Ella's fingers, but she was happy perched on a chair, her legs swinging, as long as Oscar was nearby. Hannah pulled open the fridge door – no light there either.

'It'll be a fuse.' As if she was reassuring the two little ones. They went back to the jigsaw, unalarmed.

Hannah walked back through the house, flicking switches. By the time she reached the front door, she couldn't pretend it was just a fuse.

Sean hesitated. 'We should go around the side. The torch is going to stand out like a sore thumb in the street.'

In the tunnel of the side passage, Sean unlocked the padlock, pulled back the bolt, and tugged at the gate, which groaned and protested, swelled by the rain. He wrenched it far enough to squeeze through. Hannah watched the street warily. There was no light from any of the houses – even the streetlamps were out. Only the last rays of twilight illuminated the scene. On the other side of the fence, Stuart and Natalie's house was as dark as theirs. No light showed through the closed curtains.

Sean glanced at the street and then back into the fuse box. 'I think we can be fairly confident it's not a fuse.' As if this hadn't all been for show.

It needed both of them pushing with their shoulders against the gate to get the bolt home. With each heave, she expected to feel someone on the other side, pushing back. She didn't feel secure until the padlock was on again.

Sean marched back up the passage and she was forced to talk to his receding back. 'The food in the freezer will spoil.' Sean didn't reply. 'But if we keep the door closed, it should stay cold for a day or two.' He was still silent. 'So, maybe we should start with anything left in the fridge. And we should turn our phones off too, save the batteries.'

He reached the corner before he relented. 'Yeah, all that.'

'But, and?'

'Wouldn't solar panels be handy right now?' She wasn't going to answer, however much he made it sound like a passing thought. 'Like the water tank. Didn't that turn out to be useful?'

'I never said we shouldn't have a water tank.'

'But you had to be persuaded.'

'It's too big. It's still too big. I look out the back every day and it's too big.'

'Yet it's keeping us safe. And we could have had solar panels, enough to run the freezer, charge the phones.'

'How were you going to pay for it? We didn't have the

money. Do you remember how much it all cost? We spent every cent we had on living, remember? And even if we had, it was never going to be enough to run the whole house.'

'The freezer and the phones.'

'We don't have them, we don't have them, we don't have them!'

He looked at her the way he looked at Oscar when there was no talking to him.

'It's my fault, I'll admit to that. It was my fault for being sick and using up all our resources. It's my fault that we didn't hold off the renovation until we could afford it all. My fault. I was the one in a hurry, I was the one who soaked up all our savings.' Her confession was an accusation.

Hidden by the dark, Zac and Oscar were staring out the kitchen window. Zac with concern, Oscar with wonder.

'Get off the counter, Oscar,' Sean roared through the glass, and Oscar almost fell backwards.

Hannah pushed past Sean and ran to the kitchen. Ella stood in the middle of the room, looking lost. Oscar was hunched over the jigsaw, staring at a piece in his hand. Zac looked at her defiantly.

'Get your phone.'

'What! Why?'

'Just get it. I'll need yours too, Sean.' She didn't look at him or alter her dealing-with-a-recalcitrant-teenager voice.

The phone screens cast a small sphere of light. She checked the battery icons – hers had the most charge. The other two were less than half. She redirected Sean's and Zac's to hers and turned them all off. 'We'll check my phone twice a day.'

'And what happens when you run out of charge and we're all still redirected?' Zac wasn't really asking – he was trying to prove her wrong.

'Then we swap the SIMs.'

'But it's my phone. I can use it how I like.'

'It's not your phone, Zac.' Sean broke in, an uneasy ally. 'It never was your phone. And there won't be any calls. You can send one text each time we turn it on.'

'That's bullshit.'

'Live with it. What do you think happened before email? People sent letters. It could take days.'

'Yeah, I forgot you lived with the dinosaurs.'

'Watch it, Zac.' Sean glowered at him and then spread his glower around the room. The whole scene appeared to wash over Ella, still lost in the shadow. Hannah noticed Oscar wiping at his eyes. She put her arm around his shoulder.

Zac spat contempt at her. 'He's not a little kid, Mum.'

'That's just what he is.'

'Well, he should grow up. When I was his age—'

'When you were his age,' Sean snapped, 'you were an only child who didn't have to worry about anything yet. He's lucky because he has an older brother to help him.

308

That's how life is, the luck of the draw. You want us to make sure that every bad thing that happened to you happens to him?'

Hannah was pinned against the hallway wall by the mattress.

'Bend it a bit.' Sean pushed the other end, still wedged in Zac's room.

'Back up and come at a shallower angle.' The top sheet was hanging down, only loosely held by the edge draped over the top, and each time she blindly stepped, it caught her feet. Sean repositioned and she pulled herself and the mattress along the wall. Her face pressed into the bed-clothes, redolent of teenage boy, a little overpowering but almost warm and comforting. Even if they had electricity, she wouldn't have washed them. It was hard to imagine that Ella could care enough to make it worth wasting that much drinking water.

They manhandled the mattress around the corner, across the living room. She listed side to side as she walked backwards, hugging it to her, keeping it up by the friction of her arms. Every time she stumbled, Sean piled head-first into his end.

They flipped it down on Oscar's floor. Oscar and Ella watched entranced from the edge of Oscar's bed.

'Okay, you two' – Sean rubbed his hands together – 'there's some water in the bucket in the bathroom. Give yourself a rub over where you're grotty.'

Hannah followed to jostle them along, wetting

flannels and scrubbing when they lost impetus. Oscar grumbled about how cold the water was, how dark the room was. Ella followed the instructions impassively. As she herded them past Zac's room, she noticed a faint glow leaking under the door.

Although it was still early, the twilight was deep enough that Oscar's room was dark and she could barely see Oscar and Ella snuggled down into their beds.

She fell into the sofa next to Sean. 'What happened to monkey boy?'

'He wanted to be alone.'

Hannah yawned and squinted at Sean. 'Would you mind if we passed up the opportunity to sit here in the dark and went to sleep instead?'

Hannah started to make her way up the hall. Behind her, she could hear Sean at Zac's door. 'Don't stay up too late.'

''Kay.'

'When the battery in your torch runs out, I'm not giving you a new one.'

''Kay.'

The bed received her into its soft protection. Sean climbed into the empty space next to her. The street was quiet – all was right again. His outstretched arm closed around her. She shut her eyes, felt herself fall into sleep and wake as she fell. His side was warm and she snuggled her back against him, cradling his hand in hers. His arm reflexively pulled her in. She lay for a few minutes before again falling and jolting awake. She fell and woke, fell and woke, fell and slept.

And woke, a sound she couldn't place forcing itself through her dreaming mind. Oscar at the door, half asleep and grumpy.

'Why aren't you asleep?'

'Ella woke me up' – he sounded peeved – 'she's crying.'

She rolled over to Sean, choosing to assume he was already awake. 'Do you want me to go?' She willed him to say no.

'She's used to me, I'll go.'

Seemingly moments later, without any consciousness of having fallen back to sleep, she was woken by the door and Sean's voice, whispering loud. 'Ella's a bit scared, so I said she could come into our bed.'

'Really? Oscar's there with her.'

'She promised to sleep in Oscar's room tomorrow, because she's a big brave girl, didn't you?'

'Yes.' Ella's voice was small.

Hannah shifted over to make room for her, as she once had for Oscar and, before him, Zac. Ella's tiny body took up almost no room, but her presence drove Hannah to the edge of the bed. The way Ella seemed so at home made Hannah feel like the intruder.

She could tell Sean was still awake by his attempts not to disturb her, but attempting not to disturb her did. Her body had had a quantum of sleep. Her mind jumped between analyzing the day and conjuring problems that might never happen, problems she couldn't solve in the middle of the night. However hard she distracted herself, her brain insistently brought her back. She finally fell asleep working out a complicated plan for barricading the front windows and the side passage with recycled tin cans.

Mon	Tue	Wed	Thu	Fri	Sat	Sun

Sean waved around a small square of newspaper. 'I said one, not two, not three, not a whole handful.'

From where Hannah sat at the kitchen table, pretending she wasn't listening, she could see the kids lined up in front of Sean, a silent audience. Oscar's eyes roamed anywhere but the Kabuki mask of anger on Sean's face. Zac lounged against the door frame looking shifty, planning a quick getaway. Ella stood her ground, gazing up, wonderstruck, at the display of emotional fireworks.

'This is the third time in two days that I've had to unblock the toilet. And waste more water. It's disgusting. One square of paper. If you do what you're told, I won't have to unblock it. If you don't do what you're told, I'll make *you* unblock it.'

Zac nodded his head and shifted his weight from one foot to the other, easing himself through the door.

'Hang on a tick there.'

Zac paused like a button had been pressed on a remote.

'We now have at most a week's worth of newspaper

left. Do you want to tell me how you are going to wipe your bum then?'

Oscar shook his head the tiniest amount. Ella stared openmouthed. Zac pretended he was somewhere else.

'You're not. That's how. Because there is no more toilet paper and no more newspaper. When it's gone, that's it.' Silence. 'Are you listening to me?'

Oscar and Zac murmured an indistinct chorus.

'And do I have to demonstrate to you, Zac, how to flush again? Half a bucket, just half a bucket, poured into the bowl. From a height. Dribble it in and you're just wasting water. Not you.' Sean pointed at the two little ones. 'You ask me or Mum. But only if it needs it. Yellow water in the bowl doesn't kill you. But if we run out of water in the tank, you're going to be drinking it.'

Zac scowled and muttered something Hannah couldn't make out.

'Oh, really? Stupid? The next time any of you goes to the loo, I'm coming in to check on you.'

A look of outraged horror covered Zac's face. Oscar looked down, embarrassed, but Ella was still mesmerized.

'Go away, just go away. I don't want to see any of you again today.'

Zac and Oscar scattered. Ella stared at Sean's back as he marched to the kitchen.

'Unbelievable. Un-be-bloody-lievable.' He fell into one of the kitchen chairs. Hannah kept her eyes on her book. She was not going to get involved.

'They can't follow a simple instruction. What if their lives depended on it?' Sean fiddled with the cutlery still on the table from breakfast. 'Which they do. It's basic hygiene. Remember when we used to get the paper every day? We would have been okay for months. You can't wipe your bum with an iPad.'

'Next time I'll remember to stock up on tabloids.' And an unwelcome thought parked itself at the edge of her mind – that she was taking for granted the future presence of tabloids and iPads.

She was going to let the kids stew on it – because Sean had a point about the toilet paper. But there was one thing she could do for Zac. 'You are not going to go into the bathroom with them.'

'Yes.'

'You can't.'

'Watch me.'

'Zac will burst before he goes to the loo.'

'What would you have me do? Because something has to be done.'

Even though she knew Sean wasn't prepared to listen, she was going to try anyway. 'It's coffee withdrawal. You think you're hiding it, but I know you have a headache. Take something for it.'

'I'm not going to waste a painkiller.'

'Then have a cup of tea.'

'I don't like tea. I don't need tea. I need them' – his hand took in the front of the house and the silent, absent children – 'to take some responsibility.'

'Have a Panadol for my sake and the kids'. Or stay away from everyone until you're bearable.' Sean's face was set but she continued. 'Unless, of course, you want a headache.'

'What I want is to walk to the café at the corner, even though they don't know the difference between a café latte and a cappuccino. I want to sit on the footpath, watch people going by, have a chocolate chip cookie with my coffee, and not share it with Oscar.'

She had sneaked a look at her phone in the privacy of the bedroom this morning, just to find out. Caffeine withdrawal lasted three days. As she watched, waited for the search to return, she thought she saw the level on the battery icon drop. Right now, the electrons in those batteries were the most precious things in the house. Although she was the one who had made a big deal about only using the phone for life and death, it was a crisis of sorts, and there was no one she could ask in a nonelectronic way. Natalie would know if she ever answered her phone. Hannah tried again this morning, even though she knew it was futile. She wanted to be able to tell Ella that Mummy was still busy but she'd be home. More electrons gone.

The words on the page, the ones she wasn't really reading, started to move around. She tried to focus on an individual letter. It shook like a miniature earthquake. She felt the shake propagating from the table through her elbow. Sean uncrossed and recrossed his knees, jiggling the other one. The table took on a deeper tremor.

'Could you stop doing that?'

He stood up, stretched. Hannah looked at him expectantly, hoping he would go somewhere else. He sat down again. She put her finger on the word she was reading and waited for the spasm to pass.

He stood decisively. 'I'm going to get some coffee.'

'We're out of coffee.' Which was obvious – they had searched the cupboards, the pantry, the fridge, the freezer, and the boxes in the garage.

'I'll get some from Lily's.'

Inexorably she took her part in this irrational conversation. 'Lily's is shut, and if they weren't, she'd be out of coffee by now.'

Sean looked at her as if she had failed to grasp the magnitude of what was going on. As if she wasn't aware of exactly how many packets of rice and pasta were in the pantry and exactly how many meals were between them and having to step out into an uncertain fate. As if she didn't know how germs were spread. 'She won't be there. There won't be anyone there.'

'So how will you get coffee?'

'I'll break the lock.' He was matter-of-fact.

'You can't loot Lily's!'

'It's not looting, it's borrowing. If I leave money, then I'm buying the stuff, just without Lily. For the lock too. Why do you think we have the cash?' He had worked it through in his mind.

It seemed incomprehensible that she was mustering reasons for not looting the corner store. 'We have to shop there. If you loot Lily's I have to walk an extra three blocks for milk. Forever. I'm not walking three blocks uphill for milk for the rest of my life because you can't wait one more day for your headache to go away.' She had his attention – he might succumb to rational argument. 'And how will you lock it up after? If you break her lock, other people will take stuff and they might not leave money.'

He took the objection on board, mulled it over.

'Anyway, there's probably nothing left. She's been cleaned out by now.' The intruding thought forced its way back in – her argument rested on the assumption that Lily's would reopen, that Manba would disappear and they would all pick up exactly where they left off. But what if they couldn't?

'Then it won't hurt for me to look.'

'No.' She flung herself dramatically over the hall doorway. He ran in the other direction – there was no chance she could beat him to the back door. He had a hold of the back door handle. She slipped her hand underneath just in time to push it up before it unlatched.

'I'm going. You might as well let me out.' He squeezed her hand hard. The metal dug into her palm, but she held fast. She grabbed his little finger and pulled back on it. He let go suddenly and sprinted to the hallway door, flinging it open. 'Ha!'

She felt a chill at the thought that they had been playing with ideas. 'You can't think that's a reasonable trade-off – fatal illness for coffee. And even if you find some, bigger, meaner people than you like coffee too.'

He strode through the living room. The three kids looked up for a moment, then went back to the city they were constructing out of blocks.

'I won't touch anyone. I won't let anyone breathe on me. I'll take gloves and a mask. And even then, I'll run away from anyone I see, especially the mean ones.'

He had almost reached the front door.

'You go out, you're not coming back. Someone has to think of the kids.' She grabbed his sleeve with one hand and with the other pried the keys out of his grip.

But the door was already unlocked and he swung it open with his free hand. 'I'll bring you back toilet paper.' He kissed her, like he was going to work. 'And maybe some chocolate.'

His impish smile hung in the air as the door swung closed behind him. It wasn't funny and it wasn't a game. He was gone.

It was at most a five-minute walk to Lily's and back. She ran through the house in her mind, cataloging every surface that could possibly hold a clock. Her phone was off and she couldn't justify turning it on simply to know the time. What else? What else? The microwave, the computers, the VCR, the alarm clocks all needed power. Her mother's watch. She scrabbled through the bowl of jewelry on her bedside table. It was stopped, run-down years ago and never wound. She turned the crown and nothing happened. Not a single mechanical clock in the whole house. The front door shut out the normal measures of time. Days, weeks, hours, minutes, were meaningless. Only numbers of meals meant anything.

One clock – there was one clock. An old-fashioned alarm clock with hands that Sean bought for Oscar, the kind of caricature that Oscar recognized only from the icon on their phones. She snatched it from his windowsill. It was a chimera, a fraud. Battery powered, not mechanical at all, but it was ticking. Five to, although she had no way of knowing how long he had been gone already.

Too long. Too long. That was the only yardstick she had. She leaned against the inside of the front door, turned her back to it, and slid down to the floor, placing the clock beside her. It transmitted a tiny vibration across through the boards with every second.

And each second that ticked by was another too many. She needed Sean, she needed him beside her, for all their sakes. Without him . . . there was no without him. It was a future she couldn't conceive. If she just opened the door, looked outside, up the road, by now she must be able to see him coming back. And where was the risk in that?

Sean's keys lay in a pile on the floorboards where she had dropped them. She picked them up and flung them back down the hall. The few steps from the door to the keys would give her time, even if only a little, to find sanity if she couldn't resist the urge to escape out the front. A chance to remember that her duty was to Zac and Oscar.

'Is everything all right, Mum?' Zac appeared in the doorway at the other end of the hall.

'Sure. Fine. Nothing to worry about.' Although she could barely get the words out.

He shrugged and closed the door as he went back to Oscar and Ella. Hannah stared at the clock. Five past. He would be knocking any moment. The second hand bounced as it moved forward, a jaunty flourish. Each bounce marked off more risk that she had no say in – to him, to the kids, to all their preparations. Each one brought to mind some catastrophe that she wasn't out there to prevent. Through the door she felt the throaty vibrations of a car roaring up the street, too fast. It meant nothing to her but bad news, potentially the return of Sunday's thugs. In the street, Sean would be an easy target for them or for someone even less scrupulous.

She took a deep breath. There was no earthly benefit to them in mugging Sean. The cash in his pockets was worth nothing, he didn't have keys on him. She fantasized briefly that they lived in a world where muggers would inquire as to the value of their victim before attacking. Perhaps they would if they balanced the spoils against the chance of infection.

Ten past. She lost herself in the curlicues on the dark hands of the clock, a cartoon imitation of another age. He had been gone nearly fifteen minutes. There should be nothing to distract him, no friendly neighbors to bump into. She could feel the thoughts crowding at the edge of her mind, all the worst things she had read and seen online. Sick people in the streets, turned out of their homes by frightened relatives. Bodies dumped on the curb. Without crossing their threshold, she had no way of knowing if the quiet emptiness ended at the intersection. Beyond sight of the porch there could be a scene imagined in any number of end-of-the-world movies. Maybe the minute he turned the corner, a mask and gloves were not enough. Maybe. Maybe.

He might be lucky – she might be letting her imagination run away with her – but lucky wasn't what got you through. Easy didn't keep danger at bay. A mistake in judgment wasn't an excuse, it was the kind of failure that they couldn't afford. Every disaster in human history started with a bad judgment call.

She turned the clock over, flicked the battery door with the end of her finger. If she pulled the battery out, the ticking would stop. It would no longer tell her he had been gone for twenty minutes. Then how long would she wait, when waiting was all she could do? An hour, two hours? Would she then decide to stop waiting for a knock at the door? When was the moment to leave the safety of the threshold and move back into the house? When to tell Zac and Oscar where he had gone? When to admit to herself that something had gone unthinkably wrong?

If she stayed at the door, the moment was frozen between him leaving and returning. Twenty-five minutes. She breathed with the second hand, a meditation of panic.

The door shook her as someone knocked. She took

two deep breaths and answered as calmly as she could, 'Who is it?'

'Some random person knocking on your front door when you were expecting your husband.' His voice sounded small.

She told herself to hold firm. 'I'll unlock the gate. You can go to the office. Leave whatever you brought on the porch.'

When his voice came back, it was stronger but more hesitant. 'You don't have to quarantine me. I didn't go in – there was nothing left.'

'You're just saying that.'

'Why would I say that? If I had coffee and chocolate and toilet paper, believe me, I'd tell you.'

She scrambled down the hall on her hands and knees to where the keys lay lifeless under a new dent in the plaster. They were like hope in her hands, the temptation of a gamble.

'Hurry up. I can hear another car. Just let me in and you can shut me out again when it's gone.'

She unlocked the door but not the grille, looked him up and down, looked behind him. There was no sign of food. She would have let the food in.

His mask hung loose in his hand. 'I'm virus-free. There wasn't anything left. There wasn't anyone. I don't think they're even collecting the garbage anymore. All the rubbish bins were still out. And that's all there was, garbage. Someone did a job on Lily's a while ago.'

She was still standing back from the grille. 'It doesn't take that long to walk to Lily's.'

'I needed to breathe, so I went around the block.' He shrugged and held his gloved hands out, a sheepish confession. 'All I got was air – uncontaminated, unshared air.'

'What the hell? What the absolute hell? You went for a walk?'

'I talked myself into a state, okay? There was a car and I ran the other way. And then there was this pile of garbage on the footpath. It had a smell so strong I could almost see it. Food scraps and tin cans and I thought I saw some old clothes and a pair of shoes. I swear that was all it was, some old clothes and shoes, but I freaked myself out. And then one of the shoes moved. I think it was a rat – I'm not sure that's much better. I just had to clear my head. I didn't touch a thing. Please just open the grille.'

'You want me to open the grille and let in a big fat idiot.' All the worry, all the steeling herself for the worst, all this he had chosen to put her through. 'I told you not to, I asked you not to. But you didn't think, you didn't think about anybody or anything.' Her righteous rage for Lily's, for letting Ella into their house, for all the times he had put her plans at risk, carried her away. 'And what was I supposed to say to Oscar and Zac if you didn't come back? That their dad's a moron? That he didn't have the common decent sense to keep himself alive?

'Tell me, when did you decide that the rest of us were happy to risk death so you could go for a stroll? Seven and a half thousand people died yesterday. In driving distance of this house. And you think you're bloody Superman.'

An obstinacy settled on his face. 'A number doesn't change what is happening in this street now.'

'Then what does? What on the face of the earth would it take for you to know exactly what is outside our door? Because going out and looking is the most shortsighted, dumbest answer to that question.' She unlocked the grille and stomped into the bedroom, threw herself down on the bed, the tension in her body spent. Having each other for protection was a relief, but if she was thinking with her head and not her instincts, he'd be in the garage.

'I'm sorry I wanted to loot Lily's.'

'That means nothing. You didn't because you couldn't.'

'Yeah.' He sat down next to her on the crumpled bed-clothes. 'We're still going to need more food. How many more weeks can we survive on nothing but beans and rice?'

'Beans and rice will keep you alive. Why is this not clear to you? This isn't the time to go out shopping. That time is over – I did that when it was safe. This is the time when you stay inside and shut up about the beans and rice.' It was his fault that she had lost her resolve, his fault that she couldn't face being without him. 'And don't talk to me. I don't even know why I let you back in. Don't talk to me, don't look at me. Just go away.'

Mon	Tue	Wed	Thu	Fri	Sat	Sun

'I don't have a present.'

Two more steps and Hannah would have made it through the kitchen and to the back door. She held the phone in front of her leg and cheated it behind her as she turned around, trying to keep it out of both Zac's and Oscar's eye line. 'That's the way it goes, Oscar.'

'But you have presents on birthdays.'

Ella looked up at the sound of the word.

'We could make a cake, Oz.' Zac really was trying to be helpful. Hannah caught Zac's eye with a warning look, because she didn't need that kind of help, and used the moment she held his gaze to slip the phone into the pocket of her jeans.

'A cake?' Oscar's face lit up.

'I don't know.' She glanced at the ceiling as if help might descend. 'The stove doesn't work and we don't have any flour.' A dark cloud was moving onto Oscar's face. 'You have to understand, Mouse.' She looked to Zac to help undo what he had done. 'We would make a cake and have presents, but we can't.'

'Then it's not a birthday. It's just a day.' Oscar twisted back to the kitchen table.

'Mum, there must be something in the pantry we could make into a cake.'

'I'm not hiding packet mix and a generator behind the beans.' Now Zac stared at her. 'Daddy won't mind. He understands.' Their silence communicated how much she had let them down. 'You could make him something for a present.' Zac rolled his eyes. 'You could try.'

'And you could try to find something in the pantry.'

Oscar turned around looking disappointed and angry. 'We have to have presents and a cake and a special dinner. Not beans and rice.'

She sighed and felt a headache coming on. 'You've got a shelf full of craft books and materials. If you make something, I promise I will try to find some way of making dinner different tonight. Agreed?'

She looked across at Sean in the office, saw him pointedly not looking in their direction. Since the power went off, its only purpose was as a refuge for the two of them. The children still respected its status as a workspace even now that there was no work to be done. She waited until they were all reabsorbed into their coloring books or reading and, with her hand in her pocket covering the bulging phone, nonchalantly strolled across the yard to the office.

She closed the door behind her without looking back. 'Are they watching?'

'Zac keeps looking over.'

The phone bit into her hip as she sat down. The denim folded tight across the top, sealing it in. 'We weren't at all planning your birthday, but if we were, try to be surprised and delighted. It means a lot to Oscar.' She slowly and awkwardly turned her head to look through the window to the glass kitchen door. 'I can't see him.'

'His head is down – it's safe. Give me the phone.'

'I don't think so, looty boy. I'm still mad at you.'

She stood up to free the phone, held the on button, and put it on the table next to Sean. He sneaked his hand into hers, watching the start-up screen, impatient with its stylish and colorful animation. Finally the home screen came up. The battery had only a sliver of orange at the bottom. They stared at the signal strength icon, waiting for connection. There it was, five bars. The screen flashed bright, went to black blazoned with 'No battery remains' in white, and shut off, all in a few seconds. Hannah felt a little sick. Sean squeezed her hand.

'I'll get my phone.'

She sat anxious, waiting, playing with the dead phone. She levered off the back, reseated the battery. There was a possibility, a very remote one, that it had worked itself loose. She stared at the blank screen, wondering if Sean's battery might have run down even while it was turned off, wondering just how many days of connection they had left. Once his phone died, they were down to Zac's, and all it could do was text. She heard Sean's voice from the house, booming and overly reassuring. That had to raise Zac's curiosity, but Sean came out alone, hand on phone in pocket. She pulled the battery out of her phone again to get at the SIM.

The glass door and large window of the office didn't give them much privacy from the house as Sean took apart his phone and slipped in Hannah's SIM. He turned it on, cupped in his hands. She realized she was holding her breath, twitching with impatience.

Less than half the battery icon. 'You've been using it.'

'Come on – I was an idiot the other day, but I'm not an idiot. It was run-down before I turned it off but I can't remember exactly how much.'

Five bars of signal. 'Check the government site first.'

He was staring at the phone.

'What's taking so long?' The sun reflected off the screen, making it dark and unreadable from her angle.

Sean still stared, transfixed. 'It's connected.'

'What does it say? Has something happened?'

'Twenty . . .' He looked away and squinted, then back down at the phone, as if trying to focus his eyes.

'What is it?'

'Fourteen thousand and twenty thousand.'

'Twenty thousand new cases?'

'No, that's the number dead.'

'The number for the whole country, not just Sydney. That can't just be in Sydney.'

'That's what it says – twenty thousand people died in

Sydney yesterday. And there were fourteen thousand new cases.'

'They've made a mistake, switched the figures. There were only ten thousand dead the day before. It can't double in a day. That can't be possible. Surely. And more people can't have died than the number who are sick – that makes no sense. It has to be the other way. There have to be more new cases than people dead.'

'And that makes it better? If it were fourteen thousand dead people that would be acceptable to you?'

'Check ... check somewhere else, the paper or somewhere.'

'I'm wasting battery. Knowing a number doesn't matter.' Her voice was high and strained. 'Just check.'

He typed with his thumbs, paused for a minute.

She held out her hand. 'Let me see.'

'It's still loading.' He handed her the phone. The page filled in, ten by five centimeters of information, a banner, headlines. The text jumped around as the ads loaded but it was there, twenty thousand dead in one day.

'What are you doing?' Zac stood in the doorway. It was a glass door, for heaven's sake. How did they not see him coming? 'You said we could only turn on the phone once a day.'

'Look, mate . . .'

'Dad, that's what you said. You don't let me talk to my friends but you do whatever you want.'

'There are things that it's better we do without you, some things you don't need to see.'

'What am I, Oscar? I want to use the phone.'

'Zac.'

'Give me a turn.'

Zac lunged at the phone. It shot out of Sean's hand and, in slow motion, gracefully arced across the room. Zac leaped to catch it, grazed it with his fingertips, turning its arc into a chaotic tumble, head over tail, smack into the window. It ricocheted to the floor and skidded under the couch. Zac dived underneath and backed out slowly, cradling it in his hands like an injured bird. He was ashen, his hands trembled.

'It's still working.' Zac looked shocked and relieved. He handed it gingerly to Sean. 'I'm sorry.'

'You broke it, Zac.'

'The color's a bit different, but you can read it.'

'Do you think I can't see, Zac? I'm looking straight at the screen. It's smashed.'

There was a blue tinge over the right-hand side and a crack running across one corner, but the headline 'Twenty Thousand Dead in One Day' was still crystal clear. The blue leached across the screen, with a wave of green following behind it. As waves of colors slowly flowed across, the black text began to merge into them. Hannah almost willed the terrible words to be unreadable.

'I didn't mean to. It was an accident.' He looked from Sean to Hannah and back. The screen was now nothing but the psychedelic rainbow refraction of an oil slick. 'You can put the battery in Mum's phone.'

'They're not the same. It's done.'

Hannah could see Sean physically swallow his anger.

'I just wanted to look at the phone. I'm not a kid.'

'If you're not a kid, for fuck's sake take responsibility for what you did. You broke the phone, Zac. It didn't jump out of my hand.' Sean was holding the darkening screen up in accusation. Zac looked to her to take his side.

'Bring me your phone, Zac.' She was as calm as she could make herself.

'Oh, what? But . . .'

'Now. No buts. And you don't get to touch it again.'

Zac held still, the resentment and sense of injustice written clearly on his face.

'We have one battery left and no Internet. We can text, that's all. Bring me your phone now.'

Zac pushed past her and out the door.

The house was quiet when Hannah walked through. It wasn't until she got to Oscar's room that she heard the murmur of voices. She let her hand rest on the door, enjoying their independence, then pushed.

'Stay out, stay out!' Oscar was pushing back with all his strength.

'It's me, not Dad.' Oscar let go and the door flung wide. All of Oscar's pencils and markers were spread about the floor. Zac stood over the two younger ones, supervising. Ella had a loose page of a coloring book in front of her, the outline of a princess half scribbled in with purple and red. 'See, this is me.' She pointed to the spiky lines haphazardly crossing the black borders.

Oscar pushed himself in front, impatient for her to finish. 'I'm writing a story for Daddy. It's about when we can go out. Zac writes the words and I draw the pictures.' He held out a large sheet of paper folded in half, on each face a small drawing. 'And Zac made Daddy a notebook, but he didn't write anything in it.' From his frown, she could tell Oscar didn't think that was much of a present.

'Where did you get the paper from?'

The two smaller kids looked to Zac, who dropped his eyes and shifted uncomfortably. 'Some of Oscar's coloring books have an extra page at the back.' He swallowed his words so she nearly couldn't make out the next sentence. 'I tore them out.'

He was trying so hard to meet all their expectations. He'd come up with ideas, organized the younger ones, but still he expected to be yelled at.

'Good job, good thinking. You'll make Sean's day.' Zac didn't need her here. The best encouragement she could give him was to leave them alone.

The only room she hadn't looked in was their bedroom. She found Sean leaning against the window frame, one hand holding back the curtains, the other a resting place for his forehead against the glass.

'Hey, happy birthday.'

Sean replied with a weak smile but didn't look away from the window.

'What are you looking at?'

'Nothing – the street, houses.' He stared out as if he

333

could see beyond the nothing, beyond the street, through the houses. 'Another patrol came around. You must have heard them.'

'I heard a truck.'

Sean nodded. 'They didn't have a PA this time. Most of the time you can't even tell if they're men or women. They were all masks and hazmat suits, army caps and boots. And I can't shake the feeling that they're young.' He rubbed at his weary eyes. 'Who else are you going to send out? Young soldiers who have to do what they're told. One of them came onto the porch. She had more of those leaflets. She put one on the wall where I could see it, but it blew onto the porch just after she left. I've been trying to read it but I can't get the right angle. All I can see is phone numbers, much good they would do us, and some sort of map. Why do they keep sending them out?' He turned to look at her, his eyes sad. 'They don't bring anything we can use. They don't have any new information. They're out there, at risk, for what? How many of them get sick?'

'They keep the looters away.'

Sean looked out the window again. 'She asked about Gwen and Stuart. I told her Stuart was gone and we were helping Gwen. I told her we don't need leaflets, we can't drink leaflets, we can't eat leaflets. She said all the things we need are at the shelter, and they don't have the resources to bring them to us. She said it would be safe. She's the one walking the streets, I guess. She said' – he paused – 'she suggested that Gwen should be in the shelter. That she would be better off where she could be looked after.'

'It would make our food last longer. And we wouldn't have to leave the house to deliver her meals.'

'You think we should? We can call and they'll send someone for her. And Mr Henderson, if he's still there. Is that the right thing to do?'

'I don't know.'

'And what if it kills her? What if we make the call and they take her to the shelter and she catches it? Is that our fault?'

'I don't know.' She moved over to the window and threaded her arms around him. 'Not today. Nothing bad happens today.' She gave him a soft kiss. 'Happy birthday.'

Six o'clock and the light was gone. Oscar's face glowed expectantly with reflected candlelight. Hannah found his excitement infectious. A little bundle of presents sat on the table, tied with green garden string, its flat plastic strands picking up the flickering light.

'What have we here?' Sean was a bad pantomime act. 'Could these possibly be for me?'

'They're presents, Dad.' Oscar looked concerned at having to enlighten his father.

'Tell me, tell me, which one should I open first?'

'Mine!' Ella held it out to him. 'It's a picture of me, I colored it.'

'Thank you, sweetie, that's great.' Sean unwrapped

and examined it carefully. 'So you're a princess and a fairy.' He looked her up and down. 'Just so.'

Oscar had taken a hold of his, rolled up in a checked tea towel. He tentatively held it out. 'I couldn't get you a real present.'

'This will be better.' Sean unfurled it. He had to hold it close to the candle to make out anything. 'I think I need my reading glasses. Maybe you could read it to me after dinner.' Oscar nodded. 'And, Zac, my firstborn, what have you brought me?'

'That one.' Zac poked at a pocket-sized present, folded inside a geometric napkin. Sean pulled the string off one end and the cloth unwrapped itself. The booklet was surprisingly well executed. Zac had taken the covers off a broken *Boys' Own* hardback and glued them on either side.

'My God, paper, something to write on. I am blessed.' Zac looked quizzically at him. 'It's great. I'm very impressed.' He took the last present from Hannah. 'So what did you make me?'

'I'm afraid I bought you something. I've had it for a while. If I'd known, I would have got you a tin of coffee or a solar battery. It seems frivolous now.'

The perfectly shop-wrapped present looked unreal, somehow ostentatious and foppish. She wished its execution was more rustic, more substantial. Inside, a clear plastic clamshell surrounded a pair of headphones that looked like they had rolled off a robotic production line without ever having interacted with anything organic.

'They're noise canceling, for the bus to work, so you can be in your own world.'

He squeezed her arm. 'I look forward to using them. I look forward to the time when I can use them.'

'Soon.'

'Yes, soon.'

'Now' – he rubbed his hands together in exaggerated anticipation – 'what's for birthday dinner?'

Oscar could no longer hold it in. 'Mum made spaghetti Bolognese.'

'We have spaghetti? We have Bolognese?'

'Well' – Hannah carried a bowl over to the table – 'the request I got from everyone was not beans and rice. So . . .' She whipped the tea towel off the top of the bowl. 'Ta-daa!'

Sean stared bemused at the mound of food, then broke into a deep belly laugh. A thick red sauce smothered the top of a large pile of popcorn.

'Don't make fun of me.'

Tears were streaming down his face as he pointed to the food. 'Is that mince?'

'It might not be mince.'

'Mum.' Oscar looked at her, outraged. 'Is that beans?'

'If one couldn't get mince, one would most certainly not mush up beans and pretend they were mince. It's popcorn Bolognese, a special birthday treat. For Sean. Happy birthday.'

After the pile of food was ladled out and, however incongruous the flavors were, eaten and enjoyed, after the leftovers were fought over among the kids, after a tub delivered to Gwen, after the last glass of wine they had left was split between the two of them, Zac cleared away the plates and Oscar hovered next to him, shadowing him from the table to the sink. Sean pulled Hannah into a bear hug and they kissed in the corner, just outside the circle cast by the candle.

'Gross,' Zac muttered loudly.

'You're a legend.' Only Sean's smile caught the flickering light, a Cheshire cat. 'Best birthday ever.'

Oscar was hopping up and down next to them. He looked at Hannah, waiting for her sign, but he couldn't hold it in anymore. 'There's a cake, we made a cake. It's chocolate but Mum said we didn't have to use the chocolate for our milk but I said you have to have a chocolate cake.' Ella and Oscar had considered the issue so seriously, she'd been afraid of a hung jury.

'When he says cake ... you know, it's a loose interpretation of a cake.'

Sean looked around. 'Where are you hiding it?'

'In the fridge – it's not like you'd have any reason to look there.'

She brought it out, a small pile of thick, wobbly rice boiled with powdered milk and cocoa. They'd included anything they could find in the cupboards – the last of the dried fruit, the dusting from an empty packet of shredded coconut. The whole thing was covered with silver dragées and star-shaped sprinkles. On top, they had put the stub ends of birthday candles found at the back of one of the kitchen drawers. Even Zac smiled. But the happiness was bought dearly, she knew. The popcorn, the last tin of tomatoes, the rice, and the milk powder. It was more food than they could afford to eat at one meal.

Mon	Tue	Wed	Thu	Fri	Sat	Sun

Half of what had to be said took place sotto voce in a quiet corner, leaving out all the nouns. The other half they held on to until the kids were in bed. They took whatever opportunities they found. One presented itself as the kids played loud rough-and-tumble on the square of backyard lawn. Hannah and Sean stood under the patio roof with their backs to the garden, leaning against the uprights. Soft voices and unseen lips.

'So, now it's not my birthday, what's for dinner?'

'I'll give you half a guess.'

'We can't keep doing this.'

'We have to.'

'I know you want to think that and I know it's true as far as it goes, but we have no idea how much longer this will last.' Sean leaned his head a little closer to hers. 'Just because we have to doesn't mean we can.'

'They've been able to look at the thing for weeks, they have to find a vaccine soon. We only have to hold out until that's available.'

'Which may or may not work. Thousands are dying every day. We can't just assume a vaccine will magically arrive on our timetable. There's no good reason why we get to be the lucky ones.'

Because they had to be, she thought. But he was right, she'd been relying on hope and self-deception. 'And what? You've come up with some clever solution that I haven't thought of?'

She could see him considering how to put it. He might have a solution, but from the look on his face, whatever it was, she wasn't going to like it.

'I think it's time to consider all the resources at our disposal.'

They had made full use of all their dwindling resources. They had nothing else. It slowly dawned on her which resources he was referring to. 'But they're not at our disposal.' She couldn't find the energy to argue over this, not again, not after Lily's. 'A few more days.' She cocked her head in the direction of Stuart's house. 'He might come back.'

'Not even I believe that.' Sean was staring at the ground, considering. But not, she knew, considering her point. 'Someone is going to do it. Every day we wait, it's more likely that it won't be us.'

'It's wrong. You can make any argument you like, but it's just plain wrong. It's not ours.'

'You've got plans and pantries and principles. That stuff is great, but surviving trumps it all. I'm not sure ownership means much right now, and even if it does, we have Ella. It's her house too.' Sean turned back to the kids. 'Zac, can I have you for a moment?' Zac jogged over. Sean dropped his voice again. 'I need you to keep the kids indoors for a while.' He looked at Zac as if weighing up how much he needed to know. 'We have to do something we'd rather Ella doesn't see.'

Zac nodded. 'Hey, Oscar, Ella, want to play a board game?'

'Can I choose? Can we play a game I want?'

'Sure, Oz, whatever.'

'Can we play Snakes and Ladders?' Even Oscar knew it was an ambit claim. Hannah waited for Zac to roll his eyes, but he smiled. 'Sure, of course. Ella goes first, 'cause she's littlest.'

Stuart's house looked empty once they got into the backyard, but so did theirs and so did Gwen's. The only life was a brief glimpse of Mr Moon on Stuart's garage, surveying them contemptuously before disappearing down the back of the roof. She would be able to tell Oscar she had seen him and he was all right. Or maybe it would be kinder not to.

Hannah had brought the kitchen knife with her, just in case. She hoped her bluff wasn't called. Hoped it was a bluff. In her other hand she had a couple of green shopping bags, as if she were popping up the road. She felt a slight shiver of relief that there were no surprises in the garden, though what she had been dreading, she wasn't sure.

Sean's hand rested on the back door handle. It seemed like a long moment before he started to turn the knob.

'Hang on.' Something was making her anxious – this was the last chance she had to circumvent whatever came next. 'We have no way of knowing if it's safe to go in.'

'Ella came over a week ago – five days longer than we need for the virus to be gone.'

'But what if he didn't leave right away?'

'So we have maybe four and a half days' safety margin. Beans and rice. I'm going in.' Sean turned and pushed. The folding doors trembled in the middle. 'How did this get locked?'

'The same way it got closed.'

'I guess we were kidding ourselves that the wind blew it shut.'

Ella couldn't have climbed over the fence by herself. Stuart must have been there when they were ringing. And he had locked up after himself.

Sean pumped the handle. When it didn't irrationally jump open on the fifth try, he stood back and looked flummoxed. 'What do we do now?' He banged on the door hard with his fist. 'Stuart!' He banged again. 'Stuart!'

'Shhh. The kids will hear.' She looked over their fence, but no one moved. And no one moved in the other half of Stuart's semi, either. She searched for sounds of people and found none. The quiet seemed to hint at houses filled with unseen listening ears. 'If there's any chance at all he's still home, we're not going in.'

'He's not home.'

They looked around, like the thieves and trespassers they were, for something hard or long and strong. All they saw was a square of grass like theirs, a featureless brick garage with only a single door and no rainwater tank, and a raised wooden deck attached to the house. Hannah sized up the garden chair, the one Stuart had been sitting in when she last saw him. The metal was too flimsy to do any damage.

Under the covered kettle barbecue on the deck, Hannah found only a gas bottle, a possible backup, although not as big as their own, and a long set of tongs. She pulled out the gas bottle. 'We could use this to break the glass.'

Sean blanched. 'That would make a mess.'

She wedged the tongs between the leaves of the folding door. The tip bent, bruising the wood of the frame without moving it. They were the two most incompetent house-breakers of all time. They didn't even come equipped.

Sean was over the fence as Hannah watched the back of their own house, this time for any sign of the kids. In a second, Sean was back from their garage with a large screwdriver and a hammer. He hammered the screwdriver in between the door and the frame where the tongue of the lock was just visible. Everything about the scene told her they should stop. 'How is this not stealing?'

'It's borrowing. We're looking after Ella.'

'Mask and gloves.' She handed them to him.

The metal screwdriver parted the wood easily. Although they were breaking the peace for several hundred meters, they disturbed no one but themselves. Sean threw his weight against the handle of the screwdriver, and the wood cracked loudly and gave. The lock stayed in place, surrounded by splinters as Sean pushed the door open.

'We'll nail that shut before we go.' He wasn't convincing himself. 'We can nail it from the inside and go out the front door if we can find some keys.'

The door let into a large open-plan dining area with the kitchen wrapped around the far wall. There was a faint, musty, rotting smell. Hannah opened the curtains on the window that faced their kitchen, to the sight of the back of Zac's head. She yanked them closed again.

A door banged and she jumped, ready with an excuse, but it was the latchless back door swinging in the breeze. On the other side of the room, Sean was opening and closing cupboard doors, revealing only plates and glassware. Hannah noticed the neat rows of wineglasses in one. Six red, six white, six cocktail glasses. This was like going through Natalie and Stuart's underwear drawers.

There could be nothing in the fridge that hadn't spoiled by now, but she had a perverse need to be sure. She took a deep breath before she opened the door, expecting to be hit by the source of the rotting smell. The fridge was clean, well organized, and almost empty. Tubs of leftovers, some jars and a couple of well-wrapped blocks of cheese, all carefully arranged. When she finally gasped for breath, she could detect nothing more than the slight scent that already pervaded the room. It was probably imagination, but the air wafted by the fridge door felt a little cooler. She pulled out the vegetable crisper, anticipating a stinky sludge. Inside were two pristine onions and a wilted but intact head of celery – a bounty of fresh vegetables that she could parcel out over a few days.

Sean closed the cupboard with a sharp tap of his finger. 'No space for food.' He was bewildered. 'Where do they keep the food?' Hannah looked around. A narrow door in the corner of the kitchen caught her eye.

'They have a walk-in pantry.' She folded open the door to find a person-sized space filled with shelves of old, shallow boards painted white, floor to ceiling. 'Why don't we have one of these?'

There was only room for one in the pantry, so Sean left her to ransack it while he filled one of the green bags from the fridge.

'Only take things that haven't been opened or don't go off. In jars, not plastic containers,' she called out to him. 'You don't know how long they've been there.' In their fridge, takeaway containers of leftovers often hid in the back and only reemerged weeks or months later. She lived with an anxiety that one day when Zac was browsing for snacks he would indiscriminately hoover up a tub full of contamination. Something, it had turned out, she should have taken a bit more care with herself.

'What about cheese and eggs?' His head was in the fridge, his voice muffled.

'Cheese, we can cut the green bits off. Eggs, we can do the float thing or just break them and make sure they don't smell.'

In the light falling through the pantry door, she could barely see the well-spaced, orderly shapes on the shelves. She felt for a light switch, flicked it out of habit. Nothing changed. As her eyes adjusted, she could make out regular-sized tins on one shelf – a lucky dip of tomatoes and fruit salad. Who knew secondhand groceries could be so exciting? The first one she picked up, she checked the use by date. A month over. That was a risk they would have to take. A sealed, sterilized tin of peaches didn't go from being good on the first to dangerous by the thirtieth. She dumped the rest in the bag without checking, as well as the neat stack of child-sized packets of dried apricots beside them. On the next shelf down, there were jars. Pasta sauce on the left, and in three different flavors! Packets of dried pasta lay parallel. She threw them all into the bag, noticing the exotic names – rosemary and garlic penne, squid ink linguine. On the right were half a dozen jars of jams, all farmers' market flavors with ingredients like ruby grapefruit and Campari. The kids were not going to touch fig and ginger, but she put them all in the green bag. Although they didn't have bread, if push came to shove they could eat jam with a spoon.

She had to bend to look into the next shelf. She smiled to herself, wondering whether it was Natalie or Stuart who decided that the odd-shaped jars and tins that wouldn't stack neatly should be below eye line. A flat tin of octopus, a jar of dukkah, an oval can of pâté. They were calories. They went into the bag.

She got down on her knees to see into the dark at the

back of the bottom shelf. And there it was, a vacuum-sealed kilo packet of coffee beans. She hollered out, 'Gold!' And behind it, a couple of small packets of flour and one of rice.

She waved her hand around the back of the bottom shelf, in case something was hiding. As if a tin could hide itself, as if Natalie or Stuart had considered as they stacked their shelves how best to protect their pantry from theft. But a stolen item required an owner, a loss, and a sense of the conventions of civilized society. Surrounded by someone else's groceries, she could find none of those things. She creaked herself upright to contemplate the top shelf. What, she wondered, could be so misshapen as to be exiled out of sight and reach? She gingerly used the shelves as steps. Holding on by the ends of her toes and the tips of her fingers, she raised her head above the top shelf, almost hitting the bare bulb hanging from the ceiling. She could just see a tin can and a twelve-pack of toilet paper. She let go with one hand to bat the toilet paper closer to the edge of the shelf, grabbing hold again quickly to stop herself from falling. She batted and grabbed three times before she tipped it off the edge. Posh toilet paper, not scratchy brown recycled stuff.

She did the same with the tin, leaving it teetering, then climbed carefully down, jumped and swiped at it, catching it as it fell. She held it in her hand as she came back into the kitchen. 'They don't have a cat.'

'They did, before Ella was born, before Oscar was born, remember?' The can was slightly rusty. She placed it down gently outside the back door, trying not to attract

Mr Moon with the Pavlovian sounds of tinned food, and went back inside for a Bunnykins bowl she had seen in the drying rack.

'We're going to need some stuff from home to fix the door.' Hannah spoke to the back of Sean's head as he stared into the empty house. All she wanted now was to stop feeling like a bad guy. 'We came for food. They'll understand food. Now we have to go.'

Sean took a couple of paces towards the hall before he called out over his shoulder. 'Clothes for Ella. And some toys. They want us to look after her.' He was already through the door.

She scrambled after him. 'Clothes, toys, nothing else. Pajamas – she really needs her own pajamas.'

She ran straight into Sean, who had doubled back. 'Don't come in, don't come any further. You don't need to see.' As he spoke, she realized the subtle smell, the smell she had looked for in the fridge, was still there. She'd become acclimatized to it in the kitchen. Here it was stronger.

She couldn't help herself – she had to look in. Sean caught her with his arm, pushing her backwards. 'Out, wait outside.'

'Why are you going back? If he's in there, you don't need to check.'

'He might not be the only one. And there are still Ella's clothes.'

She opened her mouth to object, offer, remonstrate.

'I've seen him. One of us has to be able to tuck in Ella

tonight without Stuart in our eyes.' Sean gave her a gentle push. 'Out.' In the fight to spare each other, he'd decided to win.

Crap, bugger, shit. Hannah was breathing hard into her mask, the reused air hot and fetid. She knew. She *knew*. She bloody knew, they all knew the risks. Even Stuart, even Sean. Especially Stuart and he had chosen to send Ella to them. She kicked the cat food so hard a searing pain shot through her foot. The can bounced on the deck with a dull thud and hit the barbecue with a metallic clang and clatter, answered with a rumble from the garage roof as she caught a flash of Mr Moon's tail streaking across. Shit again – she didn't need a hungry disease vector of a cat as well. A cat who in the absence of easy meals had undoubtedly returned to his instincts. There were enough rats around these days to keep him fed. Much easier to catch than a bat. But if he found a dead bat, or ate a rat who had eaten . . . She made herself hold still in the exaggerated silence that flooded in behind the noise. Two seconds. The silence shrank to its normal size. Everything she'd done to make them safe, everything jeopardized just by walking into that house. Because of Stuart. He was dead, had been dead for a while, and she had known all along.

She retrieved the tin of cat food from under the barbecue, emptied the contents into the Bunnykins bowl. One more meal from a tin was one less chance of Mr Moon dining on bat.

Sean emerged from the dark of the back door. She looked for some sign he'd heard the racket, but he was shut down, preoccupied. 'Are you okay?'

'I don't know the right way to witness something like that, but it deserves to be witnessed. Maybe it was easier when people wore hats. I could have just taken off my hat as a sign of respect. Maybe it was easier to know what to feel when the right rituals existed. He deserves to be respected.' He looked beyond her, and then his eyes snapped onto her face, as if just now realizing where he was. 'Let's go.'

Hannah went back over the fence first. It was an ungainly exit. She used the crossbars for footholds. Balanced like a seesaw on top, she had to wonder if Stuart had been gone for long enough. Or what she could do if he hadn't. If there was a 'long enough' for a body. If the kids could manage, shut in, alone. She twirled herself half a circle and slowly eased to the ground, falling ungracefully for the last few centimeters. Sean handed two shopping bags over the fence to her.

'What are you doing?' Ella's voice behind her made her jump. 'Did my daddy give you them?'

'Go inside.' Hannah couldn't help but sound cross as she took a step back, pressed herself as close to the fence as she could. 'We got a change of clothes for you, sweetie, that's all. Why aren't you playing with Oscar?'

'Ella!' Zac jogged out of the house. 'Ella, come back inside.' His face was thunderous. 'I told you to stay inside.'

'And we told you to look after them.'

351

Zac's face didn't change. She was going to have to give him a few words on blaming your failings on someone else, but the look on his face wasn't directed at Ella, it was directed at himself. He already knew. Nothing she said could make him feel his error more than he was making himself feel it now.

Sean dropped down beside Hannah, his voice unmuffled, his mask off. 'Go back inside with Zac, Ella. We'll be in soon.'

'I want to go home.'

'No one's home right now. You have to stay with us for a while.'

'I want Daddy.'

Hannah saw Sean flinch. She had to say something, something that wasn't *Daddy's dead*. 'Hey, why don't you go back inside again and see if your mum's phone is answering now.'

'I want Daddy, I want Daddy, I want Daddy.' It went from a demand to a wail, screeched over and over again. She threw herself on her back, chubby legs and arms flailing, her face red and scrunched. The sounds of the words were lost in the incoherent anguish pouring out of her.

Zac stood, stunned by the demonstration in front of him of how such a small failure on his part could lead to so great a consequence. Hannah could see his mind turning over, casting around for a way to make it better, for the words to put it back to where it was three minutes ago. 'Ella!' He spoke with heightened jollity. 'Why don't you come back in with me? We can't finish the game without you. Oscar's waiting. He really wants to play.' Ella couldn't hear a word he said. He shifted from foot to foot, put out a hand towards her, and got caught by an arm flung out. He wedged his hands under his armpits and looked unhappy.

In one movement Sean pulled off his gloves, flung them over the fence, picked up her small body, and pinned it against his, wrapping his arms around her tight. Her limbs could only bat against his trunk. She squirmed and cried, but more from his embrace than her anger and fear. He marched inside, her noise subsiding, and Hannah hoped that meant she was calming, but all she could think was *Too late for a decision. He should have used disinfectant before he touched her.*

Only Zac and Hannah were left in the garden. He looked so forlorn, she would have done anything to make him feel less useless, part of the grown-ups. 'Could you stay out here for a minute? I could use a hand.'

'Sure.'

She found some planks of wood rejected from the pantry reinforcing for being too short, the cordless drill, and some screws in the garage, and clambered back over the fence – harder this time because this side had no cross members and Sean wasn't there to give her a boost – then got Zac to pass the tools over. He was eyeing her gloves and mask warily. She saw his gaze go to Stuart's open back door, gently swaying.

'Ella's dad wasn't there?'

She didn't have an answer ready but hesitation was as

good as telling him. 'No one home.' He was only an adult some of the time. She promised herself she would tell him the truth in a different setting, when it wasn't so immediate. Through the kitchen window, she could see Sean sitting with his arms still wrapped around a now floppy Ella. 'Hey, could you look after Oscar for me? Dad has enough to deal with.'

'Sure, no problem.' He headed inside, if not happy at least useful.

She searched the kitchen more thoroughly this time, knowing that if the keys weren't here, they were most likely with Stuart. The thought of having to search a body unnerved her. She found them hidden among coins and old pens in a decorative bowl on the kitchen table.

The drill in the wood of the back door made a racket, reverberating off the kitchen tiles. It battered her ears and made her deaf when the noise stopped. *Loud enough to wake the dead.* She pushed the thought away. Every few seconds, she turned to check that she was still alone. The drill became increasingly sluggish and the last two screws only went halfway in, and then only by pausing the drill for a few seconds between bursts to squeeze out the last of the charge. She tested the door with her shoulder – it didn't move.

To get to the front she had to pass through the living room and by whatever it was that Sean didn't want her to see. A few steps beyond the sofa, she stopped, too aware of what was behind her. She turned slowly to say goodbye. The curtains were closed, but through the darkness, she could still make out Stuart's face. Pale, impassive. He was holding a throw around him, lying on the couch, head at one end. Where his cheek touched the armrest, he looked bruised, as if he had dropped his head hard, but it could have been shadows.

'You had a tough choice to make,' she said to the mop of hair.

Under the top of the blanket, she could see a dark wine filigree of rash spreading across his chest. It was, she knew, the mark of the end. The imprint that said you were not going to be one of the lucky ones.

She told herself she was facing death up close, but the only thing in front of her was her neighbor, as if she had walked in on him taking a nap. She expected to feel horror, grief, revulsion. But all she could think was that he had put her boys at risk. He could have killed Sean.

She put the back of her gloved hand against his cheek. It was an uncomfortably personal gesture for a man she barely knew. She still expected to find warmth, a hint of life. Although Stuart's cheek wasn't cold, its eerie room temperature made her snatch her hand away.

'But you didn't have the right to choose for us.'

She considered pulling up the blanket, to hide the brand of the disease and because that's what you did, but from what she had learned watching cop shows, she assumed his hands would be stiff, and she wasn't prepared to risk contamination by prying the blanket out. So she left him.

She locked the front door behind her and checked up

and down the road before leaving the porch. Sticking as close to the walls as she could, she trampled some of Stuart's garden before the fence forced her onto the footpath. There was no one to care about the garden now. The plants would regrow, with or without people to look after them. She broke into a jog up their steps and banged on their door with her elbow.

Sean let her in. 'I was going to do it.'

'You were busy.'

He glared at her. 'It could wait – you didn't have to do it.'

'Zac feels bad. He thinks he failed.'

'These things matter. Let him think about what he did.'

'Because he's the one who's old enough to make responsible decisions?'

'The virus doesn't care how old he is.' Sean stomped away. She peeled off her gloves and tossed them onto the pile beside the door. With the back of her hand, she pushed the dispenser on the bottle of disinfectant on the hall table, rubbing it over both hands and up her forearms. The smell was pungently alcoholic and aggressively clean.

Sean had laid out the spoils on the patio table and hung Ella's clothes on the line to air. With gloves on, she hoped.

She sequestered herself in her bedroom away from playing children and their eavesdropping ears. Two solid bars out of five on Zac's battery symbol, too few electrons to waste. On the bed in front of her, she had one of the leaflets brought around by the patrols. For most of the organizations it listed, their roles were obvious from their names, but none mentioned death or bodies. The most likely was 'Hygiene and collection', so she rang that.

She counted twenty rings, each one was more stored electrons leaking away. At the end of twenty, she started the count again from one. If she hung up, she'd only have to ring later and waste more battery. She got to thirteen for the third time when the phone was answered.

'Hold the line please.' Music, more electrons. She paced the strip between the window and the bed. 'Health and Hygiene hot line how can I help you?'

'I'm ringing about someone who's died.'

'Do you need a body collected?' No more surprised than if Hannah was complaining her garbage hadn't been picked up.

'Yes.'

'Is it a relative?'

'It's my neighbor.'

'Is the body in the house with you?' From the brisk efficiency, she read this script all day, every day.

'No, he's next door.'

'Are there more deceased on the premises?'

'No.'

'When did the person die?'

'I don't know. He was there with his daughter about a week ago.'

'Have you any reason to believe the deceased did not have Manba?'

'Last time I talked to him, he seemed healthy enough.

We went in today' – she wondered whether the script had a question about whether you were looting at the time – 'and he was dead. He has a rash.'

'Have you personally viewed the body?'

'Yes, it was . . .'

'Was there any smell, discharge, pest presence?'

'A bit of a smell.'

'How many people are in the house with the body?'

'He's alone. His daughter is here with us.'

'Are you aware of a next of kin and have you attempted to contact them?'

'His wife is a doctor. She's at the local hospital but I can't reach her.'

'The current waiting time for non-contaminating bodies is three days.'

'You can't leave him there three days.'

'We attend to bodies in occupied premises first. The current waiting time is three days. Please leave the door unlocked. If our operators are unable to gain access to the house, they will be unable to complete the collection. For quarantine reasons, please do not approach the operators. If you have access to the Internet you can enter the details on the form there. If not, please remain on the line until the beep and record the address for collection, the name of the deceased, and any contact details you have for the next of kin. If possible, mark the front door in permanent paint with a large cross, surrounded by a circle in such a way that the cross cuts the circle diagonally into four parts. Houses so marked are contaminated and should not be entered. Two days after collection, the premises will be certified safe to enter. Do not attempt to enter the house. Is there anything more I can help you with?'

She could ask about Sean touching Ella, whether he should have disinfected himself, but that ship had sailed. 'No, that's it.'

'Thank you for taking the time.' Hannah thought she meant that, at least. Beep.

Details left, she turned off the phone, placed it on the bed, and waited for the grief. All she could find was a tiny voice of relief that it wasn't her kids who had to grow up without a dad. A week ago, Stuart had been a person, a person who had lifted his daughter, that tiny piece of a human, over the fence. Now, next door, there was a body to be collected – the Stuart-ness was gone.

She thought of the person, not the body. Had he longed to keep Ella with him? She had shut out Sean, but she couldn't imagine how hard it would be to push away Oscar or Zac. How many days had he lain there, knowing Ella was only a few arm lengths away, knowing he would be alone for his very short forever? Did he wrestle with his need for his daughter and the need for her to survive him? Did he know where Natalie was? As he died, did he have the comfort of believing she would be back to collect Ella? Hannah couldn't put herself in his place. She could only put herself in her own, and she was alive and her children were alive.

Mon	Tue	Wed	Thu	Fri	Sat	Sun

From their porch, they had a good view over the fence into Stuart and Natalie's front yard and veranda. Beyond, Hannah could detect a whiff of rotting garbage. Mid-morning on a normal day, there would have been at least the occasional car or pedestrian. They watched the front of Stuart's house side by side, holding each other tight. Pulled up on the pavement was a small white florist van with the rear doors open. Two figures stood, almost lounging, on the porch, encased in white disposable coveralls, masks, latex gloves, paper booties, paper shower caps. One consulted a clipboard, then let himself in.

Sean had set an alarm for five a.m. so he could unlock Stuart's front door before the kids were awake. It was still Stuart's front door. Hannah had worried the van might come in the night and wanted to unlock it the evening before, but it seemed wrong to leave Stuart vulnerable. She slept with one ear open for the sound of an engine approaching and fell into a deep sleep only after Sean came back to bed in the early-morning light.

'Go back inside.' Sean was talking to Zac, who had appeared with no warning just inside the front door.

'What are you doing out here?'

'Nothing, go back inside. You have a job. It's up to you to know where Oscar and Ella are all the time.'

'It's not nothing. You wouldn't be standing out there for nothing.'

Sean spoke tentatively, as if parsing what he was saying. 'We'll tell you when the little kids are not around. We need you to keep them in the house. Will you do that for me?'

Zac nodded gravely. He'd looked into Stuart's yard while holding the drill for her, he'd seen the extra food. He, surely, had a good idea of what had happened. They couldn't protect him and rely on him at the same time, and he wanted to be relied on.

She felt exposed, framed by the proscenium arch of the porch for an audience that hadn't showed up. And she couldn't help turning around to look down the hall, worried that Oscar's or Ella's curiosity would get the better of them. Finally, the two figures came out of Stuart's front door in a slow, uncoordinated shuffle with a body bag on a fold-up canvas stretcher. She watched them back and fill, like an overlong truck, to get the stretcher on the porch, setting it down gently the last few centimeters so as not to jolt the bag. Stuart, she told herself. Not the bag. Stuart.

The porch wall gave it privacy from the street but left it in their full view. She was a voyeur but also a witness.

One of the figures consulted a clipboard, peeled off a sticker, and knelt down to stick it to a luggage tag attached to the bag's zipper pull.

The other came out of the house carrying something the size of a credit card or a driver's license. They both examined it and then leaned down to the bag. She heard the sound of unzipping. They looked at the license, then down at the body in the bag. They rezipped, slipped the license in one side of the luggage tag, and sealed it with tape.

One took a can of spray paint and scrawled letters or digits in the segments of the red cross and circle that Sean had painted on the front door two days before. Hannah squinted to make them out. In the top quarter was what looked like today's date. Directly underneath, he had marked the number 1. In the left quadrant were some initials that meant nothing to her.

The other retrieved a large plastic bottle and some cloths from the van. He splashed the liquid from the bottle over the bag and, gently but thoroughly, wiped it down. The sharp smell of bleach wafted over. They lifted the stretcher and moved it to the van, putting it down behind the open doors. She heard 'One, two, three' as they grasped the bag's handles and lifted it much higher than she expected. Stuart didn't have the van to himself. They splashed bleach over the stretcher, folded it up, and slid it in at the bottom. As the driver put his foot into the front seat of the car, his eyes swiveled around to them. She had begun to think of herself as invisible. Between the bottom of the cap and the top of the mask, all she could see were dark circles. He raised his chin in acknowledgment and drove away.

They all sat down to lunch – rice, dried apricots, and milk powder mixed with water and boiled to make rice pudding. The only concession to the spoils of the other day, a dob of Stuart's jam on top. Even that Hannah added grudgingly. A few packets of pasta didn't change the equation much. Sean stared out the kitchen window. Zac frowned at his plate.

'Mum, I heard you go out the door.' Oscar waited for an explanation.

'Only for a minute.'

'But you hadn't made Gwen's lunch.'

'Oh, you know – we were just checking.'

'Checking what?'

'Yeah, Mum, checking what?'

She frowned back at Zac. 'To see, you know, if anyone was out there.'

The table fell quiet. She didn't realize her mistake until Ella whispered, 'I don't like hiding.'

'No, sweetie, you don't have to worry. There were no bad people.' *Only good people doing a horrible thing.* She cursed herself for reawakening one fearful possibility while trying to hide another. She sent the kids off to play and hoped Ella would forget while she stacked the dishes in the sink, ready to wash up.

'Do you need a hand?' Sean had his hands in his pockets and didn't meet her eye.

'No, you can do the next lot.' She didn't feel like talking.

'I might go and read for a bit.'

They had painted a big jug with blackboard paint and left it in the sun, filled with water. It warmed up a little, which helped to cut the grease. She was sparing with washing-up liquid and water, and it wasn't spent until she could see oily scum on top. It got the plates clean, at least clean enough, she assumed, since no one was getting sick.

She wanted, suddenly, to be with Oscar and Zac. And Ella, she thought. Ella too. She could hear Oscar's voice and, more distantly, Zac replying.

'Cards.'

'No.'

'Let's build a train track.'

'No.'

Oscar was standing on the threshold of Zac's room, his toes lined up along the invisible border between Zac's domain and the rest of the house. He leaned ever so slightly forward. Behind him, Ella stood at random, blocking the middle of the hall, twisting one toe on the ground, facing the wall.

'Come and play with us.'

'Maybe.'

'What about a board game?'

'What board game?'

'Whatever you want to play.'

'I don't want to play a board game.'

Oscar's voice became high and whiny. 'I want you to play with me.' He caught sight of Hannah. 'Mum, make him play with me.'

'I can't make him play if he doesn't want to.'

'He said he would play with me, but then he keeps saying no. He says I have to think of what to play, but anything I say he just keeps saying no.'

'None of those things are fun,' said Zac, from his bed. He didn't even look up from his book.

'Well, not as fun as tormenting your brother.' She could see he had no intention of moving. 'Come on, let's go out.'

Zac sat up and looked at her as if she'd lost her mind. 'Out? Where out?'

'The backyard.'

'That's not out.' He fell back on his bed.

It wasn't much of an 'out'. Three steps and you were 'outside', three back and you were 'home'. No one was fooled. 'You need vitamin D,' she told them, 'or you'll get rickets. I think it's rickets you get from not having vitamin D.'

'What's rickets?' Zac asked with genuine curiosity.

'Something people used to get so long ago that I've never seen it.' If they had the net, she could check. 'Anyway, you need vitamin D, and for that you need sunlight. I know that for sure.' She put her hand on Ella's shoulder. The little girl was surprisingly stiff.

Once dragged out in the yard, the kids fell organically into a game of tag. Or a version of it. Their playing styles were determined by their size. Zac could reach out and tag the other two from any spot on the lawn. To avoid him, Oscar darted and weaved and Ella skirted the edges of the garden, standing still and closing her eyes whenever Zac moved in her direction, as if this would keep him from seeing her. When Ella was It, she chased Oscar round and round Zac, who stood like a pole, twice their size, in the center of the lawn. But Oscar preferred to pit himself against his brother. Zac taunted him by moving his feet only when Oscar came directly at him, twisting and contorting his body to keep millimeters away from Oscar's hand. Ella squealed. Zac laughed so hard he couldn't breathe.

Hannah sat on the garden bed. The sun was warm on her skin but the air was cold. When they laughed, she laughed. It was a moment of sunshine. If her phone had more charge, she could capture it in a photo. But this emotion would evaporate and sometime in the future she wouldn't be here with these three bundles of spontaneity. The loss was contained in the moment. It felt right that it was ephemeral.

Oscar made a break from the endless spiral around Zac and jumped up on the garden bed behind Hannah. Ella lunged left around her, and Oscar veered right. Ella's face darted in front of Hannah's, laughing. Hannah wanted to reach her arms around her and comfort her in a hug that Ella didn't know she needed.

'Pause, pause.' Oscar knew he was trapped.

'No pause.' Ella's face began to set into a frown. 'You can't change the rules.'

'Oscar.' Hannah reached around behind to catch a hold of his arm. 'Oscar, I'm not a piece of furniture. Back on the grass.' He was trampling on the moment. 'I asked you nicely.'

'But then I'll be It and it's not fair.' He was full of the injustice of being, in every way, in the middle.

'Now. I mean it.' She raised her voice, trying to pull him out from behind her by his arm. 'I'm not going to say it again.' Oscar leaned all his weight back. Ella stood in front of her, still, impassive but watchful. How could she not know that her world had disappeared? Hannah's voice was getting louder and shriller. 'If you can't play nicely . . .'

'What's going on?' Sean appeared, unruffled and reasonable, in the office doorway.

Hannah was sobbing, tears running down her face. Ella stood and stared, uncomprehending. Hannah wanted to shake her and make her understand what her world was like now, that it would never be the same. And here was Sean, all rationality and calm. Shouldn't she have some special 'mother' knowledge that told her what to do?

She still had a hold of Oscar's arm. He let himself be pulled onto her lap. She wound her arms tight around him and cried into the fabric of his T-shirt.

'Mum, Mum.' He squirmed, a bewildered expression

Amanda Hickie

on his face. 'You're getting me wet.' He wriggled out of her arms and stood in front of her, searching her tear-streaked face for the meaning.

Sean swung Ella up into his arms. 'Come on, kids. Let's play a board game. Leave your mum alone.' As if she were Ella's mum, as if Ella were one of them now.

Mon	Tue	Wed	Thu	Fri	Sat	Sun
▓	▓	▓		▓		
▓		▓	▓		▓	
▓				▓	▓	▓
▓		▓		▓	▓	
	▓		▓			

'Finish your food, Ella. We don't want to waste it.' Not eating. Hannah worried that every change in behavior could be a sign of a stomach bug, depression, or something else she couldn't, at the moment, research on the net. And if she thought about it, she'd had to ask Ella twice to get her to finish her food yesterday. It was becoming harder to remember what normal behavior was, or if indeed there was ever such a thing.

Zac ate every meal hidden behind a book, a mirror to Sean and his book at the other end of the table. That certainly had not been normal behavior. Within a couple of days of the power going out Zac had finished all the books in his room. Through sheer boredom, he had started on the bookshelf in the office. If nothing else, she might end up with a well-read son.

Ella was humming, turning the spoon over and looking at herself first in the bowl and then the back. 'Can we turn the phone on?'

'Finish your breakfast, then we'll check the phone.'

369

Ella took another mouthful and dutifully swallowed. 'But what if my mum is ringing now?'

Hannah dreaded these conversations. She didn't know the right thing to say. Instead stupid things came out – lies, prevarications, nothing honest, nothing that helped Ella. 'But she might ring later.' It was the only thing that came into her head.

'Oh no,' Ella wailed, 'we can't turn it on now if Mummy rings later.'

Hannah looked to Sean for help, but if he heard, he chose not to notice. 'If she rings, she'll leave a message, then we can ring her back.' If she rings, if she rings. Hannah knew herself to be a coward, a clueless coward. Was there a website on how to tell your neighbor's child that she's probably never going to see her parents again? Normal people, competent people, didn't need to be told what to say.

From the contemptuous angle of his eyebrow, Hannah knew Zac was listening behind his book. He knew the truth, or enough of it to despise her for failing to make everything right. Oscar jumped down from the table and trotted across the kitchen.

'Where are you going?' They were the first words Sean had spoken all morning.

'I'm going to get the phone.'

'Your mum said, when Ella is finished.'

Ella bolted her food. The instant her spoon hit the bowl, both little kids streaked across the room.

Ella returned with the phone clutched in both hands,

watching each foot as she put it deliberately in front of the other. Oscar hopped around her as if the extra air movement could push her faster. Even Zac looked up from his book. Like a Victorian family sharing the newspaper, they gathered around Hannah as she scrolled down the list, the new texts redirected from all their phones and jumbled together, deciding what was worth opening on the basis of the randomly truncated first sentence.

All the snippets of information that weren't her city, her suburb, her street, she couldn't do anything about, couldn't use. 'Ah, here, listen to this one. "Europe reports some success with vaccine trials."' It was like a news ticker. 'Conditions in Sydney.' She opened and read it quickly. 'Just more of the same. Zac, I think this one is for you since it starts, "Hi Zac."' She held out the phone for him to read.

'Thanks, Mum.'

'No problem.' She went back to scrolling down. Zac's was the only personal text. At first there had been the normal number of messages from friends and colleagues, but she deliberately delayed replying. Only Kate persisted, texting every couple of days, using cryptic abbreviations and text-speak to fit into a single message, just to check they were still there. The fewer texts they received, the longer the battery would last. 'Maybe we should unsubscribe from the news service and just rely on the emergency alerts?'

'And what exactly did they tell us today?' Sean looked skeptical.

'That there will be a patrol in our area, that somewhere that's not here had their quarantine lifted, that we should boil the water. Which shelters are open, same as yesterday.' The news texts were more informative but no more useful or personal – tallies of the ill in cities a long away off, foreign governments mobilizing militaries, an earthquake in South America. How incongruous that seemed. She thought of all the natural disasters she had witnessed remotely before. How important and terrible they had been, and yet now it was just more people dead, statistical noise. She couldn't muster any more empathy for them just because they had been killed by the earth and not a virus. She reached the text she always dreaded yet looked for, opened it, and held it in such a way that only she and Sean could see it. Three people short of four thousand dead yesterday. Sean read it over her shoulder, trying to look like he wasn't, but Zac clearly knew. He had to. He watched them read it every day.

'What does it say?'

'Nothing you need to know.'

'I think I need to.'

Sean inclined his head slightly in the direction of Ella and Oscar. Zac looked at them and back at Hannah. She fumbled on the keys in her hurry to switch the phone off again.

Six days with no information beyond what could be conveyed in one hundred and forty characters. No details to be dissected, considered, chased up on the Internet. No breaking stories, nothing to be followed. Whatever was happening happened and was presented fait accompli, without any need for her to watch it unfold.

There were no more bills to pay. Inexplicably, the numbers in their bank account no longer held meaning for her, and the money they had stashed around the house was inedible notes. For all she knew, their pay was still being deposited and the mortgage automatically paid. It was possible that in anonymous server farms, digits were being moved from one column to another, but it made no sense to her anymore when stacked up against cups of water and rice.

The days now were filled with routines, in themselves meaningless, but the act of carrying them out together gave them a sense of common purpose and broke up the otherwise aimless hours. The first task after breakfast was to check the level of the rainwater tank. Zac had made a simple gauge out of a piece of packing foam that floated on top of the water. A long string attached to the float came out the top of the tank and down the side, and was tied through the roof of a large toy truck to pull it taut. It hung above the spigot, which was tightly wrapped in a couple of layers of stocking to keep them from drinking mosquito larvae. Zac had marked off days' worth of water with an indelible marker, out of step with the corrugations of the tastefully eucalyptus-colored tank.

Ella got to the gauge first and in her excitement blurted out, 'It's on the one with a five.'

'Hey, Mum, it's my turn. Tell her it's my turn.'

Hannah wavered between *She's a guest* and *She's younger than you.*

'And she's wrong. It's fourteen – the wheels aren't touching the fifteen.' Oscar turned sternly to Ella. 'It only counts when the wheels are touching.'

Yesterday they had twelve days' worth. Her heart gave a little jump. Rain overnight had given them two extra days.

She spaced the rituals out to fill the day, and midmorning's task was the pantry. Each tin of beans, tomatoes, or tuna was half a meal. As was fifty grams of dried beans. Three hundred grams of rice or a packet of pasta was the other half of the meal. You could get away with less for breakfast.

'Ella.' Hannah wanted Ella to feel included. 'You can do the weighing for me.' She handed down the partially empty bag of rice. 'First you have to make sure the scale says zero. Remember, we did that yesterday.'

Oscar's hurt tone said it all. 'I want to weigh.'

'You can do the counting. You know way more numbers than Ella.' Ella was still limited by the fingers she could access.

Ella pressed the buttons carefully, gently placed the bag on the scale. 'Three. Six. Four. Three. Another one?'

'We don't have to weigh that one, see – we haven't opened it. So we know it's five kilos.' Ella nodded seriously. Hannah couldn't read this self-possessed little girl.

'You can count the packets of pasta, Oscar.' He had wandered off down the hall. 'Oscar, you could count the tins.'

Six packets of pasta and a kilo of rice from Stuart's house – that made nine meals. Plus, just shy of nine kilos of their own rice, another twenty-nine meals. For each of the thirty-eight portions of staples, she counted out a portion of beans or fish. Three tins of fish shy of being even, but divided by two and a half a day, there was close enough to fifteen, maybe sixteen days' worth. Two unopened kilo bags of Stuart's flour, maybe another four days. Twenty days. If she measured parsimoniously, she could maybe make that stretch a couple more. Three weeks in all. Three weeks. She had a third of a bag of powdered milk and half a packet of stolen cocoa. And then there were the other little luxuries from Stuart's pantry, almost like gourmet meals, rationed out as small and occasional indulgences. Stuart had provided enough jars of olives, jam, and anchovies to make three weeks' worth of beans and rice palatable.

Every bag of pasta and tin of baked beans was an extra reason to be happy. The world was balanced, and, having verified it, she could let herself be carefree.

Sean squeezed past her. She wanted to make him say something. They had become too used to silence.

'It's Thursday, right?'

'I think it's Wednesday.'

'Are you sure? It can't be Wednesday. If it's Wednesday we have one less day's worth.'

'How many days do we have?'

'Three weeks, twenty days.'

'Then we have three weeks, whether it's Wednesday or Thursday.'

'It's Thursday.'

Sean shrugged and continued through the hall.

'It's Thursday – I know it's Thursday.'

'Then it's Thursday for you.'

'Don't you care?'

'What does it matter what you call the day? Call it Thursday if you have to. It doesn't change how much food we have.'

'It matters. It matters because we need to know.'

'You see every skerrick of food that comes out of that cupboard, you count it every bloody morning. Where do you think the food is going? In twenty days there will be no more food. So the name of the day is clearly the important thing to worry about here.'

'This is how we get through this, Sean, by knowing how much food we have and what day it is.'

'And you think that within the next twenty days they'll vaccinate everyone, we'll open the front door, and it will be over and everything will be fine?' Sean's voice was low and controlled.

'It won't be fine, but there's a good chance it will be over.'

'Vaccines take months, not weeks. Plan for that. It won't be fine, no kidding. There is no fine. We don't just pick up where we left off. There will never be fine for Ella.'

'What do you want me to do, Sean? I can count packets of pasta. I can organize the kids into games. I can keep six people alive for three weeks. That makes me a fucking hero. The rest is up to someone else.'

The house was still. In their rooms, the kids were listening to every word.

There wasn't much to do in the evenings except for the nightly ritual of wash time. A saucepan of water on the edge of the barbecue while they cooked dinner didn't get direct heat, but it was better than iced water straight from the tank and was just enough for a sponge bath. Somehow in the unspoken division of chores, the act of washing had fallen to her. While it felt natural to wrap Oscar in a towel and rub him dry, somehow the act was too intimate when it came to Ella, something only a parent should do.

The two little kids led the procession to their bedroom. Oscar firmly clasped the candle in both hands – now that they had burned through her stockpile, she was grateful for all the birthdays Sean and the boys had rushed up to the shops at the last minute and presented her with another fat cylinder in scrunched wrapping paper. She took a minute or two to clean up in the bathroom before she followed them. A moment of privacy away from the cocoon of light and family. She was getting used to feeling her way around the house at night, aware of the presence of the walls.

Sean's voice jumped from the darkness as she stepped out of the bathroom. She hadn't sensed him there. 'You could try.'

'What?' Her voice was too loud for the small space.

'You could try to make her feel welcome.'

'I am. That's what I'm doing.'

'You don't like her.'

'Don't say that. I don't know her. She's the little girl who happens to live next door and up to a couple of weeks ago, I'd barely said two words to her.'

'And don't you think she picks up on that?'

'On what? I'm being kind. What more do you want?'

'Show her a little affection. She needs a mother.'

'But I'm not her mother and you're not her father. I think she knows that.'

'You treat her differently from the boys.'

'They are *our* children.'

'If you can't dredge up a little maternal feeling, you could fake it.'

'That's easy to say, Sean. You feel a special connection with her, well, bully for you. I can't just turn it on, so unless you have something practical and constructive to say, I will do my best to make sure she is fed, clothed, and kept warm. I'm good at that.'

In the flicker of the stubby remains of a candle, the yellow walls of Oscar's room had an illusory warmth. She had painted this room in a nesting frenzy a few weeks before his birth and chosen yellow as the international color of *I don't care if it's a boy or a girl*. Oscar had added the dirty hand marks and crayon drawings.

Ella and Oscar couldn't keep quiet. They tumbled and squealed on the bed, interspersed with chatter. It was as if their brains were locked into constant activity, passing every thought straight to their mouths or their bodies.

But she was relieved to be shut in here with the noisy warmth and the candle's bubble of light. It was a break from the cold, and now dark, silence on the other side of the door.

'Okay, okay, that's it. No more monkeys jumping on the bed. Where's the book?' Ella and Oscar flapped about the room, peeking under the bed, nudging the toys on the floor with great seriousness. They wouldn't find it unless it happened to be in exactly the place they looked. Ella turned to her and said earnestly, 'Well, I don't know.'

Hannah joined the search. She gave Oscar the candle and made him stand still, holding it upright. Dripped wax was a few minutes' light wasted and a nuisance to get out of the carpet. She took apart Oscar's bed, the last place she had seen the book, while the kids stood sentry. She found it tucked between his sheet and his blanket, down at the foot.

'Where were we up to? I know, we were up to "I don't read anything until you are in your beds".' They both scrambled between their sheets, Oscar pulling the disarrayed bedclothes so they approximately covered him. Hannah sat on the edge of Oscar's bed, like she had every night since he was big enough for a bed. Like she had every night since Ella had come.

'Hey, Ella, can I sit on your bed tonight?'

Ella beamed and curled herself away from the edge, leaving Hannah most of the mattress.

Hannah twisted herself down, moving about the pivot of the candle, awkwardly supporting herself on one hand while she found the edge of Ella's mattress. As she shuffled herself onto it, the foam compressed until she was sitting on the floor. There was nowhere for her legs to go but straight out, under Oscar.

As she read, Ella gradually came closer, either creeping forward or being pulled by the force of gravity into the well caused by Hannah. But there she was, with her body curled around Hannah's back and her head peeking around her side, following along with the story, looking at the pictures. Hannah tentatively put a comforting hand on Ella. It wasn't hard with Oscar – she had had his whole life to be in love with him. In fact, she sometimes had to remind herself to pull back, give him the space to grow. She knew from experience that eventually boys grew out of cuddles.

Oscar was asleep with his eyes open, but he came to life whenever she was tardy in turning the book around and holding up the candle for him to see the pictures. As she closed the book on the last page and slid it onto his bed, she leaned forward to give Oscar a good night kiss and a hug. She stiffly turned herself around to face Ella and tried to replicate exactly what she had just done with Oscar, the kiss first and then the hug. She felt Ella relax into her.

Hannah picked the book up from Oscar's bed and put it back on the shelf, flicked the curtain open a little to let in the moonlight in lieu of a nightlight, looked at their tight-shut eyes in its blue wash. A few more serene moments.

On the other side of the door, she waited for the wailing to start. She was in no hurry to go back to Sean and Zac's cold company. If Hannah was in the kitchen when Ella started crying, which had happened every night for the last few nights, Sean would insist on dealing with it.

She pressed her ear to the door. A rustle of bedclothes as one of them turned over. A quiet murmur from Ella and an answer from Oscar, her chance to tell them to go to sleep. She hesitated, missed the moment, would have to wait for another infraction. Only silence.

Ella and Oscar were asleep, so she had no excuse to linger. She felt her way back through the house. In the kitchen, Zac and Sean were playing chess at the table by the window, making the best of the thin silver light. The white piece in Zac's hand hovered over the board. Zac settled his piece onto a square, held it for a moment, and then let go. Even in the dark, Hannah could tell by the way Sean hunched into the board that Zac was giving him a run for his money.

'Hey, Mum, give us some of the light.' Zac took the candle from her and pushed it into a minimalist candelabra that had been, up till now, a purely decorative birthday present.

If she watched carefully, she could head off to bed when the game was close to the end but with enough time to pretend to be asleep, or even actually be asleep, when Sean came to bed. It was cowardly and childish, but she didn't need another lecture about Ella.

Her mother's watch sat loose on Hannah's wrist. The

thin leather band was dry and friable, and she couldn't risk pulling the strap beyond the first hole. Gravity had worked the small circular face around during the day. She twisted it gently to look at the hands. It had taken an unmeasured hour of delicate tinkering to get it wound again before she set it from Oscar's alarm clock. It showed barely nine. In half an hour, she could make an excuse, go to bed, and check Ella on her way.

She watched Zac deep in thought. He wasn't looking at the chessboard so much as staring into the distance with his face pointed in its direction.

'Your move. I'll start counting you down soon.'

Zac opened his mouth but his arms stayed wrapped across his chest, hands pinned under his armpits.

'Three thousand, nine hundred and ninety-seven people died yesterday.' Zac still stared at the board.

'How the hell do you know that?' Sean's voice was both angry and concerned.

'You didn't turn on the phone, did you? Oh, Zac, we can't waste the battery, you know that. Every time you turn it on, that's one time gone.'

'What are you doing sneaking around in our room? How can we trust you if you go behind our backs?'

'I knew what was on there. I'm not stupid, I know. Lots of people are dead. Ella's parents are dead.'

'We don't know about Natalie.'

'You don't have to lie to me. I'm not about to tell Ella – she's a little kid.'

'Look, Zac.' Sean used his serious-grown-up voice.

'Things happen that we can't influence. We can't help what's out there, but if we stay inside we can control what happens to us.'

'We didn't show you because there's no point in you worrying. That's what we're here for. Terrible things have happened . . .'

'But you don't get it. Four thousand, eight hundred and forty-five people died the day before.' Zac's eyes were on the table as he turned over a black pawn in his hand. 'And I get that's terrible, but it's a good thing. It's going down.' He made an uncertain grimace, still looking at the pawn.

'That would be nice, if it were true,' Sean said, producing an imitation of a reassuring and reasonable tone, 'and maybe there were days when the toll was higher, but it doesn't work like that. Statistics are not that clear. They go up and down from day to day and it doesn't mean anything.'

'I wrote down every number for the last three weeks.' Zac's voice was a little shaky.

'Zac! You've been taking the phone every day?' All this time she had been trying to firewall him, he had been methodically informing himself.

'Just look.' Zac darted into the dark and was back seconds later. 'See.' He held out his math notebook, open at a roughly drawn graph. The book shook but the candle-light shone in his eyes. In them, she saw the look of power that he had when he was two years old and learned that he could change the world with a simple word like 'no'.

'You have to find a line of best fit, even if the points go all over the page, and they do a bit. There are a couple of dots from last week that kind of mess it up, but the thing is, you don't look at them. Look, it went up and here, it peaked on that day that had twenty thousand.' He looked distressed – whether from the number or the memory of breaking the phone, she couldn't tell. 'And then it started coming down. And this one here, the curve for new cases, is almost exactly the same, just shifted and bigger.' He smiled. 'They're bell curves. Kind of. Well, they look like they're supposed to be bell curves, but in real life nothing is exactly like that. But that doesn't matter because they're coming down.' Zac smiled at her again.

The world had changed. He had changed it with information and thought.

Sean took the notebook from his hands and held it to the candle. He studied it carefully. 'You know, life doesn't always fit a nice curve. There are other factors involved, complicating factors.'

Zac snatched the book back. 'I know, it's amazing. Look, you can see right here. That's when the water went off. And then, see, a few days later, the number starts going up again for infections, and a few days later for deaths. That's because of all the people who left their houses. And then it levels off and it's higher than it was, but look, if you moved it all down a bit, the curve would keep going.'

And there it was, a line that meant so many different things. If you integrated the line, math Zac hadn't got to yet, it would tell you how many people had died. You could extrapolate how many more would die before it reached zero. But it was also hope, a road map to the way out, a promise that this would end.

Zac looked at his handiwork with pride. 'If they gave us examples like this at school, I'd see the point.'

'If there are three zombies and each zombie takes two minutes to eat one brain, and five minutes to find its next victim, how long before a school of a thousand kids are all zombies?' Sean chuckled, and Zac joined in. Her planning was not for naught. There was an end.

They celebrated Zac's insight by stealing some of Oscar and Ella's milk powder and cocoa and wasting gas on making hot chocolate. Zac did the making and she turned away when he spooned out the powders, easier not to know than be obliged to spoil the fun. Sean lined up three mugs on the outside table and Zac carefully lifted the saucepan to pour.

Sean, a little out of the circle of light, was fumbling in a cupboard. Zac picked the biggest mug and took it back to the kitchen table. While his back was turned, Sean produced a bottle of Kahlúa and spiked their drinks. He gave her a furtive smile.

It was easy and reassuring to slip into bed at the same time as Sean, but the cold of the sheets was a shock to her system. Couldn't the epidemic have waited until summer? Sean inched across the bed until his body rested against hers. He was warm with life. His breath heated the side of her neck, raising goose-bumps.

He sighed heavily, rustling her hair. 'I'm glad you're here.'

She turned her head to look at him, nose to nose. 'I'm glad I'm here too. Of all the places to be stuck for weeks on end, this would be my pick.'

He smoothed down the fine, loose hairs at her temple. 'You did all that planning. I don't know how we'd cope without you.'

She sat up on one arm. 'You would. You'd cope.'

'I don't know.'

'You'd have to and you would. If I'm ever not here, if that's the way the odds flow, promise me you'll cope.'

'I wouldn't want to. I wouldn't choose to be without you.'

'Ah' – she kissed him lightly – 'I wouldn't want you to choose to cope, but for Zac and Oscar, you'd have to.'

'One crisis at a time. We did that one, it's over.'

'Unless it comes back.'

He ran his hand down her arm. 'Or it doesn't. And we don't think about it until it does.'

Right now, right here, in the warmth, she took a night off from planning a life that didn't include her.

Mon	Tue	Wed	Thu	Fri	Sat	Sun

As they sat in the winter-morning sunshine on the back patio, making breakfast, the water got to lukewarm and no more. Sean shook the gas bottle, but it and the gas burners made no noise.

'No problem.' He scrambled over the fence and passed her the gas bottle from Stuart and Natalie's barbecue, shaking it as he did. It was at most a third full.

'That's from my house.' Ella's assertion took Hannah by surprise. She realized that even if she didn't quite think of Ella as one of them, she had stopped thinking of her as belonging on the other side of the fence. 'My mum will be cross.'

'No, sweetie, she won't mind. We'll buy a new one when she comes back. But we should have asked you first, shouldn't we, because it is yours. That would be polite. We're using it to make breakfast for you too, so it's okay, isn't it?' It was a careless error. They had worked hard to avoid mentioning her mum or dad, or the house next door.

After they had restored themselves with rice porridge cooked on pilfered gas, Hannah cleared away the breakfast things. The warmth of the sunshine and the rest of the pot of coffee, bought at too high a price, enticed her. She collected her book and her mug, but Sean and Zac had pulled the table off the patio into the middle of the lawn. Sean was standing on it, surveying the neighboring gardens while Zac steadied it.

'What on earth are you doing?'

'Dad's counted three that he can see, and plenty of them will be under a deck or in a shed. I guess we can't get the ones in the sheds. Unless we break in.' Zac looked thoughtful. 'Dad, are we going to break in?'

Sean did an unconvincing splutter. 'No, of course not. I'd never break into someone's property.'

'Except . . .' Zac jerked his head in the direction of Stuart and Natalie's.

'That's different. We know them and they left us implicit permission.' Sean tilted his head towards Ella.

'I still have no idea what you're doing up there.' Hannah's outrage was tempered by curiosity. 'Can you see anyone? Is there anyone else around?'

'Nope, not a person. Not that I can see. Three gas bottles, at least, for the taking.'

'They're probably not all full, Dad,' Zac corrected him, in a serious teenage way. 'On average, they're probably half full, so that would be one and a half bottles.'

'You are not stealing gas bottles from our neighbors.'

Sean looked down at her with a smug smile. 'Since I'll

only go to empty houses, if you think about it, the bottles are abandoned. It's more like finding.'

'What about Gwen? She's home but you don't see her. Just because you can't see people doesn't mean they're not there.'

'This conversation isn't securing our energy supplies. So I'll leave you to debate the ins and outs while I get the job done.'

'And the last time you went off on your own when I said it was a bad idea, I was right and you were wrong, so the conversation is in fact over. You stay.'

'This is not the same at all. No risk because I won't be on the street – it's safe as houses. I admit the need for coffee was frivolous, but this is an actual necessity.' Sean stepped down from the table, using Zac's head to steady himself. 'If it will make you feel better, you go put some cash in some envelopes and I'll leave them in place of the bottles. But that'll increase the risk. We need a surgical strike, in and out.' Zac was grinning at him. Too much fun was being had.

Sean jumped the fence to Gwen's, lifting himself with ease, even managing not to dislodge the fairy lights. Proficiency at breaking into your neighbors' was not a skill developed in ordinary times. The most exercise any of them got was a stroll from the front door to the back, but, she noticed as he vaulted over the top, he was leaner.

Once Sean had given Gwen's house a quick look, he beckoned to Zac. In one fluid movement, Zac was over. She swore he was taller than yesterday. Sean kept going, over the next fence, and passed a gas bottle across. Zac left it at the bottom of Gwen's fence and followed Sean into the next yard. Sean jumped the next fence on, handing another bottle to Zac, who lowered it into Gwen's garden.

Hannah had lost sight of Sean. She called out to Zac, 'Isn't two enough?'

'Dad says if we don't get them now, they'll be taken by someone else.'

'How many do we need?'

'This one's almost empty.' He shook the one he was carrying.

There was an enraged yell and she saw the top of Sean's head streak across a backyard three houses down. Zac dropped to the ground and rolled into the shadow of Gwen's neighbor's fence, out of sight, beyond Hannah's protection.

She fell on her knees and pressed herself into the palings.

'Mum, what was that?' Oscar came trotting out of the kitchen.

'Shhh. Shhhh. Go back inside,' she hissed at him. The battle cry came again. A man's scream. Oscar stared, transfixed, in the direction of the noise. She grabbed his arm and yanked him down.

'Muuum. That hurts.'

'Quiet.' She could hear sounds, a door slamming, someone running. 'Did you see Daddy?' she whispered.

'Where was Daddy?' Oscar stage-whispered back.

'Don't talk.' She could barely hear herself. 'Nod or shake. Did you see Daddy?' Shake. 'Did you see Zac?' Shake. 'Did you see anyone?' Shake. She held Oscar to her tightly, her heart knocking hard against him. He squirmed in protest at the constriction.

'Crawl along the fence back to the house. Go inside. Be quiet, keep Ella quiet.' She let go of Oscar but he froze, a panic of indecision on his smooth face. 'Go.' He still didn't move. 'I'll be in soon. You have to be quiet. Inside.' She could see his chest heaving as he crawled away.

'Hey, Oscar,' she whispered after him, 'it's all right. Daddy did something silly.'

She lay still, listening for noises. Nothing, not even the sound of Zac. Between the palings she saw nothing but the next fence. She counted seconds, to calm herself and measure the moments of danger. Every minor noise – a bird in the distance, a branch in the breeze – distracted her from the count and forced her to start again. And again. By now it was minutes.

She crouched, her head just below the top of the fence, and looked through the gap between two planks. No sign of anyone. She raised her head slowly until her eyes just reached above the palings. Still no one. She climbed on the fence, just high enough to see Zac lying along the far fence two yards on, calmly staring at nothing. She waved a little, one eye on the distant backyards. She waved more vigorously.

He looked up and she gestured for him to come, but he lay still and pointed down the side of the house. She couldn't bring to mind which house he was behind – what it looked like from the front, whether it had a gate across the side passage. Even if the way was clear, he still had to make it across the backyard, all the way to the street, and past Gwen's house before he reached their front porch. And all that time he would be out of her sight.

She gestured more frantically for him to come to her. He shook his head. She tried to look commanding. He shook his head. Although he sprawled on the ground, he wasn't completely relaxed. There was something about his lounge that indicated wariness.

She mouthed at him, 'You are safe.' A shrugged incomprehension. She mouthed again, 'Come now,' and beckoned with both hands. 'Now.'

He moved into a crouch and unfurled himself slowly. Once his head was high enough for a clear view, he twisted to see behind him, his feet fixed to the ground. He darted to the fence and vaulted it without stopping. His foot caught, somersaulting him over. Plenty of noise. She bobbed down, keeping watch through the palings. As he pushed himself up on one arm, she saw him grimace and glance at Gwen's back door. He would be fine. He could outrun an old lady. Unless he'd hurt himself. Unless the yeller decided to take a tour of the houses looking for Sean. They had to make a move. She stood to her full height, a landmark in the empty scene. Still no one.

'Can you climb?' She tried to sound normal, practical, not motherly.

Zac looked up at her, aghast, and waved at her to sit back down.

'I need you to stand up and tell me if you can climb the fence or if I need to come around and help you.'

His left ankle collapsed under him as he tried to stand.

'Right. I'm coming.'

'Stay there. I can walk.' He looked over his shoulder at the palings.

'Go up the side of Gwen's house, stay hidden. Don't come onto the street until you see me.'

Zac rolled his eyes at her but he got up. He disappeared into the side passage in a couple of hobbling steps.

She rushed through the house but opened the front door slowly, turning the key in the grille as smoothly as she could so as not to make noise. She tried to keep herself concealed behind the wall dividing Gwen's veranda from theirs, although that put her in full view from the other direction. No one in sight. The only life she could see was the edge of Zac's face around the corner of Gwen's house, inappropriately impish. On her wave, he limped the gap, jumping the small wall between the properties, and skidded onto the porch.

'Mum, where's Dad?'

'I saw him run. I don't know where.'

Zac nodded, looked as if he were about to say something, stopped, and then started again. 'I saw Gwen's breakfast. It was still next to the front door where I put it this morning.'

'Oh.' She thought for a second about what to say.

393

'I should have gone to help Dad.'

'No, you should not.'

'He might have got in a fight.' Zac was rocking from foot to foot.

'Zac' – she wanted to put her arms around him, keep him still – 'he ran away.' Zac looked shocked. 'Which is exactly what he should have done.' She couldn't stop herself. 'Except what he should have done is not gone thieving gas bottles. But since he did, the very least he could do is to not get into a fight, risk contamination, and make an enemy who knows where we live.'

They waited in the kitchen. A change of scenery from waiting for Sean at the front door, but Hannah was growing impatient with his recklessness. Repetition didn't extinguish her anxiety. She tried to let the time wash over her, keep her mind away from things she couldn't control, but Zac kept getting up to listen at the front. Still, she started when Sean scrambled over Stuart's fence.

'I went a couple of houses along and waited until I knew no one was coming, then headed to the back lane.' He was smiling, satisfied with the way he handled the crisis. 'Headed all the way back to the other end and jumped the fence of the house with the brick wall. To misdirect anyone who happened to see me. I've been making my way through the backyards.'

'You're an idiot.' She turned to Zac. 'I apologize for lumbering you with the DNA of an idiot.'

'I was careful.'

'You were robbing the house of someone who was at home.'

'I was passing through their yard. I told you I wasn't taking from anyone who was there.'

'How the hell would you know? They don't put a sign out. If they have any sense, they're trying to stay hidden.'

'I could tell.'

'And that's it, you could tell. We're supposed to put our safety in the hands of "I could tell".'

'I thought it was empty but I wasn't sure, so I didn't take anything. I was passing through. What did you want me to do? We can't eat uncooked rice, and the water won't sterilize itself. Have you seen the color it is when it comes out of the tank?'

'And what if you've taken someone else's cooking gas? What happens to them?'

'We are out there every day, every fucking day, three times a day, cooking. How many of them have you seen at their barbecues?'

She could tell that he was looking to be agreed with, but she wasn't going to help him feel justified. Even if they couldn't see the people around them, they were there and their needs were just as real.

He continued in a tone filled with self-justification. 'What do you think they do, cook in the middle of the night? Those people are gone. Do you really think they're coming back for their gas bottles? We are so close, so close. We are not going to fail because the gas runs out.'

'Dad, Gwen hasn't eaten her breakfast.'

'Hasn't she?'

'We can't go next door, Zac. If she's' – Hannah didn't know how to say it – 'gone, she's gone. And either she's gone and there's nothing to be done, or she's *gone* and there's still nothing we can do.'

'I know what you're talking about, Mum.'

'You didn't go into Stuart's, Zac. You don't understand what it's like.'

'Look,' Sean broke in. 'Seeing won't help her or you.'

'But, Dad, what if she's sick?'

'Then there's more reason not to go, not less. We have no medicine. Half a packet of Panadol won't cure anything.'

'But she's alone, Dad. We can't do nothing.' Zac was close to tears.

'We haven't done nothing, we've kept her fed. That's what we can do. We have the three of you to consider.'

'I'll go.' Zac looked resolved.

Hannah held the side of the table. 'That's not your decision to make. We have a responsibility to keep you alive, and you have that responsibility to us.'

'We could get her help, ring an ambulance.'

'Zac, you have to be realistic, we can ring someone, but there's probably not much they can do.'

'I'll go and look.' Sean was somber, eager to redeem himself. 'I'll try to see through her windows.'

Before she had chance to think of another solution, Sean was out the back. From behind the kitchen door,

Zac watched his dad jump the fence. Once Sean was out of sight, he meandered around the room, as if he needed something to distract himself. Hannah cast around for some explanation to put this in context.

'Monkey . . .'

He turned around and his look challenged her to say something, anything that he could feel contempt for. The silence between them drowned out the sounds of Ella and Oscar playing, the song of the birds outside. He held her gaze, then dropped into one of the chairs and took an unlikely interest in the picture book Ella had left lying there.

Sean was back sooner than she thought, sooner than she hoped, sooner than would indicate good news.

'Yeah, well. The food's gone now. Maybe we woke her. I think I saw the container on the kitchen table, but she's got all the curtains drawn. It was pitch-black in there and I couldn't see her.' Sean looked back and forth between Zac and Hannah. 'Yesterday's food was on the table too. I'm not sure she's been eating.'

'Maybe we should call someone.' Hannah spoke to Sean as if no one else were in the room.

'It might be time to consider the shelter.'

'It would be best for her. I think you're right.'

'Oh, what? You can't be serious, Mum.'

'If she's not eating, it might mean she's sick.'

'So you're going to dump her?'

'To a shelter set up for situations like this, Zac. A place where she can be properly looked after.'

'And so you don't have to share your food with her.'

'Our food, Zac, *our* food. And who benefits from her throwing food – that we can't replace – into the compost? A moment ago you were begging us to ring someone.'

'Whatever.'

'Zac' – Sean held Zac gently by the shoulders – 'what do you want us to do?'

'Just don't pretend you're doing the best for her.'

'So what is the best for her?'

Zac looked at him and then at Hannah. 'Mum? People get sick in the shelters, I read it. You can see it on the graph. There's this big spike, and it's four days after the water went off.'

'We ring the shelter or we do nothing.' Sean was very calm. 'You have to tell me exactly what you think we should do.'

Zac chewed at his lip. Hannah could see him turning it over. 'Ring someone. I don't want her to die by herself.'

Mon	Tue	Wed	Thu	Fri	Sat	Sun

'Don't go yet. Stay.' Sean's voice was blurry. He put his arm around her, nuzzling into her neck. For a few more minutes they lay still, warm. His breathing was regular, as if he had fallen back to sleep, but when he spoke again, his voice was quiet but clear. 'I call dibs on Zac.'

'Go back to sleep,' she whispered, trying to find a voice that was almost subliminal.

'I want to make it clear before we get up, I'm spending time with Zac today.'

'I'm sure he'd like that.'

'But.'

'Ella really likes you.'

'Ella doesn't *not* like you. I'm doing all the little-kid stuff – you get to do all the teenage stuff. I've had my fill of coloring. And they ask so many questions.'

'At least you know the answers to the questions.'

'Hey, I'll take "If the electrons are negative and the

protons are positive, why don't atoms collapse in on themselves?" over "If they bury me when I'm dead, how will I breathe?" '

'Like you knew the answer to Zac's question.'

'Yeah, I do, it's "I don't know". My turn.'

Zac got up last, rubbing his face. His pajama pants stopped a couple of inches above his ankles. His preposterously long and lanky feet, corded with tendons, were white on the chilly floorboards. She could see the hairs standing up on his arm as he laid his head on the table. He held his notebook loosely in his hand, slid it onto the table beside him.

'Aren't you cold?'

'No.'

She had left turning on the phone until he woke up, and now handed it to him with the text open. He added yesterday's data point to the graph – nearly seventeen hundred, not that different from the day before, but a tenth of what it had been a little over a week ago. Each plotted point brought them incrementally closer to opening the door. There was a story to be read in the dots. Yesterday, she had spent an hour with him calculating every kind of statistic they could find in his textbook. Zac assumed she knew how to do it and what it meant, and from three days before her Year Nine math exam to three minutes after it, she had. But while she pretended to explain it to Zac, it came back to her and she taught them both. As far as their limited understanding of high school math went, the bell curve was real. Zac had formed a hypothesis and made a prediction, and the data supported it. Scientific method as well as math.

It was tempting to extrapolate from the graph, draw a line down from their curve until it hit zero, but she had a feeling that they couldn't weigh down their small amount of data with too much magical meaning.

Ella rode on Sean's back, wielding a pool noodle, Sean on hands and knees. Facing them on the other side of the square of lawn, lined up as if for a joust, Oscar perched on Zac's back, similarly armed.

'Righto, this match, the Brothers against the Others. Remember, first to touch the ground loses a point, no touching with your hands, and, steeds, no helping. Go.'

Sean and Zac charged at each other over the couple of grassed meters. Sean shied at the last minute but Zac kept up an ungainly gallop, straight into Sean's side. He shouted out just before impact, 'Hang on, Mouse.'

Oscar's grin split his face. With one hand he grasped Zac's shirt tight, with the other he swung his noodle, roughly in the direction of Ella. It flexed, missing by most of its length. Sean buckled sideways, taking his far hand off the ground to steady Ella. He teetered but leaned into Zac's blow, balanced on his other hand.

'Cheat, cheat!' Zac sat up on his haunches, launching Oscar backwards. 'Dad held Ella on. That's cheating.'

Sean started to bluster, but Zac suddenly jerked up straight, on guard, no longer listening but looking from

Hannah to Sean and back. Now Hannah heard it, the sound of an engine idling in the street. Different from the diesel chug of the patrols, a quieter reminder of the outside world.

'Hey' – she rubbed her hands together – 'hey, what about a game of cards? We could go inside and have a game of cards.' She shooed the kids in. 'So, what's it going to be, go fish or snap?' She had just about forgotten the call she had made, but this had to be about Gwen. In the sunshine and the joy of the game, even Stuart had taken time off from haunting the corners of her mind. She was mortified by how easily she could forget, how simple it was to be distracted from the misfortune of those so physically close.

While she knew they owed Gwen something, a neighborly concern, Hannah had hardened herself with the belief that she had done as much as, if not more than, was owed to someone who had neglected to prepare. Now was not the time to be breaking their quarantine – not when Zac's graph promised that they had nearly reached the other side.

Ella stood her ground, feet firmly planted, certainty on her face. 'But it's not inside play now. We don't have inside play till after lunch.'

'What about we have inside playtime and then lunch?'

The determined frown on Ella's face started to shift to a pout of distress, her eyes reflecting a growing bewilderment. 'But music time is before lunch.'

'Ella, we're playing cards now. Music time will have to be later. Be a big girl.'

'Mum, I'm just going to look out the front.'

'Stay here, Zac. You're not helping.'

'Why don't I stay here and play cards?' Sean rubbed her shoulder. 'I think Zac needs to see out the front.'

'What's out the front?' Oscar asked.

'Nothing for little kids,' Zac snapped at him.

'Mum, Zac's being mean.'

'Stay here and play cards with Dad.' She gave Sean a grateful smile. 'We won't be long.'

Zac paced down the hall with determination, Hannah in his wake. Almost at the front door, they heard voices from the street. Zac faltered.

'Monkey, we can go back and play cards.'

'Wouldn't I be a coward if I let Gwen be taken away but I wouldn't watch?'

'You don't have to be brave.'

Zac oscillated from front foot to back foot. Hannah led him to the bedroom window. When they stood at the far end, they could see the front third of a bus parked outside Gwen's. A figure in a hazmat suit, mask, and gloves walked into their line of sight. Gwen came into view, led by her hand like a child. She dropped the space-suited figure's hand and looked around, bewildered. Her gray hair was unkempt, her skin loose and sallow.

'She doesn't look well, Monkey.'

Zac half shook his head.

Gwen tottered a few uncertain steps as if unsure where she was. Across the road, the blinds in Mr Henderson's front window twitched, and she wondered, yet again, how far the circle of neighborly obligation extended. Faces peered out of the dusty windows of the bus, but the only impression Hannah could form was of blank looks of resignation. Gwen pointed back at her house and said something. She stood, as if waiting for instructions or permission. The space suit took her hand again, stroking the back of it, and gently pulled her forward. Gwen climbed the bus stairs with effort. The doors closed with a hiss of air, and the bus rumbled off. Hannah saw a child's face looking from the back window.

Zac was gray and shocked. He pulled his face into an expression of resolve. 'We should go play cards.'

'Do you want to talk about this?'

'Let's go play cards.'

Sean's voice was loud and exaggeratedly cheerful. 'Two more punters to deal in.' Zac took a seat, subdued and distracted. 'The game is go fish, Ella's house rules.'

Hannah gathered up all the cards and gave them a quick shuffle. She dealt around the circle starting with Ella. The gentle swish of the cards sliding along each other was obliterated by a noise that assaulted her ears. She leaped and fell sideways out of her chair, scared into incomprehension. The screamingly loud, familiar, unexpected, insistent sound of the phone ringing.

With as much composure as she could summon, she picked up the handset and said, 'Hello?' A phone call. The phone lines were back, on the cordless phone, which meant the power was back. The Internet was back. The computers. The fridge, if they had anything to put in it. The lights – no more shadows to skirt around at night. The outside world was back, talking to her down a long thin strand of copper. 'I'm sorry, could you say that again?'

'Is this Hannah Halloran?'

The first contact from the outside world turned out to be a cold call. 'Who's this?'

'My brother's name is Stuart. He's married to a Natalie.' The man on the end sounded as surprised to be talking to someone as she was. 'Are you their neighbor?'

All that she could bring to mind were the stock phrases of loss from American television series. While she was still trying to think of a good way to say it, it was coming out of her mouth – 'Stuart's dead.'

Sean leaped up, casting cards all over the floor. He pushed his chair back, making as much noise as he could. The kids were staring at him, not her. Thank Christ they hadn't heard. 'Come on, kids, let's see if the TV is back.'

Oscar looked disapproving. 'But what about music time?'

'They have music on TV, Oz. We're going now, come on.' He shooed the two little ones to the door. Zac lagged after them, but Hannah waved him away.

'Are you still there? That was a terrible way to hear it. I'm sorry.'

'I knew.' The man's voice was firmer, steelier in a way that made Hannah feel less appalled by what she had said. 'You have my niece, Ella.'

Have, as if she were an object they'd borrowed from next door.

'One of Natalie's colleagues rang me. They listened to her voicemail after she died. Did you know she died? They bothered to track me down and pass on Stuart's message. That he'd left their little girl with the neighbors. Didn't you think that someone might be looking for her?'

'I tried calling Natalie and no one knew where she was. And our phones and power have been out. If you knew Ella was here, why didn't you come and get her?'

'I'm over the bridge. You can't seriously think I'd cross quarantine lines. When the danger has passed, I'll come and get Ella.'

'So you're happy for her to eat my food and you're happy to leave her in danger.' She'd let Daniel go, she wasn't handing Ella over to a complete stranger. Even one who said he was Stuart's brother. Especially one who was behaving like a jerk. 'I don't know who you are. How do I know you're her uncle? I never heard Stuart talk about a brother.'

'Go and ask Ella if she has an Uncle Steve.'

'You could have got that from the net.'

'I'm her uncle. Who are you to her?'

'I'm the person her father left her with. I'm the one who's here.' How dare he suggest that Ella was at risk with them, how dare he leave her there if she was. 'I intend to keep looking after her until this is over. She's alive and she's well and she's happy. There are five people here and we're going to be fine. So you can convince me of who you are when this is done. Until then, I'm going to keep on doing what I'm doing now.' She was breathing fast and felt lightheaded from the oxygen. 'I'm sorry about Natalie. She was a nice person. I liked her. And Stuart, too.'

She hung up on a jerk who may or may not have lost a brother. Even jerks deserve to have their grief respected, and it wasn't his fault that he took her by surprise. She wanted to cry. Either he was a crappy human being or she was. Or both. But they couldn't both be nice. At least one of them was wanting.

	Mon	Tue	Wed	Thu	Fri	Sat	Sun

The kids moved feverishly from television to Internet and back again. It was as if their brains, having been weaned off electronic information, couldn't take it in. On the morning of the third day, Hannah came across Oscar in the middle of the living room, spinning on the spot, sound system playing, TV on. Ella looked on vacantly bemused.

She shooed them out to the backyard and watched them play, leaning against one of the wooden posts that held up the patio roof. The winter sun soaked into her jeans, but the breeze blew through her shirt. A flush rouged Ella's and Oscar's cheeks, from exertion and the cold.

Sean ambled from the house. The smell of coffee that preceded him started a chemical chain reaction of craving. He nuzzled a kiss into her cheek, held the mugs right under her nose.

'I put the kettle on. Aren't I clever?' He handed her

one. 'It's an amazing bit of technology. You put some water in and flick a switch. It turns itself off when it's hot. No matches and you can walk away with no fear of the house burning down. I like this electrickery.'

She put her arm around him and pulled him close for warmth. As they drank their coffee leaning against each other, they watched the kids running back and forth with aimless energy. The warmth of the coffee spread through her, a tiny satisfaction with herself and the world for getting them to this moment.

'They're going to run out of puff soon,' Sean said softly.

'Well, off you go – organize them into a game.'

'I made the coffee. Anyway, I'm an old bloke, don't want to do the knees in.'

'Zac's surgically attached to his computer, but we could get him out here. They like it when Zac plays with them.'

'He wasn't able to interface with the electrons for weeks. That had to be traumatic for him.' Sean gave her a squeeze around her waist. 'He's talking to his friends, in the strange digital way they communicate. He's re-experiencing the world.'

Hannah sighed. It was a good sign, something like a return to normality. She was surprised that, unlike Zac, she felt no compulsion to get back to the Internet. Beyond confirming what Zac had discovered, that Manba was declining, there was nothing more she wanted to know. If they just hung on, they were going to get to the other side soon, soon.

Ella flopped onto the grass, arms outspread, head turned to one side. Oscar jogged around her in slow contracting circles. A blast of cold air caught Hannah in the back, sending a chill through her. The windbreak of Sean's arm had gone, and she saw his eyes roam around the small yard.

'Come on, kids. We're going to look at the world.'

'They've been on the computer constantly for two days. Oscar's eyes are square. I think his brain will explode if he gets any more input.'

'No, we're going to look at the *world*.'

Sean led the three of them through the house and she followed with a frisson of excitement, as if they were on a dare. The closer they got to the front door, the more she felt the bubble of novelty turn to cold apprehension. It froze her halfway down the hall.

'What are we doing?' she called from the back of their small gaggle.

'We're going to stand on the porch and look at the world.'

'That's out the door, Dad!'

'Yes, *Dad*. I'd like to have a word with you about this.'

Sean reached across the top of the small heads and pulled her by the hand. 'It's a bit of excitement. How unlucky would we have to be, to stand on our own porch and get a bug that's dying out?' The thought of stepping outside, of being able to step outside, was irresistible, no matter how irresponsible. Soon it would be over and they wouldn't think twice. Why wait, why not now? Just to the porch.

Sean looked through the glass in the door. 'The street's empty – how dangerous can an empty street be?'

'Okay.' She squeezed his hand. 'But if anyone appears, we come right back in, kids. Okay? And we absolutely don't touch anyone or anything.'

Ella and Oscar were already pushing against the door while Sean was trying to pull it in. They showed no signs of having heard her. Zac appeared at the end of the hall, somehow aware despite his headphones that something was going on.

And there they were, lined up along the veranda for no good reason, Oscar's chin just reaching the top of the porch brick wall. Last time he was out here, she'd had to hold him up. Ella stood next to him, jumping up and down to try to see over. She swung herself to the opening in the wall in front of the door, holding on to the safety of the bricks with one hand. Zac lounged with one arm rested on Oscar's head.

Hannah watched them as much as she watched the street. It was like freewheeling downhill for the first time, unconvinced the brakes would work. Thrilling and seductive.

'Hey.' Sean held an arm out to her. 'Relax. There's five of us, if anyone comes along we can take them. Ella can nibble their knees.'

She squeezed in between Zac and Sean. 'So this is what the world is like now.' She looked around. 'Not much different.'

The house with the broken front door, unkempt lawns.

Plastic shopping bags of garbage tied at the top punctuated the footpath, like secret cairns marking hidden occupation. No visible people, no audible voices, only the sweet, pervasive smell of decay and the hint of movement around the bags of garbage in her peripheral vision. A tiny shock reminded her that it didn't used to look like this.

The outsideness kept their interest. It would be theirs again, they would inhabit this world, they just had to wait. For the time being, they held the battlements of her fortress and her keep. Before she knew it, they would reclaim the street as well.

'I'm done.' Sean stretched. 'Fascinating as this is, time to go in.'

'Oh, Dad, go on, Dad, just five minutes more,' Oscar pleaded. It was as if the air was sweeter. Ella looked mournful.

'I'll look after them. I won't let them do anything stupid. You can go in.' Zac looked every second of his fourteen years.

Hannah didn't have to consider. 'No, not today. In we go.'

'There's no one on the street,' Sean cajoled, as if she were an irrational toddler. 'They can be inside the second they see someone. You'll come inside the second you see someone, won't you, kids?'

The two little ones sang 'yes' in chorus while Zac looked on as though the question were beneath reply.

'And you'll do everything Zac tells you to without arguing?'

'Yes.'

They left the kids, faces into the breeze, arranged like three bears – little Ella, medium-sized Oscar, and Zac at the end. The living room felt bigger. They had the whole sofa to themselves. Without standing up, they could pick up the phone, switch on the television, or open the laptop. They could turn the world on and off.

As Sean flicked between channels – news from overseas, sitcoms – roaming for something, he didn't know what, Hannah turned away. Eventually she would have to surrender her sheltered ignorance, but not yet. She traced new lines on his face, the weariness and tension that had become habit. He saw her looking at him and smiled. She ran her finger down the vein on his temple. 'Can this be over now?'

The tightness, the weariness, evaporated. 'We just have to be a bit more patient.'

'I wish the world could stay out there.' She shrugged. 'I still haven't checked my email. I don't know if I'll have lots of messages or none at all. Which would be worse? Nobody wanting me, or too many people wanting me?'

'I want you. I need you.'

'That doesn't mean anything. I could be your least favorite person in the world and right now you'd still need me.' She lay her head down on the back of the sofa. It hung between them, the thought that if they never checked their email, they would never have to know if some of their friends were permanently silent.

'Yeah.' He wasn't really listening, and she was left free

to watch the internal mechanisms of his mind play out on his face. She saw his thoughts change track again. 'Do you reckon they'd be delivering chocolate biscuits yet?'

The front grille opened and closed with a slam. Two sets of small feet scampered down the hallway. Oscar reached the door first. 'There's something in the street. Zac said you have to come.'

'He said it's Mr Whippy. Can we have an ice cream?'

'It's not Mr Whippy.'

'That's what Zac said.'

'Mr Whippy has a song.'

'Can we have an ice cream?'

Hannah was already halfway down the hall before Sean got himself reluctantly off the sofa. He called from behind, 'It's not going to be Mr Whippy. It'll only be a truck, guys.' He caught up with them and swung Ella up into his arms. 'Let's have a look, but there won't be any ice cream.'

Zac was out on the porch, leaning over the wall, his feet off the ground. 'I heard it just before. You have to be quiet. I think it's going away.'

'Your dad says we can't have ice cream. He says it's not Mr Whippy.'

'I said they had food, not ice cream.'

'Who had food, Zac? You're not making a lot of sense.'

'I could barely hear it, it came from that way.' He pointed towards the intersection in the direction of Lily's shop. 'I heard a voice on a loudspeaker and a truck.'

'We didn't hear anything.'

'You were in the house. But they said something about food. We have to go. We have to have a look.'

Hannah was pretty sure that if she said no, he'd vault the fence and go anyway. 'Look, Zac, you've got no idea what's out there.'

'Here's the plan.' Sean cut her off. 'We go together. Everyone holds someone's hand and the instant I say, you run straight home. Promise?'

Oscar and Ella nodded solemnly and said, 'Promise.' Zac muttered, 'Sure.'

'No. Just no.' The voice inside, the one that says, *How will this sound when you have to explain it to someone else?* kicked in. 'You don't wander off into the middle of an epidemic. You don't spend six weeks inside, then risk being exposed.'

'But the graph, Mum, my graph.'

'A graph won't keep you safe. A graph is only statistics. It doesn't say anything about us.'

'Dad, my graph.'

'He's got a point.'

'You have got to be kidding me. You cannot think this is acceptable.'

'We can look, only look.'

'You trust Ella and Oscar not to touch? And what are you going to do if they slip? Give them a good dose of *statistics*? Treat them with *Who'd have thought that would happen?* No one takes a step off the porch.'

'To the corner and no further.'

'No. No. No.'

Sean already had a hold of Ella with one hand and Oscar with the other. Hannah was marooned at the front door, with no way to anchor them. Even if she could convince Sean, in the few seconds before he hit the stairs, not to go, Zac was almost certainly beyond her persuasion. She could stand firm and lose all control or mitigate what was going to happen with or without her. 'No one goes anywhere unless they have a mask and gloves.'

'Are you serious, Mum? They'll be gone.'

She stamped her foot. 'A second. I'll be a second.' She looked fiercely at Sean. 'Promise me you won't let them go until I get back. Or everyone goes inside right now.'

Hannah grabbed a handful each from the box of gloves and the pile of masks on the hallway table. She put the oversized gloves and mask on Ella while Sean helped Oscar with his.

'Pull it tight, Zac, or it'll slip off and it won't keep the contamination out.'

'I know.'

As soon as Zac had them on, he headed down the steps.

'Wait for the rest of us, Zac. I mean it. And you hold my hand or we don't go.'

'No way.'

'Okay then, you don't have to hold my hand.' Although Hannah felt a little scorned. 'Hold Oscar's hand, he can hold my hand. And you're responsible for him too.'

'Yeah, fine. Hurry up.' Zac was down the stairs, grabbing Oscar's hand on the way. 'Walk faster. They'll be gone.'

Hannah jogged, clutching for the free hand flapping behind Oscar. The farther from home they went, the faster Zac moved. Sean brought up the rear, with Ella riding piggyback.

'They were up this way. I heard them.'

'This is as far as I agreed to go. Now we go back.'

But Zac didn't slacken his pace, and Hannah could do nothing but keep up. The instant they rounded the corner, everything felt wrong. The shops were never this quiet. Even at night, there was always someone at Lily's looking for milk, a tin of cat food, or a late-night tub of ice cream. Lily's shattered front window spilled into the gutter, light glittering on the shards of glass.

Zac slowed his tug on the towline of Oscar and Hannah as they came to the shop front. The safety glass lay as four large pieces in rough proximity to each other. Someone had jimmied the expanding grille that was supposed to protect the door. The window had been smashed out from the inside. All the shops had been vandalized – only the pharmacy escaped. It was protected by a metal roller door, now covered in large dents.

Lily's cheap white melamine shelves were empty. They looked small and badly made without their rows of tins and packets. The door to the fridge was open, and an empty plastic jug lay in front of it in a pool of milk. Even from outside, the rank, sour smell made Hannah gag. Someone had played a game of cricket with the packets of flour. The floor was littered with their exploded paper shells, haloed by circular white flour spatter patterns.

Underneath, a dark, dirty dusting of biscuit crumbs had congealed in starbursts of broken eggs. A pile of Mars Bar wrappers sat next to a clean person-sized patch on the floor and an empty shelf. Toilet paper festooned the fluorescent lights.

'Shhh. I hear something.' Zac stood like a meerkat in the intersection.

Sean pulled up straight. 'It's a loudspeaker.'

'Like I said.'

'That way.'

Sean jogged up a side street to the left, Ella bouncing up and down on his back. Every few steps he wheezed, 'Lean in, hold on.' Zac followed right behind him. Hannah had to run hard to keep up and not let Oscar be dragged between them. His legs couldn't cover the ground and every few steps she had to lift and swing him. No further than the corner. That's what Sean promised. She had believed him.

The voice was getting louder. She couldn't make out words over the pounding of their feet, her pulse in her ears, the sound of her breathing pulling and pushing at the mask.

Sean swerved halfway up the street, towards the voice, and as they rounded the next corner, they ran into a wall of sound. Oscar stopped dead, pulling on her hand like an anchor. Ella pushed her face into Sean's shirt. Silence had been excised. A dense throng gathered in the middle of the street. Rising from it, she could hear individual voices layered on top of one another, distressed shouts, pleading – men, women, wailing children. A woman broke away from the group and passed them, a package clutched to her chest. She eyed them with tired suspicion, looking back as she turned into the next street, as if expecting to be followed.

Over the hiss of people, the voice they had been chasing rang clear. A man with a megaphone stood in the high-sided, open bed of a truck. 'Do not approach without a mask. If you do not have one, masks, gloves, and disinfectant are provided at the front of the truck. If you need any of these items for home use, go to the front of the truck. This district is still quarantined. You will be informed that quarantine has been lifted once your district is declared safe. Until that time, do not leave your house, do not have contact with anyone outside your house. If you require rations, take only enough for your personal use for three days.' When he finished the message, he started again.

They held hands, the excitement evaporating off them. Day-trippers at a disaster. Hannah said softly, 'Sean, we've seen. Time to go home.' But no one moved.

Three or four rows of people leaned on the backs of those in front, a forest of arms trying to reach the food. At the edge of the tailgate, a masked young woman held tight to the side of the truck. Avoiding eye contact, she wove between the grasping hands, delivering a food parcel to her target. Another sat a little back from the edge. Above the mask, her eyes looked scared. She held a box between her knees like a shield and threw packages at the crowd as fast as she could. The third crouched at the back, watching the upturned faces. At best, her eyes were businesslike but Hannah felt they hid distaste. Her ease was unnerving.

Oscar pulled back hard, slipped his hand out of Hannah's, and circled around behind her. Sean had deposited Ella on the ground and she scuttled the two steps to Oscar.

A pair of hands seized the arm of one of the women on the truck. She waved a parcel as she lurched forward. The woman behind her holding the box lunged at her and caught the other arm.

Parcels exploded upward, spawning scuffles where they fell. High-pitched, angry swearing streamed out of the young woman pulled between the sea of hands and her colleague on the truck. A man with a thin face and dirty hair was pushed over by a woman beating him to a package on the ground. Hannah recognized him with a shock. When she used to walk to school with Oscar, she had seen him waiting for the city bus, in a jacket and tie, carrying a leather briefcase.

People were pushing, tripping over a tangle of fallen bodies. The man with the megaphone was shouting. 'Move back from the truck. Clear a space, move back.' But they surged forward. The third woman joined the tug-of-war and pulled the first onto the truck. They fell backwards as if yanked. The attacker followed, grabbing boxes and throwing them to his companions.

The megaphone voice became more strident. 'Move

back or people will get hurt.' Hannah could hear panic in his voice and so could the crowd. 'Move back. Move back. No one will get anything if you don't move back.' He dropped his megaphone and flung the boxes behind him, out of reach. The disdainful young woman shoved her foot into the interloper's chest, tipping him off the truck.

The pack howled outrage at the mistreatment of the food liberator. A wave of people engulfed the truck. Hannah jumped at the bang of a car backfiring. Desperate people scattered like a shoal of fish. Another bang. It took her a moment to connect the sound with the object that megaphone man held above his head.

'Sean.' Her voice couldn't reach him over the sound of panic.

The mob spread out to form a front crashing towards them and she was already running before thought had time to catch up. The kids. She had no sense of where the kids were. She looked behind her, to the side.

Ella lay in the shadow of a front fence, squashing herself into the bricks, screaming as Sean attempted to pick her up. He carried her in his arms, her flailing limbs tipping her out again. At last, he held her by her middle, like a sack. Oscar was running erratically on his little legs. Zac pelted diagonally across the street and scooped him up. She saw his legs strain to outrun the front.

The crowd kept coming, not towards them, just running. She was scared of these people, although each one of them had no more intention of hurting her than the water molecules of a breaking wave.

'Zac!' she screamed. 'Zac!' She beat an arc to Sean, pushing him down the driveway between two houses, into the sudden quiet.

Zac ripped off his mask and dropped to the ground next to Sean, his throat rasping. Oscar tumbled out of his arms. Hannah trembled, her body cold from clammy sweat. She heard the memory of a gunshot. She saw a window, some curtains, Sean spread out on his back, ferns, a garden tap, Ella curled in a ball, Oscar's mouth open in a silent cry, the pebbles on the drive, blood on Oscar's shirt.

'Breathe out.' She filled her voice with command. 'Breathe out.' Oscar started to cry. She stripped off his fleece and pulled at his blood dappled T-shirt, looking for a hole.

'It's all right.' Zac was white and shaking and his eyes were on Oscar. 'It's me. I banged a wall.' A scrape covered almost the length of his forearm.

She wiped at the trickle with her sleeve. Blood on her shirt, his shirt, Oscar's shirt. Zac wobbled as he tried to stand.

'Zac, kiddo, you have to sit down.' Zac obeyed his dad's voice. He cradled his arm in front of him. 'Put your head down.'

'I'm okay.'

Sean gently eased Zac's head forward so it touched his knees. 'You're good. You got Oscar.' Sean stopped to swallow and blink. 'That's more than okay.'

Hannah wrapped her arms around Oscar, pulling him

back a little to give Zac space to breathe. 'Don't you have a great brother?'

'I want to be with Zac.'

She held him tighter for Zac as well. 'You could do something for him.'

'What?'

'I need your shirt.'

She bandaged Zac's arm with it. Speckles of blood slowly oozed through. It was more psychological comfort than physical, but they both felt better having done something.

Sean moved to the front of the drive. He looked both ways down the street they had come from, beyond Hannah's sight line. 'Time to go,' he called back to them, in a voice that was trying to simulate certainty.

She stepped closer, pretending to herself that somehow it would make their conversation private. 'We can't take the kids back that way.'

'I'll go and check around the corner, but the truck's gone.'

'No, Daddy, no.' Oscar threw himself at Sean, entangling himself in Sean's legs. 'Don't go out there. We can stay here.'

'You can carry Oscar, I can carry Ella, but we'll be slow and Zac's still shaky.' She needed to get them home, and for that she needed them to stay calm. The kids could hear every word they were saying – there was no way to avoid that. The road would only terrify them, as would talking about why. 'I think we should stay hidden. Out there is too dangerous.'

'And I think being here's too dangerous, but we're here and we have to get home. Via the roads.'

'We're going through the backyards.'

'It's less than four blocks to home. Five minutes at most. Being in someone's backyard is what got me into trouble last time.' His voice rose with exasperation.

'We shouldn't have come out in the first place and we should have turned back, but we are here and we are staying off the road.' Hannah breathed in deep. 'The house over the fence almost faces Lily's. We only have to jump that one fence and we're in the street next to ours. If we go through one of the gardens to the back lane that saves another block. We skip two whole blocks and we only have to cross one road.'

'I don't want to go back up the driveway.' Zac's voice was quiet but firm.

'You can't climb the fence with that arm.'

'I can.' He looked less confident than he sounded.

The drive opened up into an overgrown garden. The trees gave them privacy to look over the side fences, size up the area without being seen by anyone but the hopefully absent occupants of the house.

'Once we're all over, keep moving. If you hear anyone, run straight home. Now, not a sound.' Sean lifted Ella over the fence and began to lower her down the other side. She clung to his shoulders. He tried to disentangle himself but she grabbed and thrashed, clawing her way up his arms and onto his back, raising welts as she went. Sean swore silently. He puffed with pain, then gently twisted himself to put her back down.

Zac spoke softly. 'I'll go over first, Dad. Hand her to me.'

Zac's arm began to tremble as he put his weight on it, and Hannah placed a steadying hand on his side. Sean delivered Ella into Zac's arms. Hannah followed, then Oscar, boosted by Sean. Oscar's fleece rode up, leaving his naked torso goosebumped and shivering.

The garden was quiet, the house was quiet, the street beyond was quiet, the shops were quiet, the back lane was quiet, and so was the house next to Gwen's where they jumped the fence. The absence of noise, identical to the absence yesterday and the day before, and the knowledge that all those people had come out of all these houses was as unsettling as the noise of the crowd had been.

Mon	Tue	Wed	Thu	Fri	Sat	Sun

The days moved slowly, like the beginning of a rainy summer holiday – those first days when six weeks in the same house as the kids felt like a lifetime. But the sun shone through the window and she felt winter through her toes on the wooden floors.

There was not enough room in the house for the unspent energy in her legs. It infected them both. Sean prowled from room to room like a zoo animal, testing that the artificial edges of their territory still held them in. The lines that carried the Internet were too small for her to squeeze her thoughts out to freedom.

From the kitchen she heard Sean open the front door, felt the cool breeze of the outside sweep down the hall and out the gaps around the back door and the windows. Then the sound of the door closing again and Sean's heavy tread down the hall.

She tried to concentrate on the screen even though the work in front of her, the documents to be read and written, couldn't hold her interest. All she could see was that the movement of electrons that had up to a few weeks ago seemed full of meaning was in fact pointless and irrelevant.

But the gears of civilization were turning. One by one the markers of an orderly society, the infrastructure she had always assumed was easy and ordinary, were coming back. They had even been promised water within days. There was so little else to distract her that the prospect of turning on a tap was enough to make her heart beat a little faster. She had to believe that the words she read would matter again, that in time she would see the importance of irrelevant trivia. She yearned for boredom, just not this boredom. The boredom of P&C meetings, swimming classes, going to the office, and grocery shopping. The boredom of the ordinary.

Sean came through the hallway door, crossed to the kitchen sink, leaned on the counter, and stared out their window at the sun reflected on the window opposite.

'Can't you find something to do?'

'Nothing that can't wait.'

She turned her attention back to the screen.

He slunk to the back door. 'I'm just going to check the back of Stuart's.'

'Nothing has changed.'

She glanced over after a few moments to see him hoisting himself up on the fence. She sprinted out and pulled him down by the belt loops. 'Come down, crazy man.' He let himself be towed back to the kitchen. 'Aren't they expecting some work out of you?'

'Whatever I start seems so . . . ' He shrugged.

'Play with the kids.'

'They have the TV and each other. No one really needs me.'

Her laptop beeped at her. 'Damn, this will be Kate.'

Hey, babe. I'm so bored I'm going to die. I've started talking to my television. It answers me back. My television wants to know how you are all doing.

Hanging in. Desperate for some fresh air.

Here's a little breath of air if you haven't seen it.

There was a pause, as if to let her click on the link, and then underneath the lines continued.

I don't want to hassle you, but do you think you're going to send me the doc today? I want to get a jump on things before it all starts up again.

Turns out, I have plenty of time on my hands. I'll get it to you.

The link to the article opened over everything else. Blazoned along the top of the page, 'Miracle Girl', and underneath was a photo of a toddler with a tube coming out of her nose, purple rash on her chest and shoulders, lips parted and a toy elephant lying on the pillow beside her. Hannah skimmed the page looking for the information that counted and there it was, buried at the bottom. A quote from a doctor saying that although it had been effective against the final stage of the disease, the drug-intensive treatment took more days and resources than would make it practical for widespread use. They had pulled off one limited miracle for a disease that had almost run its course.

We could meet for lunch at the café on the corner. I'd be the one with the tin of tuna and the survival rations. It'd be safe. And if it isn't, we can get ourselves some of that cure.

I'd trade you a tin of beans for the tuna but I'm not ready to enter the miracle lottery yet.

The sound of Ella's small feet running down the hall broke her concentration. Sean jumped out of his chair. 'What's up, Ella?' He lifted her up.

'I hear it!'

'I didn't hear anything.'

Oscar's heavier feet followed her in. 'I heard it, I heard it too.'

'They're back.' Ella squirmed in Sean's arms.

'It's a bit early in the day for a convoy.' Hannah held up her hands to stop them. 'Even if it is one, we don't need anything yet.'

Sean cocked an eyebrow. 'Eventually, you are going to have to take food parcels and, if it doesn't rain, water. Why not make it today?'

'Because it *will* rain. Because we still have a week's worth of food.'

'Or, you could take the food parcels now and then you'd have more in the pantry, just in case. Just think – they might enrich our lives with a little variety.'

'Yum, I like the ones with the extra germy ingredient. They taste good.'

'You know they don't come with germs.'

Ella twisted herself in Sean's arms and pointed to the front of the house. 'Can we see the trucks? I want to see trucks!'

'You saw yesterday's. This one will be the same.'

'I saw guns.' Ella looked proud of the statement.

Zac appeared in the kitchen doorway. 'A convoy's coming.'

Ella wriggled out of Sean's arms and tore down the hallway, Oscar right behind her. Hannah didn't catch up with them until the front door. Ella was on her tippy-toes trying to reach the lock, but Oscar stood back, looking guilty.

'What do you think you're doing?'

'But I want to see.'

'From the bedroom.'

Ella held her hands up to Sean.

'I guess I'm doing the heavy lifting.'

'Please can we open the window?' Ella smeared her hands on the glass.

'Yeah, please, Mum.'

'Come on, Mum' – Sean smirked at her – 'a bit of fresh air.'

She unlocked the windows and swung them back. The air was brisk, and she could smell a hint of diesel and hear a soft rumble. Down past Stuart and Natalie's house, near the corner, a large truck with an open bed lumbered forward, a smaller dull khaki jeep following.

'Mum, I can't see anything.'

Hannah lifted Oscar up to the sill. He bent himself into a right angle to get his head as far out as he could. They all watched the truck inching slowly towards them.

'I told you it was a convoy.' Zac stood a little back from the window, feigning indifference. As the engine got slowly louder, she began to hear a voice over the top.

'Do not approach the truck. We do not have facilities to treat the sick. Do not approach the truck if you are sick. If you are sick, return to your house and call triple zero. We can provide you with limited first-aid kits. If you need supplies, signal to the truck and wait where you are for one of the workers to approach you.'

Mr Henderson was out on his lawn, watching the vehicles, watching them. When he turned his gaze on her, it seemed to be with accusation. She told herself off for imagining things, and just to prove her courage to herself, she held his eye for an instant before looking away. When she looked back, he was still watching her.

Oscar teetered on the windowsill and she leaned out next to him to try to see the other way, past Gwen's wall. Up the block, clusters of people stood on three of the front lawns, and there could be more watching from inside their houses like they were, behind curtains. Every truck was bound to have an audience – there was nothing else to do except watch television. However uneventful watching a truck drive past was, it felt more real than TV.

The most distant two groups were too far away to make out clearly, and the wall limited her view of her side of the road and anything beyond the next intersection. The only group she had a good view of were the family she'd seen leaving and coming back in the night. The mother and father with their daughter.

The woman was pallid and thin and her husband supported her arm as they walked out, holding her up. Yesterday when the truck came around, the girl had sat at her mother's feet, but today she was standing, pulling her mother forward. The woman smiled at her daughter straining away. Their hands, clasped together, were skeletal.

Sean gave Hannah a nudge with his elbow, inclined his head towards the idling truck. Two people sat in the cabin and four more stood on the bed, all of them in fatigues, paper masks hanging around their necks. And Ella was right – several of them were conspicuously carrying guns. One, a young woman, looked down at something, then towards their house, and spoke to the man standing next to her. They jumped down and headed, with the wide-legged saunter of people in authority wearing baggy pants, in their direction. The woman said something to the man. He laughed in the way he would if he were walking down the street with a colleague at lunchtime. As they walked, Hannah could almost think they were deliberately not looking her way. When they reached her fence, the man pulled up his mask.

It felt like the whole street was looking. The woman

waited at the bottom of Hannah's steps. The man strode up to the window, pulling gloves on as he came.

'Is this your daughter, sir?'

'She's our neighbor . . .'

The man bent down to Ella and talked over the top of Sean. 'What's your name, sweetheart?'

'Ella.'

'Ella what? Is this where you live?'

'Ella Cope. That's my house.' She pointed. He tried to hide his glance to the woman. She nodded almost imperceptibly.

'This child is listed as missing. I'm afraid she has to come with us.'

Hannah jumped in. 'Who reported her missing? We still hope we might hear from her mum. She was working at the hospital.' Hannah noticed how young the man was, not ten years older than Zac. His fatigues, his sidearm, his mouth twisting into a frown, gave him a thin veneer of age.

Sean let Ella slide down from his arms and she darted farther into the room. A look of unease came over Oscar as he slid down and sidled next to her. Hannah felt Sean take her hand and stand a little closer, a little more defiantly. If she kept her feet on the ground, what could these people do? The guns were for show – they weren't going to fire on them.

'Her father left her with us.' Sean spoke with a measured calm designed to make an impression on this kid in khaki.

'Look, mate, I understand how you feel. This is happening all over. But I still have to take her into care. This is the contact details of the shelter.' He had a card prepared. 'If you can show some proof that he intended for you to keep the kid, you might have a chance.'

Ella and Oscar sat on the ground behind them. Zac had his head turned to the view down the street, not looking at the scene unfolding but paying attention, wary.

'We've been looking after her. She knows us.'

'It's not up to me. There are kids all over that don't belong to anyone.' The young man put his hand on Sean's shoulder. 'I have to take the kiddie. She'll be well looked after. Lots of other kids. It's like camp in there.'

'Hang on.' Hannah considered the open window and how quickly she would be able to slam it. Not quickly enough. 'You're telling everyone to stay at home but you want to take her to a place full of strangers? All those kids, people coming and going. You could' – she dropped her voice for the word – '*kill* her.'

The woman stepped forward with a nonchalant truculence, broadcasting with a voice the whole street could hear. 'Don't worry. There's staff there, there's nurses and stuff. They know what's what. If she gets sick, there'll be treatment for her. Not for idiots doing stupid things, but for the kids in the shelters, there's enough.'

Sean let go of Hannah's hand, crouched down, and took Ella's. He breathed hard a couple of times. 'Ella.' He breathed in and out again. 'Ella, you have to go with these people, okay?'

The woman came up the stairs, leaned in the window, so close Hannah could hear the crack of the paper mask as it inflated and deflated with her breaths. 'If you could get a few things for her.' The woman looked Ella up and down with a faint wrinkle of her nose. 'A clean change of clothes and if she needs a blanket or a toy.'

Hannah recognized the stale smell coming from them all, a smell she had lost awareness of. The woman's pressed uniform drew attention to the grime on Oscar's shirt.

'Hold on to the rest of her stuff. Someone will come and get it when she's sorted out.'

Despite every part of her body urging her to pick up Ella and run, Hannah found herself nodding. It wasn't about the guns. It was about two soldiers, clean and well fed, right in front of her, and four more on the truck. It was about the social agreement of civilization. It was inevitable, and her actions could only make the situation more or less difficult for herself, for Ella. But nothing she could do would stop it.

'No, Mum, no!' Zac was standing in front of her. 'You can't. She has to stay here.'

'I can't do anything about it.'

'Yes, you can.' The edges of his mouth were turned down and trembling. 'You can say no, don't get her clothes.'

'Your mum's right—'

Hannah held up her hand to the woman soldier.

The man spoke to Sean with casual authority. 'Bring the girl out here now, sir.'

Zac grabbed Sean's arm. 'She lives here. She has to stay here.'

The young soldier ignored Zac. 'You're not doing her, or your other young one, any favors by making it harder. You'll do the right thing, won't you, mate.'

'You don't know what it will be like there. It might suck. She'll be alone.' Zac's pleading lost any teenager he had left. 'Who will look after her? There'll be no one to look after her.'

'Look, kid.' The man leaned into the window, over Zac. 'She'll be looked after fine. That's their job.' He reached down and swung Ella through the window and onto his hip, and called out to the woman soldier. 'Catch up with the truck when you've got her things.'

Ella hung passively like a sack of potatoes in his arms until he hit the path at the bottom of the steps. A switch flicked and she started to wail and thrash.

Zac looked at Hannah, his mouth open in outrage. She was pinned in place by Ella's screaming.

'Look, ma'am, I have to get back to the truck. If you don't get her things now, she's going without them. Is that what you want?'

'No.' She could barely hear her own voice – she cleared her throat and tried again. 'No.' She kept her eyes down, ashamed, as she pushed past Zac. Sean grasped at Oscar's legs as he scrambled onto the windowsill, but he slipped through Sean's hands and down the other side. Oscar bolted down the steps and grabbed the soldier's leg. Ella wailed, Oscar screamed, but the soldier walked on, lopsided.

Sean flung open the front door and took the steps in one pace. The soldier stood rock still while Sean pried Oscar off his leg. Sean, his face dark and stony, carried the screaming Oscar up the steps as Ella was carried, arms flailing, to the truck. At the top of the stairs, Sean mumbled, 'Sorry, Zac. That's the way it is.' He kept on going straight through the house. They could hear Oscar shouting all the way to the backyard. The truck drove by, bringing Ella closer again. The guttural rasp of the diesel engine and the fumes could barely cover the sound of her calling between sobs. 'I want Mum, I want Mum.' The truck was gone, Ella with it, without even Oscar's purple teddy bear.

Hannah had never got around to charging the camera. She didn't have a single photo of Ella.

Mon	Tue	Wed	Thu	Fri	Sat	Sun

In the kitchen sink, Hannah washed the few clothes they had brought over for Ella from next door. When they were dry, Oscar helped her pack them up, with Ella's teddy bear and a couple of his picture books, into a small backpack. Oscar placed the backpack next to the front door, ready to be collected, and stood looking at it, as if it could explain why Ella left.

'Should we ring Ella again, Mouse?'

Hannah had called the number they had been given for the social worker, in hopes of talking Ella back to them, but it was clear that Ella's uncle could prove who he was. As soon as quarantine was lifted, he was free to pick her up.

When Hannah asked to speak to Ella, the pause on the other end indicated that she had committed a faux pas, but she didn't care. She let the silence hang until the social worker put Ella on the line.

'Hi, Ella. How are you going?'

'Good.'

'How's the center?'

'Good.'

'Do you have other kids to play with?'

'Yes.'

Hannah was running out of things to say. 'Do you want to talk to Oscar?'

'Yes.'

She handed the phone to Oscar.

'Hi, Ella.'

She watched him listening, looking far ahead as if he could see her if he squinted. After a moment, he said 'Okay' and held the phone out to her.

'Hello?' She couldn't hear anyone on the line.

'She went to play, Mum.'

The third time she walked by the bag of clothes in the hall, she found Oscar sitting in front of it. She moved it inside the door of her bedroom.

The house felt quiet, even though Ella had not been a noisy child. At the kitchen table, Zac and Oscar went back to school, with email and Wikipedia as teachers. Insistently, electronically, they were flooded with communication from the outside world.

'I was right – it's gone.' Zac had appeared noiselessly. His voice startled her.

'What's gone?'

'I put today's number on my graph and it fits. I think it's exponential, or the opposite of exponential. I think that's still exponential.'

'You need to give me some context. What is exponential?'

'The curve. If you just take this week, it dropped yesterday, a lot. It's still, like, two hundred deaths, but compared to a couple of weeks ago, hardly anyone new is getting sick.' He stopped to consider this. 'The people who are dying are people who were already sick.'

'Or you might have a couple of days that are anomalies and the numbers will go up again tomorrow. That's what happens in the real world.'

'It's gone.'

'It can't be *gone* gone. These things don't disappear overnight. If you've got one sick person, they'll be infecting others.'

'Not many, which means they infect fewer people. And only some of them are going to die, because they can treat lots of them.'

'Then it's not gone.'

'But it will be, in, like, a week, it will be. Even if we got it now, we'd probably get better 'cause the fewer people who are sick, the better they can treat them. If we got it now, by the time we ended up in hospital it would be almost over. I saw some guy on the Internet dancing. Outside. It's weird.'

'I'm taking the TV, kids.' Hannah changed the channel.

'But, Mum, we were watching.'

'This is important.'

Zac pointed at the screen. 'What, an empty stage with some suit hanging around the back?'

'Give it a minute.' The suited man stood self-consciously to the side of the podium as if he wasn't sure whether to stay put or slink off. 'There's some big announcement.'

Zac sat forward like he had money on it. The image didn't change. Two commentators filled up the dead air with chatter that said nothing.

Sean wandered in holding his laptop. 'Are you watching this? Oh, you're watching this.'

The prime minister finally reached the podium, alone. Hannah noticed that the suit had taken a step into the background. Maybe no one wanted to be responsible for losing the highest-ranking member of the government to a virus that was supposed to be on its way out. Odds were the PM had been wearing a mask, gloves, and gown the second before she walked into the pressroom. Her suit was perfectly ironed, and her hair formed a satiny bob. She was immaculate and healthy.

She spoke of pulling together in a time of crisis, of the unwavering spirit of the Australian people, of the sacrifices made by us all in this time of hardship. She pressed her lips together in a thin smile of solidarity, she furrowed her brow in concern and grief. She smiled at her own words of hope, but not too much, not disrespectfully. Something real needed to be said, but this wasn't it.

The PM leaned forward on the lectern and gave a tight smile as she invited the first question.

'Prime Minister, there are already cities in Europe that have declared themselves disease-free. Can you tell us how you will define "disease-free" and what criteria you will use to decide that this epidemic is over?'

The prime minister smiled and nodded, as if the journalist had asked just the right question. Her answer referenced the experts who were working on the problem, the post-pandemic role of various organizations, the patience of the Australian people, the complexities of the issue, and the necessity for caution. She promised the nation she would give the matter the serious consideration it deserved.

The coverage cut to news footage from around the world. Celebration in Europe, a roundup of cities, all looking much the same. A succession of crowds jumping in unison as if to unheard music in front of iconic buildings lit in bright colors. Hannah searched the jubilant faces in case one was Sean's sister, but they knew from her emails that she wasn't in a celebrating mood. She'd lost too many friends. On-screen, youth hugged in the street. A young woman ran at the camera, arms outstretched. 'Kiss me!' she called out. 'I'll kiss anyone.' Hannah was torn between deploring her recklessness and celebrating her optimism.

When she wasn't looking after Oscar, Hannah worked diligently. Not because the work was important or engaging but because it was a reason to delay reading her emails. They sat there on the computer, gathering weight, demanding attention. She didn't need to open them to know what was in them. They were an invoice for her random and unfair survival.

It was a bleak roll call. The first one was a client of Kate's, a man she didn't really know. She sat with the email on the screen, trying to remember something specific about him, the tone of his voice, a time she'd spoken to him, a meeting they had both been in. If she could make the electronic message real, she would know that he was dead, say goodbye.

An email from the convener of her book club. Two names. Not women she was close to, but one she had been sitting with at the last gathering. And in her mind, Hannah could see her, leaning across the arm of her chair, admitting in whispers that she hadn't read the book. Her abashed and conspiratorial smile was more real than the pixels on the screen. A woman she knew only to drink a glass of wine with.

A single line from Yvonne – 'I lost Damien last week.' And it was as if she were again sitting at the big table in Yvonne and Damien's backyard, as she had been only two weeks before it all started. Kate had been there and complained because they had talked about schools and real estate and nothing that mattered.

Hannah made herself read on. An email from Zac's school advised that once the school reopened a memorial would be held for teachers, children, and family lost. Like a note sent home that the Sports Carnival was coming up, or Tuesday would be cupcake day. Her inbox still held five more emails that she knew would be like this. It was as if the universe had decided that it was time for her to allow room for other people again, that emotions were no longer a danger.

Even to look at the subject lines brought to mind Victorian mourning announcements, black-bordered and florid. They formed an unseemly deluge of memorial services, as if everyone realized that if they didn't lock in a time next week, the best slots would be gone. When she had read them all, with their bold typefaces and their funeral director-approved phrases, she wiped her face, breathed. Her head felt as if it were crushing in, as if the act of crying had desiccated her.

She gave herself permission to go to the kitchen for a glass of water. In the small hall just outside the bathroom, she passed Sean. He whispered conspiratorially, 'What are we going to do about Oscar's teacher?'

'Not her too?' Mrs Gleeson's face was in front of her, her way of smiling when she was annoyed, the after-school conferences about Oscar's misbehavior. Someone she never really knew.

Sean gave a slight and somber nod.

'Do we tell him?'

'He's going to find out, but I don't know the right words. Or what to do. Do we take him to the funeral?'

The apprehension in her chest spread through her body, as if looking for release, as if she couldn't hold much more. 'I'll tell him.'

Zac and Oscar were propping each other up on the couch. 'Hey, Mouse, can we turn the TV off?'

'I'm watching something.' Eyes fixed to the box.

Hannah perched on the arm of the sofa. Better not to think, better to start speaking. Anything to release the pressure inside.

'Zac, can you mute it?' She moved herself down to the sofa and sat beside Oscar, with her arm along the back. Was that normal? Was that how she usually sat? She didn't like this new world in which such a conversation was normal.

She needed to get it over, say it, spit it out. 'Mouse, it's about Mrs Gleeson.' He sat patiently. 'Mrs Gleeson got sick.' He was still looking at her. 'Mrs Gleeson died, Mouse. I'm sorry, she died.'

'Oh, okay.'

'Do you want to talk about it?'

'That's sad.'

'Yes, it is.'

'I love Mrs Gleeson.'

'I know, Mouse.' He was silent, waiting to hear her out. 'There's going to be a funeral for her. Do you think you want to go?'

'How do you know she really died?'

'She did, Mouse. That's why we have a funeral, so we can understand that she is gone and remember her.' To really know it, like she'd been trying to do with the emails.

'Mrs Gleeson's family must be sad.'

'I'm sure they are.'

'All the kids must be sad too.' His eyes went to the TV. She stood up. 'Mum, it's good you're not dead.'

*

The curtains glowed and slowly faded as the sound of a car's engine flowed and ebbed. Hannah kept her eyes closed, but the light diffused through her eyelids. There were people out there, people in cars. She was nearly asleep when it came again, the pulse of the outside world. Glow and fade – long, slow, urgent Morse code.

It came again, the distant hum of an engine, reminding her of the people passing by, hermetically sealed inside their tin cans, kept fresh by their air-conditioning. A day, two days. The thought of waiting made her muscles twitch. It was a physical yearning, like a crush. A lust for the world, and she couldn't think herself out of it.

'Are you asleep?' she whispered softly.

'No.'

'What are you thinking about?'

'Nothing. Sleeping. I'm thinking about sleeping.'

'I want to go out.' Once the words passed her lips, she had to confess all. 'Not be running away from anything, not afraid. Just a stroll, to see. Like we belong there.'

In the long pause before Sean spoke, she knew he was weighing up just how irresponsible she was. 'Word on the net is it's pretty much gone. We could go out, for a minute.'

'Zac will hear.'

'Then don't make noise.'

She slipped a jacket over her pajama top and pulled on the day's worn jeans. They carried their shoes until they got outside, tiptoed down the stairs, and trod lightly past Gwen's house. The breath in her mask kept her nose warm, but the thin disposable gloves didn't hold any heat. She wedged her hands into her pockets.

She walked briskly in order to get back home as quickly as possible. Sean put his arm around her shoulder and slowed her. He walked with false bravado. Their steps rang out, daring the quiet houses to take notice of them. The streetlamps were like floodlights, banishing from the open spaces any shadows that an escapee might hide in. In the dark crevices that remained, she caught glimpses of the occasional rat scurrying out from a garbage bag.

Sean hesitated at the corner. 'Where are we going?'

She smiled at him. 'For a walk.'

'Left or right?'

'I want to see normal again.'

By unspoken agreement, they bypassed the little local shops and headed to the main street, keeping to the safe, larger, well-lit roads. Seeing people walking, being, even from a distance, was exhilarating. Sean slipped his hand in hers and even through the glove, his warmth made the cold ends of her fingers burn. The shops were lit up, switched on, empty, but there were people in the street. The crowd was thin at this end of the short main stretch but the farther down she looked, the more dense it became, until the groups were so close, people could reach out and touch each other. A buzz rose from them, friend calling out to friend and where there were no friends, strangers chatting. The crowd was skittish, like teenagers playing chicken for the first time, daring each other on. So many people shouldn't be in one place.

What a stupid, stupid, impulsive thing to do. They should have waited. It could only be for a couple of days, a week at most. She had chosen not to think it through. Now was too late to realize how foolhardy this was.

They skirted the edge of the boisterous crowd, as if it were a dangerous animal – slowly, keeping an eye on its movement. They had become tourists in their own country, wary of the vibrant, ordinary, everyday danger of life. The normal that she wanted to see was not here, perhaps never would be again. At the first corner, they took the turn into the relative quiet and safety of a side street. There were fewer people here, scattered in ones and twos, walking with purpose and keeping to themselves. Halfway down the block it seemed to Hannah as if one of the storefronts glowed a little brighter than the others. She could hear a choppy jumble of conversation. They slowed their pace, Hannah pulling Sean's arm in a little tighter, the fear of the crowd returning.

As they passed through the light from the restaurant, a woman stepped out, anonymous behind her paper mask. Hannah involuntarily shied.

'You're welcome to come in. We haven't got a full menu but the chef's come up with a few dishes from what we have on hand. The Desperation Stew is not bad, considering. It's no mask, no service tonight, so we ask that you keep your mask on unless you're sitting, and whenever the waiter comes to your table.'

Inside, half the tables had been taken away, leaving the remaining ones like quarantine islands. Steering a course between them to maintain the greatest distance, the masked staff carried plates and glasses.

'There's a complimentary glass of champagne for every customer, to celebrate. Until it runs out . . . then we'll see what's left out the back. It's possible we drank a fair bit of it the last few weeks.'

Hannah felt impolite and shy and touched. 'Our kids will be looking forward to your desserts when they're back on the menu.'

Above her mask, the woman's eyes filmed with tears. 'You tell the kids that the second we can get the ingredients, we'll be making puddings again. You tell your kids that.' As they moved away, she suddenly spoke again. 'Every regular I see tonight is someone who is alive. Keep safe. You look after those kids.'

Mon	Tue	Wed	Thu	Fri	Sat	Sun

'What time is it?'

'You're the one in front of the computer, Zac.'

The math books were spread across the kitchen table in a radial pattern from Hannah's laptop. At the point of convergence, as if absorbing all their knowledge, sat Zac.

'The numbers might be available by now.'

'What time is it?'

'Nine thirty, but they were up early yesterday.'

'Not half an hour early.'

Oscar was doing doughnuts around the kitchen floor. 'What's your guess?'

'It's not a guess, it's an estimate.' Zac used his superior tone.

'But you don't know.' Oscar wasn't going to be dismissed.

'It's not a guess. A guess is when you make it up. I estimated and I've been right every time. Close enough.'

Oscar stared blankly. 'You didn't tell me your guess.'

'Thirty. That's my estimate, thirty. And we can go outside if I'm right, can't we?'

She had never seen him look so full of longing. 'I don't know, Zac. It depends.'

'On what? What does it depend on?'

'Lots of things.'

'What does it depend on? How can you decide whether we can go out if you don't know what it depends on?'

'It's not that simple, Zac.'

'Yes, it is. It is. You tell me what it depends on and then we see the numbers. Otherwise, you're just making up a number that fits in with what you want. You can't keep us inside forever.' Hannah thought she might. 'Dad, there has to be a number, right?'

'He's right. We should be able to come up with a number.'

'I don't know . . .'

'Come on, Mum. Like, ten. If there were ten deaths yesterday.'

'There's not going to be ten.' Sean tried to be the voice of reason. 'Be realistic, Zac.'

'I know there's not going to be ten, but if there was.'

'Fine, then.' She could play this game. 'If there are only ten, you can go outside.'

'What about twenty?'

'Twenty, yes. There'll be more than that, though.'

'Fifty.'

'No, not fifty.'

'Dad?'

'You wanted a number, your mum gave you a number, so live with it.'

'Okay, thirty.' It was Zac's final and desperate offer.

'I don't know.'

'Come on, thirty people dead in the whole of Sydney. That's nearly halved in two days.'

'Twenty-five.'

Sean blanched. 'You can't bargain about this. This is actual people dying.'

'Zac wants rules, I'm laying down the rules. Twenty-six and we stay inside.'

Zac furrowed his brow and sent her a dirty look. He started mashing the buttons on the computer.

'You can type all you want. It's still not time.'

He sat back from the keyboard and stared at the screen. 'It was early yesterday.'

She came around behind him. The screen showed yesterday's figures. Two hundred and fifteen new cases, forty-eight dead. The numbers no longer had absolute meaning for her – they were only better or worse than yesterday. Six and a half thousand last week was cause for optimism when you compared it to twenty-five thousand the week before. And yet she knew that six and a half thousand people saw no upside. Neither did their families.

'Since when were there fewer deaths than new cases?'

'Haven't you been paying attention, Mum? There are two curves, and people don't die for about five days, so the deaths depend on how many people were already infected. There were only more deaths when the infections started to come down, but the deaths were still going up. That was, like, two weeks ago.' He rolled his eyes.

He hit the refresh button, a heavy moment of expectation, and then the same figures filled the screen.

'There's still five minutes to go, Zac.'

He clicked refresh again. It took a little longer to load. **THIS PAGE CAN'T BE DISPLAYED.**

'Oh, what?' Zac hammered his frustration on the mouse button.

'Hey, be careful of my computer.'

The table's lines appeared in a sputter followed by an unbearable pause. A long moment later, the numbers materialized in place.

'The same, that can't be right.' Zac was beside himself.

'That's yesterday's. They've put yesterday's first. This column is today's.' She rested her finger on the top of the next column, but it made no sense.

'Twenty-three new cases, twelve dead.' Zac looked up at her, confused. 'That's good, right? That can't be right.'

'You've got it the wrong way round, Monkey.' Sean was leaning over his shoulder. 'Only twelve new cases. In all of Sydney, only twelve.'

'Then I was right. I said thirty dead and it's twenty-three.'

'But, Zac, only twelve new cases. That's nothing. That's noise.'

'Where? They might be near here.' There was a catch somewhere. If she wasn't careful, they would let the numbers on a screen lull them into a mistake.

'What does it matter where? They could all be on our street – if there's only twelve, it's gone.'

Hannah felt agitated and flushed. Somewhere in the details she risked being conned by the data. 'Click on them. I want to see where they are. Now, Zac.'

Zac clicked. 'See, they're all over the place.'

Sean grabbed her around the waist. 'That's it, it's done.' He pulled her into a hug so tight, she had to breathe deep to loosen it.

She rubbed her cheek against his. 'It's over.'

'So we can go out, right? We can go out.' Zac had his feet apart, planted squarely on the ground.

'What, now?'

'You said twenty-five, it's twenty-three. So we can go out, right now.'

'I guess we can't argue with that.' Sean clapped his hands together. 'Get your shoes on. Let's see if we can't find chocolate or an ice cream or' – he turned around to Hannah with a wicked smile – 'a cappuccino.'

'I'd settle for a bottle of fresh water.'

They scattered, getting ready. The house was filled with insistent, jangling anticipation, like Christmas. She could feel each individual activity, locking doors, putting on shoes, searching out the cleanest shirt, all driving towards one joint moment. She found herself out on the porch, impatient. From inside the house she could hear Sean. 'You can't wear those. For God's sake Oscar, where are your sneakers? Look under your bed, look under the sofa. How can they be lost? You haven't been out of the house.'

Zac walked out the front door on the balls of his feet, as if they were springs. He stepped down the first stair and then up again. She watched him pace to the footpath and back, measuring the distance with his steps. He considered the pavement and then came back to her, his attention still at his feet.

'I think I'll go for a run.'

'What about the ice cream? What about coming with us?'

'I'll have an ice cream later. I think I'll go for a run now.' It sounded like a statement, but he was waiting for permission.

'Where are you going?'

'I don't know, not far.'

'Do you want us to bring an ice cream back for you?'

'Yeah, if you want. I'll be back soon.' The springs in his legs released and he took off.

He was once a baby, she was sure of it. She had the memories in her head, although this long straw of a person didn't look anything like the bundle of baby that used to be. When he had first learned to crawl, he would take off, fearless, curious, an explorer. She remembered saying to the baby health nurse, 'He doesn't need me.' And her saying, 'He knows you'll be there.' How strange that realization was, that the better she did her job, the less he needed her. That was how it was supposed to be. She had survived everything else, she could survive that.

She felt the weight of the ephemeral moment. And then it was gone, unrecorded, irretrievable. She watched Zac's back as he ran. He's never coming back, she thought, not this Zac, not the one that exists right now. Someone else will be here when I get home. Someone who looks and sounds like Zac, who thinks he is Zac, someone I only think I know. And that was good – she couldn't wait to meet him.

Acknowledgments

My thanks to:

The people who kept me afloat in 2001 – Ruth, Debbie, Charles, and Janet, who were normal in abnormal circumstances. Mum, who encouraged me as a child to tell myself stories when I couldn't get to sleep. Although it turns out stories are more compelling than sleep. Dad, who taught me to think and question. My dear friends Maree and Ruth and my sister Cait, who suffered through the early version and made me feel like there was something there. Pam, who gave up very rare spare time to talk me through medical issues. Jodie, who talked me through practicalities. Anything that is right is due to them, anything that is wrong is my misunderstanding or pigheadedness. Most especially Gordon, for patience, an always attentive ear, support and encouragement, and the time to indulge my folly, and K and X, for referring to what I did as 'working' all those years.

My fairy godparents – Anna Solding for plucking me

Amanda Hickie

off the pile and having a totally unrealistic vision of just how far we could go. Kim Lock, Peter Cassidy, and Lynette Washington for all their hard work on the Australian edition. Everyone who has supported MidnightSun or contributed to their success.

My second fairy godparents – Anna again, who has worked so hard for my book and against all reason achieved that unrealistic vision. Our agent, Daniel Lazar, for picking up and championing my little book, taking Anna and me on an unexpected and wild ride. My editor, Asya Muchnick, for her gentle passion, her thoughtful and insightful guidance, and her practiced and delicate handling of a fragile author ego. All at Little, Brown for taking a chance and giving me this extraordinary opportunity, especially Reagan Arthur, Judy Clain, Genevieve Nierman, Sarah Haugen, Karen Landry, Susan Zucker, Alison Miller, Barb Jatkola, Zea Moscone, and Pamela Brown. Everyone at Writers House, especially Torie Doherty-Munro, Maja Nikolic, and Angharad Kowal.